Above the Salt

Above the Salt

KATHERINE VAZ

FLATIRON
BOOKS
NEW YORK

ABOVE THE SALT. Copyright © 2023 by Katherine Vaz. All rights reserved. Printed in the United States of America. For information, address Flatiron Books, 120 Broadway, New York, NY 10271.

www.flatironbooks.com

Designed by Jen Edwards

Illustrations courtesy of Jason Lazarcheck and Ece Manisali

Grateful acknowledgment is made for permission to reproduce an excerpt of "The Portuguese Sea" from *Fernando Pessoa & Co.: Selected Poems* by Fernando Pessoa. Translation copyright © 1998 by Richard Zenith. Used by permission of Grove/Atlantic, Inc. Any third-party use of this material, outside of this publication, is prohibited.

Library of Congress Cataloging-in-Publication Data

Names: Vaz, Katherine, author.
Title: Above the salt / Katherine Vaz.
Description: First edition. | New York : Flatiron Books, 2023.
Identifiers: LCCN 2023017238 | ISBN 9781250873811 (hardcover) |
    ISBN 9781250873835 (ebook)
Subjects: LCGFT: Novels.
Classification: LCC PS3572.A97 A65 2023 | DDC 813/.54—dc23/
    eng/202304413
LC record available at https://lccn.loc.gov/2023017238

Our books may be purchased in bulk for promotional, educational, or business use. Please contact your local bookseller or the Macmillan Corporate and Premium Sales Department at 1-800-221-7945, extension 5442, or by email at MacmillanSpecialMarkets@macmillan.com.

First Edition: 2023

10 9 8 7 6 5 4 3 2 1

for Christopher Cerf

Ó mar salgado, quanto do teu sal
são lágrimas de Portugal! . . .

O salty sea, so much of whose salt
Is Portugal's tears! . . .

—FERNANDO PESSOA,
TRANSLATED BY RICHARD ZENITH

Through desire a man, having separated himself,
seeketh and intermeddleth with all wisdom.

—PROVERBS XVIII: I

THE HOLY BIBLE . . . TRANSLATED
OUT OF THE ORIGINAL TONGUES
FROM THE CENTRAL PRESBYTERIAN
PORTUGUESE SUNDAY SCHOOL LIBRARY
JACKSONVILLE, ILLINOIS, 1866

Genesis

When God first made the world, He forgot to invent ice.

He poured the last of His longing into the final acts of creation.

What is the color and shape of God's desire?

It is a white blaze. It might rip off your skin or dazzle you blind. It is the same shade as His favorite animals, the fish that wander over the deepest floor of the sea. They are pure light. Their bodies pulse, and they call that speaking. God embeds prismatic colors in ice just as He blesses glass: A fuchsia that aches. A blue that darts. The same gold of the tiger's eye that blinks in a topaz. Only His vision can see the mad castle He builds in every pinprick of snow.

But listen to the wind: His howls lacerate the land because He neglected to design a lover worthy of heaven.

Why on earth should passion drive us so, when God Himself can find no one to marry?

THE SKY IS MADE OF TEETH

MADEIRA, 1843–1846

FOR A LONG TIME WHEN HE LIVED IN JAIL WITH HIS MOTHER, HE ATE nothing but the music of birds.

Serafina Alves was a thirty-five-year-old widow on the Portuguese island of Madeira, condemned to die for heresy, for chatting like friends with the Presbyterian God. John, screeching, had gripped her skirts when the soldiers seized her, and they decided to use him to break her. If she did not return to the communion of her youth, she and her son would starve to death.

The jail was in their village outside the capital city, and John stayed barnacled to her middle. Their cell dizzied him with its scent of lime and salt.

"Hungry?" asked Tónio Dutra, the guard. "Accept the true faith, Senhora Alves." John lunged for the key dangling from Tónio's belt but only smashed his face against the bars. Tónio pivoted away, laughing and devouring a mango.

"We'll eat some songs, John," she whispered.

Music would feed them; they would feast upon sounds. Seabirds squawked and chattered close by, and their melodies tasted sweet. Mother said that John and she were birds themselves. He was a hawk with talons, she was a rock dove, and at first, they both dined very nicely on quite the little orchestra of their fellow birds.

My boy has blue wings, sang Mother.

I fear no evil, my love is a sword.

———

JOHN WAS ONLY FIVE YEARS OLD, BUT HE WAS TO REMEMBER HOW THE hunger went into him strongly enough to sprout vines in his stomach that were white, like soft, leached bones.

O for a thousand tongues to sing / He sets the pris'ner free.

"Listen to the Little Birds," said Tónio. Os Passarinhos! His eyebrows were caterpillars, and his hair was ginger.

"Mama," said John. He needed to help her escape. This was all his fault. She smelled of papayas; her black hair was parted precisely in the middle.

Tónio declared, "Repent for reading the wrong Bible, Senhora, and we won't hang you." His former job had been hauling guests at the Hotel Jardim up and down the hill in a rattling wicker sleigh; he was strong enough to break a horse's neck; flowers wilted in his wake.

She said, "Maybe if the priest stopped wearing a skirt and got married, he wouldn't be so angry all the time."

When Tónio extended his arm through the grated door to wag a scolding finger at her, John bit the guard's hand. Tónio bellowed, unlocked the door, and punched John so hard he flew backward, and Mother caught her soaring child.

———

ON THE FIFTH DAY OF HUNGER, JOHN FULLY LEARNED THE LANGUAGE of the birds. They tend to ask, "Where are you?" For every fifty notes about fright, eight are searching for beauty.

"Mama," he said, "I want to go home."

"I am your home. God is your home."

Your eyes are windows, Mother. Your skin my walls. But I'm dreaming of our pine table, the blue ceramic bowl, my toy piglet, and Nikka gathering mint while Rui rocks in the striped hammock. As the hours expanded hot and large, John got mad at the Lord: What kind of "home" was He? God is hunger, God is baffling. John huddled on Mother's lap, his nose denting her throat as he inhaled a remembrance of her gardenia powder.

Often he heard Nikka pleading in the distance, begging for their release.

John asked his mother why the Reverend Robert Kalley, the Scottish missionary who had converted many of them to the Protestant faith, was not coming to the rescue.

"He's hiding in the valley," she replied. "He's no good to us dead."

He almost shouted that her death would not be good for anyone, either.

Tónio grinned when he announced, "Senhora Alves, return to the Lord of your birth, and I'll bring cake."

The word "cake" poured over John.

Lemon and cocoa-nut were his favorites.

At night Tónio brought them water, and Mother gave most of it to John. The basin held his blurred face split into ribbons. A fragment of star streamed through the window and struck the back of his head, burning a hole as he bent to swallow his face.

Mother talked to God, sometimes aloud and sometimes in her head, and she seemed, always, very sure of what He told her. She believed that every sound—every sigh, groan, or murmur—got writ upon the human record, *and so did every thought.* Nothing—*not one thing*—in the universe is lost; each person *at every second* designs creation. No action is truly hidden, and no intention is merely scuttled into the ether. Every pin dropped, or kiss stolen, or furious reaction swallowed, every whisper of gossip or flicker of feeling, no matter how well it stayed concealed: Everything adds its beats to the lyrics within the ears of God, and He replies to the faithful.

But John could not hear any divine Voice, because he wanted jam on corn bread more than the Lord's Supper.

———

BLACKBERRIES AND NUTMEG! . . . TOAST SO HOT IT SEARS THE ROOF of his mouth. Banana fritters; swordfish in port; rosemary like black earth sugarcane paraffin on jelly jars hens' eggs with salt and days long as longing and craving contracts into a white point that grows into a band. And you float in the band. Even after a feast when you're old, you'll put your hand below your heart and there is that white band, ravishing you. This is desire. This is love.

—

RAVENOUS, ON HIS BACK WITH ARMS AND LEGS SPREAD, JOHN WATCHED the birdsong break apart as it sailed through the grate covering the window. The whole notes, and the circles of the half-notes, pressed onto him like Nikka's tambour and held his skin taut while the stems of the notes pierced like needles.

Mother grabbed Tónio's collar and hissed, "You're killing a child." He squeezed her hand until she let go; she refused to yelp in pain.

"Don't worry, Mother, I'll get us home," said John, but she did not hear him because his words melted as they puffed from his mouth.

"What?" said Tónio. "Say that again, John."

His birdcage rib cage was expanding. He spoke. He wanted to beg, "Let Mother take me home."

With a victorious shout, Tónio dragged Mama away. John was knocked aside, a disgrace, because he had uttered, mumbled, one word, echoing now inside him, despite having first been released so softly.

"Cake."

—

THE GRATE OVER THE WINDOW CHOPPED THE SKY INTO THE SHAPE of teeth.

The cake had been a wedge of rough-ground corn and olive oil that stabbed his stomach. Mother would tell the priest he was a fool, and they would burn her at a stake. She would die before denying God as she had come to know Him—all Spirit, everywhere.

—

INSECTS THROBBED IN THE HOLES OF THE WALLS UNTIL JOHN FELT watched by blinking black eyes.

———

HOW MANY HOURS WAS HE ALONE, IGNORED EVEN BY TÓNIO? THE stillness reverberated, and inside deepest silence was a mermaid's chanting. He wanted Nikka, large-eyed as a lamb. She liked to wash their clothing in the creek and lay it over lavender to dry, a chore that prompted her to hum. He longed to be cast down upon the grave of Father in their yard, where Mother planted a morning glory that twined through the kitchen window so that plum-toned flowers sent from Father's body laid their aching heads on the cutting board, under the pots blackened by meals, twisting slightly, clacking with pleasure despite hanging from hooks. John listened to his house, to the living and the dead. If he stayed quiet, God might speak to him as He did with Mother and describe how to rescue her.

But then he erupted in squalling, hurtling against the bars, calling for her, for Nikka and Rui, and for the Reverend Robert Kalley, and his shrieking rumbled toward the city of Funchal and skimmed over the hardened lava like sinew shouldering its way out of the buckled ground and carried onward, to tilt the hypnotized boats in the harbor.

He gasped when his throat offered nothing more, not even raw bleating. Awash over him came music. People were singing the hymn "Pouring Out Our Rapture Sweet," the sounds traveling, he guessed, from the hillock between the dolphin-flecked sea and the jail, men and women and children funneling words to heaven that heaven in turn was raining upon him.

The tunny-fish in the tides swished and salted the wind that blew the melodies of these unseen souls to him.

Someone was splitting pineapples with a machete, commanding the breezes to carry the juice's spray.

O Happy Home, Where Thou Art Loved.
Light of Light, Enlighten Me.

The songs commanded him to abide by Mama's anthem: If you live through one minute, you can survive the next, *drink us up, eat us up*, the world is a musical instrument. The banana trees sway like tall, jeweled women with violent hair who are mad to dance but only in one spot, such a racket, and someone, somewhere, is splitting a guava or beating egg whites until they form castles. Listen! Someone is opening a fish, lifting the spine by its tail to get to the meat still printed with the memory of its bones.

Nikka was unlocking the door and giving him bread. She begged him to stop crying. *People heard you, John. You're free.*

The protesters, Catholics, too—their leader was a Catholic—demanded your freedom. Mother must stay in another prison, but they'll feed her. Kalley got arrested, and they are praying in the same place. You were brave.

———

FOREVER JOHN WOULD HOLD A VISION OF HIS OLDER BROTHER, RUI, weeping in relief and of Nikka in a cloud-colored dress, her necklace of volcanic glass swaying like a child's swing as she lifted the cauldron of kale soup off the fire. She was old enough to become a second mother and took in laundry to earn money. From a secret new Bible, they read Genesis. The Reverend Kalley believed in the education of everyone, including women and girls. How else to obtain God's words?

They absorbed English. *Wait. Watch. Year. Yearn. Sleep.*

John learned to dive and excelled at holding his breath for inhuman lengths as he collected shellfish, scraping limpets in their tiny-volcanoed homes off rocks. An onslaught of needlefish once wrapped him in a silver bow. When the salt stung his nostrils, he kicked to the surface, where the air sighed like a church organ's coda. He wanted to write that down in a way that allowed him to hear it over and over, his breath marrying that organ's moan.

Whenever he set out to reclaim Mother, he usually got no farther than the ravine marking the border of their village of Santa Cruz, where Nikka nabbed him, assuring him that Kalley was struggling to get her released. But one morning John eluded his sister and hurried toward Funchal. People had been whispering that Mother was in a filthy dungeon, where men and women, godless criminals, seethed together. If Tónio was the guard, John would kill him with the knife in his pocket.

His legs ached because Madeira was full of pumice crags, jagged gaps, vertical hanging gardens, and pillars of vegetation, and he paused at a trail into the interior. Rui warned that its one inhabited spot—Curral das Freiras—was still littered with the skeletons of pirates pierced by swords thrust into them by nuns. God had split the earth with an axe to discover what was fermenting below, but then He speared laurel trees toward the fissures to stop the groaning devil-bodies of nuns and pirates from crawling out. Dwelling there now was a colony of humans like knotty saplings who ate flaming wood and bared charcoal teeth at intruders, and John drove himself onward.

Madeirans used a language of whistling to cover expanses, and John stopped because a harvester tending grapevines and a man hoeing fava beans were rolling up whistles and sticking them into make-believe bottles to pitch to each other across an abyss. They spoke in his direction, too, and he offered the yodel he used to announce suppertime to the pigs. The men volleyed back something John could not decipher, but he felt rocked in the netting of the sounds.

Funchal churned with people as he hurried past houses with shutters painted crimson or Chinese blue. He asked a shopkeeper selling wicker dolls where the prison was and got pointed down the avenue overlooked by the bluffs with the mansions of the British who built the embroidery factories and molasses-works.

Two young guards held bayonets outside a fortress, and when John demanded to see his mother, they were polite in apologizing that they needed to keep her locked up.

John said, "Where is Tónio Dutra? I need to kill him."

The soldiers glanced at each other, and one said, "You're too late, little fellow. He drowned himself to save you the trouble."

They persuaded a man with a mule cart to take John back to Santa Cruz, where Nikka was frantic. Why had he given her such a fright? Yes, Tónio was reported dead of suicide. He had left a note, but his body was missing.

A grotesque clarity dawned, stopping John from heading toward

Mother's rescue again. She had willingly risked the starvation of her boy. She could have ended their hunger in the jail, and she could end her absence now, by declaring she loved Nikka, Rui, and John more than Kalley's God. This haunted him as much as the image of their tormentor bloated underwater, a soft green banquet for the crabs.

———

HE FORGAVE HER AS HER IMPRISONMENT STRETCHED PAST A YEAR, into eternity, and Nikka's crooning of "Soon, soon she'll be home" was a torment of endurance. The heat thickened and curdled to form bouquets of white mums and white roses, as if Mother were tossing these to him and singing, "Catch this, Birdie. I'm God's bride."

Past the second year of waiting, Nikka provided a distraction by turning seventeen and marrying a fisherman named Miguel, and the only thing good about him was that he was gone for immense stretches at a time. He once twisted her arm when she refused to fetch his boots, and John and Rui punched him until he let Nikka go.

One lilac-striped morning, after the pile-up of hundreds upon hundreds of motherless days—Rui was twelve, and John was almost eight—Nikka exclaimed, "The Reverend Kalley wants us to visit tonight." He had been freed from jail months earlier and was back from a trip to England.

During the cart ride with his sister and brother, John was petrified that they were being summoned so the Reverend could offer solace after breaking the news that Mother was dead. John pictured her feet swinging midair, her neck broken inside a circle of rope, and his terror gave way to the Portuguese affliction called Wearing the Nerves on the Outside of the Skin, and the jangling worsened during the ascent up the hill to Kalley's dwelling, a haven suggesting that it was not a sin to partake of the earth's majesty. Sunset tossed violet scarves that drifted onto their shoulders as they knocked, and the Reverend flung open the door and boomed out, "Enter, faithful ones!" Kalley's white hair was a lion's mane, and his Scottish skin was climate-toughened.

"Mama," John croaked out.

"John, my friend in Jesus," said the Reverend, bending lower,

forcing John to look into his burning eyes, blue as if the sky had compacted to form them, and he wore beige trousers and a plain shirt but
no cross, since no one could claim the Lord for himself alone. Kalley
proclaimed, "Your mother has survived the petty laws of men by ad-
hering to the decrees of God!"

Nikka cried, and John and Rui collapsed onto either side of her.
Kalley ushered them toward the library with its cypress pews. John's
quaking kept him from shouting, "But where is she?" as he was introduced to a sensation that would endure the rest of his life: The Reverend insisted they offer thanksgiving to God at once, while Mother
was finishing a recitation of prayers upstairs with Kalley's devout wife,
Margaret. She and her husband had come seeking subtropical warmth
to cure her frailty, and they decided to stay and spread the gospel and
rail against slavery, the earth's greatest stain. The two minutes of John
knowing Mama was above but not yet in his arms was an acuteness of
agony surpassing the steady distress during her long spell gone.

He would have bolted upstairs had his legs been capable of it while
Kalley folded his massive hands and declared, "Accept our gratitude,
Christ Jesus, for convincing the queen of England and the queen of
Portugal to commute the death sentence of Serafina Alves. All honor
to You, Lord, for guiding me in my voyage to petition them! Hosannas
to those who protested the jailing of our kind, and I humbly request
blessings upon Augusto Freitas, a Catholic, the primary organizer in
those early dim days, for we are all Yours in the realm of glory. Extend
Your mercy over Your flock of Presbyterians here, almost two thousand
strong. Grant peace to Serafina, who remained willing to die for two
and a half years."

When they lifted their heads, John shook off paralysis because his
mother had soundlessly reached the bottom of the stairs. He did not
want prayers; he needed her physical being.

"Mama!" he shrieked, flying to her. "Mother!" She stagger-knelt
as if for a beheading to let him stare at her impoverished teeth before
they embraced. His memory of hunger dropped a halo around her,
a blot-mix of reds and yellows. She smelled like a mossy cellar. Rui
tucked under her other arm, and Nikka kissed their mother's cranium.
Humans turn into what they devour, so John hugged her fiercely so

he could feed her. He wanted to gasp out, "I love you more than sugar, Mama, more than bread," but he failed to produce a word. Because her gospel was adamant that even glints of yearning are as real as a spoon or a cat, her skin roared as she pressed him closer. Bodies are a language, how he loved her and loved her loving him, let their embrace contain volumes.

———

HOW LONG DID THE NEXT ROUND OF PRAYERS TAKE? THE CHANTING went on for an eternity, broken at last when Margaret Kalley, with the fragility of a corn husk, tottered downstairs to serve tea and biscuits. The Reverend declared, "Let us end this happy reunion by exulting in the wonders of the Lord."

He liked to claim the only paintings he needed were his library's windows, with their vista of the harbor, the waves like shards of glass slitting a green-fabric sea, and an orchestra was no farther than the ruffling choirs of goldfinches and warblers. He undid the brine-rusted latches to open the windows, and a whooshing rope of bats gushed in and swarmed over the bookcases, eating the insects that crawled over the bindings and endangered the greatest of treasures, words enclosed in multicolored covers. The bats were cleaning the library, the collections on the shelves of what Kalley called "the voices that talk on pages" and the tomes on lecterns displaying tinted plates of shells in cutaway—whelks like turrets, scallops like fans—and Catholic Bibles, too, because he admired their gilt illuminations.

John strained to hear the high-pitched cries of the bats. Bones were visible in their crepe wings as they chased bugs that scrambled into crevices, and the flying creatures tucked like black rags onto the dusty tops of books. Mother's head tilted upward, and her hand gripped John's, the best kind of chatting; it sufficed. Rui sighed with gladness. Nikka ate a biscuit and wondered aloud if it contained rosewater. Margaret said yes. The preacher's lighthouse-bright eyes cast beams in a weave with the trails of the bats as they finished purifying the library, and, fed for the evening, they shot like writhing lassoes back outdoors.

—

THAT NIGHT, JOHN WENT TO CONFIRM SHE WAS ALIVE ON HER COT and discovered her missing. He burst outside to find her near the pigs, stroking the head of Glória, his favorite. John erupted with, "Mama, I should have saved you." She was wrecked and racked but aglow as she said, "You did nothing wrong, Birdie. The priest asked why I'd rather speak directly to God than speak to God through him. I told him that the Lord will whisper me a message one day, and I won't leave the world until I get it. It'll be the answer to solve everything that's wrong everywhere. You and I did not starve, John, and I did not betray the God of my heart. One day He'll tell me this special secret to share with everyone, but I'll give it to you first."

"Why won't He tell you now?"

"God's time is not like ours." She pressed her forehead against his and said, "Can you hear what He's saying?"

"No, Mama." He stayed extra quiet, in case God deigned to give him the message, and what joy to be able to inform his mother: He speaks to me, too!

"Listen." She smiled until he giggled. "He's saying, 'John has a mother who loves him so much that instead of bringing her to heaven one day, I'll let her grow through the trees so she can always hold him, no matter how old he gets.'"

He was too daunted to reply, *Ask God never to take you away.*

She said that the stars offered the alphabet of the Most High. Portuguese navigators used the constellations, deciphering God's script to find their way. He writes like a mad artist upon the book of the night.

She led John back to rest, to the brilliant strangeness of sleep. When he got up again to check on her, God had tucked a blanket of speckled starlight over her. *Upon the body of this My beloved,* went the penmanship of heaven, *I write a love story. What will yours be?*

—

GOD AGAIN TESTED HER LOYALTY BY HURLING DOWN HEADACHES that knocked her flat in the spring of her release and into summer.

John guessed these were triggered by people sneering at her. Her suffering was worsened by quarrels with Nikka about fetching a doctor. Mother kept retorting that only the Lord could cure her.

One morning John hollered that since God *made plants that created medicine*, and made men *who knew how to use them*, why was she refusing earthly help?

When she fell asleep, her forehead wrinkled, John whispered, "Mama, I'm sorry I raised my voice. I'll save you." He vowed to give up happiness itself, food and friendship, all, all, *if, O God, You let her live to one hundred.*

After sharing a ride with cane reapers into Funchal, John stood on a beach of black-sugar sand hemmed with red hibiscus and stared upward at the Botanical Garden that seemed to float on a high terrace. It was common knowledge that a wizard of healing lived there, tending an estate where lorico birds and emerald bilingual parrots swerved past avocado trees, and experiments produced remedies, and flowers could pick up their roots and walk about, some so lovely that beholding them might inflict blindness. Sopping towels of heat tried to smother John as he climbed the path. A vantage point past the entrance allowed visitors to absorb how this shelf of land was transformed into a tapestry.

And it was beautiful—beds shaped as pink diamonds or yellow parallelograms—so sharply beautiful. The musk he would transport home saturated in his shirt might be enough to cure Mother's headaches. Wandering past drowsy birds-of-paradise, and a species of green globes split by cascading purple buttons, he wondered why he was completely alone. But then a few shrubs rustled, and he waited for the rare gift of spotting the magical plants going for a stroll, and his heart let fear pool in its bottom chambers while excitement flooded its top chambers. Because her dress was dark green like the leaves, and the fabric's red dots resembled the berries, he at first mistook the girl with a watering can for something born out of the garden. Only when he was close did she turn to him, her eyes green, and her black hair had one of those little arrows pointing at her forehead—this arrow had a name, but he forgot what it was. She looked to be almost his age and gave off the brave air of someone who had lost a great deal even amid this grandeur, making her seem out of a storybook that he was sure—a *knowing* possessed him—had a line or two including him.

"I was hiding, and you found me!" she sang, as if they had agreed beforehand to play such a game. "I'm Maria Freitas."

He gave her his name, and the right side of her face landed a kiss on the right side of his, and making a cross between them in the air, the left side of his face finished the kiss on her left side, like grown-up strangers meeting at a party. "I need medicine for my mother's head pains," he said. Already he was violating his oath with God to have no friends, no worldly pleasure, in exchange for Mother's well-being, and this girl seemed to sense he was rattled. Did she understand vows that were bigger than a person?

She pointed toward a grove where a gentleman who looked like a doctor was laying hands on some bark and said, "That's my father. He's talking to the coffee trees."

John had no memory of his own father, who was asleep in Jesus. Never on the earth, not at any time, would he be able to utter such a sentence—*this, that is my father*—but he managed to ask, "He talks to trees?"

Regarding him with impatience, she said, "They're living things." Maria plucked a red berry and flipped his palm skyward to receive it, and she grabbed a lemon from a tree and slashed it open with a knife seized from a tool bucket. The dripping half extended toward him suggested a fruit not so much split as decapitated. "Eat the berry and then chew this lemon," she commanded, "and it'll taste sweet."

"No," he said.

"Yes. These are miracle berries. Would you like a miracle or not? Look, Papa is on his way. He always guesses when I need him."

"What happens after I try the lemon?"

"Have you ever had a lemon turn into sugar? What more do you want?"

They laughed. Summertime is spongy and full of citrus, and life is stalky and rigid. What seemed miraculous was that someone very smart could be very funny while also seeming very sad. He regretted being in Rui's hand-me-down trousers and a shirt befouled with sweat. The berry he consumed was mild, and he set the lemon on his tongue—

Stars! *Glory be.* Within him was not just a dot of sweetness but a waterfall, bursts and sparks.

The white-haired gentleman drew near, and Maria Freitas could read John's mind—later, he realized she was accustomed to people thinking her papa resembled a grandfather—and she said, "I tell myself the parents who first had me went to live at the bottom of the ocean but left me here above."

This sounded like the first line in the book of the tale of her life.

As manicured as his gardens, mustache and goatee trimmed, with a sun hat and clogs but also a spotless tan suit and vest, Maria's father introduced himself as Augusto Freitas. John had heard that name before; where?

Maria announced, "His mother has headaches, Papa."

When Senhor Freitas asked if there might be a cause for her suffering, John mentioned her death sentence, now lifted, and the hounding that continued. Augusto genuflected, gripped John's arms, and said, "Serafina Alves? Child, I led the protest. I am a Catholic, but we must love others as our own. You're special to me, John. I'm honored to assist her again." His timbre grew decisive. "Feverfew."

The greenhouse had panes the color not so much of lettuce but of the souls of lettuce. Augusto located the feverfew and told it, "You have a new job," and he clipped two dozen flowers resembling daisies. Senhora Alves should dry them for tea, double infusions when affliction struck, then a single dose every four hours.

John blurted, "Why do you wear a suit, Senhor? For gardening."

With a magnificent smile, he said, "I'm a guest of the plants. And you are ours. Come along! You look thirsty."

His cottage with Maria had honeysuckle coaxed over shutters an eye-searing orange, and John averted his stare from the shrine to Saint Francis—saints are human, and to venerate them is wrong, though John secretly liked how they were in the special category of people granted unearthly powers. Augusto showed him a map of Madeira, which looked like a rock that had crumbled off Portugal and come to rest in the Atlantic like a bright thought above the Canaries and the brainpan of Africa.

We live on a dot in a sea salted by the world's weeping.

Maria asked if they could drink shrimp-water. While her father sliced a peach into a pitcher, she set out a tray with cocoa-nut tarts and candied almonds, white and pink, like the petrified eyes of blind rabbits. (Was it a sin, for this bounty to make John so awfully happy?) She plunked a tart onto a ceramic plate for him and gently asked, "Tell me what it was like."

He knew instantly what she was asking. "I was afraid Mama would die in jail. I still worry about losing her. Losing everyone." It unnerved him how she was looking right inside him.

She replied that she understood that sort of fear, very much. Papa had told her that John was from the family called Os Passarinhos because they were birds who dined on their singing. She had been only three, half her age now, but she remembered the voices swelling together. He already had a hero's real-life story!

Maria clapped when her father toted in the pitcher with the curved slices of peach resembling shrimp bobbing in an aquarium, the tendrils that had clung to the pit wavering like frail legs. The feverfew was in a parcel, and he had added a packet of fennel, excellent for digestion. "I'm handing you a bit of our city," Augusto said, an amusing remark because Funchal took its name from the word for fennel plants.

John's ease permitted him to ask, "What was everyone singing at the jail?" He had recognized a few hymns, but much of it had been a blur.

Senhor Freitas sang some Protestant lyrics he had not feared voicing. *To my listening ears all nature sings, and 'round me rings the music of the spheres.* Maria was deliberately, bemusedly intent upon cutting a tart with a knife and eating pieces daintily with a fork while radiating pride in her papa's steady tone, and John almost shouted, "I wish I could write that down! Not just the words, but the sounds. I would listen to them all the time." He admitted that was an impossible wish.

Senhor Freitas said, "Not at all. Composers write notes, and when any musician follows them, the same tunes happen."

"But I wish sounds could be put on paper, and then the paper sings back at me, whenever I want." The way written words entered the eyes but stayed available, or a camera could freeze an image and it could be looked at without end.

Maria strode to a cabinet, took out a heavy book, slammed it triumphantly in front of him, and proclaimed, "Men are studying that. About capturing sounds."

"Look inside," said Augusto.

The author was a Jesuit named Athanasius Kircher, and the title was long and in Latin, but the book itself was in English. Illustrations filled many pages. There were depictions of trombones—a hand gripping their metal could clutch music agitating like a wasp. A diagram of an ear canal displayed a circle called a "drum" that quavered when noises tapped it. Humans walk around like instruments, thanks to a tissue called a drum!

"Take it home, and bring it back on your next visit," said Senhor Freitas.

When John protested about taking anything so valuable, Maria cried, "Make paper that sings. Just don't spill water on the book or rip the pages! You have to return it so I can see you again."

Augusto wrapped the tome in a cloth and renewed his insistence. "Can you read English? I know your Reverend Kalley teaches it in his schools." Or he had, before the authorities shut them down.

All of a sudden the world felt oversized, with men galloping ahead of John in the pursuit of auditory inventions. He had never met a girl who believed something mysterious should be rendered matter-of-fact.

He had given no thought to getting home, sixteen kilometers, but Senhor Freitas offered to arrange the trip. He led them single file on a narrow ash-powdery lane, with John following, and Maria leapt in order to land her footprints dead center in the indentations John left, traces that looked as if he had carried her perfectly centered within himself. He hugged the herbs and the book by Kircher. A gardener agreed to transport John to Santa Cruz, and Augusto and Maria Freitas helped him climb into a hay wagon.

"When you come back, John, bring your family," said Augusto. "It would be a special honor to welcome your mother."

Maria could not stand still, was jumping in place, and despite the heat she had put on a capelet just to escort him on the farewell. John said, "Thank you for everything."

"Oh, John," Maria replied, coating him with her green-eyed stare, "isn't it a wonderful day." She dashed to him for a goodbye kiss, and he vowed to bring her a gift out of the ocean. He knew she knew that by speaking of such a present he was referring to the story of her parents living there, and enveloping her was that joyful melancholy he recognized as the heat source of the Portuguese soul.

The horse-drawn wagon clunked over the Marginal, where a shopkeeper sold sugar candies slick as glass, bordering the sea where Tónio got eaten by crabs and Maria's blood-parents were developing ways for abalone shells to light the travels of the schools. John dismissed a craven thought of becoming one family—Augusto liked elegance, and he was Catholic. Mother would disapprove of a man dressed like a wealthy Briton even though he lived in a cottage, and the girl was assertive in a way that did not befit Christian humility, and she wore pretty clothing and walked with too proud a spine, and her laugh was boisterous, though it would be quite nice to pin that laugh onto paper replicating the skin of an ear's drum, letting it vibrate on and on.

As the wagon crested a hillside, the white, squat homes with black chimneys in the distance looked like tumbled dice. Everything he had seen today, or tasted or heard or touched, starting with the berries that sweetened a lemon, and the peaches changed into prawns, were things of the actual world, not nonsensical fantasies—*real* miracles—and this set off a roaring in his chest so loud he could weep.

Mother threw out the feverfew and fennel, arguing, "My life is in the Lord's hands." Wounded, he tamped down a flare of anger. But he shared the Kircher book, conquering his worry about the author's being a Catholic priest, because there was an illustration of a king holding a tube to his ear to listen to prisoners in a dungeon. "Birdie," said his mother, rapt at this, "God wants us to find out how everything sings His praises."

Oh, Mother! They spoke loudly at water in a cup to watch how circles formed. John's idea was to draw a picture of it, and Mother called that idea genius. He was elated. This was how to cure her, by making her gleeful.

Inspired by a diagram, Mother whispered into a feather, "I am a servant of the Lord," and it rustled. They immersed it in wine, and when she spoke toward the drunken feather while touching it to paper, God painted purple wisps.

John wanted her to meet Maria and Augusto, but their Catholicism kept him from suggesting it, and he was reluctant to return a sacred book that had so enlivened Mother.

And then history decided to hammer all their triumphs flat on its anvil. Scarcely three weeks later, glad that Nikka's husband, Miguel, was off on a fishing boat, John and his sister were tossing corn to the pigs while Rui was dawdling over porridge inside and Mother was scouring the dishes. John heard what sounded like the rockets normally launched to signal a festival, leaving smoke trails overhead. He gestured at one and said, "Nikka? Look."

It was a mercilessly hot day in early August. They stared toward the valley below. Houses were ablaze, with flaming palm trees swaying like metronomes. Nikka jumped at the report of a cannon issuing from the direction of the harbor. John threw his arms around his sister. He must be ready to die for her and Rui, and above all, for Mother.

Because three men stomping quickly, snorting like charging bulls, were ascending the slope toward their yard, bearing torches.

THE WEAVER OF ANGELS

MADEIRA, 1840–1846

THE DEATH SENTENCE FOR MARIA CATARINA PEREIRA VAZ GATO DE
Freitas came at her birth. She was left near the stone well of the old
woman whose name had long ago been replaced with the title Tecelão
dos Anjos. This was in Camacha, right outside Funchal, so the girl
was in a wicker basket, since the local industry was to shape reeds
into dolls, chairs, and bowls. Everyone called the woman Tessie, the
nickname bestowed by the British who could not pronounce "Tecelão"
but also used her services. Her job was to smother or drown unwanted
newborns, weaving their immaculate souls into garlands while they
were still angels, before hardships drove them to sin.

The baby—nameless at the hour of her execution—kicked off a
blanket to reveal a lacy gown, as if she were dressed for a pageant at
the palace in Queluz. Tessie's fee bought her secrecy (for whatever that
was worth on an island) about love affairs, about girls spirited into
hiding as their bodies swelled, but this child had the most shocking
parentage of Tessie's career. The crank shrieked as she lowered the
bucket and drew up water while the baby gurgled. Tessie dipped a
clamshell and intoned, "I baptize thee in the name of the Father, Son,
and Holy Ghost," while trickling water onto the baby's forehead and

racing through the sacrament, the denouncing of Satan and so forth. She was suffering double her usual hangover.

"Now you'll fly to paradise," said Tessie, but she paused. The mother was a silly rich girl now locked up in a nearby convent, but the larger-than-life father was a famous wielder of cruelty who claimed to be divine. Likely he would be grateful to be spared another bastard. Or would he order Tessie's guts wound on a windlass? Her grandmother and mother had been Weavers of Angels, and she enjoyed being re-garded with fear, which is far better than reverence, and how many women made enough money to buy freedom from other humans? Due to her sore shoulder, she figured pressing a pillow over this tiny face was easier than stuffing her in the bucket and working the pulley again.

The pillow's underside was amber from the choked exhalations of the by-products of mortal mistakes, of nuns and priests or wealthy, straying spouses. Some angels were deformed, or unwanted girls, and sometimes commoners could not afford an eighth child.

Tessie was a spiritual midwife, a creator of instant saints.

Parakeets screeched overhead, swooping in parabolas.

She nestled the infant in a dirt indentation, grunting because a diet of firewater and goat made her inflexible. A pity that the last earthly sight for the babies was Tessie's cracked molars and goitered neck. Her flesh got increasingly disfigured as she absorbed the crimes that the true guilty ones were too cowardly to own—part of the bargain. Under the raised pillow, the baby giggled, and that rocked Tessie backward, scared of what sounded like defiant amusement.

It would be sweet to think her pausing was on account of the ba-by's being special, or especially lovely. But this angel held vectors of the highest corporal powers, and Tessie could sell her bloodlines to an eager parent for an excellent fee.

———

AUGUSTO PEREIRA VAZ GATO DE FREITAS CALLS HIS NEW DAUGHTER Maria Catarina—to honor his wife, who died in childbirth two de-cades earlier as their son emerged strangled on the umbilical cord. His grief is well known. Delivered in a reed basket, Maria Catarina is his uncanny Moses, bearing back to him his wife's lime eyes and black locks. He is forty-six, head gardener of the Botanical Garden owned by an aristocrat, though the flowers and trees, reveling in their view of the sea jostling itself into curls, whisper that they are really his.

The gargoyle who brought her offered a tall tale of parentage to maximize the extortive price—Augusto could laugh at the fairy-tale rudiments of a crone tottering out of the woods with the prettiest child in the kingdom—and caused him to investigate and conclude that *it is possible* his daughter has such a powerful birth-father that she might be kidnapped or killed. The birth-mother resides in silence-insuring shame in the convent.

A wet nurse gives Maria Catarina's scalp an odor of milk and marzipan.

Upon exiting their cottage every cantaloupe dawn, the scent of honeysuckle so heavy she dons it as a coverlet, he sets her near custard-apple trees as he prunes the rosemallows before descending the hill to soothe her with the sight of black sand, a beach the shade of ground-up darkness, with sparkles; the moment is everlasting. When he carries her into the city, people fawn over this treasure in a widower's arms. *Everything is yours, darling,* the manicured yards where dragonflies stitch up and down, the factories and kirks of the British invaders. The basaltic pieces called dragon's teeth turn the sidewalks into mosaic pictures—O Meu Mais Do Que Tudo, let us stroll upon a black-and-white caravel, a compass. Observing the skiffs at the tide-line, their hulls painted with Phoenician eyes to see through fog, he shares a lesson: Never sail away without a woolen hat, because if you get lost, you can wring the mist out of it to survive on unsalted water.

He brings her when he dines at one of the hotels along the beach, in the cool, pink-tinged dining room where utensils tap china and the pearls dangling from the throats of foreign women shoot off bite-sized panes scraped from a rainbow. His suppers are light, often clams in garlic broth.

Basting in the humidity, the tourists at the tables speak of leaping east across the water to Casablanca. Augusto tells Maria Catarina to listen to their news of the globe:

A place billed as the first nightclub is open in Paris!
Avoid Greece! A rebellion has ruined it!

Find a photography studio and buy an immortal image of yourself! An
Englishman named Fox Talbot got a chemical from an astronomer and is
producing portraits from glass negatives, and that heralds people captured
forever, thanks to a silver liquid from someone who loves the stars.

When the wet nurse uses saliva to adhere filthy threads to the baby's forehead, so that demons will find her too ugly to steal, Augusto
snaps, "None of that foolishness under my roof," though "my" is a
stretch, since his cottage belongs to the estate's owner. Augusto's father
in Aveiro, in the northern mainland of Portugal, is a municipal judge
who despises superstition. When Augusto's wife and son died, and he
migrated to the steam-cleaning, pain-leaching languor of the subtrop-
ics, the reminders of his birthplace were the ovos moles his mother and
sisters shipped from their shop—confectionary shells filled with yolk
pudding—and a wish to better subscribe to his father's belief in the
supremacy of reason.

An attack on tranquility came brutally quickly.

Despite netting around her bassinet, Maria Catarina contracted
malaria. Infusions of fenugreek did nothing; his talent as a magician
with herbs deserted him.

While bargaining with a God he scarcely trusted, including an
offer to swap his life for hers, Augusto rushed Maria Catarina to a
physician named the Reverend Doctor Robert Reid Kalley, whose
conversion of Madeirans to Presbyterianism was inflaming the powers that be. Jarred from the wicker sleigh that two giants had pulled
up the slope, and with his child panting with fever, Augusto burst into
tears the second he entered Kalley's home, weeping that had been
accumulating since losing his wife and son. Kalley steered him into a
tapestry-covered chair. Sun enveloped the Reverend, turning him into
an expertly shadowed portrait study as he said, "Your grandchild? My
wife and I are not blessed with one of the Lord's children. I needed to
learn that everyone I meet is His offspring. Pardon me, Senhor Freitas!
I speak Portuguese, too."

Augusto replied that he knew a lot of English, and out gushed his
story: gardener, widower. He would abandon Catholicism if the doctor
saved Maria.

"I require no conversion from a faith in which you are comfortable," Kalley said. When Maria Catarina shrieked, he added, "Your daughter agrees. We come to Jesus as we are, equal." He winked at Augusto. "Even girls. I suspect the root of my troubles is my refusal to hold Eve responsible for men's folly. Let me acquaint you with the properties of quinine, from cinchona trees. My Margaret has had cause to praise our Lord for its curative power."

He administered a tincture to Maria Catarina from a vial, adding, "You're looking less than hale, too, Senhor. Tobacco? A glass of port? I do not indulge, but I keep some for visitors."

"I partake of neither." No point in Augusto admitting how separate he was from most society. He lived with plants, and a foundling he had failed to keep well.

"A lemon drink? I flavor it with papaya, as sugar's history with slavery gives it a taste of blood. No? All right." He set a benedictive hand on Maria's forehead. "She is cooler already. Let us pray, Senhor Freitas, you to your God, I to mine, an easy convergence." Kalley closed his eyes and achieved that muscling into communion with the ether that people of faith found innate but that Augusto thought puzzling, almost embarrassing. Prayer seemed at root a pleading for God to change His decree that everyone must die. Kalley intoned, "Lord, in Your infinite wisdom, allow Maria Freitas the great destiny I am sure awaits, as she is clearly loved, and such things are sadly rare upon the earth You entrusted to us."

———

MARIA CATARINA PEREIRA VAZ GATO DE FREITAS STANDS WITH PAPA and many strangers on a hill. Behind them the tides ripple in the manner her skin does when she hears music, when Papa sings as he is doing now, ribbons of notes unspooling, and she joins in while a soprano chants like a sorceress, the whole day is a song! Papa shows her the hymnal with its tunes shaped like black wires and hooks. A little boy is locked in that building past a salt-dashed field. He is a caged sparrow. This is called a "vigil." With tunes they are demanding his freedom. She hits a note high enough to get through the window to greet him. A taste of pineapple pours down her throat, since a protester wields a machete to open fruit so the juice will travel like edible yellow birds into the jail.

Papa says her wishes are forged of iron; she is made of iron.

Why, then, does she often feel so frightened? He vows to protect her, and as she drowses with him in the rocking chair, he recites the Portuguese Night Blessing that counsels a child to dread nothing, neither sleep, darkness, age, nor illness—Deus a abençoe, e a faça uma santa muiiiiito grande, boa noite, durma bem—God bless you, and make you a biiiiig saint, good night, sleep well—and he tucks her into her feather bed while wishing her sonhos cor-de-rosa, pink dreams, the Lusitanian way of granting sweet dreams, night-rest in the shade of peonies, the raptures of sunrise, and the tint of the camellias that got the best of God's paintbrush . . . sail into pink and seize it as yours, my living angel, my own dream incarnate.

———

WHO IS MY MAMA?

Your mother lives at the bottom of the sea. She tends the beds where sand sneaks inside oysters and irritates them while it buckles into pearls.

Alert to Maria Catarina's fear of the dark, Mama comes to play at night. Salt water fills Maria's room to the ceiling, and her neck cracks open with gills like Mama's, and they somersault as the hairbrush and gardening clogs spin, and the dresses and Saint Francis statue swim-dance. There is proof every morning—a low-tide twinkling after the draining of this tank, and a wet thread linking Maria's lip to her pillow.

Papa's skill at plaiting vines enables him to braid her hair. He calls her "Cat," short for Catarina. It is also the English word for their name Gato.

They like dragon fruits and bananas and chard, red yellow green. He praises her sowing of carrot seeds—each is tinier than the heart of a flea, they pulse, she can feel it, her fingertip pushes them two and a half centimeters deep. The epiphytic orchids are unsettling because their roots attach to air, but she is communal with earthworms, and with trowel and hands, she works the soil until it resembles the cocoa from the Dutch. She tenderizes the hydrangea patch with lava dust so the flowers will turn vibrant purple. These will be worn as shoulder puffs on dresses during festivals. Into the mouths rampant in the dirt, she spoons vinegar, the way other girls feed dollies, which is stupid because dollies are not alive, but the earth is.

She and other workers in the Botanical Garden shuck fava beans out of their pods, where they nestle like peridots in the padded lining of jewelry boxes. Islanders declare, "Favas!" when they mean something is ridiculous, and she finds this hilarious.

Is that my mother? she asks, pointing at a boat's maidenhead.

Favas, Cat-Cat! responds her father, guaranteed to unleash her glee.

That Senhora with beauty marks?—favas, your mother is a pearl-maker in the sea.

That is a story for *babies,* Papa. Just tell me the truth, tell me tell me.

She pictures Mama writing a book inside a castle, where she is drenched in a sunlight that melts the words so they will re-form into the language of any reader who picks up her story.

———

ONE DAWN THE WEAVER OF ANGELS CORNERS AUGUSTO TO HISS THAT she wants more money to keep quiet about the girl's birth-father. He grabs an axe and threatens to chop Tessie in half if she goes anywhere near his daughter, and her grin as she waddles off plagues him. One of the tyrannically worst aspects of living is that someone minds his own business, wants *to be left alone,* in peace, *for God's sake,* and yet forces come to prod and poke and forbid it. O Meu Mais Do Que Tudo, My One More Than Everything, where can I hide you, what ends of the earth?

To distract Maria Catarina from inquiring about a mother who is profoundly locked away, Augusto elicits the help of the gardeners Edite and Alberto Teixeira, bereft since both their sons left them for America. Alberto creates a topiary cat to honor her nickname. With her auntie-titia Edite, Maria makes rice puddings dusted with cinnamon, and she learns broderie anglaise and Guimarães whitework, extracting threads from cloth to form cutwork as if she has done it for one hundred years. It is deliciously disquieting how she feels born to it, and even this young, she suspects girls can go a lifetime not knowing how to match who they are with what they do, but she is already united with gardening and stitching, in her flesh every bit as much as her own lungs. She convinces herself she is fine without others her age, which saves her from having to apologize for being who she is. She perfects bullion knots using a milliner's needle, the kind with the eye end as thin as the point end. "You have the gift," Edite purrs. Madeiran needlework is ornate and world famous, but each generation has only a few goddesses, though everyone has at least a nearness to someone with a talent, the men, too; the men are the ones in the households who stitch buttons onto clothing.

Edite and Alberto watch over her—as Maria plies threads, or reads her English and Portuguese books, or they feast on roasted chicken, salad with nasturtiums, and the baked meringues called suspiros—on Wednesday evenings, when Augusto descends into the city to visit a retired madame named Amparo, her forearms weighted with bracelets.

To camouflage these visits, Augusto buys supplies or stops at the Howell embroidery factory to purchase an exotic dye from the manager's collection. Maria-Cat best endures his absences by thinking he might bring home a new color, liquid or powder, such as synthetic lazurite, or *French Ultramarine*, which Jean-Baptiste Guimet invented for a contest, and *Tyrion Purple*, from a concentration of murex shells. He buys *Quercitron*, from black oaks, and *Indian Yellow*, from the urine of cows fed mango leaves, and *Mummy Brown*, from the resin of bandages that wrapped the dead. A spectrum of reds glisten in their bottles—*Amaranth*, called the eternal shade, and *Orange-Poppy* and *Carmine*. Best of all is *Cochineal*, a shade of fuchsia, the pink of deep dreaming, and *fuchsias* are also ballerina-flowers, each stamen with its drop of honey far inside the dancer's body.

He buys a tabletop object with glass facets set in a circle and whispers, "It spins, Cat. Go ahead!" A horse is etched on each rectangle. Every pose is different. When she sets this carousel in motion, and the horses melt into a single animal galloping round and round, she is so flabbergasted she could fall to pieces.

Because sometimes she feels as breakable as a teacup, or a fragile plate that is kept in a cupboard after all the other plates in the set got broken long ago.

———

THE GARDEN'S OWNER SENDS HIS FLOUR-WHITE NIECE NAMED SUSAN Ashe to boss everyone around, and when she snaps at Papa to trim the fig trees more severely, Maria grabs a shovel and shouts, "If you talk to Papa or me like that again, I'll hit you." Susan is a shit-smeared cow too stunned to answer. (No, she's not a cow, their lowing is angelic, and they are sweet, and so are goats, bunnies, chickens, and pigs.) Papa steers Maria-Cat toward a walk. Halfway up a crag, he laughs and chides her with, "Be careful about offending the people who pay me, minha princesa."

"I hate her."

"I hate her, too. But before you speak like that, go on a stroll and calm your nerves." On days dedicated to the trees, he wears a bow tie, because in Portuguese it is called a butterfly, and the trees appreciate that.

"I'll think very loudly how much I hate her." Even without looking at him, she senses her father trying not to grin.

"A good plan, darling."

Agitated, her skin too tight, she leans into the climb but pauses to explore a cove carved into the side of a hill. A shrub with glossy dark pointed leaves and red berries has tucked itself behind a boulder, under a lofty umbrella of a palm tree. When she touches a few leaves, the bush stirs. Her father dissolves into reverence. Tone hushed, he says, "Do you realize what you've found?" He greets the plant by asserting, "Aren't you lovely," and he declares to Maria, "It's *Synsepalum dulcificum*. The miracle-berry or miracle-fruit plant. A pity more people don't know about it."

She relishes the stealth required at night to dig up the plant. They transplant it to an unobtrusive spot in the garden and hope to keep it a secret. Their *Synsepalum dulcificum* does its best to hide in a gaggle of other shrubs, and then the greatest thing ever in her whole life happens. In their kitchen, he urges her to chew a berry, and when she hesitates, he pretends to be hurt by saying, "Don't you trust your old papa?"

She grinds a berry with her teeth and swallows it. He provides her with a wedge of lemon and encourages her to gnaw on it.

Her entire being expands, her feet leave the ground. Such an uplift from expecting acidity but receiving a candied taste! The miracle the berries perform, he explains, is to change anything sour or stale into sweetness, and she cannot sleep from the elation.

Scions of their *Synsepalum dulcificum* are swiftly created. She goes out-of-her-skull mad with the know-how he imparts about taking cuttings at a slant. *(Don't pester a stem with timid nicks, make one confident strike, sweetheart.)* She plasters mulch on the wounds before embedding the new growths. When her first successful cutting sprouts its first berry, she insists they celebrate by descending the slope in the evening to traipse on the sea-basted black sand, where she points out how the moon has tossed a shimmering ladder of light onto the water.

Gone are the fables about a mermaid-mother climbing out to her. Maria Catarina is long past being an infant. She whispers, "Look what fell out of the sky for us, Papa. Isn't it beautiful?"

Minha princesa, he breathes, *it is, it is.*

———

ONE SUMMER'S DAY, AT THE HEIGHT OF WHAT SEEMS POSSIBLE—IF they grow too many *Synsepalum dulcificum* shrubs, they will be discovered, and the space is limited—a boy startles her out of a reverie. That very morning, hand to heart *that very morning!*, the idea pierced her that tapestries exist that are the size of walls, but what if she stitched one of the Botanical Garden with every detail replicated *to scale?* That would exalt her as the most fabulous embroidery artist under the sun, and her handiwork would be exhibited in Paris or over an expanse in America's Wild West. She would buy Papa his own garden (and raise her miracle plant in it), and—and—suddenly a boy appears, as if instructing her to *include him* in that vast project. He is tall, with huge brown eyes.

What compels her to divulge the secret about her plant? She has been lying to herself about needing no friends other than Papa, Edite, and Alberto, and this boy will save her from an existence that is not as large as she wants to think. It is closed off, and she is not adept at dealing with strangers or altering her plans—if something is not *perfect*, it might as well be in *ruins*. It tickles her when he acts as if she wants to poison him with a berry, until he bites into the lemon and his gaze floats into her eyes.

Papa kneels upon meeting him, since this is the boy who was jailed with his mother, when Maria sang to him. He has lived a tale of adventure already, and this terrifies her. He knows about the world! He carries wounds. She gets show-offy lest he discover she understands nothing outside her little kingdom. Papa does his trick of floating cut peaches in water so they swim like prawns, and they loan him the *Phonurgia nova sive conjugiam something something*, because John admits to dreaming as she does, God-large: He wants to trap music on pages! No one she has met thinks as he does ... this, too, frightens her, and she becomes loud and giddy and suspects she scared him away.

—

ON A SUNDAY THICK WITH FLOWERED HEAT, AUGUSTO AND MARIA Catarina attended Mass, despite Papa's dislike of the priests' insistence that humans are disgusting meat-bags. The owner of the Botanical Garden had forbidden them to dispense free vegetables to the needy, and getting the Church to intervene might first require displays of devotion. Maria donned Papa's montecristi hat over her lace veil and was experimenting with assorted tilts to bolster her daydream of being on an Italian riverboat, when suddenly the priest in the pulpit began thundering about "heathens" and "holy war," and congregants muttered assent. An old couple nodded furiously as Father Silveira tipped into ranting, "The infidels are responsible for our drought! Herd them into the sea!" Cheering erupted. When he bellowed about "putting a stop to that foreigner Robert Kalley!," Maria gave Papa his hat and led him down the nave, their urgency attracting stares.

Set upon warning Kalley, they reached the incline leading toward his vista-perfect house, but black clouds billowed from it and rafters snapped, releasing embers. It was a spewing volcano on the hilltop. A duo was descending with torches, and Papa demanded to know the whereabouts of the Reverend and Margaret.

The rioters cackled. What fun to have the dogs released, the mayhem sanctioned by men who decided they were in charge. "You're too late," crowed one of them. "He escaped with his wife, but don't worry, we got his house."

Augusto and Cat had visited him recently with a thimbleful of lapis lazuli powder, meant for use in depictions of the Virgin, and Kalley had been touched by something so precious, and costly, and now rabid jesters had consigned it—everything—to cinders. Papa said, "Let's get you home, minha princesa. Now."

But as they hastened through the main square, a mob poured in. Maria had never seen such a churning mass of arms, legs, and sticks. Men were being beaten. A plank slammed into a head that geysered blood. A woman pointed at Papa and shrieked, "He's Kalley's friend!" and another one grabbed him and hollered, "He goes to whores!" The storm swept him away as Maria screamed, "Papa! Papa!" and shoved and scratched and fought to go where a riptide conveyed him. But she tripped, and a boot pinned her calf, and she called his name over and over until her eardrums were bursting.

THE TRANSLATION OF "MADEIRA" IS "WOOD." THE NAME COMES FROM THE FORESTS BURNING SEVEN YEARS WHEN SETTLERS TRIED CLEARING THE LAND, BUT WILDNESS ROARED OUT OF THE ASHES

1846–1860

THEIR NEIGHBOR AMÉLIA, A CATHOLIC WHO HAD BROUGHT OVER octopus rice when Mother was imprisoned, was racing to John and Nikka, frozen like statues, as men with fire trooped up the slope toward them. Mother was the prize everyone still wanted to capture.

Amélia yelled, "Hurry!" She shoved a sweater at Nikka—what comforts to give?—and when another cannon boomed out, Amélia cried, "The warships, British ones, they're saying they'll take you. To Trinidad. Go!"

John glanced downward at the men before running into the house, Nikka behind him, and he shouted, "Mama, they want to kill you again!" and Nikka reported the news about protection in the harbor. Rui set down his spoon. Mother said, "God will take care of us," and John shrieked, "Our book!" and darted for the Kircher treasure, but Mama nabbed him and said, "It's too heavy, my baby." She unlatched the chicken coop and pigpen and stamped her foot to force his beloved Glória to join the others galloping away. The men were only the length of one Our Father from finishing the hike to the yard.

Past bougainvillea and dragon trees, John plunged with her and his sister and brother into thickets where branches cut their faces.

He glanced backward to see the Alves house engulfed in flames. The book holding his dreams with Mother, that he had sworn to return to his new friend and her father, was being destroyed along with their bedding, rugs, and morning-glory flowers. A twitch of fury slowed him for a second.

Getting to the harbor of Água de Pena required crossing a thirty-meter bridge with vine banisters and a gap-filled floor of planks. It was not capable of holding more than one person at a time. Mother, ignoring John's protest, volunteered to risk it first. As she skimmed her hands along the vines, the bridge swayed over a chasm, but she reached the other side, where the land descended toward the shattered-sapphire sea.

A boar appeared at an outcropping of rocks, snuffling up yams. John adored pigs, sensitive and smarter than most humans, and ached for Glória, who used to play fetch but might already be dead. As the men's hooting grew near, Nikka insisted her brothers head toward refuge first, and there was no time to argue, so Rui scampered onto the bridge—too vigorously, and it veered side to side, but he held on, while Mother radiated calmness. Beyond her the ship awaited. John refused to cross until Nikka was safe, and a few boards tumbled as she hastened, and he hesitated until the bridge quit rocking before he began storming over it. The men arrived when he was halfway, and one roared, "There's no fleeing the true God!"

The drop to oblivion was so far that John had a sensation of floating. In the jail he had wanted sky and far vista, but now they were making him ill.

"Look, a hog," said Manny, owner of a sardine cart. "Dinner." Mother used to buy fish from him, gleaming pieces of silver; John had had no idea Manny hated them. Manny picked up a rock to kill the boar, and John bellowed, "Run!" at the animal. It reared its head and tore away, and Manny shouted, "Goddamn it!"

The man next to him crouched and set fire to the bridge. The air spoke in John's ear as he inhaled a draft of singeing. It is possible for children to die. *The wolves shall not spare the flock.* Mother called out, "John! Come to me! Don't look down!"

"That's a child!" said the third man, taking off his shirt to extinguish the burning.

"He scared away the pig!" yelled the fire-setter.

His compatriots stomped on the fire, but sparks landed on the wood, and planks spiraled down. The men had impeded their own pursuit, and they gripped their snapping torches as John barreled forward with wild swinging, burning wood behind him while Mother, opening her arms, summoned him to fly.

Help her slide down the sand, toward the small boats crammed with refugees, a wonder they did not sink on the way to one of the three warships. British sailors dropped rope ladders after securing the little boats, and they aided with the climbing, especially with children, the elderly, and the infirm upward while the jaws of the sea opened and shut on the hulls of the boats and any feet that slipped near the water. The pilots of the little boats returned to the shoreline as exiles, hundreds more, scrambled out of hiding.

Huddled on board was John's best friend Francisco de Melo, with his parents and brother. Francisco whispered, "Isn't Jesus supposed to save us?" and John wondered why Mother did not ask Him for aid. Old Ronaldo Mendes, his eyebrows gone, smelled like the custard Nikka once reduced to tar by cooking it too long, and the deck was crowded with families. Word came that Kalley's house was smoldering, but he had disguised himself as a woman and been conveyed with his wife on a palanquin to the ship *Forth*, already gone, the only one destined for England.

Faraway sounds rode fast on the wind to wrap John and Serafina. Animals screamed with slaughter while attackers brutalized children, women, and men, pausing only to cart off anything valuable. Incinerated books in Kalley's library were transforming into bats, joining the black-ash bat of the Kircher book to flit over bleeding livestock and clothing-ripped girls, over homes expiring and flowers bellowing because they could not run, and over stones finding their targets of human torsos. "Nikka," John said, "what about Miguel?"

"He'll come back from fishing and find us gone," she said.

"Good." John hoped Augusto and Maria were safe as Catholics in their roost above the sea. The water heaved under this vessel called the *William of Glasgow* as it sailed toward the unknown. He scavenged the length of the deck to find a blanket for his shivering mother. He heard her insides chanting: *I am frightened.* And this scared him.

—

IN THE BEGINNING WAS TRINIDAD. THE PORTUGUESE PROTESTANTS took up the labor in the sugarcane fields abandoned by enslaved people freed a decade earlier. John spent his tenth birthday cutting underbrush on an estate lit for parties with pale-green Chinese lanterns, and his eleventh birthday was spent wondering if the sun had baked the sheen clean off his eyes.

God at last decreed it time—He seemed determined to try the faith of the Alves tribe in two-and-a-half-year dosages—to lead them from captivity. He said, Reports of your distress have reached American ears.

A first covenant of jobs will appear like a dream and will not come to pass, but be watchful, despair not, for I intend to deliver you thereafter to the heart of a state that is shaped like a heart, buried in the heart of the country.

—

IN THE BEGINNING WAS NEW YORK.

The United Hemp Company in Illinois responded to the American Protestant Society's search for a solution. Jobs would be provided for these pilgrim souls, along with homes or the land to build them on the frontier, if they first sailed to New York City, whence they would be guided into the paradise at the center of a limitless nation.

One hundred desires, most of which he could not name, galvanized John when they arrived in the river-encircled realm of enormous buildings and fast horses and people hurrying as if from floodwaters, only to hear that the hemp company's intentions were greater than its abilities, and it was bankrupt. The exiles were stranded. A further message arrived from Illinois: When the cholera along the roadways lifted, the Protestant churches would indeed make the Midwest a haven. Charity was long, and hopes must not be dashed, and the Madeirans would find shelter, food, clothing, and work, mostly in the far-stretching fields.

The refugees waited in New York for so many months it became home. Mrs. Eula Brooks of the Presbyterian Church took Nikka, Rui, and John to the coffee-room at the Park Theater to discover hot chocolate. It was splendor. It dissolved the crystals John's marrow had become.

Nikka's fingers laced through his as they hurried to Washington Street and Little West Twelfth to see where a fort had been ripped down. They learned the word "block," as if the city could be broken into immense bricks to move around. At a fresh-provisions store, they were enchanted with horror at the metal boxes of meat. Men had invented a way of putting animals into tin so the flesh did not spoil.

Mrs. Brooks was impressed by how well many of them spoke the language, thanks to the Reverend Kalley, who was busily chatting with great leaders in Illinois and praising this land of bounty. It struck John anew that everyone, including his mother, always used his English name, had done so ever since he could remember, because the British had a devil of a time pronouncing "João." Missionaries in New York lectured about men of accomplishment who hailed from elsewhere, and a rhapsody about John Jacob Astor—a German immigrant who had risen to the highest wealth—caused John to insist that his friend Francisco join him in breaking into Astor's mansion, to search for clues as to how he had gone from *nothing* to *everything*. Astor had died not long before their arrival, and maybe he haunted his property, ready to divulge the secrets of becoming rich enough to pay for one hundred years of whatever Mother needed.

Francisco's skills with picking locks were tested at the sumptuous door, and passersby eyed two ill-clad boys pretending to wash the façade with rags. Francisco, with his liquid eyes and long lashes, said, "I don't want to get shot." His genius with locks had been used to break into a lord's manor in Trinidad to steal some Warburg's tincture when Nikka was ill, and they had sprinted away under rifle fire.

"We're only going to look. Hurry up."

"You want to try?"

"All right. All right! Sorry."

Francisco angled the wire he had brought along, and a snap admitted them to the palace of the dead richest man in the city. They tiptoed up a curving staircase to the grandest room in the universe, and

John slid on the polished floor below a chandelier of a thousand glass droplets. Drapes covered statues in niches.

There were so many corridors and closets. A dressing area offered top hats, and John tried one on. "Well, well," John boomed, grabbing Francisco's hand for the grip-shake Americans did. Mrs. Brooks had explained that it evolved from a wish to prove no weapons were carried. John twirled a walking stick, and Francisco, though wary, put on a top hat, too. They entered a parlor with prints of birds, including a roseate spoonbill. John had never seen a floor with dark strips of wood containing lines of paler wood. America must have a tree with different colors entwined. All at once he jumped, and his top hat spilled off, and so did Francisco's, as their collars were seized by a humorless caretaker.

In the police station, Francisco's skills with English deserted him and John's were sorely tried, though he protested that they had only wanted to pay their respects to Astor.

"No one taught you boys to stay out of homes that aren't yours?" asked the officer with eyebrows that reminded John of Tónio's. Iron doors clanked nearby.

"About Astor we think a museum, that it to be a museum, sir," said John.

"What? Where are you from?"

"Sorry." But he did not regret finding the gleam of those floors, the smoothness of the hat, or the watercolor of the pink bird signed by Audubon, whom Mrs. Brooks had said was another immigrant to find fame.

When Serafina Alves entered this locale of justice, her face stayed immobile over disappointment with him but also fear as an officer sized her up as penniless. John had stamped her impression of the new world with a reminder that imprisonment would always threaten. Her English broke into pieces as she smiled at the officer, and John detected the tremor as she said, "My boy make a mistake, ai such nice houses here, but it is wrong to go in, say sorry, John. Francisco."

"I'm sorry, sir," said John.

Francisco echoed John's apology.

"We should put them behind bars, teach them a lesson," said the officer. The walls were greenish, and a bellow of someone unseen entered this anteroom.

"I pay you for I take them home." She fumbled in her pocket for coins.

The policeman laughed and told her to keep her money but stay out of trouble or they would get sent back where they came from. Mother ushered them out, and when John tried to thank her, as they shuffled in chilly air past one grand home after another, she snapped in Portuguese, "Have the decency to keep quiet."

Shame began slashing his muscles and worsened when she went missing the next morning from their temporary home at Twenty-fifth Street and Seventh Avenue.

He found her in her favorite spot for praying, near the Hudson River. When he perched beside her on a low wall, she pointed toward some buildings and said she loved how immense they were and how tall he was, so much taller for his age than most Madeiran boys. And it seemed glorious to build something so towering that when you sailed to heaven, and God asked what you had done to help with creation, you could point to what you had made, and He could see it from where He was and be well pleased.

"I'm sorry for looking inside Mr. Astor's house," John said. Nikka had spent breakfast-time calming him; no, Mother was probably on a walk, not under arrest. But one day she *would* be gone forever. That this should dawn with the heft of a surprise was itself the surprise. They fell into that lullaby she had invented when he was a child frightened that Tónio would hurt her. *Who is my canary-pet?* she would whisper, and as they sat near the Hudson, she repeated the words of her old consolation. Shall Mother tell you how she will never leave you? Will you know how to find me when I die, my love? It is so simple. It will be the first time Mother will be grand, so you must rejoice when my spirit moves over the waters.

Listen, John. It does not matter that spiders eat us after we're buried. Do you know why it would grieve me to think of you crying? I'll be inside those spiders, and when they spin their webs, across doorways and in corners where walls meet other walls, or when the webs get hung as earrings on cattle or draped across space to your collar while you lie in the grass—get up and walk through me. Walk through cobwebs, since that is how I'll kiss your face. If you're wounded, use cobwebs, mashed up the way Nikka showed you, to stop the bleeding. That will be your mother to your rescue.

Because Mother had remarked upon tall buildings, the Lord reminded him that kings and nobles always built monuments dedicated to God, their names on plaques, so John declared, "I'll help you build a church in this country, Mama." Such a purpose would keep enormity from swallowing them.

"Yes. It's a sin not to be grateful."

The message of the gulls overhead translated into *Hearken! Listen to this land's music of welcome.*

He could hear the citizens far away in Illinois scurrying around for them:

Our Christian duty is more than lip service. Pots with dents hammered out and cloth wearing what looks like a mist of itself lifting off, a kind of cloth meant for midwestern weather, hurtle into the mass of goods being assembled. The women of Jacksonville and Springfield are in a flurry, preparing for the newcomers, collecting lamps that use whale oil, and so the smoke, the vapor of the dead out of the sea, fills the nostrils in the prairie with leviathan fantasies. Jars of pumpkin chips swimming in syrup shall be bestowed, and cucumbers pickled white and green, and tongue in aspic—such unheard-of things emerging from cupboards for the Portuguese Protestants, along with hats that are thick; Americans wear a nearness to the size of cats on their heads!—and hollows of fur called muffs that eat the hands of women—how does invention follow dream, and how does it come to belong to others? The spirits of the whales shall rise nonstop out of lamps like the genie in the story about wishes that Nikka once read to him, the flames going strong because Americans demand, *must now have,* light beyond God's daylight. Women with the heat of stoves biting their faces crimson are speeding to receive the exiles. Here praising God is *action.* Here praising God is about putting everything to use. Take this *rushlight:* a stalk soaked in grease and burned in a minute stand in place of a candle, poor man's light.

But first: Dusk bathes New York, with wrens and jays glad-swooping to join the gulls, trilling so as to make John clutch his mother as if that would cure all that besieged her, and the song was:

Twilight is a paint spill, all jeweled, and here you are, and here you are born.

———

IN YET ANOTHER BEGINNING WAS THE FUNNY TRAIN THEY RODE slowly over wooden tracks lashed in place with iron strips down their middles, the ties wooden, too. The cars were open and flat, and the air was so freezing that everyone's words came out *white. Cold is white. Sounds have colors.* The Reverend Daniel Lathrop, their escort, said they could not be expected to guess it was unusually warm for a November in Illinois. John knew from New York that breathing can be white, but he had never seen it amassed like this. Almost 350 of them filled the twelve cars of the train. Refugees were shrouded with blankets. Did exhaling this much white mean their spirits were leaving their bodies, and did that prove they were very alive or very dead? Surrounding them was nothing, nothing but the train; he had never seen *nothing* before. Exhalations rose and dissolved to form an enormous, chilled curtain the shade of gauze, and the train kept piercing it.

They had taken a steamship out of New York City and assorted canal boats before boarding a lake steamer to Chicago, followed by more canal boats down the Illinois River to Naples for the purpose of riding these Wabash rails. He whispered to Rui that they could get to Jacksonville faster if they walked. On crutches.

Feathers of laughter blew out of their mouths.

A missionary lady with hair the tint of pineapple was distributing shawls, and Mother got draped with one stitched with a design of bamboo, and Rui brushed her with its tassels as if she were a lady being dusted with rice powder before a party.

She grinned and said, "Oh . . . you."

John sat and rested a hand on her clavicle as the train clanked, and God warned him: *I charge you with guiding her if she becomes afraid* due to her shock at a vastness unlike anything they had seen. To the west the land was so flat he wondered why the citizens had chopped down the hills. There was one distant line where the sky met the land. If you sliced open that line, maybe the hills jumped back out.

The Reverend Lathrop at last strode into their car to shout that they were in Jacksonville. A platform held the group ready to receive them, including musicians, with a tuba coiled around a man who was like an excited stamen inside an American-sized golden metal flower. The wheels screeched from the pain of braking, and the travelers knocked into one another from weariness. Rui pointed out a man in a top hat and a suit who consulted a watch attached to a fob that shined in the frigid light. That had been a discovery in New York, that in addition to having good teeth, people were in constant need of knowing or, even stranger, *wearing* the time.

The band swelled with "The Race That Long in Darkness Pined," and even the older exiles knew hymn-English and Lord's-supper-English and sang a little.

After the nation's anthem, the song-marked wind was crying lightly as everyone cleared a path to let Mother be the first to step onto this new earth. The man in the top hat and other gentlemen approached, along with women resembling friendly bears in their ample coats, the faces so pale they looked like biscuit dough rolled thin. They were all doing the American smile as they clasped Mother's forearms to assist in lowering her from the train.

As reporters ventured closer, Rui let John step in as Mother's translator, saying, "You were the one hungry with her. Go on." The journey was burning upward through everyone's donated shoes and the soles of their feet, riding the rails of their nerves as the trip spun in a circuit inside them. He peered around to spot Francisco, but the de Melo family was on a different flatbed car.

One reporter had such slight features that he looked partially erased. Another had a handlebar mustache like the kind worn by a gleeful villain on a stage in New York, and he asked, "Many converts were jailed, Mrs. Alves, but why were you the only one sentenced to the gallows?" He pronounced their name ALL-vez instead of the Portuguese way of one syllable with a *shh* sound at the end.

When a priest had insisted that Mother believe that the communion loaf was the actual flesh of Christ, she had snapped, I would not even call that good bread, much less the body of the Lord God.

John shouted this without waiting for her to speak, and he felt bad that she stiffened as amusement rippled through the crowd. First chance to guard her, and he had failed, and despite his amazement that they were being preserved forever in words in newspapers, his eyes were going blind from exhaustion and his ears were shutting down. Rui caught John as he collapsed and told him later that the man with the top hat had been the governor of Illinois. The train had pushed onward, taking the other half of their group to their new lives in Springfield.

John awakened inside their cabin in the undulating lands north of Barton Street, in the patch of Jacksonville newly christened as Madeira Hill. The porch was covered with dead squash vines. Stalks leaned against each other in the yard.

—

HE RESTED.

—

ON THE TABLE, A BOWL WAS FILLED WITH EGGS SMOOTH AS RIVER stones.

—

THAT GAUZELIKE SCREEN MADE UP OF EVERYONE'S BREATH CONTINUED filling the sky. He imagined people cooking and chopping wood and comforting their babies, all with that backdrop. Mother perched with John on the single step leading to the porch and said, puzzled, "I'm cold, but my feet are burning." He told her he felt the same. Maybe this was how a person came to live in America: with a chill that set you on fire, while everybody moved around on white film.

—

IT TOOK A FEW YEARS FOR THE REIS FAMILY TO TRANSLATE THEIR name to King and for Diogo Teixeira to turn into James DeShara. The Pereira clan became the Perrys. There was so much English still to learn: *Snow. Slavery. Stun.*

Weasels live in the *grasslands,* and rainwater collects in the *wallows* formed when *bison* roll around to scratch themselves.

John pictured the numbers filling the days: Town was 1.8 miles away. Hundreds more Portuguese Protestants continued flooding into the heartland. When the exiles first rode into Jacksonville, the rickety Wabash had been the only railway in Illinois, before the state's face combusted into a mass of iron suturing as French calico, kettles, awls, gun flints, cotton and list cloth, buckwheat flour, sewing machines, and cattle traveled up and down and in Xs, Chicago to East St. Louis, Galesburg to Champaign. Like a Colossus of Rhodes, Raimundo Silva— Ray Silva—stood astride these streams and reeled in items to start his business, comparing this to fishing, a Portuguese talent. He spent eight hundred dollars on a Chickering piano to celebrate his general store's success. Americans created buildings called *banks* owing to such overflow of prosperity that they required temples to store it. What an exaltation of *things:* The Dr. Keller's Rheumatic Lotion that Mother needed cost thirty-seven and a half cents a bottle at Corneau & Diller's Drug Store, thirty-three miles east in Springfield. John longed to harness the velocity of the wind, grass-cologned and unimpeded as it tumbled over the prairie, to lift his mother into some safety he associated with the air.

Before and after school, he undertook field labor for ten cents an hour, and the outdoors swallowed Rui. Nikka worked at the Joseph Capps Woolens Factory, where the generous owner hired refugees to produce the linsey-woolsey cloth, yarns, and rugs. She loaded whipped-cream cloth into baths of boiling color—woad, saffron, madder root, beet leaves—and used grainy borax soap to scrub the dyes off her skin. On annatto days, her arms were red and orange, as if she had reached into a sunrise. She left the factory upon discovering a profitable talent for making wine, which she sold along with her milk brandies at Ray's General Store.

Noises new to John and Serafina—owls, wolves, demons with ember-red eyes—kept them awake in the dark, and they huddled, alert to protecting each other. When he was thirteen, God commanded her to walk him to the nationally renowned Illinois Institution for the Education of the Deaf and Dumb, not far from their home, to ask if they might visit its library. They had heard about this place of charity during church services. She later admitted she hoped he could learn how signing might ward away night terrors.

John was aware of how she was seen by people ignorant of her grand story: ragged clothes, haunted eyes. But she was not viewed dismissively at the deaf school. He wanted her to stay famous, and together they would fund a cathedral. She would write a message from God with John's help, and no one would look at her in a way less than she deserved. A skinny man with threads for a mustache introduced himself as Philip Gillette, the superintendent, who rang out with, "Certainly you can use our library! You're from the exiles, aren't you! I was on the welcoming committee."

John suspected their dark skin would always announce who they were.

Mother said, "My boy, he is smart, good to study sounds."

As they conversed in an echoing corridor, Mr. Gillette declared, "I applaud your English! Is there a deaf person in your family?"

It was impossible to describe how feeding upon birdsong in a jail had caused them to fall in love with the idea of everything giving off music, so John said, "We read a book by a man named Kircher that was interesting, sir." Mother radiated approval of how he translated her wishes to this kind soul.

"You're in luck," said Philip Gillette, ushering them into a domain with floor-to-ceiling books and glass cases displaying the latest ear trumpets. He located the *Phonurgia nova* of Athanasius Kircher and set it on an oak reading table as if handling a Bible. Mother's hands folded in prayer style. To John this was like witnessing the resurrection of someone dead. "May we borrow it, sir, please?" John asked, but Gillette laughed and said no, John could read it under a librarian's supervision, but it was worth seventy-five dollars—

"Heavens," gasped Mother.

"How much?" John wobbled. They owed a fortune to a girl and her father on the other side of the globe.

Gillette urged them to turn the pages. Diagrams of ears showed their tiny hammers, and in one engraving, eavesdroppers held cups against walls. It seemed too grand to state that John longed to help children imprisoned in silence, so he said, "I'd like to learn hand-speaking and be a teacher, Mr. Gillette." Mother nodded. In truth, John was skilled with languages but bashful, and words lodged in his brain and grew claws as he struggled to dislodge them.

Mr. Gillette gestured, signing, and John felt jubilation at figuring it meant: *Begin*. What a brisk country! Mother said in Portuguese, "Birdie, now I can rest a little," because she had helped him find a blessed pathway.

She entreated John to quit fieldwork. When his schoolday concluded, Nikka escorted him to study sign language with a deaf teacher salaried by the school. While a librarian watched, John paged through Kircher and other volumes until his eyelids dropped toward the common human silence of sleep.

Francisco de Melo had become Frank Meline, and his parents Jorge and Teresa and brother Hugo were George, Teresa, and Hugo Meline, and despite preachers railing against "godless entertainment," they opened a theater on North Diamond Street amid the harness shops, tearooms, and dry-goods stores of a downtown split by tracks, where trains left the air misted with coal dust and lungs grew a lattice of the mist. Frank helped organize shows of traveling magicians, ventriloquists, and actors, and John used the storeroom to tinker with what he called, unimaginatively, his Sound Machine. Why not try to replicate a large ear? He formed a papier-mâché cone and stuck a bouffant feather pen in it. When someone spoke into the feather, it vibrated, and a razor-sharp nib protruding from the cone's aperture marked a square of vellum positioned with prongs.

Fascinated with the Sound Machine, his mother exclaimed, "God, He will speak through people into this!"

Frank once said into the Machine, "My friend is crazy." Grinning at the result, he pronounced, "Looks like two whiskers off an old cat. Now what?" How could lines and blots be prompted to utter "my friend" again?

Amused, John admitted, "I have no idea."

Madeira Hill existed as a fulcrum between prairie and town, and Mother suggested toting the Sound Machine to where the wind stirred the quill. John added ink, and the moaning of the outdoors got snared as *dot splat*. Sensing her ongoing wariness about immense spaces, this gaping open country, tenderness prompted him to tell her, "God is writing that you're safe."

It was a season called *fall*, with leaves flashing bellies of flaxen and maroon. Howling wind nipped at her hem. Smiling, she replied, "Then maybe He shouldn't try so hard to knock me over."

John transferred the marks onto staff paper and played notes on the piano in the Meline Theater, but his arbitrary notation had no chance of reproducing the symphony of Illinoisan breezes.

—

FORGIVE, O LORD, OUR SEVERING WAYS / THE RIVAL ALTARS THAT WE RAISE / THE wrangling tongues that mar Thy praise!

Arguments simmered a few years before combusting. The Reverend Kalley, residing in Springfield, decreed that the converts must be baptized in their new faith, while a faction insisted that declaring their original Catholic baptisms invalid offended God. Despite slavery and the threat of war in the new land, *this* was the division eating the refugees alive. The Scottish firebrand became a fanatic. When John turned sixteen, after Kalley fled the uproar to preach in Brazil, he soured on the religion of his youth—once based upon charity, literacy, and free medicine, now reduced to foaming-at-the-mouth raging about whether God *was* the water of baptism or if the water was merely a *sign* of blessing. The Reverend António de Mattos led the non-rebaptizing schism by establishing the Second Portuguese Presbyterian Church of Jacksonville.

Mother took to her bed in sorrow at Kalley's abandonment, and John felt a hardening of his heart when she refused any comforting.

—

AS A YOUNG MAN OF TWENTY-ONE, JOHN EMBRACED JOY AT TEACHING ten-year-old deaf children, but this was tempered with a tragic reminder that his new country could, on a whim, turn inhospitable. Missy Baker, daughter of a cordwainer, delighted in meeting him out by the granite fountain of a boy and a girl under an umbrella, her devotion stirred ever since he had amused his students with the confession that pigs had been his favorite pets on an island, and every morning she gave him a drawing of one. "Thank you!" he would sign, a flat palm to his mouth, then the palm tipped toward her.

Delicate as an egg and tiny, she skipped to keep up with even his slowed gait as he led her by her hand to the classroom. Missy spanned both his worlds—then and now—because her flyaway red hair reminded him of the British people of Madeira.

At a first crackling of springtime, Missy told a friend she wanted to search for wildflowers, and she vanished into the prairie. Children were warned not to wander into those grasses as high and far as could be seen—they possessed the same drowning power as water—but on occasion caravans of westward-bound travelers erred in letting their children range, or local citizens forgot about the danger—and the swaying grasses swallowed them. Search parties tramped in daylight and darkness, far down the Old Jacksonville Road toward Berlin, parting the sea of reeds, rustling the bluestems, calling out her name, John foregoing sleep.

She was never found. Thunderstorms rinsed the earth, and each winter drifted toward the next. To encompass the memory of the lost girl and his failure to save her, John pictured her emerging after many years. Missy Baker had swum purposefully into fortunes beyond the grasses, and she had returned, a grown young woman bestowing a bouquet, hair still like summer's apricots and her smile still wide enough that an ordinary person cracked in two imitating it, signing cheerfully to John that it had taken her until now to find the best wildflowers everywhere on the earth to bear back to him.

——

SOMETIMES HE STILL PAUSED NEAR AN OVERGROWN FIELD IN THE hope that Missy Baker might be returning, though what he feared seeing was her skeleton lashed to grasses that had sprouted enough to bear her aloft, her body turned into a wind chime, hoisted into view.

—

ONE EVENING WHILE PASSING THROUGH THE DOWNTOWN SQUARE with Nikka and Mother, after purchasing flour and salted yellow butter, John witnessed a preacher bellowing from a soapbox. He was as brittle as a praying mantis and with a patchy beard, as if he had struggled mightily while someone kept trying to ram him toward singeing flames. Flimflam men often ranted here, droning out Bible passages or extolling elixirs. Usually few people paid them any mind. But this preacher, arms wide as if commanding the sea to part, had gathered a crowd that also magnetized Mother. Rather than comprehending every word, the audience seemed to be riding the waves of musicality. The man of God joked about welcoming every facet of everyone present, because "each of us is a schism, separate in birthright from one another and even from aspects of ourselves!" His voice pealed and swerved, slowing at times to gather propulsive force.

John could swear a Pentecostal lick of flame descended over the man's crown as he crested high, lyrical and fulminating, "The Good Word declares that wheresoever we convene, sinful and yearning, in His Name, there He abides, whether below His heavens directly as we are today, or under a roof we raise in the richness of our hope— hope is the essential American attribute!—that we be forgiven our lusts and banalities. Sisters, brothers, I speak to you as I am, a man of constant faults! Does my demeanor appear carefree? No, I am troubled by being named Isaac! Abraham was ready to roast his son like a lamb shank when the Lord commanded it. Why would God impose such a test, if murder is against His law? I endeavor to understand, hence my wish to lead like-minded searchers in a churchly dwelling. What if we cease to battle among ourselves? God would declare we have attained a holiness that inspires Him to withdraw His death sentence upon us!" And on he exulted, with listeners going into raptures, and Mother lapsed into a deepness with her Lord that John had not witnessed since the days of jail. She gripped John's arm and said, "He is like Kalley!"

Every coordinate in John's emotional axis, every instinct, was to usher his mother and sister home. When Mother protested that she wished to meet this Preacher Isaac, John pointed out that their butter was melting, and the man was intently conversing with other admirers. He detested how Isaac, in addition to releasing melodious conjurings, had been eating up Nikka with his eyes and zeroing in on Mother. Preachers rolled through town all the time; let this one roll on out, especially since Mother got so upset with John that when they arrived home, she snapped, "He talks of unity! God, He sends us answers in human form!"

John replied, "Beware of false prophets." Doubly upset when Nikka took Mother's side—did not the Reverend Kalley, and St. John the Baptist and others, appear wet eyed and half mad?—John subdued a pang of wanting to return to a village on a small island, far from this country where large people were obsessed with large dreams.

—

EVEN HE COULD NOT ESCAPE THE ATTRACTIONS HERE. HE REGARDED with awe the home of the charitable banker Augustus Ayers, a cube-and-cupola stunner. During a train ride through upstate New York, Ayers had glimpsed a mansion and caused the locomotive to be halted while he inquired if he might buy the blueprints, so that a dwelling he loved at first sight could be replicated in Jacksonville.

It was an American magic act, *to want* and almost simultaneously *to have.*

When John took Mother to see it, she frowned at the Italianate façade as he asked what she thought of it. She replied, "It is the house of a rich man, and it is not ours."

"But what if I buy a place like this for you? Someday."

"For such money, I thought we were to build a church. This house is not humble."

She intoned from the Bible, "Do not store up treasures on earth, where thieves break in," which John took as a rebuke for his grubby materialism, and for the incident at the Astor mansion, and for his arrogant hope of making an auditory discovery that would cause his name to be honored in books.

Was it wrong to imagine financing a church in his mother's

name—what woman had that honor?—its spire going up and up, *and* a sturdy home? Maybe not in College Hill—all right, that was naïve, since each one cost one or two thousand dollars, or double that, triple, and then came upkeep over a lifetime—but why not a well-tended place like Asa Talcott's on Grove Street, where convivial parties featured piano music and Talcott, an honorable, religious soul, aided those fleeing bondage in the South?

—

A REMINDER THAT JOHN WAS AND ALWAYS WOULD BE FROM SOME-where else was a brief foray into a romance with Julietta Price, blasé about everything, which he took at first for worldly charm. Their alliance was frosty, banter-y, and maddeningly non-carnal other than a kiss at Watson's Confectionary, where she revealed herself prone to biting. She remarked that John was handsome but should stay out of the sun, since he was too dark already and might be mistaken for . . . well, for the person he actually was. He never introduced Julietta to his family, since having a mother willing to die for her beliefs failed to miter with pursuing a girl whose moral spindle was wrapped in frivolity.

—

BUT IT WOULD TURN OUT TO BE RUI WHO WOULD MOST REVEAL TO John how their years in Illinois were slipping past. From the outset, Rui plowed the furrows where he got hired, from what the natives called the can't-see of dawn to the can't-see of nightfall, and each passing year he wafted to a more distant field until, from where John gazed out, his brother shrank to the size of the little roosters inside those peek-hole Easter eggs that were coated with glitter and trimmed with ridges of pastel frosting. If you looked inside, you saw a tiny farmhouse with a tiny heart on its roof, and those minute barnyard hens and chicks and that rooster beside it, and who could say why it touched you so. Something had happened to Rui in Trinidad that he refused to talk about. One day John discovered him in an abandoned shed on the other side of a cornfield abutting their yard, where, before shutting the door in John's face, Rui stated his wish to be left alone in order to invent the finest perfume in the history of the world.

TAKE MY VOICE, AND LET ME SING

MAY 1860

JOHN HESITATED, REMINDING HIMSELF OF HIS VOW NEVER TO RETURN to the weekly five-card-stud game that the Dane conducted. The devil on John's left shoulder whispered that he would only risk the treasure trove of six dollars he had won the previous Friday.

An odor of pelts assailed him as he stepped toward the rear of the tannery while the Dane shuffled a deck on a barrelhead. As a familiar figure approached, John blinked in disbelief. Dry as jerky, resembling the marionettes at the Meline Theater, the holy drifter who had been channeling God a while back on the soapbox loped into view. With a grin upon spotting John, he introduced himself in full as "the Reverend" Isaac Unthank. John reluctantly offered his name, and Isaac drawled, "I recall you with your mother and bewitching sister. I see that you too participate in contests of chance, though money be the root of all evil, and eager for it, men have pierced themselves with many griefs. One Timothy, six-ten. I aim to preach in better settings than the one you witnessed."

John said, "I don't plan on any grief myself." He had nickels, dimes, and quarters in his pocket totaling four dollars plus two silver dollars, nigh on a week's pay.

Isaac volleyed back with, "I detect an accent. You have a col-or-ation not quite native."

"I'd call it a sight more native than yours."

Roaring with delight, Isaac said he liked taking cash off people with wit, adding, "I meant no offense, seeing's how I am myself a man of nowhere and therefore everywhere. I lack domestic centering."

"What's a preacher doing playing cards?"

"Same as you. Those of us not born to means must acquire it. God helps those who help themselves, whilst He attends the lilies of the field or some such."

Even the Dane dropped his deadpan expression, and John was speechless, as Isaac set out a stack of twenty silver dollars and a gold twenty-dollar piece. Flashing it from his oversized jacket was already a demented act of a fool—most hardworking men did not earn that much in a month and a half—but the Dane collected himself and said, "Do we resemble commodity traders? I run a clean nickel-and-dime game."

Isaac rummaged in another pocket and produced smaller coins. "As a matter of felicitous fact, I did take a tidy sum off a fancy man in Cicero, but I require more. I intend to build a dwelling of the Lord, and He rewards those with the faith to risk everything."

"I understand Him to better reward good sense," said John, but his brain was giving off sparks at the sight of weeks' worth of cash flung around by an idiot.

Another player approached, a Madeiran knotted strong in his limbs, a vineyard laborer who introduced himself as Joe Gouveia and exclaimed when he heard John's name, "Is your mother Serafina? With First Presbyterian? We're in the Second and would love her on our side."

John shut his eyes and opened them, hoping this semaphorically conveyed a wish to conceal his mother's story. But as the Dane dealt a card facedown to each of them, Isaac insisted on an explanation. Joe described her readiness to die for her faith, and how arguments over baptism had split the congregation, and this was known to trouble her.

"She's ready for peace," said John, promptly wanting to kick himself. Despite aiming to shut down the topic, he had circled the essence of the preacher's soapbox harangue. Isaac directed white-hot eyes at him. All of this felt distinctly like a mistake.

The Dane snapped, "Ladies, I forgot to bring the tea." He distributed the second cards, faceup. Isaac's three of clubs was low card to John's visible queen of hearts and Joe's jack of hearts, and Isaac opened the bets brazenly with a Liberty silver dollar. Joe whistled but saw the bet, following John's response to call it as well.

Isaac said, "Proverbs, I forget which one, declareth that a mother shall be clothed with dignity and can laugh at days to come. John, your mother seemed a repository of devotion, which transfigured her otherwise humble raiments."

John ignored him. His hidden card was a king of spades, with that queen as his door card, followed by a king of hearts for a faceup third card. Joe showed a six of hearts to accompany his jack, and Isaac had a two and a three of clubs displayed. Isaac said, "King and queen, John. You a fellow of regal tastes? Got a woman who's costly?"

"My mother needs a home where air won't rush in through the siding."

"Ain't she a squaw?" said the Dane. He had tobacco teeth. "Get her one of those cones with a pole."

Joe Gouveia tensed. Mother got called an Indian on occasion, and so did John, and no doubt Joe did, too. The Dane liked to rattle players, and John refused to be prodded, even as the Dane flapped on with, "Those ain't farmer's tans. Sure you boys ain't from Africa?"

"We're from an island near there," said John, "but I think of myself as born in New York."

This fine little biographical sketch did not appear to be captivating the Dane. John said to Joe, "Não deixes este fodido caralho irritar-te."

Joe guffawed in shock. John had not learned those words from his mother.

"You Injuns in cahoots? Talk English," said the Dane. He asked if John, being a teacher of sign language, were signaling Joe.

"I don't cheat," John muttered.

"You're a teacher?" asked Isaac, staring at the fourth card flipped toward him, a nine of spades. He folded. "At the deaf school?"

That too seemed like something John preferred he not learn. Isaac stated with heat to the Dane, "Their people speak English a sorry sight better than half the mutts born here, and I am spellbound by the beauty of their girls and admit to ungodly spec-u-lation that one day I shall wed one, much as cowboys get themselves a Mexican girl—"

"Shut your mouth," said Joe. A pair of jacks was now visible with his six of hearts. John's fourth card was a good decoy, an eight of diamonds.

Isaac Unthank gaped skyward and said, "The spirit is great, but the flesh is heir to other things."

After fifth cards landed, John's pair of kings won the round. With a thrill juddering into his gullet, in a match of unconscionably risking the highest stakes he had ever dared, he had gained three full days of livelihood.

"You damn dog," said Isaac, whistling.

The Dane's practice was to sit out the first few hands and turn into a player thereafter. Instead of give-and-take with his fellow players, John hit a winning streak. Isaac's luck rose scantily before plummeting for good. When John obliterated him, Isaac joked about requiring prayers from John's God-linked mother. At the hour's end, John had fifty dollars, forty of it from Isaac, a staggering seven weeks of teaching pay, because Isaac was a terrible player. Joe was slightly in arrears, and the Dane was below even, but Isaac, sweating and mumbling, had sacrificed the most toward John's windfall.

The Dane performed his usual vanishing act, leaving the players in the last jolt of sunlight. "I hope you donate some of that to a charitable cause, teacher," said Isaac. "I would not look unkindly upon a loan, seeing's how you've got all my savings. I came in a spirit of fraternity."

"He won fair and square," said Joe. "Get on down the road. Not his fault you threw away a fortune."

"Much as God allows an ugly musician to produce glorious song, so do I share His tunes when I preach, despite my gangly aspect." He smiled. "I require cash money to achieve, as suggested in my sermons, a traditional structure where harmony doth reign."

"Get going," said Joe, "before I make an aspect of your face more than gangly."

They watched Isaac's hunched shoulders recede before John offered

Joe some coins back, and Joe replied, "No, you had a once-in-a-lifetime day. I shouldn't do this anymore. The vineyards are growing fine."

John said, "My last time as well." The school would not thrill to a report of a teacher engaging in vice behind a tannery, though upstanding men constantly plied their money in a spin-the-wheel way to stockpile more gold. Seeking overnight fortune—instant mobility—was a creed in this land.

"You looking for extra cash, head to Springfield," said Joe. "Lots of us show up for day labor at the Lincolns', us and the Germans. You might meet the next president, Alves." Women stitched and chased after the boys, while men did odd jobs. Mrs. Lincoln was a frantic sort, but the Great Man was wise and welcoming and told good jokes.

John informed his mother and sister that the dollars were from Rui's invention of a perfume that had hit a jackpot. Rui was so removed from their lives that the lie would almost certainly stay concealed, but meanwhile ecstasy fed new tributaries into his usual flood of thoughts. He could save up to buy Kircher's *Phonurgia nova*! Or he could give some money to fix the dormitory roofs at the school and use the rest to buy wine supplies for Nikka and to replank the cabin's floors and increase its worth.

Exhilaration lasted until only a few days later, when he straggled home from Flash Card Day to find Isaac Unthank, decked out as a man of the cloth, lolling in Serafina's rocking chair while she set out a plum cake. Discomfited at the wood-fire stove, stirring a vat of wine, was Nikka. Clerical collar askew, Isaac was casting an appraising eye over their single-roomed home, the oat-colored curtains, the threadbare Indian rug, and the piano with teeth missing, a gift from the First Portuguese Presbyterian Church, a naked gesture to secure Mother permanently on the pro-Kalley side. Her bedroom was in an alcove, with John's cot by the door and Nikka's by the hearth.

"All hail the professor! A calling as noble as my own. It was a simple matter to make inquiries and locate this woman of God."

Demurring, Mother said, "I said to him, he make a good sermon."

Nikka added, "John, he says you promised him a donation? To start a church."

Ignoring the dried starfish of a hand thrust in his direction, John

joined Nikka at the stove as he said, "I did nothing of the sort." The
floorboard under which they had secured his winnings of Isaac's gold
and silver pieces, and the Dane's and Joe's dollars, had been pried up
and the sack disgorged.

Mother rebuked him, in Portuguese, for being rude.

Unthank veered on his haunches to bore into John with, "Your
mother has regaled me with the tale of you being jailed! I told her I've
heard of her anguish about the quarrels besetting our Presbyterian
family. I'd thank Jesus for your blessing as I establish a sanctuary for
those who support peace and oppose the idea of armed conflict. Your
mother judged that to be a fine solution to strife. A haven for non-
conscriptionists of all Protestant persuasions!"

Serafina nodded in a way that glued John's teeth together. Dollars
were stacked on the table between Isaac and her.

Nikka tapped a packet of powder—made from the air bladders of
fish—into the wine to clarify it, and the red brightened apace with
John's growing temper. He said, "Mother, the Reverend Kalley was
strongly against the enslaving of men and urged us to oppose it, and if
war comes, I plan to fight."

"God does not wish us to die because of the faults of other men,"
said Isaac.

"The Lord Jesus Himself did exactly that, as I recall."

Making a show of forebearance, Isaac chided him, "He took it upon
Himself, that death on the Cross, to spare others. You and your mother
would be vital to welcoming those from every walk of life. Maybe not
the Catholics, who are liquored troublemakers. People desiring peace
could build a fortress championing it, dare I say a well-funded one.
Men of deep pockets would support an institution that fought to keep
their sons safe."

"You don't say." This country was massive, John thought uncom-
fortably and not for the first time, and it pained Mother that she
was no longer a central star. He stepped away from Nikka, sat beside
Mother, and counted the dollars she had unearthed. Ten. Reading his
mind, Mother said, "It is a simple idea about union that nobody has
described like this holy man." She looked small and alone. Was it so
awful that she wanted to keep her acclaim as special, something he
wanted for her, too?

Isaac, gaze level with John's, said, "I hear your perfumery-brother made a fortune, and you did not want your share to go toward mammon. Your avowal to assist me must have slipped your mind." Gripping Serafina's forearm, Isaac spiraled into lyricism. "Your son and I met at a prayer breakfast at his school, and he was enthusiastic when I mentioned my intent to be a peacemaker. His contribution—in your name—will encourage others to do likewise."

John confiscated the dollars as he barked, "Get out." He peered into the sudden alarm of their visitor, who glanced backward, as if Jesus might materialize to aid him, before he replied, "It would be prudent to keep your promise. I would hate to tell your family, or your school, of some behavior of yours that leaves much to be desired."

Mother looked confused. Never once had she seemed perplexed in John's youth.

"Get out of our house before I break your arm."

"John!" said his mother sharply. Nikka hovered on the periphery.

John had Isaac on his feet, and his wheat-chaff weight made it embarrassingly easy to hoist him outside. Clutching the front of Isaac's shirt, John hissed, "Don't ever bother my mother again." He shoved him away.

"I'll tell your employers."

"You won't. A congregation saddled with you can also find out about your own affection for lady luck. Take your schemes elsewhere, or better yet, take them nowhere."

Isaac said, "I'm empty of purse, and you took my savings. I do want to build a church. That much is true. Your mother's prominence would aid the cause mightily."

"No."

"He who stiffens his neck will be broken beyond healing, Proverbs twenty-nine. We could be allies. I hope you don't mind my saying that your sister, though a mite too old, is entirely comely, and I sense there are no suitors, so if on my behalf, you could—"

John's fist cut upward against Isaac's jaw, and he landed a kick that doubled him over. It was only when his mother and sister were pulling him off, with Nikka yelling, "John, what's the matter with you?" that Isaac stood, brushed off his shirt, and straightened his collar. Touching the blood leaking from his nose, he murmured, "You will be sorry you did that." He bowed and said, "Ladies, most of the afternoon was splendid. The cake was akin to nectar. Until we meet again."

His mother did not wait for Isaac to be out of earshot before she cried, "You treat a guest in this way? A man of God who for us wants a church to put people together? You go to fight men, leave me for a war?"

"A guest ready to help himself to whatever he can get out of us, Mother."

Nikka said, "John, I can't look at you," and she flung an arm around their sorrowing mother.

———

RUI, SCRAPING FRANKINCENSE INTO A BOWL, BARELY GLANCED UP when John entered his downtown shop. A walnut grandfather clock ticked. Shelves displayed canisters of desiccated plants, and pestles held rose petals bruised with a mortar, separated into pink, red, and yellow. Orange rinds hardened into ancient pottery shards littered the floor's sawdust. Rui's neroli extracts were in demand due to their eloquence at bridging the top and bottom notes of his perfumes. John sounded like a gored animal as he intoned, "I miss you, Rodrigo. We all do."

"Been busy."

As if adding "I have" would siphon away too much energy.

Hovering between them was a floral scent in a dimensionally perfect cube that encased John's saudade, the longing that was the presence of an absence—Rui embodied it, this missing of someone John still had. Rui survived in an apartment near the tracks, and beyond it lay the Morgan County Poor House, and rills and Mauvaisterre Creek, and sandhill cranes and pie-billed grebes in tall grasses. That John must be sole household custodian and guardian angel of their mother pressed on him heavily. No point in any brotherly joking about using Rui as a cover for an ill-gotten trove of dollars.

Even less reason to wail: *What in God's name happened to you in Trinidad?*

———

"MA?"

The glory of how this country said *Mother* as a bleat, the shortest possible syllable to get from you to her. She was sleeping. An open prayerbook on her nightstand offered an underlined passage: *Ai de mim . . . Já minha alma assaz de tempo habitou com os que aborrecem a paz . . . Alas, my soul has already spent so long living with those who disturb the peace.* When she sensed him, he helped her sit up, retied her blouse's neck bow, and said, "I'm sorry I raised my hand to someone and went off angry."

"I am sorry, too," she said, wincing. Her stomach hurt, but she refused to let him take her to the surgeon in Beardstown. That would be the best use of the money under the floorboards, Isaac's savings. She might have a stone that needed cutting out. "I think God will tell me what to do. I want to give Him a church, but in this country, I don't hear His words so well. I'm lost here, Birdie."

What moved him unutterably was that sometimes her speaking was broken into pieces, an immigrant's unglued mosaic, but often the words and their tunes were paved, and at other times her melodies flew out of the hymnal of the Lord Himself, and it was this mystery driving him the most toward wanting to understand sounds without end; without end, Mother. Forever they were the Little Birds. He pointed to himself and then crossed his arms over his chest before gesturing at her: *I love you.*

Birdie Mother, sleep. Safe now. Rest.

Things can change overnight, but it is also good to exist in a slipstream of stillness, nothing yet ventured.

She had once proclaimed that if the Donner party had not been in such haste to take a shortcut, their voices might yet be praising Our Lord.

He could hear their rattling last breaths, and beyond them, the rocking, rocking of the coffins that prospectors in California were converting into washers, screen-bottomed cradles with handles attached: searching and panning for gold although the Lord saith that breath is gold, bread is gold, and thy mother's hand in thine is beyond all treasure.

———

TONIGHT'S CONCERT AND FUNDRAISER FOR THE ILLINOIS INSTITU-
tion for the Education of the Deaf and Dumb would cap the sacro-
sanct day when his students turned peanut shells into parrots. Fifteen
ten-year-olds filled John's room, surrounded by a riot of wildflowers
done in tempera paints on butcher paper during We Love Our Prairie
Week. One wall featured a gigantic diagram of an inner ear with its
ossicles—the bones of stirrup, hammer, and anvil—and the snail-spiral
cochlea. Into the classroom's globe he had stuck a dragonfly pin where
Madeira was missing. The children found it hilarous that he claimed
to be from somewhere not on a map. All morning they had teased him
about his Sound Machine, which would be unveiled to public scrutiny
after the concert.

While handing out the cobalt robes, the satin rustling, he allowed
himself a final image of Isaac Unthank, a self-appointed preacher—
though weren't they all?—storming in, accusing John of disgraceful,
speculative game-playing, with Superintendent Gillette in tow to lead
John away to face every Portuguese Protestant waving a hoe and driving him into the Illinois River while his family watched in shame.
Maybe his mother would give him a last push with a rake.

The hair-brushing and ribbon-tying reduced his agitation. But-
tonhooks got plied on shoes. The peanut shells painted the reds and
greens of parrots roosted on the sills, reminders that birds have only
membranes for ears but that this does not stop them from unleashing
full-throated songs.

We look like blue ghosts, signed Sammy Byrd.

No, we are bluejays! John led them in a cheer.

Students enrolled here from all over the country. Normally the
schoolday ended with the female teachers escorting the girls past the
icehouse to their dormitories and the male teachers corralling the boys
while the Jacksonville residents returned home, but tonight everyone
trooped en masse into the gloaming, leaving the horses, cows, and
goats to roam the seven acres. Foxes shot past in some milkweed as
they strode through the stateliest part of town. Illinois College's young
men streamed by, their destinies enhanced by proximity to the grandeur of these homes with their eyebrow-dormer windows, columns,
and buttresses, and buoyed by such good works as digging tunnels
under their college or building hidden rooms to aid runaways.

He marched with his children through the college's quad to Rammelkamp Chapel. Sammy Byrd signed that he was excited (chest taps plus twirling), and John signed back that since Sammy was a bird, he would perform well. Rammelkamp was nearing full capacity, and John noted the attendance of banker Augustus Ayers, cattle king Jacob Strawn, and Benjamin Grierson, an abolitionist and musician never without a jaw harp. Mother was absent due to a stomachache, Nikka tending her. John had been looking forward to impressing on them that he was a force in a prominent institution of charity and education that summoned the likes of Ayers, Strawn, and Grierson.

Frank entered with Hugo, George, and Teresa, and Elizabeth Hampton, Frank's fiancée. John waved in greeting, and his friends did the same. Frank was judged daringly American for his betrothal to a native Illinoisan. Willowy, unfussy Elizabeth was able to plow a straight line in frozen ground, a bookseller who promised a love that was clear-eyed and therefore lasting. Being happy for Frank proved that he, John, was decent, might even be good.

The ceiling's apex collected the sound of the hearing and the non-hearing and pulverized it into particles that sifted over everyone as John hurried his flock toward the front pew. He scanned the audience, racked by an unshakable certainty that someone was lurking to surprise him. Surely not Julietta Price, though it would not be beyond her to show up to flirt and needle him. He had let all contact with her drop, a coward's way of moving on.

He paddled through the torrent of welcoming words from Julian Sturtevant, Illinois College's president, while an interpreter signed next to the pulpit and John adjusted Claire Clearwater's hair bow. During the Reverend Josiah Semple's invocation prayer, John dropped into a fugue state . . . what if Isaac, lusting after Nikka, found out about the husband she had not heard from in ages? The marriage was not unknown in their community, but everyone (so far) guarded Nikka's secret. She was reluctant to meet someone as it was, but widespread gossip would kill her. John stole another fruitless look at the packed house. Maybe he was anticipating the ridicule of his Sound Machine later. Superintendent Gillette was promulgating an account of his school for the deaf's achievements, and then it was time for the choir to raise music to the welkin.

John directed his blue-robed pupils to assemble on the platform. As the organ wailed its opening gambit, he conducted their signing of the lyrics, his lovely children, look at them, rocking like minia-ture waves detached from the sea. The Reverend Newton Abernathy unleashed an out-loud rendition of "Safely Through Another Week" while John led his students in using arms and fingers to model sounds as if they were clay, to amplify the rhythm with their full beings. When Hiram Lattimore faltered, John signed encouragement, with a nod to Sammy in appreciation of the clarity of his gestures and his swaying. *Use your bodies to speak like actors on a stage.* That was his signature embellishment to their language, the use of limbs, facial expressions, entire selves.

Here are my own Little Birds. If only the Sound Machine could capture this, to be heard by generations, the whole world over.

They concluded with "The Life in Christ," adapted from Mozart.

Take my hands, and let them move /At the impulse of Thy love. / Take my voice, and let me sing /Always, only, for my King.

When he hugged his chest, the children copied him. *Let the music tap the xylophones of your ribs; sense the applause. Feel everything through the floor. Don't allow deafness to be a prison.*

He trundled his victorious children to the reception in Beecher Hall, past the portrait of Edward Beecher, the college's first president and brother of Harriet Beecher Stowe, whose *Uncle Tom's Cabin* had been inciting a rallying cry. Cookies were arrayed next to punch bowls with red-currant fizzes. Within the mob, a line was forming at a table to write checks for the institution for the deaf. Thirty, forty minutes into talking and signing with the parents of his children, and visiting with Frank and Elizabeth, John got grabbed by his colleague Max Jef-fers, who thundered, "Your choir was the showpiece!" After exchang-ing pleasantries, John steered himself toward the displays, primed to get the reactions to his Sound Machine done with. Even to him it looked like a bad art project. People jammed near the audiophones, air-conduction fans, and bone-conduction devices. There was an au-rolese headband with a tiny fabric-covered trumpet to blend in with a hat, and a velvet carnation harboring a hearing aid to be tucked coyly near an ear, and a vase that collected sounds through receptors in artificial daisies. A merry child perched on a throne with hollowed armrests—tigers' heads with gaping maws—leading toward a resonance box in the seat, with a tube for the king to collect the chatter pooled under his hindquarters.

And near his Sound Machine, there for deities and humankind to behold, was a young woman in a coat with a cloth peony. Her dress was a green like drenched emeralds, as if the contents of her eyes had spilled over her. Her collar had the orange-trimmed cutwork he recognized as Madeiran. No woman was dressed like her, no one alive dressed like her, there was no one like her. Banish all the rest of the planet. A little black arrow of hair pointed to her forehead. *If I were blind, Maria, I could still see You. My ears hear Your heart beating out a loss so great. You're telling me it's Your father.* She was examining what he had made, his invention. He approached, and stopped. Let God strike him dead, because his silly vows as a scared boy to give up love and friendship, to give up home and money and whatever else of the earth would weigh him down and away from his promises to listen to God—all dissolved at once.

The young woman turned; she saw him, too. A tall blond man hovered behind her. Her gasp preceded her hands covering her mouth. The lighting was dazzling, and a spot of it landed like a ring on her finger; was that a ring? When he stepped to her, and she stepped to him, he said, "Maria Freitas?" *Your face so lit up I just about fall apart, remembering it.*

And yes, yes it was, and this was wonderful, and she breathed out with, "John Alves? John! My name is Mary now. What on earth? Oh, my dear. Yes."

He would lose her toward the end of that tumultuous, shocking best of evenings, would lose her before learning how to locate her again. His recollection of the night only got him as far as knowing she lived in Springfield.

He would take the eastbound train thirty-three miles, a voyage of an hour and a half, to ask the Madeirans laboring at the Lincoln household where she might be. But as a Catholic, she was not part of their circles.

And so he would enjoin his heart to call her, and one night, in the

Meline Theater of Jacksonville, during a magic-lantern show celebrating the arrival of the exiles, she would rush in. Late, confused in the darkness, she would pause in the lantern's projected beam. Her timing would land her in the colored-light image on the glass slide someone had painted of John Alves as a boy being lifted through the ceiling of a jail by a stork.

Mary would wear, for a brief moment, that picture, done in yellow, green, and blue.

She would stand in front of the audience, wearing him sailing to freedom on her chest.

She would help him encompass in full what happened on the night of the concert, which had commenced with her pitching herself into his arms. Here she was again, in a darkened theater. Let the Sound Machine record him repeating her name and her repeating his while she exuded that gardenia fragrance from their youths. Let the feather scratch out the music of every syllable they uttered for all recorded time. This was happening; the other name for God is Now—God is always, always *Now*.

TANGERINE DRESS IN THE RUBY CITY

1846–1860

PAPA WAS FIGHTING HIS WAY TO HER, PUSHING ASIDE ANYONE JOSTLING him. Maria's calf was sore from that rampaging fool stepping on it. The ocean of arms legs mouths surged east, clearing his path to her, and her elbows flew chicken-winged outward so nobody would dare ruin her getting to him, and he bellowed, "Cat!" and she screamed, "Papa!" His hat was lost. She clamped her arms around him. He steered her homeward while monsters shoved people toward ships. The air was smoke gray. Animals were dying, they would be eaten. The climb to the garden put stitches in their sides, but the plants waved them forward, so sweet were the plants, stirring as if to tear loose and run toward the two people they loved best.

Maria-Cat wept, and so did Papa, because men can feel sad, too.

"A convert got killed," he said, "and won't be allowed to rest in the cemetery. I'm going to find a shovel and bury him somewhere. I'll take Alberto. You'll stay here."

"They'll put you in jail. I'll have to steal something so I can go to jail with you." Hadn't John refused to let his mother go alone to that fate? Her muscles slackened . . . of course John and his family would be gone forever.

Quietly, Papa said, "Faith and hope are different. Hope means you wish very hard. But faith means you know something will come true, so you don't worry. I'll come back, and you'll learn the difference between hoping I do and believing it, minha princesa."

He left her alone with the ache of waiting, the longest hour of her life stretching past two, then three. *Worry is a sign of hoping, and hope is not faith.* She cut an oval out of a cloth, and inside this locket-shaped space she suspended a portrait of her father in threads. Time itself dissolved when she did her best work. But she was not perfect, she missed him too much, the *waiting* throbbed.

When he reappeared, dirt-covered, they held each other and he studied the thread-painting of himself and said, "What did I do to deserve you?" When he told her he could be at peace now that a body was at rest, she cried out, "I was afraid you'd get hurt!"

He remarked that the only thing that would hurt him would be if anything bad befell her. "Since I won't let that happen, I'll be fine, Cat." They retreated to a ring of frangipani trees bending toward each other at their crowns, where salted blue sea air funneled down, an arena they considered their best church. Their prayer was visible, it was just being side by side, safe, safe.

He was summoned to the owner's mansion, and upon returning he needed to lie down. She soaked a rag in camomile water for his forehead. His mustache and goatee were unkempt. "I'll no longer be in charge," he said. "I'll be allowed to keep working, but people are furious that I buried that Protestant man and call Kalley my friend."

Susan Ashe appeared with a crew of the owner's nephews, and they ordered Papa and Maria to do tasks, and Maria bit her tongue for fear of Papa losing his job entirely. One day, Susan stood in her hat, enormous because the sun hated her even more than Maria did, and brayed, "Augusto, explain this." She pointed toward a bush he had left fan-shaped instead of what she called "sculpted." These people sailed here, bought houses, and built factories where native women did embroidery that helped them get richer, and yet they learned hardly a word of the language. "Well?" Susan said, as if Papa were a schoolchild instead of the greatest gardener on an island of sensational gardeners.

Gesturing at the unruly top, he said, "It's going to bloom and put a red arch around the bush." Maria tensed up; Papa detected things before they appeared because he sensed what was birthing inside the stems.

"I don't see any blooms," said Susan, lobster-colored even with her straw hat.

"They're there, Miss Ashe."

"Show me. No, don't." She grabbed some shears and chopped the shrub into submission, more of the hacking of limbs she was undertaking to wreck years of his work, Maria's most vivid early acquaintance with how jealousy savagely seeks to wipe away beauty. For the sake of his dignity, she swallowed her screams.

Papa and she were never included in whatever the new bosses got jolly about. She and her father put their heads down and tilled, and weeded, and the plants were like pets with unconditional love, faces tilting to greet them. She was aware they were mocked, since people relish biting into a body they perceive as vanquished. Now and again, she wondered how John was, because Edite said the Presbyterians were in Trinidad, where the labor was merciless. What nourished Maria and her father were the berry shrubs, three of them now, and the real miracle continued to be that everyone else glanced past them. The plants were smart enough to camouflage themselves.

The single blessing of the new regime was a plan for a swath of lavender, to be sold in sachets, and Augusto and Maria Catarina, and Alberto and Edite and others, dropped into waves of fragrance so heady they imparted a spell.

Maria shut her eyes, and upon opening them she had grown half a decade older and was conversant in two languages and specialized in portraits of people in thread.

She hurt her father by protesting that she was too old for the Portuguese Night Blessing.

The headwinds blew, and the rippling lavender revealed a white carpet of undersides.

The Reverend Robert Kalley wrote to Papa sporadically, reporting that the Madeirans had fled the plantations of Trinidad for the liberty of New York City before taking up residence in Illinois, where Kalley was absorbing the wisdom and humor of a gentleman named

Abraham Lincoln, who bore the hallmarks of a grand leader. Margaret had died, but Kalley rejoiced in a Christian new bride, Sarah, a lively pianist.

And the lavender field got riffled by trade winds, and from a high ledge appeared purple, undulating, soporific, and once again Maria Catarina shut her eyes, and upon opening them, she had reached seventeen, and Papa was in his sixties.

One day she told Papa she wanted to surprise him with a new color from the Howell factory. She bought pistachio-green powder, and a packet of pink glitter to decorate the dirt of potted plants, before continuing upward to the mansion where David Hamm, the Botanical Garden's owner, peered down at the city. When she told the Madeiran butler she required an urgent word with Senhor Hamm, he paused but left her in the foyer with its mirror rimmed by belly-swollen cherubim.

She was ushered into a study where milk-colored David was gazing out a window while keeping his back to her. A chief attribute of wealth was that it kept people at bay, it imposed a moat, and this was, she had to admit, highly desirable. His failure to turn around immediately signaled that although he would receive her, he would stay in command. What a bore. Instead of books covering the walls, there were paintings of the early Hamms, whose fortunes hailed from "shipping," which Papa said was the word used by rich men for buccaneering. Hamm was so eerily tall he appeared stretched on a rack, but having jelly for bones meant he was elongated instead of broken.

"To what do I owe this honor?" he said, wresting himself away from the vista greeting him each day, gesturing at her to sit. He seemed amused.

"I'm the daughter of Augusto Freitas. He should be head gardener again."

"That hasn't been the case in years. Why are you here today?"

"When you took it away from him, I was a child. Now I'm not." As if a span of time should make a difference to the mandates of her heart.

"It's good you want to defend him, young lady, but—"

"Maria is my name. I need to know why you stopped letting him be in charge."

"We had complaints about his work."

She could not do this, could not contain herself. "That's a lie."

David fidgeted at a desk where he doubtless did no work. "I require you to guard your tone, Miss Freitas."

"He does a beautiful job, you know that, and he did back then, and that's why the garden was better. Susan is terrible, and you know that, too." Maria wanted enough money so her father and she could stop renting a cottage from this man and his clan, could quit laboring for absentee and present masters.

"I admire your admiration of him." David had a rushed voice due to having a soul that, on its way to dying, was abnormally thin and had to flutter twice as fast as normal. "I'm Anglican, but we must get along with the Catholics, and your father was noted burying a heretic during that unfortunate convulsion years ago, and he led a protest at a jail. We fought to keep him employed but judged it best that he be removed from the top spot. He's nearing retirement, maybe, eh?"

"No."

"Your choices are to keep enjoying that paradise, with others relieving your father of the highest burdens, or you can move to town and, I don't know. Garden for others."

She considered smashing his paperweight in the face of one of the ruffle-collared Hamm pirates. Instead, she reached into her handbag for the packet of pink glitter from her expedition to Howell's and flung the contents over the carpet and at the walls and shelves. "What are you—" David Hamm lurched backward.

She said, "It's glitter. You'll never get it completely out of this room."

—

ONE SUNDAY AFTER MASS—ATTENDANCE CONTINUED AS PART OF their efforts to appear docile—a fellow sidled near while Papa was off chatting with friends and invited her to dine. He was from Gibraltar. His name was Eduardo. He added, "But call me whatever you want, if you'll whisper it in my ear," and this boiled the fluid in her spine.

It did not occur to her to wonder how Eduardo from Gibraltar got her name and had recognized her. And how had he known to pick Friday evening, when Papa made a weekly trip to the countryside to pick up manure?

The moment Papa set out on this errand, she chose an embroidered dress and raced down to the city, to the Hotel Jardim. Eduardo awaited her in the dining room and ordered the jugged rabbit for them both, after which he growled, "I should eat you instead." He asked if she drank wine. One of his front teeth was crooked.

"Yes," she said, though she did not care for wine, its sourness.

When he teased her for having no mother, she replied, flustered, that she supposed she did have one.

"I sense your father has never divulged your true origins." A glint of cruelty flecked his eye. "Innocent child, aren't you?"

"No, I'm not," she answered, except that she was. A waiter brought over a selection of wines with their rabbit on a trolley. While the server dished their dinner out of its clay pot, Eduardo leaned forward to gesture at a bottle, and she spotted a dagger held in place by his belt. The only time she tried trusting an outsider, all she found was peril. She stared at a pearl onion on her plate, the aromatic blood-gravy. He held a glass of wine below her chin and said, "To your health. I'd love to walk with you by the harbor. After dinner. You came to a hotel to meet me, but I'm not going to take advantage of that."

"Would you excuse me?" she said. "I'm going to refresh myself." The hotel had a fancy water closet in the hall outside the restaurant.

"Don't take long."

She walked outdoors fast and began to run. Papa was not yet home. She changed into a plainer frock. When he returned, she confessed and mentioned the dagger.

His jaw unhinged, he located a knife and moved a table in front of the door. He explained about the Weaver of Angels. Maria's mother was a wealthy girl whose parents had wanted to force her into the convent to avoid dividing their estate among too many sons-in-law, and an aunt carted the rebellious girl to Rome so that the Holy Father would order her to consign herself to her fate. "Our King Miguel the First was in exile there." The deposed king who ordered torture and killings as he sought to reclaim the throne, inciting rabid followers and enemies. "It's possible you're his child, though you might also be the daughter of a Roman shoemaker. Gentlemen can carry daggers, but I sense trouble has come. I should have paid the Weaver when she insisted on more money or she'd spread the rumor about your father. Republicans want to prove the monarchy is corrupt, and they'd make your existence a misery. Royalists want to keep a line pure, and they're dangerous. Illegitimate children ruin the myth or show up with demands."

"Are you upset with me?"

"No. A little. I should have faced years ago that our chapter here has closed, querida." Forget about kidnappers paid to bundle her into a boat and toss her into the brine. Look at their life, tidy and circum- spect, a soap bubble, his work plundered by envious simpletons while he fetched fertilizer.

They sold the cabinet of exotic colors and booked transit on a barge. The Reverend Kalley had built a permanent channel for the Presbyte- rian Society to procure legal passages to New York via London and, if any refugees wished, onward to the prosperity of the Midwest. Augusto took three cuttings from a miracle-berry shrub, wrapped their wounds in damp cloth, and, unbeknownst to his daughter, conducted a linger- ing goodbye with his mistress, Amparo. He destroyed all traces of the miracle bushes; the lone virtue of the dullards who made him miserable was their lack of curiosity about this treasure, but best to ensure their ignorance.

Alberto and Edite escorted Augusto and Cat to the ship. Maria, weeping, accepted a fig cake and an etui of fresh needles from the couple like grandparents. "There, there, pumpkin," whispered Edite. "He's taking you to something better."

Edite and Alberto waved handkerchiefs as the boat pulled away, and Maria smiled for the first time in days and said, mildly, "So I might have a king for a father."

"That is correct."

"Is that why you call me princesa?"

Cooling spray dashed them. "No, I call you that because you're my princesa."

When they approached the gull-pulsing harbor of New York,

Maria Catarina joined him at the railing. She ceased mourning the selling of their color cabinet, because look what it had bought them, look at this city as if the tints had splashed out of their bottles, a multitude of hues! A person can fall in love at first sight *with a place.* The grandeur made her cry out, "Papa!," as if declaring that such a skyline was synonymous with his name.

They had been given the address of a Madeiran couple who had correctly translated their name from *Ferreira* to *Smith*, but their drafty house at Twenty-second Street and Sixth Avenue was packed, with one newcomer using the bathtub as a bed. Mr. and Mrs. Smith helped them locate a boardinghouse at Twenty-eighth Street and Seventh Avenue, with a water closet shared by the five families on their hall— marvelous! In their room was a broken radiator where the steam kept the miracle-plant cuttings alive in a bucket, and they fed them coffee grounds. For dinner they toasted bread on the radiator and ate it with strawberry jam. A charity bag of clothing arrived, and Maria was the perfect size for a dress dyed a color called *tangerine.* It had a neckline like the lip of a bowl.

Mr. Smith found them jobs in a private greenhouse thirty streets uptown, owned by Lawrence Jamison, a banker, and his wife, Myrtle. Their three children rattled about and were friendly in visiting the enclosure where Augusto nourished the gladioli bulbs with Hudson River sand. The Jamisons allowed the miracle-plant cuttings to bed in the warmth, and the roots clawed the soil near the nodding ladies' tresses.

The Jamisons and the boardinghouse residents called her "Mary." She tumbled head over heels in adoration of the city and convinced Papa to wander with her and stretch his aching back. The tenements, with laundry like tattered flags on clotheslines, were unlike anything they had seen even among the poorest Madeirans. But New York overall was a jewel box. Its bands of color suggested a prism, like something a priest should brandish in a homily about wonder. Horse carriages rang with their music; gas lamps flickered. It *hummed,* this town. Life glowed a ruby red . . . one could be thrilled, because what might happen next, a turn around a corner, might be *breathtaking.*

Often the sky was lemon, and it poured and splashed.

At the Fulton Fish Market, as men hauled their nets onto the dock, she spun in her tangerine dress, full skirt twirling, and a fisherman called out, "Look at Miss Sunshine."

For old times' sake, conjuring those parents inhabiting the sea, she said, "Are they towing my father out of the tide?"

Yes, Cat-Cat, he's that gray fish flapping about—your dying father.

Through springtime and summer, and on the verge of something called *autumn*, she embroidered hand towels with leaves in satin-stitches, gold and red for this season new to her, laying the threads so closely together they melted into an unbroken gloss.

One crisp morning, Maria-Mary was walking up Fifth Avenue, toting a dozen towels to show Mrs. Jamison. A grand lady stopped her to admire the collar Maria-Mary had embellished with swans, and Maria-Mary showed her an autumn-leafed towel, and after proclaiming, "My word! I must have that, dear girl," the lady handed over a dollar. Maria-Mary was thunderstruck, more so when Myrtle Jamison surveyed the other handiwork and said, "Heavens, Mary, I'll buy the lot." She paid her fifteen dollars.

Knocked asunder, Maria-Mary could afford tinned *apricots* to bake pies—one for Lawrence and Myrtle Jamison, their teenaged boy, and their twin girls; one for Mr. and Mrs. Smith on Twenty-second Street; three for her Twenty-eighth Street residence. The fruit was a tint so gorgeous that should the sea turn apricot, Maria-Mary would be the first to bathe in it. A lady on the first floor showed her how to *crimp* the crust and dot butter on the fruit, and the pies were set in the foyer—and you would have thought to a person everybody had discovered where the stars hid in daylight.

Papa and she plunged ivy into vessels of rainwater in the Jamison hothouse, and when the insides of the leaves decomposed, they pressed them between flannels to lift away all but the networks of veins. For pure-white skeletons, Papa added chloride of lime to the rainwater. They sold framed pieces for fifty cents each by the fish market. Maria-Mary left a white-skeleton pear leaf for Mrs. Jamison.

One afternoon held the stirrings of a cold unlike any Maria-Mary had known, and she was alone on the job. Papa was resting at the boardinghouse, having admitted to feeling unsteady. Two of their cuttings had died, but one was thriving. There was no earthly reason why it had not only rooted but exploded toward abundant growth in only a few months. A tendril held several new berries. Red berries were "bagas vermelhas," but she thought of them as "amora," despite this meaning "blackberry," since that was close to the word for love.

Mrs. Jamison appeared in a champagne silk dress cut on the bias and a ropy string of pearls. In a flurry of desire to share her first berries in America, Maria-Mary insisted Mrs. Jamison enact the ceremony of testing one, and it made her rapturous. "Mary! Isn't this a marvel, and you along with it!" In repayment, Mrs. Jamison fetched a flyer about the Horticultural Society sponsoring a painting contest, and she exclaimed, "You must try! The prize is twenty dollars."

Entries had to feature plants or trees. Papa reminded her that since she was skilled at stitching portraits with thread, she should try flowers like that. Everyone else would use paint. She commenced sewing on linen, aligning threads to be smooth as oils, pink gradations as a background for an apricot orchard.

She won.

Art can plow a safe passage through the wider world!

During the award night, in yet another grand home, her disbelief at winning merged with panic, since Papa had not arrived. Propped on an easel, with people sauntering toward it, was her miniature thread-painting. She was in her tangerine dress, with a rose pin from Myrtle Jamison, who was wearing the most shocking thing Mary had ever seen—a "stole" consisting of a dead fox with dried eye sockets. Mrs. Jamison whispered, "They wish to start the ceremony, dear. Where is your father?"

"Ma'am, I don't know." Mary's voice was tiny. Papa had planned to install batches of dill and thyme at the Jamisons' greenhouse before hastening to this capping event of a day for Mary of a lunch and tours of home galleries that had put her in the company of self-assured, intelligent women who were kind but did not realize how they strained her social skills to a snapping point. He was never late to anything and would not have missed this. The blood in her veins slowed into sludge.

The ceremony featured applause and attentive demeanors, and a floor blinding in its shine. When she got tearful with thanks, especially for the Jamison family, everyone thought it a foreign girl's timidity. Dead fox still hanging from her shoulders, Mrs. Jamison took command at the finale and said, "We'll find him, Mary."

He was not in the boardinghouse, nor in the greenhouse, nor at the flower-district's outlet he favored. In her horse-drawn carriage, Mrs. Jamison put a lap robe—a thing to protect against a cold that was worsening—over Mary. Maria.

They found him in a bed at St. Luke's Hospital, run by the Episcopalians at Fifty-fourth Street, and Mrs. Jamison stood by as Maria shouted, *"Papa!"* What prevented her from fearing he had gone to the Silent City was the tube in his arm. Mrs. Jamison patted Maria-Mary's back and excused herself to find a doctor to make inquiries.

"Papa, Papa, I'm here," she whispered.

Blinking, he came to, murmuring that a man had discovered him collapsed from dehydration on the sidewalk and transported him here. "If I'd had more water, I wouldn't have ruined your evening."

"I'll take care of you, Daddy," she said, like an American girl. "Mrs. Jamison gave me a rose pin, and people clapped."

"Tu és O Meu Mais Do Que Tudo, minha princesa, minha filha."

"Deus o abençoe, e o faça um santo muiiiiito grande, boa noite, durma bem," she said, the first Portuguese Night Blessing she had ever bestowed, returning the favor for all the ones in her childhood. She requested a cot to stay with him. Mrs. Jamison, who always got what she wanted—what a model of assertion she was—helped her make sure that happened. In the night, Mary rested a hand on his back, to take the measure of the air of breath confirming he was alive. How I love you. It is my turn to care for you. We'll always remember that this is the city where in such a short time I fully grew up.

She had figured on growing old in ruby-and-tangerine New York City, but the doctor suggested Papa needed open air to breathe properly, and that meant land with a garden under his care. Myrtle Jamison not only understood, she said firmly, "You'll come back one day, Mary Freitas, and Lawrence and I and the children will welcome you, and you'll invite us to the gallery with your paintings."

The Presbyterian Society aided Mary in reaching out to the communities in Illinois, and a position on an estate sorely in need of his talents was secured for Augusto Pereira Vaz Gato de Freitas owing to his never-to-be-forgotten courage on behalf of the converts. He might save enough to own property near the spot where Madeirans were concentrated in this colossal nation. Mary accepted extra money from Mrs. Jamison "so I can claim to be your first benefactor, dear heart."

When he protested that he knew how Maria-Cat loved New York, she countered that she cared about him far more. They dug around the base of the surviving miracle plant, where roots and hairlike filaments fought to remain. Mary whispered, "Anda," a word that means *walk* but also many actions involving forward motion.

When the steamship's wake sent out froth, Mary's heart erupted with frazzle cracks from an abiding worship of New York. "I've heard Illinois is very cold," she said. The deck tilted, and the buildings shrank. And still farther west, onward, there was gold, gold pried out of crevices. According to Mrs. Jamison, where they were going was extremely flat. Perhaps the winds there were like curtains that blew all the way to California and dipped into the Pacific, where the gold had run off in rivulets, and then the curtains made of winds blew back to the center of the country, brushing gold upon everyone's head.

———

"I'M LUCKY. I'D WAGER NOT MANY WORKERS HERE CAN RAISE PINEAPPLE," said Edward Moore, brushing at his shirtfront as if his words had spilled there. Mary sized this up, not unkindly, as a nervous gesture. They were inside his greenhouse. Never—not anywhere—had she seen such an unusually large private one. It stretched a full Springfield block, and his estate itself consisted of three lots combined as one. His blond hair held the furrows dragged by a wet comb, making him appear determined to tame himself. Edward had tasted Hawaiian pineapple during his life out West, and now fronded tops floated in a bucket, slicings from a rail shipment. Observing Papa acquainting himself with the flowers, saplings, and vegetables awaiting their embeddings, Edward said, "What a warm-hearted father. Some day I'll reveal why I envy your closeness."

She remarked that yes, Papa and she were twins, and since

Madeirans were expert with pineapple, they would be honored to grow
some. She felt utterly indebted. They would make this place theirs.
"He's grateful for the job, and for you letting us grow our transplant,
Mr. Moore." Her animation was in no minor part due to the arrival by
wagon of the miracle-berry survivor, still sprouting despite its exasper-
ation with constant uprooting.

"Call me Edward. Or Ward. We're all transplants, since I'm from
San Francisco." He had only been in Illinois for six months. His joke—
she smiled at it—made him blush. Poor man; it was impossible to hide
even minor embarrassment with such paleness. "I hope to grow even
more pineapple on my land in Florida."

How much property did one man require? She wanted only this
secure realm with her father, an American version of what they had
once had. Edward was in his late twenties but lacked a wife. Everyone
was stuck inside a casing called a body, but this seemed to burden him,
and she stifled an impulse to tease him like the brother she suddenly
wished she had. She said, "Why not go there now?"

"War is coming. Florida is in the South. I'm thinking toward the
future."

Edward Moore—Ward—took the train west to Illinois College in
Jacksonville twice a week to lecture on botany, a fertile spot for hearing
about events in the world. She knew nothing about a war.

He mentioned that his specialty was grafting. "Care for a look?" he
asked, and he called Papa over and led them to a yellow Lady Banks
rose scion bound with string to an exemplar of Beau Narcisse. "I'd
like to develop a thornless breed," he said, and Papa, appraising where
the slant wounds were cauterizing together, muttered, "This is good."
Worth a try, since a Lady Banks and a Gallica varietal had fewer,
wispier thorns.

"Fame and fortune await the inventor of a thornless one," said
Edward, excited, then ashamed, as if for besmirching an act of creation with a vision of cash. Holding out his hands palm downward,
like a boy presenting them for inspection, he said, "A farmer's or
gardener's nails are checked when he's in his coffin to see if dirt
is there, so mourners can say, 'Look, he died happy.'" He flashed a
desperate smile. "I like plants in theory, mostly, I'm afraid. Despite

dabbling in grafts. As you can see: clean hands. Augusto, August, I suspect you'll win this one."

Papa liked this enclosure he would orchestrate into harmony, and he liked Edward. A Portuguese nervous system meant either possessing anxiety or sympathizing with it. Game, he displayed the trim blackness marking his nails, like the kohl lining the eyes of certain animals or the tattoos of shamans. "I die happy, Mr. Moore."

Mary laughed, and Edward did the same. Unlike that unforgivable Hamm crew, their new boss confirmed her father as the maestro. Papa abandoned them to go strip detritus off boughs, since half of gardening is clearing away the dead stuff. Alone with Edward, she stared at her gardening shoes.

"I trust you're finding the cottage acceptable," he said.

"The climate it is colder than okay we think," she murmured, English slipping, but Ward overlooked that and offered assent. "It's December," he said, "but I agree, Mary. I'm called a stoic, but my blood is thin from my being born in California."

She had no idea what "stoic" meant. "I'm worried about my father," she blurted. "It's so cold, he gets so cold. Please, do you have a coat? A coat for him."

"I do. Come with me."

Winter's air put her in mind of stinging jellyfish tendrils. A minor farce ensued in her not knowing if she should walk beside him—too companionable, and he was the height of a cornstalk with yellow hair, and speaking required him to incline in a way she reared away from, the whole operation slowed on account of the snow. When she skidded, Edward offered his elbow and said, "Take it. My arm. I fear it'll be necessary." She did. He pointed out she needed proper boots, and he would acquire them.

A lion's-head door knocker guarded his two-story white house. What arrested her, this first time in a dwelling so imperial she wondered if one could be lost in it—who can imagine a house where one might be lost?—was the wallpaper in a whole room given over to dining. It was white with white raised dots, and she walked to it and ran her hands—she could not stop, could not help herself—over the dots the way the blind read Braille before she breathed out, "Crisântemos."

"You have a good eye," said Edward. But her heart detected the pattern of chrysanthemums before her sight had, it was her heart that was good. This pointillism like gooseflesh was a new kind of delicacy, this was remarkable in America, which was stormy-big but also tucked with plenty of wisps, whispers, and things you would miss if you did not peer carefully. And there was a library. Waist-high cases displayed glass flowers, with their Latin names on cards in handwriting faded to the color of honey. A raven was perched on a bookcase with volumes behind gilt-framed glass, with tasseled keys in the locks. Edward said, "There's a story behind the stuffed bird that I'll share some day, though it does not cast me in the finest light. You may borrow my books. They're mostly about botany."

"Oh, thank you! Thank you, Edward!"

Her bubbling enthusiasm took him aback, and he said, "I'll get that coat."

When he presented her with a tawny fur, she momentarily dropped her face into it because its thickness was so welcoming. He insisted upon escorting her back, and their tread was unsteady, with her holding his arm, and both were relieved to say goodbye.

Papa dozed soundly below a stack of blankets, with the coat burying him further. Their new home offered a table, a basin, cots, hearth, plates, and towels. They had looped back to a cottage life, and laboring for someone else, except Papa kept repeating that America held endless space and promise.

At dawn she awakened to him coughing outside, in his lion's wrapping, so as not to disturb her. Ghosts shot from their mouths in the cold. Maple syrup had been poured onto fresh snow to harden, with a rock-pinned note explaining it was candy for breakfast. She was touched that Edward was smart enough to use objects to affirm his generosity, knowing words and manner might fail him.

—

DOWNTOWN SPRINGFIELD WAS A PLATTER OF SLUSH AND DIRTIED snow (where did those rust streaks come from?), trash-strewn, disheveled, crowded, and marvelous. This hub lay north of Aristocracy

Hill's narrow, deep lots, where Edward Moore and his monied tribe fashioned rural-like estates not far from the vortex of commerce, a city with the prairie as a fringe that then cracked wide. Fronting the Globe Hotel were hitching posts for horses that shuddered. The water pump creaked in its sentinel spot near sidewalks winter padded yet drummed on with boots (including her new ones from Edward). An oyster sky flooded over the buildings, some displaying false fronts but with all shops bursting with wares, and sleigh bells on the doors announced the customers, singing out, *Here I am!* She counted the offices of attorneys, sensing a cardinal churchdom of law. Slip-sliding with Papa, her scarf got spit-frozen to her face. Her woolen hat had ties that ended in yarn balls each with a cat's face, ears, and whiskers. When Papa had found it at Julian Barr's store, he needed to make it hers.

Their errand was to fetch more Lady Banks yellows to continue Edward's quest to breed a thornless rose. The vaulted nursery rested on an expanse hedged with Osage orange shrubs bred as fencing because they grew *horse-high, bull-strong, and pig-tight.* Buyers were examining plants that would brave the winter. Swaddled Lady Banks cuttings waited at the cash register, and a young man said, "Mr. Freitas, I hear you're a genius." Papa bowed his head, disagreed, and handed over coins from Edward.

The young fellow showed Mary a sprig of sharp leaves and red berries—a new kind of red berries! She asked what it was. "Mistletoe, for Christmas. You hang it in a doorway, and anyone who stands under it must be kissed." He dangled it over his head, and to Mary's own amazement, she pecked his cheek. He said, "That's for good luck, because next week a few friends and I are heading west to strike gold."

Some love stories are like this, scarcely a minute, but their brevity keeps them sweet.

As they rounded the last corner before Springfield's bustling gave way toward widening spaces and the estates on their substantial lots, they were blocked by two men teetering out of a tavern. Brandishing a bottle, one said, "Why, looka this Mexican gent with his baby bride whosa Mexican of the nice light kind."

It was dumbfounding how people hurried past. Fire ignited her, but she needed to let Papa be the one to steer them. He whispered in Portuguese, "Don't look at them."

The second man retorted, "You gotta nerve speaking Mexican. You lost that war, and I shot your kind. Pay up." A grimy paw was extended.

"He only I'll bet got Mexican money," said the other, reaching for the cat head on one tie of Mary's hat. Papa grabbed his wrist and stabbed a warning gaze into his pupils.

The man backed off with his hands up. "In the spirit of the up-a-coming birth of our Lord, Mexico grandpa, I apologize."

Papa hastened her along, and they hooted and one yelled, "Come back when you get tired of old men, girlie!"

She ordered herself to be calm so her father would quit shaking. At the cottage, she picked up the envelope that Edward had propped against the door with their pay and a toting-up note: "$1 per day 6 days, August Freitas; 50¢ per day 6 days, Mary Freitas, bonus $1 pineapple progress = $10." But under this was written: "Minus $2 for coat, 1st week of 5 payments." The combined salary for the week was $8.

He had started charging Papa for that coat, a further thing to ruin a day of being introduced to mistletoe. She hid the note and put the dollars into their money box. Myrtle Jamison had cautioned her, "The saying nowadays is, 'A dollar a day is very good pay,' and you must ask for that, dear." Mr. and Mrs. Jamison had paid her a dollar and Papa two every workday.

They ate buttered bread with hothouse tomatoes. A bit of décor from Edward was a plaque with a slogan burned into the wood: A WISHBONE AIN'T AS LIKELY TO GET YE AS FAR AS A BACKBONE. Papa asked, "What is a wishbone, Cat?"

"Fúrcula, Pai." Tugging a prong of a dried fork-bone of a chicken and hoping to crack off the crux part to win one's desire—the superstition was universal. "We work hard," she continued, "but we're from a race of wishbones in the land of backbones," and they choked with laughter, the skittish kind after a fright. She would conceal from him that the owner of a triple-sized lot on Aristocracy Hill and acres in Florida had charged him for the use of a coat. Papa insisted upon spending one dollar on a map of San Francisco as a Christmas gift for Mr. Moore and left it with a card on his porch.

Edward was planning a holiday gala. Caped workers toted in provisions, crates of brown bottles of stout, and squawking hens carried by their feet, and men cleaned the rug in Ward's "great room." The bursts of bounty helped Mary and her father pretend nothing threatening had assailed them. On the day of the party, she met Perpetua Roderick, with close-set eyes and a hooked nose—formerly Rodrigues, from a family of Protestant tailors, who was mustering a dervish energy to polish the silver. Mary showed up with hothouse pomegranates as requested by the host, and Perpetua sang, "You're one of me!" and their hug became a dance. Perpetua's family's Springfield hovel was so crowded it was hard to keep a thought for more than a minute! She had heard about Maria Catarina Freitas and her holy papa of the Botanical Garden. A cook shrieked, "Stop dilly-dallying, girl, and go squeeze oranges!" Perpetua made a face when the cook turned her back, delighting Mary.

Men on ladders draped garlands from the ceiling of the great room, and papery flowers called poinsettias were carted in in pots. Edward, directing the transformation, spotted her sneaking a look and said, "I need you, Mary, please," and gestured at a crate of pineapples. "I couldn't wait for the greenhouse ones. Tell me how to serve these. By the way, the map is already framed on a wall upstairs. Thank you."

Was he being a touch short about a gift meant to keep him from being homesick, or was this the abrupt manner displayed by perfectly nice Americans?

His light matte blue eyes suggested a paintbrush saturated with water before it swiped up blue from a color-block. She described skewering peeled pineapples, grilling them, rolling them in cinnamon, and slicing coated pieces onto plates. Repeat: Grill, roll in spice, and keep cutting off portions to the core.

"I was sure you'd know something like that." He produced a miniature wrapped item and Madeiran wine. "The bottle is for your father, and the present is for you," he said. She thanked him, and was about to voice worry that her dress would not be smart enough for the party, when Edward added, "Get some rest. You and your father deserve it. Apologies if the festivities keep you awake. I'd say I'll see you in the morning, but likely it'll be noon."

A worker summoned him, and Edward abandoned her. She toted the gift and the wine that had traveled from her birthplace (the expression "this is like carrying bananas to Madeira" came to mind) to where Papa was shining his Sunday shoes. His mustache and beard were lightly waxed. She said, "We're not invited."

He clutched the cloth streaked with black paste and stared at her, and she repeated the news in Portuguese, and he said, "What?"

She unwrapped her gift—a hair ribbon, green—and said the wine was for him. "No reason for him to know we don't drink, Cat-Cat," he said. "Maybe you misunderstood about the party?"

"No, he apologized that the noise might keep us awake." On their table were presents from Mrs. Jamison, one hundred skeins of silk thread for Mary, and five types of lettuce seeds and an elegant handkerchief for Papa. Mary had sent profuse thanks, along with monogrammed hand towels for Myrtle and Lawrence Jamison, and Teddy and the twins, Gemma and Clarisse.

The carriage drivers shared pipes and endeavored to warm themselves by stomping, while the horses nickered and tossed blindered heads, all of them exposed for the duration. Guests in finery drifted as phantoms toward the strains of an orchestra. Mary and her father went outside twice, as if expecting Edward to investigate where they were, but when guffawing tipplers invaded the greenhouse, Papa could not watch. A banging on their door revealed Perpetua holding out a dish. "I stole this for you," she trilled. It was milk frozen, shaved, and flavored with vanilla, and they downed every trace of it. They hauled blankets out where the stars were like knots on the back of satin that God and all the dead were stitching; what handiwork was on the other side? Perpetua pretended to smoke a cigarette, puffing out white air, and to Mary's delight, Papa joined her, so she did as well. But Perpetua could not linger and soon threw off her blankets and cried out, "The cook will kill me!" She clutched her throat, entertaining them with strangling noises before dashing back to serving at the party.

Papa offered to unlock the map of heaven for his daughter. Look at the Big Dipper, and see, there's Cassiopeia the Queen, and Cygnus, and the Dog Star. "There's so much left to teach you, and not enough time."

Blood bolted to her nerve endings. "What do you mean, Papa?"

"I just want to name the stars for you." Softly, "I'm much older than most guardians of someone nearing twenty." He was wearing the lion-colored coat, the one Edward was charging him ten dollars for. "I should have left my job in Funchal sooner. Be patient, but don't pretend something isn't happening when it truly is."

"Then I won't pretend Edward is decent."

"Cat-Cat, he's a fine person. Most men use wealth to dominate people, but some use it to insulate themselves. That is who he is, and I understand that wish, and so do you. He's reserved but obviously fond of you. You should trust him. I'd be at rest to think you lived in such an elegant, protected house. What a height of success for you, querida."

Terror compressed her so hard it made her eyes leak.

She requested the Portuguese Night Blessing after climbing into her cot. They heard some guests departing early and a few horses giddying-up. "I love you, Papa," she said. Crystals of weather decorated the window. Ice is like lace; it's a form of water; it is not scary. "I love you so much. There's so much ahead of us."

"Happy almost-Christmas," he said gently. "O Meu Mais Do Que Tudo, child of my heart."

Three days past Christmas, she banged on Edward's door, and when he opened it, she spat out, "I work twelve hours a day, and you pay me almost nothing!"

He invited her into the sitting room, where she shouted, "You bill my father for a coat? He makes half of what he got paid working for a nice family in New York! How are we supposed to save up and buy our own place? You don't even invite us to your party! You give Papa wine, but he doesn't drink, and I get a hair ribbon for a schoolgirl, and—" She dropped onto a sofa. She had meant to sound forceful, like Mrs. Jamison, not petulant and juvenile.

Ward occupied a chair, keeping an end table between them. He said, "I've been writing a lecture for Illinois College, and—"

"I don't care!"

"Mr. Freitas and I were discussing the potential of tropical fruits in cold-climate greenhouses, and I promised to mention him by name in my talk, Mary."

"Stealing his knowledge." A red screen dropped across her vision. Her line of sight absorbed the great room, where remnants of the party's décor dangled.

"I'm crediting him in an article for a journal. As to your wages, women make less than men, do they not, and Mr. Freitas's skills are—well, I suspect you'd agree they are superior to yours." His expression was pinked-up, confused in the manner of earnest men.

"I deserve a dollar, and he deserves two, at least."

"Very well. I'll pay what you deem fair. As to the coat, he insisted it not be charity. It was new, and I bought it for fifty dollars, though I concealed this amount. And I snuck in bonuses for pineapple growing." A large hand raked his yellow hair, and Mary ceased gnawing her lip. "As for my Christmas party." This was the one time in the year, by the way, when he honored his Catholic faith by attending Mass. He let his eyes meet hers for a flicker. "People would have asked your father, or you, to fetch them drinks. I'll be even more honest and ask your forgiveness. He is my gardener. So are you. It is not a world in which it would be judged appropriate to include you at festivities. Such a world doesn't exist anywhere. Surely this is not a shock."

Edward Moore was not a brooker of tides, but few people were. He went on, "I thought Madeiran wine might give him a taste of home, much as you gave me something about San Francisco. Your ribbon was a last-minute folly. Your real present is upstairs. I've been hesitant about showing it to you. Would you care to follow me?"

She debated skulking away but was curious. He led her to a room with upholstered sofas, a cabinet for notions, and a Singer sewing machine with an iron-lattice foot pedal and a needled proboscis, the Queen of Inventions. She could not stop herself from petting it as if it were a cat. He said, "There's not enough space in your quarters, so I'll keep it here. We'll have an understanding that this room is yours. Despite these last minutes, I find your company wholly pleasant."

She wrapped herself with a protective carapace of air. A man widening her pathway was a novel kind of jeopardy. She had seldom missed having a mother but yearned for one to advise her while she drummed up a wariness of someone who bestowed a gift so frankly conditional, since he still possessed what was given. And yet she forgave him about the coat, who would not, and without much contention she had doubled Papa's income and her own. Edward would sharpen who she was, toughen her, and she murmured, "I appreciate the sewing machine, Mr. Moore."

He blurted, "Causing you distress would be terrible to me," not perceiving that he was distressing her now. She needed a mommy. He concluded, "The sewing machine is yours to claim. I mean to say, your presence is welcome, but it belongs to you, no matter what. However, I would miss you, dare I say substantially, should you go elsewhere."

She said—and this was weak of her—that they had only just arrived.

She caught her father coughing up blood near the rose-grafting experiment, where he said, "Cat-Cat, I didn't hear you come in," while kicking at the red splatters in the sawdust. He was eager for the wild-flowers he had heard burst onto the prairie in the spring, still months away, adding, "It'll be like our color cabinet finding us." Only now did it strike her that for her sake he had pushed as far as imagination, as strength, as flesh and faith and talent—as geography itself—might deliver her.

—

THE LEAVES OF HER MIRACLE PLANT—THE SURVIVOR NOW A NASCENTLY blooming shrub—erupted with pinprick-sized holes, the borings of a disease that even he could not identify. He mixed neem oil with warm water, and when she begged him to rest—*Papa, please*—he said, "Don't you worry, Cat-Cat. I'm going to save this." Her plant was piercing itself already with mourning for him, the pocked leaves imitating the picture haunting her of his lungs. What grade of grief is it during the trickling-away part when someone is not yet gone, the phase that is like trying to carry water in open hands?

Side by side, they washed each damaged-lace leaf, every single one, devastated or mildly afflicted, topside and underside, at dawn, again at noon, and a strong tender dosage to last through each fall of night.

The white-haired physician in town informed them that Papa's lungs were indeed leaking, but what was killing him were the calci-fying branches, fast-growing tumors, attached to his spine. Since the doctor also had a goatee and a kindly manner, his paleness ushered in a preview of Papa's ghost.

Her father told her, "I've enjoyed a perfect life because you're at its center, Cat-Cat. Now you'll carry me at the center of yours, my darling."

As they worked to save her plant that day, she sobbed, and he put down his cloth to hold her. *Remember this, this right now, he is still drawing breath. Bless the action of gardening, the sowing, its conduciveness to being silent together, call it never-ending.*

———

WHAT WERE THE SMALL THINGS—FOR EVERYONE, IT IS ALWAYS THE smallest things—that ejected her heart straight through her chest, blowing out of the jailhouse of her ribs? It was Augusto Freitas donning his suit and hat each time he doctored their transplant.

His mustache was never untrimmed.

Once as he stood before the tin sheet serving as their mirror, she took the tiny scissors—in the shape of a crane—from him because his shaking might cause an injury. The crane's beak snipped the white ends above his lip, and she said, "Now you're beautiful." At forty-six, he had insisted her story would not end with her being murdered by a weaver of baby souls. He would end at sixty-five, short of his birthday in the year 1860, just shy of her turning twenty, an enclosed garden of time, a parterre.

The hour arrived in the first week of March when Papa beamed and said, "Congratulations to us both." The holes in the leaves were sealed up, and the oil had burnished her plant to a gleaming. Berries appeared, primed toward profusion. "I'll rest now, Cat-Cat. Would you please bake me a pie?" He craved this dessert. The word for it amused him, owing to its being identical to the Portuguese word for father—pai—and his passion was for a lattice top, an edible trellis.

When she knocked on Edward's door and he admitted her, she eyed two suitcases. "It is not a good time to leave you, Mary," he said, "but I have a lecture tour out East. It's been arranged for a while. A visiting botanist will take my classes for a few weeks."

A spike of terror tore into her, as if this abandonment guaranteed Papa would not survive the night. When she asked if she might use his oven to bake a pie, he said, "I'm glad your father is well enough to consume something rich."

"Were you going to leave without letting us know?"

"Not at all." To welcome her toward the kitchen, he produced a humorously exaggerated gesture as if inviting her onto a dance floor. She stifled a pique of anger. He had found the doctor; he praised Papa unsparingly. She was glad that his once-daily visits, like clockwork, were devoid of hovering, and she could imagine the indecency of most bosses toward someone who would not last long on the job. His tour had been set before Papa's illness. But she was beset with a judgment of *You're running off because my father is dying.* Edward could not hide relief at having an excuse to avoid a deathbed. When she scrubbed her face with her hands as an attempt to wash the contents of her mind, he said, "Believe me, I'm sorry about your father."

Forcing herself not to fall apart, she said, "Do you not have a family? Parents. Brothers or sisters, or cousins. In California." Had he ever grieved?

"My father died years ago, and I have no contact with my mother and brothers. The feeling, or lack thereof, is mutual, trust me."

Before she could ask why he had chosen Illinois—he seemed to have arbitrarily picked a thriving spot, whereas Papa and she had followed a Madeiran trail—he said, "Order what you need from the grocer. Use my account. Your father insists upon tending the greenhouse and yard, but don't permit that to be your main concern." He proferred a set of keys from the lowboy. "Do not hesitate to summon the physician at my expense, and please use the house."

Afraid of bursting into tears, she managed to thank him. Annoyance got tempered with a grasping of one manifestation of decency: *He is aware of unlocking his door because he lacks a history of completely opening his heart.*

A man in livery arrived to take him to the station and carried away the luggage. Edward said, "Let me pay my respects."

Papa was trimming the pink-tomato plant in the greenhouse, and he turned to face Edward lingering in the doorway. Mary could feel passing over Papa the knowledge that he would not see this man, their benefactor, again. Edward said, "Mr. Freitas, I'll let Mary explain, but I must leave for a while. I wish you to rest, and not to worry."

"You hired me for these tasks, and I'll do them as long as I can," said

Papa, gaunt but at peace. Despite his being here only a few months, the greenhouse was filled, brimming with color.

"You're an artist, I can say that much." Edward looked downward, then reared his head up. "Mary will affirm my hope that you inhabit my house." Sometimes containment is a hatchery for eloquence, because Edward concluded, "I wish you ease and some miracle of health, sir, and farewell."

The downstairs of the white two-story house held the great room, library-study, kitchen, living room with the annexed parlor, and the largest bedroom, with tartan throws and a dresser the size of the monsters that had lurked in the dark in her youth. She peeked at Edward's clothing hanging in his closet, and the empty shirts and trousers were disturbing, as if men had dissolved out of them. Upstairs, along with her sewing space and a water-closet, an assortment of rooms included one guest quarters with two single beds. She baked many pies, apple, huckleberry, and cherry. Papa insisted upon gardening, that gorgeous coaxing of life into such frail things.

She awoke one night with a start and found him missing, as if he had ascended to heaven out of rumpled winding sheets. After confusion about where she was, she threw on her night wrap and bellowed, "Papa?"

He was in a chair at a window in the parlor, seeking a strength of moonlight to read Edward's book about raising orange trees. She rested the side of her head onto his crown and muttered, "You promised not to leave me."

"Forgive me." He breathed scantily. "I'm not in pain, not so much, querida. Mr. Moore agreed to put you in charge. I asked him to. Isn't that nice of him?"

"I can't."

"When you think you can't move, listen. I'll be telling you to do one small thing at a time. You're the daughter of a king. You can do anything."

Laved by moonlight, he allowed her to be unable to answer. By morning, a sifting of snow late in the season had melted, and everything was held in the salivating mouth of the world. He used her paints to dab smooth rocks with reds and pinks, adding black dots and green tufts to turn them into strawberries, and she copied him. They set the strawberry-rocks in the yard to herald a springtime he would not live to see. He said, "Watch," and a bird zoomed down to eat a strawberry, smashed its beak, and tore away. "They're the prettiest scarecrows you can make," he said, grinning. "It's an old gardening trick. I have so much more to teach you."

—

"I REGRET NOT VISITING CALIFORNIA," HE SAID. HE WAS FLAT-OUT ON one guest bed, and she was on the other.

"Let's travel there, Papa." They had played this game when she was a girl.

And they closed their eyes and flew to the Sierras. The air of the West was layered butterscotch and orange. "I read that tall-masted ships entered the San Francisco Bay and ended up buried in the streets," she said.

In the East, in New York, the sky was blue, gray, and white.

Illinois held aerated banks of green and yellow from the bleeding corn.

Why not visit Chinese pagodas, and Italy, where her rebellious mother had conceived her before getting handed off to God?

"I pictured San Francisco, New York, China, and Italy," she said. "Tell me where you flew."

The darkness was enveloping, and velvet. He replied, "I did go to San Francisco to look at the buried ships, but then I only wanted to stay here with you."

—

IN THE END, PAPA WISHED TO DWELL INSIDE THE GREENHOUSE, ON cots dragged from the cottage. The heating pipes were sibilant as snakes. He asked, "Do you think it means anything that the English word 'exit' is so close to our 'exito'? We think success means leaving, that it always lies other than where we are."

"I think that's a coincidence, Papa, about the words. But I don't know." She helped him swallow the dregs of his morphine.

"Angel mine, this is a place beyond what I dreamt for you."

She replied, "Yes, Papa, all right. I agree. Rest, knowing I'll be here."

———

WINCING THE NEXT MORNING, HE SAID, "LET'S GO INTO THE OPEN AIR, Cat." This would be the only miracle: He could stumble a short distance. She assisted him because of the weight of the tree stretching its boughs on his back and into his limbs. And he smiled! Plants were straggling upward despite the cold earth, greeting him before their proper season. She eased him to the ground, to lean against an oak. Plants respire a gossamer of the water they drink, and they were conspiring to exhale all at once at him, bathing him in thanks.

"This is entirely fine," he said, eyelids shuttering. He kissed the fist they made together by holding hands. March the twenty-ninth would get branded hard on her bones. He had invited her to watch on the last shore, so that all the other deaths to come, and her own, would not frighten her as much. "Sonhos cor-de-rosa, Pai," she said. "Deus o abençoe, e o faça um santo muiiiiito grande. Boa noite."

"I love you. You are my life, Maria-Cat. What a wonder it's been."

"Daddy, I love you, too," she said near the scarecrow-strawberries and dormant foxgloves that would be up to her to untangle. She stopped herself from shouting, but her cry was loud. "Father! You are my only, only father. You know that, don't you?" Shaking their joined hands. "Father, mother, everything. Only you!"

And then his last word: "Yes."

———

"I HOPE THE HOUSE WAS A SMALL COMFORT," SAID EDWARD.

Lying on her cot next to Papa's, her muscles welded together, she did not turn over to face him. He had tiptoed into the greenhouse, smelling of weeks of travel. An irrigation pipe had burst because it was wailing for her father, and she had not fixed it.

"Mary?"

"Go away."

"The job is yours if you wish it. Have you eaten?"

"No."

Papa had wanted to be buried on the prairie to greet the season of wildflowers. She enlisted the aid of the physician to take care of what were called "arrangements," but the priest would not allow Papa to be interred out in the open. She had raged at him, but her father in a pine box went to rest at the Oak Ridge Cemetery. A Presbyterian minister had officiated, and Perpetua Roderick had come.

"I'll pay you his salary, two dollars a day." Ward laid a hand on her shoulder, but she refused to move. Grime coated her forehead, but her arm was too heavy to wipe it away. He said, "It's painful to see you like this."

"No."

"No. What does that mean?" He stepped away.

It means *you understand that you left me alone, using obligations to avoid looking at someone dying, and I won't ever entirely forgive you.*

"I am heartbroken at the loss of your father, and heartbroken for you."

She should move to New York City and work for (and get adopted by) the Jamisons . . . except her *plant* was here, and *Papa* was here, and he called this her place of success and safety, and she had little money, and *besides*, she could not lift her arms and legs.

"Tell me what to do, and I'll do it. Should I leave you be?"

"You're good at that," she mumbled. The retreating footfalls paused, and the air held his attempt to reply, but he could not produce anything, other than a bowl of chicken soup that he set by her cot. She forced herself to sit up. (Also, she was ravenous.) Ward crouched to meet her at eye level, that well-meaning, good-looking face bothering her with its belated kindness now that the requirement of large emotions was done. "I'll leave you to it," he said. She finished the soup while alone. Stretching supine, she released a howling.

She awakened with a fresh pillow below her head.

Upon the occasion that Ward handed her a framed pressed purple trillium lily as she sat in the yard, staring at ivy that was hoarding space, he shook her elbow and said, "For you." Perhaps she did not wish to hear about his lecture tour, but at Amherst College in

Massachusetts, he had met Austin Dickinson, a lawyer who attended Ward's talk on "The Value of Gardens" and invited him to dine. Austin's sister next door had sent over one of her pressed flowers. Ward had witnessed red-haired Emily at her second-floor window, lowering a basket with her homemade cocoa-nut cake for the local children. She wrote poetry. "Emily reminded me of you," he said. "Let me help you return to the living. Harvest some pomegranates and walk them to Julian Barr's store, to sell."

The lily's veined petals were splayed in a triad. Anyone else would have dismissed her by now, coldly, a solitary girl. It might be overwrought to think he had owed her courageous deathbed attendance, because she would not have wished to share her father's leave-taking with anyone. Edward appeared to be the vessel for Papa telling her to do one small thing so she could do the next small thing. He added—as she gripped the framed flower—that she needed the company of someone who doubled as an assistant. "I'll ask Perpetua Roderick to join you in the cottage, and in your work. Her home situation is less than ideal. You'd be in charge, and she'll work for a dollar a day, and you'll receive two. Enough now, Mary."

That "enough" infuriated her again. She had run out the timer on his allowance for sorrow. But she had promised her father to continue what they had begun, and she hugged to herself the gift from Emily Dickinson.

———

BECAUSE I CANNOT SEE YOU, YOU'RE EVERYTHING, FATHER. YOU'RE lightning streaks, an arbor. You have no legs, so I must walk for you. The birds chatter about your stone strawberries. In Madeira, we made lavender sachets, and I'll sew bags for miracle berries.

———

PERPETUA RODERICK PROPPED UP MARY ON HER BED COME MORNING, washed her face with water from the pump, and brushed her hair. Admiring the gift threads from Mrs. Jamison, Pet said, "You must sew the biggest, best tablecloth ever. Ever! Stitch the story of your life like a Madeiran girl, Maria Catarina."

Fix the irrigation hose.

Trim the branches of the satin-apple tree (same family as her plant). Groan at Perpetua's jokes.

Perpetua commands Mary to set her hands upon a massive sheet of linen as if she were playing a piano, and transformation arrives. Gone is the fleeting plan to stitch a replica of the Botanical Garden done to scale. Here is the new work of a new lifetime.

She stitches a likeness of the red-berried plant that keeps her in Illinois. In threads, she creates a likeness of her father.

Blow a kiss. Let the spirits catch it.

The world is strange.

But like a book, it ruffles open.

THE SWEETEST TASTE

MAY 1860

SHE WORE HER CAT-HAT, PRAYING JULIAN BARR OF BARR'S SUNDRY
Goods would recognize it as his former merchandise and remark about
Papa buying it. But he was wincing at her, and at Perpetua. Using the
Singer machine, Mary had sewn sachets with seven miracle berries in
each and had written the instructions on slips of paper. Spilled onto
his counter were the contents of one sachet and half a lemon. Customers in that dreamy waltz of all shoppers eased through his aisles.

Mr. Barr, in a spotless apron tied at his waist, giving him the ap-
pearance of a high priest of butchers, glared when offered a berry. He
snapped, "So what'm I supposed to tell folks about this?"

Mary said, "They're good at parties. People can admire that they're
a real thing. They make old food taste better. Pay me three cents a bag,
and you can charge five."

Holding up the slip with instructions, he read aloud in singsong,
"'Then you chewened something stale or sour.' What is 'chewened'?
Where are you two from?"

She would need Edward's help with the writing. Because she
hoped in future to sell full kits, he had bought lemon trees at her request, though she still had not disclosed the secret of her plants.

"We're from Aristocracy Hill, Mr. Barr." Do the tiny thing of meeting his grimace. Mary could try other outlets, but in addition to this being Papa's favorite, Julian was renowned for high-volume sales. This was a way to join the world but hide away. Out the berries would go on her behalf, a small enterprise.

"Her, too?" He thrust a chin toward Pet, who got called a Berber and an Arab but was so fearless in laughing at fools that Mary worried about her. Pet snapped back, "Try it. Are you scared?"

After Julian ate the berry and chewed the lemon that Mary offered, his eyebrows shot up. He said, "A penny a bag."

"That's not fair," said Perpetua.

"I don't need black witches telling me what's fair. This is trickery."

"Yes, we are witches!" Perpetua raised her hands and shimmied.

"Get the hell off my property," yelled Mr. Barr, and Mary ushered a giggling Perpetua to the exit as an older couple materialized to ask if he required help. So many night women and snake-oil salesmen swarmed in Springfield.

Mary did her sewing when Ward was at Illinois College, vacating the house before his return. While she was sensing how pointless it was to pile up stitched bags as fruit shriveled, the front door opened, and she felt eerily trapped. He was startled to find her at the Singer, and she apologized for her timing. He replied, "I took an early train." Gesturing at his briefcase, he dropped his head in pretend-sleep and droned, "Essays on the genetics of wheat." When she laughed, he added, "Don't be sorry for being here."

It was well past time to disclose the properties of her crop. She invited Ward to sample a miracle berry in the greenhouse and was expectant when she handed him a lemon slice. He set the gnawed rind on a seeding bed, mentioned that the chemical properties had escaped his research, and instead of a ringing exclamation, he said, "You mean to sell these, don't you? I can assist."

"Yes. But Mr. Barr didn't appreciate them." Why wasn't he more excited? She was hoping for—what? Blissful leaping? She had once shared the Azorean legend of the blue-eyed shepherd not allowed to marry a green-eyed princess, who wept out a green lake and drowned, and his tears caused a blue flood in which he too met his end but also eternal joy, with the lakes forever side by side, blue and green. Edward had stopped short of calling it ridiculous, but he had remarked, "Instead of drowning in sorrow, why didn't they run away together?"

"It provides a spot of pleasure, this fruit, but what's it for?"

She shifted in place. "It's for a spot of pleasure, I suppose." She had never heard of pleasure being called a "spot." She added, "It makes stale things edible. That's useful. Children would eat things they don't like but are good for them."

"I'll give this some thought," he said, turning on his heel as if the student papers on wheat had issued an urgent summons.

Several nights later, he invited her to dine in his home. Was it her aloneness that made every person seem either threatening or unreal? Visitors came to the property, and gales of laughter, female laughter, male laughter, emanated, guests wafting in and out. Papa told her to do the one small thing of showing up at the residence of Edward Moore. An Indian corn pudding and a turkey pie awaited on a table illuminated by beeswax tapers. "I read about Madeira, the cuisine, but I don't trust the fish in Illinois, even from a river," he said, setting out plates. What man had ever done this for her? "I bought bananas for dessert. Fried with cinnamon, a variation of what you taught me."

"I've never known a man to cook."

"I'd hate the pitying stares were I to dine nightly at a public establishment."

She said, mildly teasing, "It's a pity more men don't know how to be good wives. Someone like an aunt to me in Madeira used to say that."

She was thunderstuck when he answered, "I was engaged to a woman in California, but Rose was Jewish, and both families were against us. She was not adept at cooking, so I undertook some study of culinary arts."

Speak; say something. "I'm so sorry." She tried to read pain below his held-in-place visage, but his skin shifted to submerge it.

"You've asked about my past, and I suppose I can let you know I have a firsthand acquaintance with religion-based idiocies, as you do."

"Edward." It seemed a slender kindness to pronounce his name.

"Have the pie before it gets cold. No point in dwelling on ancient

history. I have a proposal." He downed a quantity of ale before choking out with, "I mean I'll invest in your crop. There's potential in an
item found nowhere else. I view women as capable of business. Your
father would approve. Tropical berries won't grow here indefinitely,
and never in abundance, but as you recall, I have land in Florida. We
should breed a longer-lasting strain. I'm assuming the potency fades
soon after picking."

"True." She was still reeling about Rose, and this was written on
her, because Edward set down his utensils and said, "I don't wear my
heart on my sleeve, Mary, but it doesn't mean I don't have one. I could
learn from you to be more—I don't know. Emotional. Dare I suggest
I might teach you to be less impetuous? No, I take that back. It's
who you are. But you could assert yourself with bigger plans. We can
experiment with your plant, try desiccating it to see if that's the best
form for shipment. How is the turkey pie?" He was not meeting her
continuing stare. "I use lard, not butter."

"Lard. It's nice. I don't want to move to Florida."

"You might prefer that climate. Part of thinking large is trying new
things. Another part is realizing you don't have to do everything yourself. You—I—can hire workers. We invest in a farm, find distributors,
people who know the railways. You took berries to Julian and want to
make something of what you brought here. I'll help."

Fumbling for words, she asked why he would do that.

His gaze involved a small shake of his head. Ignoring her question,
he said, "You've wondered why I'm in Illinois. Getting far from my
clan after my broken engagement was a driving force. But the answer
I generally give is that the prairie has few trees, so clearing property
for homesteading makes the value of lots practically double overnight.
I prefer dropping money where it'll multiply."

He set out the banana slices fried in cinnamon. She asked for water,
and he poured a glass from the pitcher. It was still cold from the well.
He said, "My father was a genius with land speculation but started
selling deeds to worthless lots to more than one eastern investor at a
time. Very few of them would show up. They would just sell again later.
But two investors arrived and found out they shared a parcel of sand,
and they tracked down my father and beat him so horribly he died a

week later. I inherited my portion. You are regarding me with judgment, but you also live on some of the ill-gotten gains. He made even more legitimately, sowing and reaping without dishonesty. His need for duplicity is something I revile, and therefore you can trust me."

His eyes were red-rimmed, from lack of sleep or an internal combustion that made him seem like the loneliest man on earth. She said, "The bananas are good."

"Too mushy." He smiled as she did. "You and I have a good deal in common, being on our own and from other places. Though you grew up with affection. Care to hear what my parents and brothers would do when I was six? I'd wet the bed, and my mother would hang the sheets in our front yard. When I outgrew this, my brothers would stick my hand in a pan of warm water at night so my curse would return. That's just one thing. I stuttered, and the ridicule was constant. When my father got killed and I had money, I ran to Princeton, as far as I could think to go and as refined as I could imagine. Where my being a Catholic, and my money from uncouth sources—never mind how industrialists make their cash, and I've no idea how my family's shame was discovered—meant I was mocked even more. The way Catholics treated Protestants where you're from is merely reversed in this country, because people need hatreds to thrive."

A last disk of banana was congealing on her plate, a coated eye.

"I got drunk once at Princeton and kept muttering variations of 'never again' or 'nevermore,' so they gave me a stuffed raven, lest I forget humiliating myself. I keep it in my study as a reminder of how people treat those who presume to advance themselves. I have sympathy for your striving, Mary."

"You said the bird suggested something wrong about you. But the other students were the cruel ones. I don't understand. About a bird and nevermore."

"It's from a poem. Never mind. Never mind, nevermore. I think I said the bird embodied what did not show me in the best light. Forget it. Let's turn your crop profitable and make your father even prouder of you. I would expect to earn back my expenses and take nothing beyond a low percentage. The rest is yours." While clearing the plates, he remarked, "I'll pay whatever is due to you, should you move on."

Abruptly he said, as if peeved, "Thank you for a lovely evening. I'll walk you to the door."

But he summoned her to dinner several more times, with the plans for her crop involving numbers and ideas that thrilled but wearied her, like a tidal wave crashing over someone who preferred only to paddle in the ocean. One night he said, "People are beginning to talk. About you being a woman on my property. You might have to reside in the women's boardinghouse in town."

She was silent as her face drained of everything in it.

He burst out with, "It's excruciating to be around you. No, I don't mean that." He opened a drawer in the buffet and set a tiny box in front of her.

A platinum band with a dotting of diamonds rested in the velvet slot. Unsure of what was required, she snapped the box shut.

"Mary," he said. Their steaks exuded pink juice. "Your father gave me his blessing. When I asked. I'll honor working as a business partner no matter your decision, I hope I can do that, but I would like to ask as well if you would make me a happy man. I'd do my best to make you happy. I know you don't love me, not exactly—no, don't deny what's true. But we could make a fair run of things."

"I don't know what to say, Ward."

"I shouldn't have said that about moving out, like a threat, marry me or leave. You can stay. But people do talk. I have to live in this city, and so do you."

Who were these "people"? After thanking him for dinner, and the new cabinet to dry berries to test the extension of their potency, she was at the door when he caught up with her, the ring in its box, and said, "Keep it, whatever you decide." He looked gargantuanly sad.

It still unnerved her that Perpetua Roderick slept on Papa's cot. When Mary showed her the ring, Pet cried, "You didn't say yes? Mary Freitas! You were wounded when he didn't start dancing about some berries, and he wants to give you everything, including himself, and you aren't sure? Go back before he changes his mind!"

"But—"

"Don't talk to me!" Pet flung around on her cot to face the wall.

Mary used the door knocker lightly. He appeared pensive but

pleased to see her. She whispered, "All right," and he sighed and said, "I'm painfully aware of being ten years older than you, but we are in accord, entwined, in many ways."

"I was afraid you'd change your mind." Perpetua had voiced that. Could Mary not even locate her own thoughts?

"I would not be the one with the changed mind," he said softly. "That's one thing I know." He extracted the ring from the box in her hand, slid it onto her finger, kissed her widow's peak, and said, "We'll have an engagement party. You'll meet people. They'll be the ones who won't care that you're a foreigner and we're Catholic and I'm a non-aristocrat in Aristocracy Hill." Her hand was tiny, but he had had the idea of taking her gardening gloves to the jeweler's. "I wanted to get it right the first time. I'm glad I did."

That was touching, and so she replied, teetering with confusion, "And I'm glad we'll be together," and he lapsed into clear-stated fondness by declaring, "I couldn't have dreamt you up, Mary," before bidding her to sleep soundly.

On the pathway back, her ring glittered. Tears fit a film over her corneas. Who was watching, what owls spied when she entered the house of a man? Papa, what did I do; what should I do? She was from a place where every eyeful held something fringed or protruding; here there were dense whites and clear whites and nothing to hold on to. Nell Clark was a friendly presence a few houses down, but who were the others set to flood in? She missed Papa among the coffee trees and might sob until she was tossing in a salty lake. She wanted winters that allowed for sauntering in a thin dress. She longed to set crocuses in a parallelogram and dab lapis lazuli powder on her eyelids, an extravagance even for a queen. The homilies about gossip being akin to murder—the killing of a person's reputation, a knife in the back—made her tremble about marriage meaning cold-climate strangers and their cool whispers.

Shouldn't love feel like faith, not hope and worry?

Their first outing as an engaged couple was in late May. They held hands in the carriage on the way to a concert at Illinois College to support the nearby institution for the deaf. Though aware he had picked an event that avoided the scrutiny of Springfield's society, she said,

"I'm excited. Thank you so much, Edward." But the horses got stuck
in a muddy stretch for so long that they arrived after the reception
was underway.

Was it half an hour into that tumult when she first spotted his
name, on a little card declaring he had invented this thing that looked
like a conch shell married to an ear?

His hair was black. He uttered her old name. He was walking
toward her.

She was riveted. Tall as a boy, he had grown taller still. The entire
body of John Alves funneled into his smile. There it was, oh, the aston-
ishment, look who is here, here he is, imagine. She must have dashed
to him, they were magnets, he was lifting her, her feet were off the
ground, he was strong enough to manage that, and the pulse of her
blood adhered near as could be to the pulse of his blood.

The cloth peony on her coat crushed against him, and he smelled
like home, they understood that they understood one another, and he
said, "Your father?" He could tell: Her father had gone away. She nodded, yes. The adventurer had found her, this boy who used the senses
and art to do as he liked and be where he chose, unfettered by others.

Edward stepped in and offered his hand, and she said, "This is
Edward Moore. Ward."

"Her fiancé," said Edward. "We live in Springfield."

"Ah." John's eyes went to her. "It's nice of you to attend."

"Not at all," Edward replied. "I teach at Illinois College twice a
week. Botany. I fear we missed the concert."

"My children were beauties," said John. "I led a signing choir.
Botany? Your subject, then, I see, Mary."

She felt Edward's strained patience as John described his work in a
rush and mentioned his Sound Machine and a belief that his mother
might say something into it from God, at which point Edward interjected, "I suspect the Lord doesn't talk to her more than to anyone
else."

Mary said, "No, everyone said that was true about her, Edward,"
and to John she concluded with, "It would be nice to have a picture
of what her words become." *Right away he saw Papa within her, along
with the loss of him.*

"We should write our check to support your school, John, and Mary, we should depart. It's a long way back. John, you and Mary should meet in future and catch up. Do give us your address, so we might invite you to our engagement party. It will be on the twenty-third of June."

She cried that they had only just arrived! But the man who had given so much to her, and promised still more, led her through the black-plush air of the quad. John, trailing them, called her name out in the open, and she waved, and Edward offered a good-natured salute. She watched John watching the footman offer his hands as a stirrup to hoist her by the soles of her caramel-colored shoes. Edward steadied her entry into the luxurious encasement set to transport them. Threads needle-poked their way through her every pore and were waving, frantic as an anemone's legs. How utterly new to feel the need of . . . another body, that best refuge beyond isolation. Halfway through a mud-free journey, Ward described how thoroughly uncomfortable he found the inhospitable cold of this state before proclaiming, "Men with great resources in Europe, in labs, are studying auditory science. He'll find that out in his own time."

—

PERPETUA HEARD ABOUT A MAGIC-LANTERN NIGHT AT THE MELINE Theater in Jacksonville that would feature the Portuguese Protestants of Illinois. She and Mary stopped at Ruark's for raspberry-and-cream sodas, thinking they were early. But Pet had gotten the time wrong, and they rushed late into the packed theater. In a projection of colored lights against a wall, a bird was lifting a boy out of a jail.

Mary made the error of stepping in front of the beam in the dark, and it lavished her torso with the essential tale of John's childhood, and it moved, this picture, it moved its tinted lace over the front of her.

She put her hand there, and then he cloaked her hand.

What the Conch Shell Sings When the Body Is Gone

You were always shivering.
    You and I come from a land of heat.

A person can't help but think: The old stories are true—
the earth is flat. Meadowlark, deer, hawthorn & plum,
bluestem, homestead, wild cherry, plow, quail—we
sharpened our English. We learned the names of every-
thing.

The eye gets stunned. The land has the hills carved off so
we can see forever.
    My sweetheart—
    You were my new country—

FATHER TO US ALL

QUAKING LIKE A BATHED SCHOOLBOY, SKIN STINGING AFTER A CLOSE shave from a barber who slapped him with bay rum, John knocked at the green-shuttered yellow house on Jackson and Eighth. It was mid-June, and he had turned twenty-two on March 11. Despite elation at winning a dollar during one-on-one impromptu blackjack with a bored dealer on the Wabash, he was riled with anticipation. Mary opened the portal to the most exalted home in the land, and he stepped onto a red carpet with white flowers bunched in threes. A golden chandelier blazed. "Oh, John," she offered shyly, "you're here."

Thanks be to Mrs. Lincoln for bellowing overhead while Willie and Tad bashed around, giving Mary and him something to grin about. Bashful, too, he removed his hat and responded, foolishly, "Yes, here we are." The previous Saturday had been so easy, meeting at his suggestion in this neutral spot known to be tended by Madeiran workers. Her engagement ring had diamonds with blue veins. When would it feel resoundingly that they were detouring outside their lives? Suddenly she was stitching for hire on Saturdays for this family instead of tending her business on her fiancé's property. John usually spent the weekends tinkering with the Sound Machine. Fido scampered downstairs, sniffed him, and galloped back to the battle-ground. John picked up a towel that Mary had been embellishing with log cabins in almond hues and murmured, "There's a lot of blindness in this."

Her lips parted. It was a Madeiran compliment to evoke the seam-stresses who labored until their eyesight was destroyed, a whole bodily capacity sacrificed for beauty.

"Sometimes my eyes hurt, and I see double," she said.

Before John could roar that any affliction besetting her was un-bearable, they met Abraham Lincoln for the first time as he entered his home and wondered aloud if his guests might be stars of a stage, since their looks suggested as much.

Mary introduced herself, and John stammered his name, his tall-ness compacting into average as he received Mr. Lincoln's two-handed welcoming grip and proclaimed, "We need you in Washington," a ver-bal equivalent of blundering about like a circus bear. But Mary looked pleased, and the Great Man's aspect seemed bred of rubber to allow infinite configurations of wryness as he replied, "Shame all folks don't feature it like that, John Alves. Pleasure to make your acquaintance."

He declared that knowing me is a pleasure. John said, "I'm on my way to tend your yard, Mr. Lincoln." His black trousers, and a cream shirt of a rough weave, with sleeves rolled up, signaled a readiness to work.

"Sit a spell," said Mr. Lincoln. "We toss chicken bones toward their cemetery out back, and they're in no rush for burial." Mrs. Lincoln blazed down the stairs, huffing from exertion, and insisted upon tea. Admiring Mary's towel, she asked, "Young man, have you ever seen anything so fine?"

No, ma'am. Never. He felt shoved under a bell hard-struck.

Mr. Lincoln said, "Mary, when you visit us in the nation's capital, I hope you'll honor us with more of your handiwork."

Mary affirmed how much she would love to do that, and John nearly collapsed with pride—for her, certainly, but also because she embodied the whole of Madeira's beauty.

When they entered the dining room and prepared to settle at a respectful distance from the homeowner, Abraham Lincoln insisted they come closer, and John and Mary exchanged glances. Back home it had been rare for a worker to be a guest in a British home, much less to get invited to a main table. They had been ready to sit below the salt line—below the middle where the salt and pepper shakers stood like chess pieces guarding the crucial divide. But they were being urged to move within reach of someone preordained to lead the country. John pulled out a chair for Mary on the right side of the head of the table, and he claimed the seat on the left while Mary Todd Lincoln grabbed the screaming kettle. Out of the pie safe emerged a cake that she cut into squares. John was stunned that *she* was serving *them*. The cake was vanilla with pink icing. He knew from Nikka's former job at the Capps factory that fuchsia tints for cloth or food came from cochineal insects, such a merry color from a pulverizing of bugs. If he described this, would everyone laugh? But the chance passed him by; Mr. Lincoln petitioned John "for his history." When John got tongue-tied, Mary rescued him by stating, "As a small boy, John was jailed with his mother. She was ready to die for choosing the Presbyterian faith. My Catholic father led a protest."

Mr. Lincoln asked them to air "more particulars of your origins, because they're quite something." Mary described the Botanical Garden, and John discussed the Reverend Kalley—*Mary, the man destined to be the Father of the Nation affirmed to us, two fatherless children, that our stories are* something—and he complained about Trinidad with its soupy sicknesses. God bless Illinois.

"Mud and ice included?" said Mr. Lincoln. "Very well. God bless Illinois, her muddy drawers and icy ways." His wife scolded him for being "off color." He brought up his court case defending William Dungey, of Madeiran extraction. "Called Black Bill, accused of having African blood by his brother-in-law, Joseph Spencer, after a family dispute, on account of Dungey's dark skin."

John guessed aloud that William's surname had been Domingues, broken down to Dumigues and then Dungey, and he inquired about the nature of the quarrel, cautioning himself not to overstep in his need to impress Mary with how easily he could converse above the salt with the Great Man.

"Perhaps he left his boots in a smutty condition on Spencer's porch. The closer the family, the pettier the fight," said Mr. Lincoln. Spencer defamed Dungey everywhere; if judged a man of color, Dungey stood to lose everything. He charged Spencer with slander and sought a thousand dollars. Lincoln won him a six-hundred-dollar judgment but suggested he pay four hundred dollars to persuade Spencer to remove references to race that he had caused to be written into official records. It was unpleasant that simply being a descendant of the tribe of Ham, or being described as belonging to it, required a defense or denial. "But Spencer sought to prevent him from owning property," said Mr. Lincoln, "and I must play the existing laws until a higher moral order forces the passage of better ones."

John decided to confront him mildly. "But surely, sir, the higher moral order will come sooner if you insist, as our Reverend Kalley did, on immediate equality."

"I've helped Billy Fleurville, my Haitian barber, obtain deeds to lots by signing on his behalf. Change is often created, John, the way water wears down stone."

Mary shot John a look indicating that she not only did not object to his speaking his mind to the Great Man, she admired it. Mary Todd Lincoln finished her pink-frosted cake. The boys had possibly slaughtered one another and Fido, because supreme quiet filled the house. Mr. Lincoln said, "Tell me more about being refugees."

Mary said, "Here and in New York, I've received kindness."

"Your community is also a voting bloc for Republicans," remarked Mr. Lincoln.

"With respect," said John, "our being abolitionists wasn't the only reason the Presbyterian Society sponsored us." (Would Edward Moore have the self-possession to talk politics with the man running for president?)

Mr. Lincoln did John the honor of considering this. "A fair point, but your group's presence certainly aids me."

"As Mary said, I like to think it was mostly American generosity that gave us homes and jobs." John aimed for a courteous but non-servile tone.

"People are magnanimous when there's plenty to go around," said

Mr. Lincoln. "Doesn't make the charity less real. But you do tilt the balance away from the influx of Catholics and that sorry lot of slavery-espousing Democrats flooding in from the South." His cheekbones were a pronouncement of strength, with a face marinated in thought. He said to Mary that he meant no disrespect to her Catholic faith, and she replied that she took none, and naturally she could only dream of voting.

"We're known as hard workers, if I set aside the irony that I'm supposed to be raking your yard, and instead I'm partaking of your hospitality," John added.

Mr. Lincoln laughed! So did Mrs. Lincoln! Chattering, everyone finished the tea and cake, the last ingesting of the creatures that bled fuchsia, mixed up with eggs and flour and heat. Soon the country would claim the Great Man, but for a time—and therefore for all time—John and Mary had him to themselves. John had risen from a jail cell in a tiny village on a tiny island into one of the two highest seatings next to someone poised to become the highest man in the highest country. And this soaring moment forever included Mary.

When they paused outside, her head rested against his shoulder, and he set his hand lightly at her temple. His heartbeat looped through her and emerged back toward him through the parting in her hair. The afternoon floated in equipoise, nothing perilous yet said or done. So many pieces defied assembly—Edward, greenhouse, religion, a prominent school for the deaf at a distance from her, *his salary*. She had mentioned her father's wish for her to remain in the ease she had found. Was she also puzzled, and wasn't that part of the ache, that they were reading one another this soon? She asked if he had received the invitation to her engagement party.

He vowed to do his best to attend—a direct lie after a day that, however splendid, was a postponing of truth. A shadow was attached to her heel, and to his lights it resembled a silhouette of her father, as if Augusto inhabited her to such a degree that he seeped out of her. John would pay his respects at Senhor Freitas's grave. If the timing had been different, John rather than Edward might have received a father's blessing. Instead, today was akin to the thrill of holding a hand close to a candle's flame.

At their leave-taking—he walked her to Sixth Street and gawked at even a distant glimpse of the magnitude of what would be hers—their looks conveyed full knowledge that they were going to lower their palms onto fire.

GALA

JUNE 1860

MARY'S FIRST SHOCK WAS THE PUNCTUALITY OF THE GUESTS. WHEN she arrived for her own party, a crowd was already swarming under the wedding-cake ceiling in Edward's great room, people forming eddies with innate skill at knowing how to break free and join a new eddy. Invitations put the start at eight . . . and they all must have arrived at eight! (Once, in Funchal, Alberto and Edite had appeared under a sugar-glazed midnight moon for a nine o'clock supper.) The women seemed stuck inside encrusted balloons, though perhaps only Mary felt like that, in a frock the shade of well-watered grass, with beads forming lilies, a gift (another one) from Edward. Perpetua had pulled the stays to reduce Mary's waist from tiny to unnatural. Despite Mary's pleas, Pet refused to attend, because Edward had neglected to invite her. In a dark suit and waistcoat, he was chatting with a gentleman and signaled that he—*her almost-husband*—would join her when he could politely tear himself free. She had consented to marry this man who wanted her to travel a short, final distance from where she slept and settle into his house. Her house? In April, she had turned twenty. Papa had picked the day of receiving her as her birthday, the twenty-second, a number like two swans swimming.

John would arrive shortly . . . *what on earth was she thinking?*

Guests were studying the instruction card Ward had propped near the miracle berries and wedges of citrus on the buffet table, which also offered Roman punch, ham and turkey, hothouse tomatoes, a cucumber salad, and persimmon cake. Servants replenished platters and carried drinks. She recognized Philo Beers from the newspaper—a legislator and farmer even before Sangamon County was born—and after he tried a berry and sampled a lemon, his ancient face was incentive for others to follow suit. Ward insisted that tonight was not merely about their wedded future but about a crop that needed to be widely discussed among "local citizens of means." She did not deserve such generosity. Barely an hour before, she had nursed a vision of leaning out a train's window with John, the country racing past, her hair torn like a flag in the wind, and she being amused by his comments, though she had not felt clever enough to invent what those were. As big as Edward's resources were, John seemed bodily connected to the airy world—thanks to him, she had met the man who would surely be the *president.* They had been invited to *Washington*!

Breaking her trance was a woman with a beauty mark who whispered, "Well done, child. Fast work of it, to go from nothing to this."

"I didn't come from nothing, ma'am."

"You're not from here, and now you'll be the lady of the house. That's all I'm observing. Your complexion is full of—how to describe it? It's full of sunshine." Beauty marks were deliberate blots, Papa once explained, to suggest that someone is so dazzling that she requires a flaw.

On the rug were knights in poses of hunting. The brisk neighbor whom Mary recognized as Nell Clark appeared and sang out, "Salutations, Dottie. Did you introduce yourself to Mary Freitas? Mary, this is Dorothea Willis. Her husband trades in coal. I don't see George anywhere, Dottie." The cameo at Nell's throat featured a goddess-like profile on a coral background. "Perhaps he's off penning his memoirs." Nell would later confide that Dottie's husband was a skirt-chaser, and mentioning his absence often took Dottie down a notch.

"No, we leave any writing to you, Nell."

Summoning gaiety, Dottie professed to Mary, "Nell wrote a poem for the *Sangamon Journal* when the lot of you showed up. How did it go? '. . . those exiles brave beyond all fears, rescued from their vale of tears.'"

"My father and I weren't in the original group of refugees."

"I stand corrected."

Nell squeezed Mary's hand and said, "Dottie is jealous of my passion for the arts. I laud those who reinvent themselves, and Mary, you selected a land that allows it."

"Our host is the epitome of reinvention," said Dottie, gesturing at Edward as he got waylaid by another band of well-wishers. "Mary, what secrets lurk about his family in San Francisco? I've asked Maud to disclose them, and it is unlike her to be tight-lipped. I assume you've met Maud Dieterman."

"I don't know anyone by that name, ma'am." Mary would never betray Ward and his troubled past to this duchess of the prairie.

"So much larking about in the world, such fortune-seeking, this country is losing its character. People should stay where they are born."

"Then you should be in Chicago," said Nell. "You're implying Ward should have remained in California, denying us this genial celebration."

"I mean people should dwell in their native countries, as I suspect you know I meant, Nell." To Mary, she said, "Meaning no offense, dear."

"Of course you mean to give offense," said Mary. She relished studying the immobile features of Dorothea Willis. Mary was not unaware of the tiny wars happening constantly, everywhere, the reason she did not seek out humans or company at large. How odd, to realize Ward—or his money—could draw this amalgam of strangers who had been all this time in close range.

"Bitty sprite with large nerve," muttered Dottie, showcasing her dexterity in pivoting toward another group.

Nell said, "Mary Freitas, you've learned a thing or two. I heard that you set up a table near Julian Barr's store. True?"

"It is, Mrs. Clark." Mary grinned to recall the downtown slathered with a mocha froth of mud, the passersby sampling her offerings and exclaiming over stale bread turned into candy. "He insisted I couldn't sell merchandise without a license, and I told him I was giving out the berries for free."

"While instructing people to beseech him to carry them in his shop."

"Yes."

They laughed. Nell said, "I'll pay Mr. Barr a call. See that gentleman talking to your intended? That's William Farnsworth, and he'll be easily persuaded to buy a supply for the front desk of his hotel. Julian is a rhinoceros, and it'll serve him right if he's the last in town to turn a profit with you."

"You're very kind to help me, Mrs. Clark."

"I wasn't welcomed with open arms when I came here and married Oliver, I assure you." He had been twenty years her senior, and after ten years of marriage and no children, she was nesting comfortably with the inheritance of his rail stocks, thank you very much. "There are plenty of good souls, dear. You just need to identify them. For instance." She pointed toward Sullivan Conant, who manufactured resplendent chairs, chatting raptly with his wife, Lydia. Mary thought: How sad that precious few couples seemed so connected, and even more startling to realize that *Edward and I don't look at each other like that, but John and I do.*

Where was he? It was close to half past nine. Artificial light dripped down, felt wet. How is it that light can liquefy?

"Who is that person who keeps looking at me, Mrs. Clark?" A large-boned woman with upswept brown hair had been flitting about like an instructor in a school for pickpockets, eyeing Mary from various vantage points.

"Speak of the devil, that is Maud. Maud Dieterman."

"Ward has never mentioned her, Mrs. Clark."

"Please call me Nell. I doubt he invited her, but lack of an invitation never stops her from popping up where she fancies. She swooped in when he first came to town, but she now entertains the affections, and I use the word loosely, of a fabulously wealthy ne'er-do-well named Billy Mars. Like Dottie's husband, Billy is doubtless at a tavern, with a barmaid on his lap. I was lucky with my Oliver, as you are lucky with Ward."

A flush mottled Mary's neck. "I don't understand."

"About Maud? Ward is no pushover, but he is mild-tempered. She is imperious. They were engaged for such a short time it doesn't count. She is no threat to you, but I'm surprised you haven't seen her around here before."

"People come and go, and I work, and I don't notice them."

"Calm yourself, darling. This is your engagement party, remember? You don't seem entirely aware of that. You have a gentleman devoted to you, and it is not his style to toss anyone out on her cushioned rear."

Mary tamped down a distaste for how Edward was courting these people, coming out of his shell to win their favor, making her ache to race back to Pet in the cottage, to stitch her masterwork tablecloth until it was room-sized.

"Do not permit her to get under your skin. That's her sport. You won, Mary. I mention her because being savvy about games means identifying the players. Most of us commit romantic errors, and she is his."

"He should have told me." She had some nerve being upset, being in an anguish about John, pretending to be innocent.

Nell patted her hand and said, "Likely he deems her of so little note that she is beneath his utterance. Your gallant intended has been corralled by another parcel of folks. Go mingle with your guests at the buffet. Go on." She shooed her.

A huddle near the miracle berries included Ellie Whistler, an author of ghost stories and a columnist for *The Ladies' Wreath* magazine, who extended best wishes to Mary, as did Sadie Pilcher, a schoolteacher (John's noble calling), both uninterested in the usual single woman's practice of scanning a party for available men. Sadie exclaimed, "Miss Freitas, I'll use these as rewards for my students."

Mary agreed that would be sublime. The income from her fledgling project was approaching break-even, but even if she garnered an exhilarating profit, such money would be a drop in the bucket compared to what this crowd possessed. She regretted judging Ward's wish for their approval. She wanted it, too, didn't she, along with security, and he was bestowing that to a remarkable degree while supporting her strange crop sheerly out of his considerable goodness.

An older man ate a berry, tasted a lemon, and noting Mary in her lily-adorned dress, he shouted, "Good heavens, such magic, young lady!"

Mary beamed, but deflation set in as Maud grabbed Edward's arm, pulling him close. Mary gaped toward the door . . . but why should John put himself through what she was struggling to endure? Edward slipped from Maud's grasp and headed toward Mary, and studying her oversized hooped skirt, he whispered, "You seem to be hiding a flock of chickens. I wish we could sneak away. You look stunning."

Inflamed with self-consciousness at his comments about what might be below her skirt, she asked, "Why did you invite Maud? Nell told me about her. Since you've never bothered."

"Those are the first words you wish to share with me? Tonight. On your night and mine. I did not invite her, but she knows the entire town, and having chatted with me briefly, as I saw you noting, she is turning her attentions upon her next victim, because her own *affianced*"—he delivered the word with a deliberately humorous flourish, but she did not crack a smile—"is a dissipated boy who does as he pleases, which gives her license to do as she pleases, an ideal match. Instead of being upset, you should be pitying me. I barely escaped with my life, Mary."

"She has neither greeted nor congratulated me."

"Because you've only stared daggers at her. The evening is hardly over—more's the pity, since I feel about these events as you do—and I'm guessing others have yet to vocalize how momentous it is that you will be living here, with me. I greatly wish for that. Do you?"

"She came to ruin my evening."

"Only if you care more about her than me. She could help with your business if you were of a more expansive mind. I should have mentioned her before. You're right. But honestly, Mary, what's going on?"

They were conversing in a hiss, with glances darting their way.

As if addressing a tribunal floating above, Ward said, "We invited your friend John, and I didn't want to bring this up, but I've heard you and he have met more than once at the Lincoln household, and you did not see fit to tell me any details beyond your mysterious wish to perform menial labor for Mary Todd on Saturdays. Several people tonight, and in the past week or two, have enjoyed filling me in."

This was not false. She said, wanly, "He is not here. John."

"I find that worse than if he were. You are agitating about ludicrous Maud Dieterman because you are upset that he is not present."

When she said that made no sense—though it did, and the strength of his clarity caused a flare of genuine love for Ward to engulf her—he inhaled in his bellows-long way and said, "Don't insult my intelligence, or yours. Attending would torment him."

She took his elbow, a doleful bonding, as someone hollered, "A toast to the bride and groom!" Guests lifted glistening glasses. Everyone and everything swam before her, edges dissolving. Philo led the tributes by stating, "Mary, your warmth in this cold yet hospitable land increases our own. May married life to this upstanding man be in lockstep with your miraculous product's fortunes."

Courtly hotelier William Farnsworth chimed in with, "Mary Freitas and Professor Edward Moore—I hear praise of your lectures at Illinois College—how radiantly you increase the luster of our city, and together you shall be unstoppable."

Nell Clark intoned, "Kudos to Mary, a valorous exile. There is plentiful talk that Jacksonville is the Athens of the West, the mother lode of art and music, of institutions for those in need. Mary proves a combination of expressiveness and business can dwell in our very own Springfield. In abetting her exploits, Edward confirms that he is an unusually supportive, worthy man. May your marriage grow in commerce, and in love."

It was the first time someone had used that word about them. Mary and Edward had yet to use it themselves.

Maud, near Dottie at a fringe of the assembly, hoisted her glass and yelled, "To the happy couple! Give her a kiss, Wardie!"

Ignoring the raucous urging that he comply, he stretched an arm around Mary, pressed her side to his, and raised his glass to say, "I've encouraged the horticultural talents of Mary Catherine Freitas, who carries on the work begun by her late father Augusto." He pivoted to observe her with a steadiness that would be wicked not to return in kind. "I cannot believe, Mary, that you consent to be my wife." He gently asked if she cared to offer a few words. Feeling like an understudy in a play that was in fact about her life, she managed only, "Thank you to everybody," prompting companionable laughter. He whispered, "Everything will be all right, Mary."

Life unfurled from its bolt, long, long life.

Musicians in their string ties tuned up. Queasiness overtook her; dancing with Edward would entail being able to peer up his nostrils, a prelude to the raw truths of marriage, and she ducked through the churning of guests, their hilarity and dishing up of food, to seek the stabilizing calm of her sewing room.

She was arrested outside the realm considered hers, destined to be fully hers, because voices were inhabiting the space. A shriek shot out as someone pressed the Singer's pedal and her machine leapt alive. It was easy to break the needle or jam the bobbin. Her spine adhered to the wallpaper—white with gold stripes—while the floor vibrated from the music and deft maneuvering below. Low chattering in the sewing room ceded to someone—Dottie Willis?—raising the volume to proclaim, "Who knows why? They're wanderers temporarily come to rest. Against each other." This produced tittering.

"She pretends she didn't seduce a man to save her from poverty." Mary could swear this was Maud.

"Catholic girls are bred to twist men around their fingers." Who was proclaiming such a thing? What had Mary done to any of them?

"Men are such predictable animals." During their giggling, an actual physical rending ripped Mary's body. This voice belonged to Maisie Mauzy, a shopkeeper who often confided in her and whom Mary thought was a friend.

She descended the stairs. (Where was the girl who had confronted David Hamm and Susan Ashe in Madeira?) Attendees gasped in delight with their stomp-dancing, and she coursed through packs of revelers. Papa used to caution that if we could invisibly eavesdrop, we would be scalded to find that most friendship is a lie, but that was why true friends must be cherished. The Bible issued a warning about those *who whet their tongues like a sword, whose words are arrows . . . O homem que diz um falso testemunho contra o seu próximo é um dardo, é uma espada penetrante.* In the foyer, countable steps from escape, she heard, "Are you ill?" Edward reached out as if to detain her from where he stood but then dropped his arm.

A whooping erupted as the band burst into a polka. Were the boots damaging his floor? She didn't know. She didn't know anything. Edward's hair was longer but thinning. He approached, emanating a male scent of tobacco, though he did not smoke.

She confessed, "I was going to rest a minute in the sewing room, but women in there were saying awful things about me."

"I'm not surprised that others are jealous." His fingers elevated her chin. "Consider the episode practice in ignoring a common, detestable impulse that will continue hounding you. Dare I suggest they might envy that you are with me?"

She looked at him—profoundly—for the first time that night, the first time ever, and funneled all her effort into not bursting into tears.

"Mary. We wish people were purely one thing, but they aren't, and you think love is pure as well, but marriage is many things. I trust we'll do well together. I hope so."

"I'm sorry we quarreled."

"Pay that no heed. You look lovely. You break my heart."

"I don't want to break your heart. I'm very fond of you."

"I know. If you're unwell, I'll give your regrets to our company."

But she said no, she must not act like a scared child. She brought out petit fours from the kitchen and endured a waltz with a drunken man. Maud exited early, taking Dottie Willis with her. Midnight chimed as Mary conjured her father, like a steam-creature who then evaporated. Dancing with Ward revealed his unexpected talent for deploying arcs that bade others to back away. She talked with Sadie about her students and discussed ghost stories with Ellie; she tolerated an obscene comment from a spindly woman about Edward's tallness compared to Mary's smallness requiring creativity on their wedding night, and she shared persimmon cake with Maisie, who gave no sign of having uttered vicious things and who was among the last to collect her coat and wander out, after which Mary said to Edward, "Forgive me."

"I shall, if you also forgive me." His lips were papery as they brushed her forehead, and he did not linger to watch her return to the cottage.

In her nightdress, Perpetua was gnawing a rusk and offered one to Mary. She had stolen the box from Ward's pantry as revenge for his failure to invite her. She helped Mary de-encase from the dress, and when it was hanging on their laundry-line cord, Pet said, "It looks like we robbed an infanta of her clothes," which entertained them both. She asked about the party, and Mary replied, "It was very nice."

"Mmm . . . exciting. Sorry I missed it."

"Pet. It was good."

"I'm sure it was." As they climbed onto their cots, Pet said, gentle as rain showers, "When you talk about John, he's a part of you without my needing to ask if it's love, and Edward makes you say things like, 'It was good,' but what do I know, because his 'good' looks wonderful. Comfort is nice. I'm happy you're moving into the house, as long as you don't boss me around." She extended her hand across the divide, and Mary took it, as she had when Papa offered solace upon sensing her terror of the dark.

"But I already boss you around. You work for me in the greenhouse, Pet." A spill of moonlight fluttered like a manta ray on their floor.

"Oh. Right." They laughed their way into tears.

"You're my true love, Perpetua Maria Deolinda Rodrigues."

"And I love you, Maria Catarina Pereira Vaz Gato de Freitas."

"Let's grow into two old women right here," Mary said.

In the days to come, she would receive a terse note from Julian Barr, agreeing to carry her sachets; Nell Clark had ordered him to do so. That was how the world worked. Mary's brave stunt setting up a table as a hawker nearby? Not crucially persuasive. This seemed allied to Edward's grasp of how to navigate a monied circle in the Midwest, and by working with him, and certainly by marrying him, Mary was on the brink of an entry into something not entirely clear, a conflation of territory and acceptance.

And yet on the night of her party, as a new summer began, she could not sleep. Specks of light coalesced into creatures, the way stars dot out archers and bulls. There was a man whom Mary needed to love, and a lovely man she needed, though he was a decade older and engaged twice before, once to Rose from a religion deemed forbidden, once to Maud—an error likely born of grieving the loss of Rose. What else did Mary not know?

She flattened herself against the window to wear the white-hot moon in place of her head, and she reached up, pretending to hold the span of this immensity.

Stepping backward, she observed the ( ) marked into the condensation.

Your body drew John's open arms.

Press yourself into the space between them.

He is as far away as the moon, but he pours over me, he paints my skin, he forms himself out of the light in the sky, to come to me tonight, as he swore he would do.

THE LOVE SONG OF AN OCTOPUS
IN A MOVABLE SEA

0:13

The octopus clung to the artificial kelp in the closet-sized tank. John bobbed inside it, holding his breath as in childhood when hunting with Rui for an animal that required pounding to tenderize it into a salty cloud. *Exhale slowly, boil the water.* Mary was blurry through the glass. She had delivered miracle sachets to Ray Silva's store, had sent John a note that she would be in town, exquisite timing: The impresario of this traveling show was stopping at transcontinental venues to lecture about aquatic kingdoms.

0:33

Pearl divers hold their breaths for inhuman lengths while plunging to oyster beds, 6:15, 8:50 minutes. The head of the octopus was in the very shape of an ache, sagging worse than John's preposterous bathing costume loaned by the showman.

0:57

With his lungs in spasms, his hands spelled out: *I won't harm you.* His summer-session children signed in a frenzy: *Mr. Alves is talking to the octopus! Hearing people can't speak underwater, but he's showing us that we can!*

1:15

Mary grew agitated. The octopus reached toward him. *This isn't your real home, but you're going there, whistle-stop by whistle-stop, until you're released in the Pacific.*

1:37

How long can he hold his breath he's over a minute and a half the clock ticks the children watch it and Mary's hand is over her mouth, I'm going to burst. We're in the Jacksonville Female Academy also known as the Jail For Angels first of its kind in Illinois, Mary, I believe as the Reverend Kalley did in women being educated as for instance the impresario said before I climbed the ladder that it was a *seamstress* who devised a means of studying marine life in aerated tanks, I volunteered to hold my breath because men do bull-dumb things so a woman will think they are brave, the octopus's body was first green now blue-white, coloring its flesh merely by wishing for it.

2:12

Mary, this octopus's arms encircle my chest, head pulp-soft on my neck. What terrifies me: Pearl divers can walk around *for years* after quitting their work, and suddenly their lungs catch fire, their eyeballs combust, and they die.

2:22

My children gesture with animation at the timer, and Mary You rise from Your chair. With a puff of ink, the octopus tightens like a gelatin jacket bunched on top of me, *can't stay, sorry, goodbye!*

He kicked streamlined to the top of the tank and gulped drafts of air as the octopus tumbled downward. His deaf children clamored, stomping loudly. Mary was smiling at him and at the children smiling at him. He disentangled the octopus now clinging to his shins, they are escape artists, they can cram a whole marshmallow body into a flask of ginger beer by drinking it instantly.

The octopus will get transported in an aquarium in a wagon, along with the drained tank. Neither distance nor storm shall hinder this showman who entices landlocked citizens to swim with a creature born for solitude.

Teacher held his breath two and a half minutes, forever!

Mary said, "How did you learn that?"

In jail his mother told him, "If you can last one second, you can last another." He admitted he used to dive for octopuses and eat them. "But this one forgave me."

She likes humor; she glows, Mary does. She asks, "Since you live nearby, may I meet your mother? We can talk about my father."

He has not mentioned her to Serafina. Should he present her as a Madeiran friend or ally? His dread of Mary's sizing up the cabin, and of risking his mother's disdain for Catholics, added to the likely sharp inquiries as to why an engaged woman exudes unbridled affection in her son's company, causes him to whisper, "Someday." Like a dividing wall between them, too, is a silence about her party and his missing it.

Children dancing and leaping surround them. The impresario has a conch shell, and though you would imagine its music would be lost on deaf children, he puts it to their ears. *Just feel it,* he signs. They pass the shell around, its smooth peony lip darkening toward the twist of its insides.

He holds it to Mary's ear: Listen, love.

This is what a conch shell sings when the body is gone.

—

A WHIP-POOR-WILL DELIVERED A GRACE NOTE OUTSIDE EDWARD Moore's home during a day—John had checked—of his lecturing at Illinois College. Persuading Frank to ply his lock-picking skills had taken some doing, but curiosity had gotten the better of him as well, at least until they were at Edward's door. Frank said, "We're spying because you think love should make you suffer. She is betrothed, Alves."

After an interlude of ignoring that, John insisted that peeking inside would allow them to check out where one of their own would live. Frank replied dryly, "It looks acceptable." It was traditional to await an *invitation* before entering a house. Though this recalled their John Jacob Astor debacle, Frank, sighing, inserted a wire into the lock and inclined his ear. John was not clear on the mechanisms in play; metal prongs of various lengths got manipulated to match what a key would do. But how, by listening and feel, was that alignment discovered? "Hurry! Hurry up," he said.

Frank trained camera-lens-large eyes on him. "Locks are individuals. Some open fast, others never do. Unlike you, this one's the devil to hear."

"All right, all right."

Frank said, "I am again breaking the law because of you, Alves. Elizabeth will box my ears and then yours. Aha!" A click, and the door opened to an enshrinement of repose. John could hardly blame Mary for appreciating such bounty, though it did not resemble her taste. A room with a chandelier was by itself bigger times three than the Alves cabin. The grounds were gigantic, and the home was grand but plain and male, with no-nonsense furniture and a kitchen with paneling so muted it looked as if it had once housed the sun. The bed in the main bedroom was made crisply, as if only a sheet of paper had slept in it. Or two sheets side by side. Edward's study arrested him: Mary would love those glass flowers, causing terror to stipple his backbone. Riddling him with remorse for violating Edward's privacy, even more than the raven jabbing its beak toward him, were the golden cages securing volumes behind glass, with keys in the locks. Instead of seeming regal, the bookcases looked like gilded prisons.

"What in God's name is going on?" The voice was dulcet but sharp.

John spun around to observe Mary clutching an armful of striped cloth. Frank offered a pathetic wave from near the desk. She asked—vexed, bemused?—"How did you get in? Por amor de Deus."

"I let myself in—this is Frank Meline, whose family runs the theater you've visited—because I knew Edward wouldn't be here, and I hoped to see you. It's been so long since—" He had been in an agony of suspense after the outing with the octopus, because she had not shown up the subsequent Saturday at the Lincoln household.

"I sew here when he's in your town, teaching. Shouldn't you be doing the same?"

Another reasonable scenario, that her entry would hardly be forbidden. He choked out that he had the day off. Suddenly he could not bear to view the greenhouse that would keep her here, nor her cottage-quarters saturated with the floral scent she natively possessed. "I needed to see you, Mary," he said.

With Frank attempting to recede into the woodwork, John stepped out of a study where he had no right to be, and she followed. He held on to her arms, with only pristine striped linen between them, and said, "Since I was born, my mother's independent nature was preparing me to find you. To find you as you are. To love you, I mean. I love you, Maria Catarina. You deserve fortune and a house like this. But I'd like to stay in your life somehow. I'll do anything, anything you ask, including going away, and I'll tell myself I'm alive and you're alive somewhere, we're in the same world together."

"I don't know what to do," she said. "Your name is written on my heart." She appended something he was sure, even then, that he would carry to the end of his days. She set down her cloth. Her right hand grasped John's left, and his left held her right, and their gaze created an arch. She said, "It's already a sacrament, how I long for you."

SPECTACLES

AFTER EDWARD'S CURT NOD, MARY DROPPED INTO A CHAIR NEAR THE case with the glass flowers. Papers were heaped on his desk, and he did not stir as she took off her engagement ring, set it in front of him, and said, "I'm sorry I can't accept this, Edward."

His words emerged in a splat. "Why not? I know the answer, but am I supposed to make this easy on you, Mary?"

"No. I regret ending our engagement." And violating her father's wishes for her.

"You might have thought of your *regret* before a party announcing our future to everyone. You think this is a huge surprise. Say his name."

"John."

"How gracious am I expected to be? Sell the ring. I can't use it." He gestured in a fury at the disarray on his desktop. "Do you ever wonder anything about me? Why, given my ease of circumstance, do I teach? An ill-paying, thankless job suitable for those who won't ever rise far."

Meant as a slap at John, but she would endure it. She could not recall another occasion when she had deliberately hurt someone.

His blue eyes were clouded. "Illinois College keeps me active. Else I would crumble. I require bright young students pronouncing brilliant things. I do not need work for hire."

But I do. They were Catholic, and Catholics must be punished for wrongdoing.

"Are you even slightly aware of the mockery I've endured about you, and what awaits me now? The world will dash your romantic notions soon enough. I refuse to fight with some other man for you. I won't."

"Edward, I like working with you, I care about you, love you."

"Have you considered finding another job?"

She gathered her strength not to cry. "You said no matter what happened, you would be a guardian with our business, fair about it."

"I meant that if you left, I'd be the same honest person I've always been, but staying on my property means rubbing my nose in your being with someone else. I suspected this was coming, but you consider me without intuition or emotion."

"I don't." Except that she did, a little.

"You've complicated our lives, Mary. I worried that I was too old for you, but I'm not dashing enough. Or something. Stay in the cottage. For now. But leave me in peace."

———

SPECTACLES ARE LUCKY-CHARM MIRRORS THAT PEOPLE PUT OVER their eyes. Everything then becomes clear and shiny, as if coated with glycerin.

They were in the Springfield office of Dr. Benedict Gladwell, and John had paid him seven dollars. On her face, she would wear hours of his teaching. She struggled to recite minuscule letters on a wall chart. "'A,'" she said timidly, *wrong, all wrong*, squinting. "Is that a 'T'?" She sensed John thinking the answers loudly to help her. The doctor exhaled a whiff of oil of clove that she prayed was not to mask drunkenness as he set two glass circles into the slots of two large disks attached to a movable metal arm.

The black letters became as lucid as cross-hatched stitches! She announced, "That's an 'X,' and 'Y, K, E.'"

John reacted as if she had solved an enigma of the galaxy, but Dr. Gladwell seemed less amazed—she almost laughed at his

moroseness—as he swung the metal mask away and leaned in with
an instrument that positioned a dot of light so close to her eye that
the veined jelly, the cushion for her optic nerves and irises, got emblazoned throughout the room as a wallpapering of forked lines. As
the doctor examined the other eye, projecting the black and white-
yellowish in that as well, John got up to touch her splayed branches,
her pathways spilled over. Perhaps whatever roads he walked would
turn into the interior of her eyes.

The doctor assembled her glasses, using nearly invisible screws in
gold-wire frames.

And there John was, etched and crystalline, with what muscularity
and presence, her heart so replete it expanded and broke her skin so a
red flood swept them onward, and John's dark eyes were chanting, *Only
You*—such abundance, her arteries were vibrating into a SONG but
the song was too fast for her to catch. They stepped into an outdoors
burnished and new, and his flesh and hers might as well be humming the hymn "Awake, My Soul, Stretch Every Nerve" or delivering
a psalm: *Your eyes are doves. Our couch is verdant.* The city is a flying
carpet of glossy threads, I've never seen such brightness! Come night,
the Gas, Light, and Coke Company's streetlights will glint.

Clamor rang from the foundries, and John and she were haloed
with the smells of industrial inks, dry-cleaning fluids, and the famous
cream crackers at Billington's stand. How could hunger be satisfied
and thirst be slaked because her eyesight was sharper, how could
the *scent* of wood shavings drop before her like an opaque screen?
Look, she cried—*that dog wagging its tail has so many spots!* Some
towns are cradles; others are cauldrons. Funchal was chasms and
gem-teeming sea, and Springfield was speed and *possibility*—and
sludge and mares. Madeira had thinness—in its clothing, petals—
but Illinois was *thickness*.

They reveled in the grotesquerie of a shop's display of teeth, sets of
dentures hanging on threads. Who can contain a yearning like mine,
let today prick my veins, let my wellsprings gush. Break me into wet
pieces, liquefy my organs and nails, turn me into a body of water. Everything about John pointed to . . . desire. *With this body I thee wed.* No
girls—not even Perpetua—owned up to such pangs; they whispered

about what must be endured to have a family. She held him with all she was worth. These feelings seemed intrinsically bound to her impulse to create *so many many things*. But then stillness came so as not to mar infinitude. Bless this hour; bless the tremulous communion of everyone everywhere. They fell into a kiss, mouths sealed. Then they kissed more deeply, in front of God and man, and after gathering breath, they kissed hard again.

———

TIME-DISTANCE-MONEY-RELIGION-WORK SURGED INTO FOCUS. THE Lincoln household was their meeting zone, visits blending with the tasks of fellow workers, and having only Saturdays available imparted a rhythm that swept them through August, into September. John played games of agility with the Great Man, slapping a rubber ball against the outside of the house. Mary once fixed Mary Todd's coronet braid as she spoke of a dead love Abraham Lincoln had had, someone named Ann, whose ghost wafted through the halls.

Mary and Edward did their utmost to avoid one another as the success of their enterprise increased. A woman whom she did not recognize began to come and go, to and fro, into and out of the house that might have been Mary's. This shook her, the loss of a self-made man at a pinnacle of the basic American dream made sumptuous ... but it was his, they had not forged it together. This got muted with unfair upset that he could so swiftly replace her.

The dehydrator (purchased by Edward) revealed that desiccated *Synsepalum dulcificum* kept its power much longer after plucking. Eager to share this with him, she pushed past his ajar front door. A female voice caromed within, and Mary pressed ahead despite an instinct not to, expecting to meet the unknown woman who had been steadily visiting. Instead, she pulled up short outside the sitting room at the sight of Edward with Maud and her bright red mouth, as if her diet featured raw animal or human leg. Maud was manhandling the parrot nutcracker sent to Mary from the Jamison family. She had loaned it to Edward and forgotten to retrieve it.

Whitening, Edward said, "Mary, I didn't hear you knock. I mean, yes, you don't have to knock, no." His stuffed chair was burgundy, so he looked padded by jellied wine.

"The door wasn't shut, and I have news. It can wait."

"You've never officially met Maud Dieterman. Maud, this is—"

"Your weed-puller. Garden*ess*." Maud stuck a walnut into the parrot's beak and crunched it. After devouring the meat, she announced, "She's as petite as a ballerina, Wardie. No wonder she eluded your grasp. Mary, we have that in common."

He said, "Mary, sit," though she stayed immobile.

"Care for one?" Maud stuffed another walnut into the parrot and slammed it shut, and the nutcracker snapped in two.

"That was a gift!" Mary cried as Maud shrugged and put the pieces of the bird on the coffee table, and Edward said, "A shame. I'll replace it."

"No, I'll buy one," said Maud. "That could have happened to anyone. Let's have tea." She gripped the armrests to marshal breasts and buttocks from her chair.

Mary near-shouted, "I'll do it." Despite having no right—none—to think this, it was ghastly to contemplate Maud spreading her spoors in the kitchen, but as Mary set down a rattling tray near the ruined parrot, she did not appear in command so much as subservient. Out of Maud's mouth came, "Are you still living in his adorable cottage?"

"I work here. Edward is kind about that."

"Kind of pathetic. You still collect a salary from the cavalier."

"Maud, enough!" he barked.

He was letting this woman strike out so he could remain dignified, could point to being so. Maud did not seem like anyone Edward would find remotely appealing, much less worthy of even an impulsive, brief engagement. What was her hold over him?

"Tra la, I'm only playing. Right, Mary?" Maud Dieterman toted an excellent wink in her kit bag of qualities. "Cat has got her tongue. Hint taken! I'll be on my way."

Mary endured the farewells and the gushing of don't-be-shy-let's-be-friends and Ward-is-so-cordial-with-*all*-his-ex-loves. When Edward returned from escorting Maud out, he said, "Her teasing is harmless."

While she stifled an impulse to overturn the tea tray, her words blasted like steam through a volcano's fissures. "It's not harmless. You allowed her to mock me."

"Nonsense. I spoke up."

"You said her name, and the word 'enough.'"

"Exactly. Now explain why you're here."

Nell had counseled Mary to grant him his unromantic, socially valuable alliance with Maud. But she couldn't bear it. Snatching up the broken nutcracker, she burst into tears.

"That seems an extreme reaction. I'll find you a new one."

"This was from my friends in New York! You can't replace that!"

"Again I say, she can be tedious, but she has sway regarding whether newcomers are accepted. Her father works in rail shipping and could help you. Us."

"Never." Mary set down the halves of the parrot and headed for the door.

"I am free to invite whatever guests I please into my home. You—" Seizing her arm, he directed her into a chair with a strength that alarmed her. "You have voiced a dedication to John, but you forbid me similar freedom."

She said, "I want to keep our work, Edward. If this is difficult, I'll— I don't know." She had not thought about where to go, what to do . . . she had built so much here. Any other man suffering a broken engagement would kick her out and cut her off.

They regarded each other. "I've helped significantly with an endeavor you commenced in my space," he said. "No boss would let a worker, especially not a woman, get away with that. I permit it despite what you have done to me. I've debated buying you out and asking you to leave. But banishing you feels cruel."

She was tempted to ask the identity of the new female caller, because Mary *was* jealous of her; forget about Maud. Instead, she replied, "You were right, dried berries have longer-lasting potency. We can ship farther."

"I'm conducting lab experiments at the college to improve our current breed."

"You should have asked me if you could do that."

"I'm telling you now. I look forward to shipping cuttings to Florida, where the climate is ideal for this plant and for me. But it seems prudent to wait out the war."

"The war won't last long." John had assured her of this, that whatever call to duty interrupted their lives, it would not take more than a few months. She could not begin to address what it would mean if Edward moved far away.

"I've been to Florida, which counts as the South, and the people there are fanatics. An army of the republic will battle them for years. I don't say this to wound you, Mary."

This dropped John in a soldier's uniform into their presence, and she perceived something else. Not in one hundred years would Edward feel he had to risk his life for a nation that gave him shelter.

Did he detect her alertness to this? He created divergence by remarking, "I'm loath to give up on a promising, unique crop, but I dislike how you take me for granted."

"Ward, I don't."

"You do, but let's not quarrel. You barged in, so I assume you can find the exit." He paused in his departure to turn to her and say, "I trust John is well."

She said yes, he was.

"I apologize for speaking brusquely."

She concurred that theirs was a strange situation, and it was all her doing.

Regarding her with colossal forlornness, he said, "I know about lemon verbena, but you taught me to use it in tea. Everyone ridicules me for keeping you around, but no one makes daily life as beautiful as you."

EVERYTHING THAT HATH BREATH

MARY POUNDED OVER THE GANGPLANK AS THE RIVERBOAT PUSHED off from its Naples dock. Men on the train had deluged her with teasing, since a woman alone is comical, and the effort of concealing fright made her a wreck, and then had come the bump-bump-along of twenty-five miles more on a carriage to the Illinois River, which was blasting up stalagmites of water-wind.

Music issued from the riverboat. She passed sightless children and women whose minds were not right. Deaf boys were signing. Squadrons of bugs found entry, and underneath came the lilt of water. The main floor revealed an orchestra. People in wheelchairs held the hands of escorts twirling them in rhythm with the notes. Jacksonville embraced the broken and the beautiful; this excursion was for them . . . and then John was staring at her, his expression tenderness harnessed to alertness.

He felt like home to her. Going toward him was a going home.

People drifted; he was appearing, then getting blocked. Then re-appearing. He walked steadily, and she drew toward him. The boat's rocking sang of the undulating mosaic sidewalks of their childhoods. Students signed at him, and he signed back. She guessed the meaning:

Precious day. A wheelchair stopped him. Another step. A blind child led by a grandfather passed in front of Mary. In prolonging the dance of getting to John, these strangers were a gift.

He took off the light coat he had worn for a day on the river, an evening verging toward October, and put it on her because of her shivering. She understood then what it means to deem an hour *stolen,* wrested from the usual barreling into plans, all her plans, so much new-world existence was about galloping toward further success instead of registering how wondrous it is when neither solid footing nor ground exist. The floor vibrated with the circling wheelchairs. He rested a hand at the back of her neck, where her downy hairs sprang up like feelers, and asked, "May I have this dance, Miss Freitas?"

"You may, Mr. Alves."

A ballad swelled. His hand adhered to the small of her back as they moved through the hosts of wheelchairs. She touched his arms, the years made into muscles from his building strength for so many things. Every part of you is alive, every part of me is alive. She sensed that he felt her feeling this, and he was feeling this, too, she knew he knew she knew.

Sunset flattened itself onto the river: red sky onto blue water. Bach and Mozart spilled from the instruments. The faces of those being wheeled stayed lifted toward the partners guiding them, everyone content to veer quietly. John and Mary played that game of whispering: Would you love me if I couldn't walk? Would you kiss me if my hair fell out? Would you still want me?

Would you love me if I stopped knowing how to speak? If I forgot my past and everyone in it? You would have to remember for me that we wanted to die of happiness as the wheelchairs circled. This is desire. This is love.

The river is slow, and the boat is slower.

The water is scarlet; the heart is halved.

The sky is red and will wash blue by morning.

They stopped, dead halt, and their foreheads rested together, skin to skin as the boat heaved and her life went from all it had been to what it was.

The body sends its tired blue blood to the heart, where, in the divided chambers, hidden but ceaseless, the work goes on, minute by minute, cleaning it to red again.

Bless its repetition; bless that old washerwoman, the heart.

———

WHEN HE TOLD HIS MOTHER ABOUT AUGUSTO'S DAUGHTER, SHE replied, "But you cannot marry her."

She brought up Surfina Dias from their church, and John said, "Surfina talks constantly about nothing and makes me want to slam my hand in a drawer to redirect the pain of it all." His head was going to explode. He would postpone Mary and his mother encountering each other; he would, he realized, downplay the truth when Mary again begged to meet his family, as she had after the riverboat, rupturing the enchantment.

CONTESTS

AT THE SANGAMON COUNTY FAIR, JOHN AND MARY STROLLED PAST men on bunting-draped stages as they waved brooms and shouted about sweeping Washington clean, while other decriers denounced the widening gulf between rich and poor. John felt himself to be escorting her guardedly through the spread of the raging world itself. A scent of hay rose near the latest wonders of farm machinery from John Deere, and fairgoers milled. Everything, this commotion swirling under the sky, was added to what he could give her without a price tag. They had been bred as outdoor people, especially Mary. Even a perfect greenhouse was still an enclosure.

They found a booth with a woman tatting lace. Over the edges of a footstool, bobbins dangled like spiders as the lacemaker plied the strands. Attached to a table's edge was a metal bird, and the thread it was meant to hold had fallen out of its beak. John pressed the tail to open the beak and replace the thread. Was it to show he was attentive, he was tender? His reward was Mary regarding him as if this simple act imparted one of the most erotic bolts ever to charge through her.

Next to where the Temperance League was handing out apple juice and pamphlets, the Ayers Bank had set up a festooned display. Pinned under paperweights were one-sheet announcements of a contest with a deadline of Christmas Eve, two months away. John and Mary glanced over the rules. Essays were invited to suggest a building, opus, or installation that might convert a lot in downtown Jacksonville, a gift from an anonymous donor, "into another manifestation of our aspirations, which are to infuse the future with charity, education, and civic vigor, not only in our fair town, but as an example to our country, in need of defining its soul. This contest seeks to prove that worthy endeavors might ring out more vehemently than the drumbeats of conflict."

Anyone was eligible to deliver a proposal for transfiguring the empty lot. A box to receive entries would be displayed in Jacksonville's Ayers Bank, and the judges would be "several of our most upstanding citizens," with the winner announced on New Year's Day. Mary pointed at the awards: One thousand dollars would go toward the creation of the "public paradise" suggested in the essay . . . and another one thousand dollars, a life-changing fortune, would be the prize given to the "most imaginative thinker and outstanding prose-stylist."

When he unleashed a variation of the Madeiran whistling language, she told him about winning an art contest in New York. His mind roiled with how a victory would unite them in the most splendidly rare way, with their art and words gaining the new world's approval. His insides raced with ideas he rapidly discarded.

A cake table offered another competition. Maisie Mauzy, the grocer, would select the most elegant one, and the winner would receive a coat from John Jacob Astor's defunct American Fur Company, donated by the Springfield Merchants' Association. John took pride in apprising Mary of the Protestant Society's lectures in New York about this being the only business at which Astor had failed. A vanilla-frosted double-layer featured dripped red lines on the frosting, and Mary said, "Do you think the baker cut herself? This one suggests a maiming." His beloved reveled in a command of English; she could joke. He answered, "A very bad one." When he confessed to the break-in with Frank at Astor's mansion, she seemed to add it to her personal storehouse of how he was bold.

The woman behind the table, the custodian of the cakes, pointed out that the confection in the shape of a crescent moon was from the wife of Joel Matteson, a former governor who had made a million dollars in rail stocks, *as if Mary Fish Matteson needed a free fur coat.* The rest of the entries were sternly plain.

Bearing a cake on a tray, bustling into view, was someone he could identify even before Mary introduced them. "Pet, what a lovely cake! This is John Alves. John, this is Perpetua Roderick. Pet, where did you manage to make that?"

John and Pet kissed; it was momentous to meet Mary's friends. Cascading over pristine fondant were tropical flowers piped in frosting—the clear winner, given the sad lot on the table. Perpetua proclaimed, "I used Edward's kitchen, and he will kill me. I used up the flour and broke a vase." She was kinetic with glee and shouted at John, "You're even better-looking than Mary said!"

"Pet!" said Mary.

Waving at a man in the near distance, Perpetua declared, "That's my Henry! There's a tent offering daguerreotypes, and for two dollars they'll put it in a morocco case! When he breaks my heart, I can reuse the frame."

"Henry won't break your heart," said Mary, "but if he does, we'll plot your revenge." They laughed, and why not. Humorous remarks were among the best joys of friendship. But a mention of heartbreak and revenge, however tossed-off, tensed John up. A baby wailed. The cakes hurtled him back to betraying his mother by accepting that oily cornmeal wedge in jail.

Before dashing away to her Henry, Pet repeated how glad she was to meet John.

Mary said to him, "Are you all right, dear?" As if to slather words over his faraway stare, she chattered about Perpetua's parents never speaking to each other. Their eight children had to convey all messages, because one afternoon, just the one time, Pet's father had seduced a neighbor lady. The mother shut the curtains over the windows that looked out at that house, never to be opened. "For a while, Pet thought that houses in America were supposed to have a dark and a light side, like the moon."

Before he could feign interest in Pet's parents' home life, he shuddered to behold Isaac Unthank in preacher's garb bearing down on them. Isaac bellowed, "Alves, fancy meeting you here. Who is this celestial creature?"

Flowing around them were hordes of families as Mary told Isaac her name.

"Mary Freitas, aren't you promised to a gentleman in Springfield? I read the newspapers. One day I aim to tend a flock, and I must keep abreast of pending sacramental vows or civic frolicking such as this fair."

"Mary's status as betrothed has changed," said John.

"Dear oh dear. What happened?"

John took Mary's elbow to steer her away, but Isaac responded, "I haven't seen you at the Dane's lately."

John stepped closer to Isaac, who backed up but sneered while informing Mary, "He claimed a pretty penny from me in a gambling match but turns a deaf ear, as it were, to my pleas for help. 'Do not neglect to share what thou hast, for such sacrifices are pleasing to God,' and frankly, who doesn't like a little gift. The least he could do is put in a good word with his famous mother. She told me he vowed to help her build a church, and I'd wager, again as it were, that what he took in our match will help finance that. A smile from her, a teaming-up, and my life's mission is set. I profess a weakness for card-playing myself, as the Lord in His infinite wisdom made me imperfect." He appraised Mary and said, "You are a delectable instance of God's talent for birthing temptation."

She replied, "We're from Madeira and have known each other a long time."

"Birds of a feather do flock together." His meat-laced exhalation coated John's face. "The path to true love is riddled with missteps, I concur. To err is human."

"Unthank, go try your luck at a booth."

Isaac bowed and said, "Miss Freitas, I bear away your image emblazoned on my brain. John, thank your mother for her continuing attendance at the humble sermons I'm forced to deliver while perched on a box."

John and Mary observed him descending on a booth with tin toys and a wheel of fortune, and she hissed, "You gamble?"

"Not much. Men do it all the time."

"You would risk everything? John!"

"I would not risk everything, Mary." This was of questionable truth.

"Promise me—promise me!—never to do it again! What did he mean, you're building a church?"

The sun burned his eyes. In the offing was the endless trip home. He said, "My mother aims to sponsor a little chapel, or a sanctified spot, I don't know, Mary. It's to thank God for her life being spared. Isaac is an untrustworthy but charismatic word-spinner, proving that even my mother can be seduced." He avoided adding that rich men often funded such structures, fearing it would underscore what he lacked.

"You might have mentioned this."

"I owe you a replacement of the Kircher book, Mary, and I'd like to give you a good home, best I can, when I'm back from the war, and yes, I have to take care of my mother and honor her wishes, as I vowed to do, and all right, I won't gamble—" and words burbled to the surface that he failed to swallow as he said, "but you have become accustomed to expecting a great deal."

Silence wrapped in tightening scarves around their necks.

"Do I seem like someone totaling up what I am owed?" she said quietly. "By you? The one thing, the only thing I've expected, is that you introduce me to your mother."

"I'm afraid her reception of you will be soured by what Catholics did to her. Sweetheart, you know about the walls every faith builds around itself, and then the faith inside those walls argues and constructs subdivisions."

Instead of addressing that, she said, "Are you sure there'll be a war?"

Strange that speaking of conflagration should bring a return to peace, driving them to hold one another again. John said, "You're the person I want to tell only true things to, querida. I'll do better about that. Here, now, don't cry. I'm not gone yet."

—

THE ESSAY CONTEST SPONSORED BY THE AYERS BANK WAS ALSO announced in newspapers and flyers around town. What if he won?

Next time at the Lincolns', Mary reported that Pet had indeed been awarded the knee-length black-beaver coat but sold it to lend support to her parents and siblings, out of guilt because living on an estate meant she did not suffer a household with parents who used their children as couriers. The proceeds of the fur coat failed, of course, to heal the Roderick family. A cake contest, an essay contest to convert a downtown lot into an Eden, the booths where accuracy won somebody a doll, the games of chance John would give up for Mary's sake: How hungry for competitions this country was, for victories and defeats.

—

AS THE AUDIENCE POURED INTO THE MELINE THEATER, JOHN welcomed the Gouveia clan, worn out from their vineyard, along with Ray Silva with his petulant wife, Faith, and their daughter, Linda, who baked pound cakes that could bludgeon a man. Nickels pinged a staccato anthem as they hit the tray at the entrance, and glancing there, he grew hot-faced. Mary was late, and he worried incessantly about her traveling alone. When he once offered to escort her both ways, she declined. Even if rail schedules existed to aid him, it would mean a six-hour burden.

Overnight this had turned into a dreadful day to fulfill his promise to present her to his mother, who had been accosted in an alley while returning alone from prayer services the previous evening. Scuffles were on the rise; the editor of *The Morgan Journal* had been pistol-whipped for publishing anti-secessionist commentary. A man with an Irish accent had shoved her around, babbling, "Why so serious, squaw?"

Mother was surrounded by fevered haters of Catholics but had admitted—this was a straw to grasp—that she was struggling toward the spot she glimpsed on the horizon, a kingdom of all souls. Then a Catholic dunce had to go and terrorize her. Compounding John's anguish were fresh doubts about Sound Machine Night being a suitable setting. His thinking had been that a jolly distraction would aid conversation. The public would have the chance to turn their utterances into scratchings, though *replicating* speech, echoing a voice with etched clarity in a leap out of time, might elude humanity forever.

He greeted Frank arriving with Elizabeth Hampton, who said, "I could bind tonight's pages into a pamphlet, John." Her hands were stained from plying engraving tools to decorate covers in her bookshop.

John thanked her.

Frank whispered at him, "Don't fret. I look forward to greeting Mary when I'm not involved in criminal lock-picking, Alves." When John expressed worry about her religion, Frank replied that John's mother would soon—soon—be among the first on the earth to help end the wars that had persisted for centuries between "us and them."

Mother's entry with Nikka was so slow as to be ceremonial. She remained shaken from that Irish imbecile. People settling into their chairs whispered. Serafina was to be the final act, with everyone curious if God would claim her as the vessel of His Voice. What would be the message, what speaking-in-tongues could she produce? "Mother," he said. "I'm glad you're here and that you'll meet Mary."

She surveyed the theater and announced, "She is late, this Mary."

As he helped Nikka settle Mother into the front row, he said, more crossly than intended, "She's not the train's conductor." It was an inopportune time to remind her that Augusto had fought for them, and John's fantasy of their being one happy mixed-faith family by Christmas grew paler. "Do you want to be onstage with me, Ma?"

She did not.

He delayed starting as much as he dared—his tactics included prolonged signing with his pupil Sammy Byrd and Sammy's mother—but the audience was stirring, and Frank was gesturing near the stage. John joined him in working the pulleys to raise the curtain and reveal the Sound Machine on a red-velvet-draped table, the papier-mâché shell backlit and the pen's luxuriant feather protruding. He had discovered a way to address the narrowness of the aperture, the limited range of the scratching. Instead of affixing static vellum, he had installed paper around a roller, with a crank to turn it as it received fluid markings. Frank welcomed everyone warmly before joining the audience.

Shaking off foreboding, John pointed at a stack of paper strips and said, "I'll wind one sheet on the roller at a time. While you speak into this feather, and the vibrations move the pen, I'll rotate the crank, and then I'll write down the actual words you spoke." He lifted a notebook to faint applause. He cut short his speech about auditory science as the sea of nickel-payers got restive, concluding, "If certain syllables produce identical marks, an alphabet of ciphers might exist. How can recordings reproduce those sounds? It would mean that what we say can last forever, like words in a book. At the very least, tonight's scribbles will commemorate our madness." He had hoped for more laughter. Mary had missed his whole presentation. The sill held wind-up toys—a dancing bear and a clown with cymbals—that he swore had not been grinning like that when his recitation began.

When John requested a first volunteer, Ray Silva lurched to the stage. As John turned the crank, Ray pronounced into the feather, "Thou art Peter, and upon this Rock I shall build My church!" Applause accompanied John's detaching the strip and holding up the jottings. People in the back shouted that it was hard to see, and Frank jumped to his feet, ready to pass around each strip to allow for scrutiny.

Joe Gouveia came next, and John feared he would bellow, "He won money from me while we gambled with the Dane!" But Joe flashed an affable smile and thundered, "Winter ruins grapes!" and a spiral resulted. As participants clamored forward, John fretted about reports describing trains as ideal for robberies. Ray had mentioned that the demand for patterns to copy ladies' dresses had men forcing women at gunpoint to open trunks, since couture dissected into blueprints for mass production fetched high profits. John regretted laughing and pictured Mary forced to undress in front of bandits.

And then she arrived, bursting in, his darling, with flowers wilting from the journey. Mother flashed a scowl at such tardiness. Flustered, Mary slunk into a peripheral seat as old Ronaldo hobbled to the fore and produced a recording of scratches like swipes of a bear's paw.

Elizabeth's offering into the Sound Machine was, "There's a sale this week at the Hampton Bookshop!" and delight was general when the audience viewed her lines and dots like exclamation points. At last a catch in his throat trapped his leaping heart as his mother mounted the steps, Nikka guiding her, Mother aging with each increment of forward motion before setting her hands on either side of the earlike funnel. With John willing her to release something, anything, she bent toward the feather and waited for God's Voice to exit her. John plied the crank to turn the papered roll. Her whisper was brief and low, and Nikka and he failed to catch it.

He undid the page from the roller and held it up—and it was empty. Mutterings rose, and when Ray shouted a request that Senhora Alves's words be revealed, or could she please try again, Mother replied, "Not today." No telling if that meant she refused to repeat her mumbling, or if that was indeed what God told her, thereby issuing a blank. She begged Nikka to escort her back to her seat.

"The marked-up papers and original words will be displayed for a week in the theater, and afterward Miss Hampton—don't forget the sale at her shop—will produce a book." John's voice was hollow. "Thank you for humoring my experiment."

He hastened to Mary and said, "I was so worried."

After she poured forth irritation about a man whistling at her on the train, he said, "You don't have to meet her." The prior evening, he explained, Mother had been accosted by someone identifiably of the religion that, despite prayerful efforts, she had yet to trust.

"I'm here now. What'll be different in a month?"

He guided her over, and Mary lifted the drooping bouquet and said, aiming to lighten Mother's impassive face, "They were more alive when I set out. I'm Mary Freitas. Senhora, I admire you." She smiled at Mother, then at Nikka. "Is Rui here?"

John cringed, and Nikka said, "We don't see him much."

"Oh." Mary glanced at John. Serafina's lip quavered.

"I should have mentioned that, Mary." John rested an arm around her shoulder.

Nikka kissed her and said, "Dear Mary! Mother, isn't it sweet of her to come all this way for John's show, and to meet you and me?"

Serafina accepted the flowers gingerly, and Mary pulled a handkerchief from her purse and said, "I embroidered this for you. With fennel plants."

"To remind us of Funchal!" sang out Nikka.

Serafina peered at the handkerchief, too fancy for her to consider using. Mary's dress was embroidered with seashells, and she seemed like a body in it; it was not a Christian woman's subdued attire. Serafina deflated before his eyes. She was seldom perplexed, but accepting a

Catholic remained beyond her reach, and with a beseeching tone, she asked John, "What is it that is happening?"

Nikka chimed in with, "What remarkable stitching, Mary. Mother, look."

Serafina brightened. "You can convert!"

Mary said, "Pardon, Senhora, but I'm my father's daughter. I'm satisfied with who I am."

John wished Mary could play along. He said, "Mother, Mary is the other half of me, and that's Presbyterian enough."

But Mary shook her head and said, "I'm not Presbyterian at all, Senhora."

"I worry that you are not saved, you will have children blind to the light."

Noting Frank and Elizabeth heading over, John gestured to ward them off. He croaked out, "Mary is the kindest person I know, and that is enough for her to be saved. Maybe she'll convert one day."

"No," said Mary, "I won't."

In distress, Serafina said, "The Catholics, they want to kill me."

"Oh, Mother. Mary is hardly capable of that," said Nikka. "I'll kill you long before she has the chance." The joke did not even begin to do its job.

People trickling out of the theater eyed them. Mary finally seemed to detect how John wanted a release of adamancy. More temperately, she said, "I liked the blank page, Senhora. God said, 'Tell me how you plan to fill Me.' He left it up to us to invent something."

"I do not presume to know what the Lord says unless it is clearly from Him, not some girl who likes the things of this world," said Mother to John. "'No inheritance shall transfer from one tribe to another, for each tribe of Israel shalt hold on to its own.'"

Mary went rigid with hurt, and John retorted, "We're not in Israel."

"All of God's kingdom is Israel," intoned Serafina.

"Hallelujah, a miracle," he said, fed up. "Snow falls in Israel. Mary, let's get you home." The plan had been for dinner in the cabin and a stroll to look at the sort of houses he envisioned buying, fully aware that *she could claim an estate where her work already thrived.*

At the station, he enlarged the day's errors by suggesting, "Since you don't care about religion, you could convert. Or we should have lied about your background. Why didn't we lie?" He kept encouraging Nikka to do precisely that to find a suitor. Why should his sister suffer for having married some fisherman who jumped into every bed he could while she honored pointless vows? Nikka had believed their mother would be executed—he understood this now—and had panicked about caring for two little brothers.

"I won't lie about who I am. Why? Why don't you convert?"

"It would destroy her. I could strangle that Irishman who bothered her." He took Mary's hand, but she withdrew it. "If I have to choose between you and my mother, it will always be you. Give her time. I'll help her come around. She's trying to get there. She will. I'll see to it."

"How can she forget that my father spoke up for her? You said she's tired of divisions and wants unity."

"Unity for Protestants. She's fifty-two and unwell. The size of this country shocks her. It makes her cling to who she was, when she was at war with the priests and everyone was in awe of her. She prays about that, too."

"I thought she would love me."

"I'll love you enough for us both."

They failed to kiss goodbye as the screeching train came to a halt, and he suspected it would convey them into a spate of avoiding each other. When he next went to the Lincolns', she was absent, and then came a second Saturday without her. Brain on fire, he reasoned: A breather will cure everything. I'll remind my mother that once upon a time, *we were Catholics, too,* and she'll recognize her blind spot, and the quarrels over religion since the dawn of time might be ended once and for all by an exasperated Lord.

Though probably even He had no idea what to do except confirm Mary's idea: Here is a blank. Draw on it yourselves. Your planet exhausts Me to death.

———

HE DID NOT WAIT FOR YET ANOTHER SATURDAY. AFTER THE TRAIN pulled into the flat-topped Springfield station and everyone disembarked, a lout told him to go back to wherever he came from, and John replied, "I come from New York," and the man called him a jackass and landed a fist on John's face before John kicked the man's feet out from under him. His nose seeping blood, he went in a straight line to Sixth Street and the greenhouse the size of a fiefdom, mastering his fear of running into Edward. Her hair was tied with a green ribbon as she raked a trowel near miracle-berry shrubs, his first time entering her kingdom of tints and shapes and scents. Her lips parted as they had when he said her stitching bore the skills of those who would rather lose their sight than give up their work. Rumpled and bloody, he looked like an escapee from a battlefield, having crossed mountains, lashed through forests. In his arms, she was lifted, her knees drawing up, up and around his waist, let me carry you away. Mary, my balm in Gilead.

"You're hurt," she said, slipping from him to find a rag.

No, the bleeding was nothing, it was from a disagreement with someone who did not like his looks.

"I thought I'd give you time, and your mother time," she said. "I thought that's what you wanted."

How to express how little of that they could afford to waste, all the young men about to be packed up and shipped?

"Oh, darling," she said, "I didn't mean to make you cry."

She fetched her coat and mittens—*You were born warm, forever goose-fleshed from the cold*—so they could go for a walk. He had forgotten gloves, and she stretched a mitten and said, "Slide a hand in with mine," which he found almost lethally arousing.

They wandered into an open-air party, with stands for drinks and desserts, hemmed by the oaks on West First Street and lit by colored lanterns, blue, yellow, and red. The air was switching from bright gold toward evening's oxidized gold, as if thousands of wedding bands had been melted and poured over the trees, flowers, and well-clothed men and women clinking glasses. Musicians tuned up with sobbing violins.

They found a table, and he bought glasses of fruit punch and told her that he had entered the Ayers Bank's contest. Because of her, he had suggested a public park with a greenhouse that dispensed medicinal herbs for free. A thousand-dollar prize might finance a home, not in the style of Aristocracy Hill but in a form of restfulness. "Mary, let's go to New York. You could work at the Jamisons', and I'll get a job. At a school for the deaf, or anywhere." Voice straining, he gamboled on, "Mother liked it there, Nikka, too, and you said Edward would share any profits, and—" And he sounded unhinged. They had already run from so much. A black ash tree seemed to be talking on account of the rustling of birds and the leaves shedding in the cold. On a but-tonbush shrub, a caterpillar dropped onto a diving board of a leaf and bounced into the air. "We could go to California, Maria-Cat. Labs are experimenting with sound in Los Angeles. It's the right climate for your plant. Please say something." Instead of one or the other of them giving up everything, they both would.

As if to ridicule him, a band of Wide-Awakes swept in, drowning out the musicians. Young men with militia fever banged drums and toted torches and banners with giant eyeballs, and they crashed cym-bals. The attendees at the party became upset. When the Wide-Awakes quit clamoring, Mary whispered, with surpassing reasonableness, "Why go anywhere if you're about to leave me to join the Union army?"

"I won't die, I'll try not to. Everyone agrees it won't last long, the war."

"Do you have to go?"

"When you and I visit the Lincolns in Washington, when you bring them handiwork the way Mr. Lincoln invited you to do, I can't tell them I shirked my duty. I'll fight for all of us from Madeira." He was going to combust from suppressing an outburst about Edward's undoubtedly considering it acceptable for poorer men to die, and no one would blink twice at his cowardice.

She said, "I go over and over in my mind how we fought at the fair."

"We didn't fight, not really, Mary. Disagreements happen, and se-crets, or almost-secrets, come to light, but there's no harm, it's all part of loving each other, isn't it? I should have told you more about my mother, and what I'd like to give her, but I want to give you much more." He thought: You are beautiful, and beautiful, and like a garden, beautiful.

"Please stop thinking so much about money. It sounds ungrateful, but I don't love that big fancy house and yard. I like having money enough to garden and stitch and not have an orphan's fate. I want something to call my own. That's all. I don't like parties." She grinned. "Or people, not so much."

"Then we'll be fine, querida. We both want freedom on our own terms. I'll never forget being a boy without it, locked up. We'll send students and unusual, good things into the world, things we make and invent, won't we, when I come back?"

Did she nod? She said, "Such a well-lit night." Her father had taught her that the stars formed pictures.

He replied that his mother described them as God's alphabet. He slipped a hand again inside one of her mittens and said, "Marry me."

"Yes. One day, I'll marry you."

They agreed to wait until he returned from the war, and then they would be free to go where they chose, not frantically, not in flight. "I'd have to leave Papa here," she said.

"You already carry him with you everywhere. Even if I don't win that contest, Mary, I won't die before I buy you a house. You asked me not to talk about money, but I need to tell you I'll shelter you. On my life, I promise that."

The lanterns coated people with primary colors, and the musicians let a tune swell, and a golden quietude swept in from the prairie, the fields, praise it all, all the cornucopias under the sun under the Lord.

Waiting: It would be the biggest mistake of their lives. Since already they were offering all they were, what better time could there be?

Had I foreseen all that would come to pass, Mary, I would have held You until my bones shattered from old age.

"May I kiss you?" he asked.

You may my love, my love you may.

The stars dissolved and became the souls of stars.

Then they changed from being the souls of stars, into souls.

We have our whole lives.

Frank once remarked, Look at all your name holds, Alves. *Sea, slave, lave, salve, save, seal.* And *ave* and *vale,* hail and farewell.

THE CITADEL OF WOMEN

SHE NEEDED TO STITCH TWO HUNDRED BAGS TO FULFILL THE LATEST orders for outlets in St. Louis. Perpetua was sowing saplings of lemon trees, and Mary's entry into the house was at her usual time, on one of Edward's afternoons at Illinois College. Her mind was a blizzard of bits and pieces about John, Protestant dogma, secessionists, and a woodworm infestation in a cinnamon-apple tree. Aggravating her unease was the discovery that over two dozen of her shrubs had slashed limbs, evidence that a marauder had stolen some cuttings. Pet, in a tense moment, had sworn she was not to blame.

The woman whom Mary had glimpsed from afar as a frequent visitor appeared at the top of the staircase and descended several steps. She stopped, fingers whitening as she gripped the banister. From the bottom of the stairs, Mary called out, "I'm Mary Freitas. I care for the greenhouse and grounds. We finally get to meet."

The young woman answered, "What are you doing here?" Her ecru dress was cinched high, and her hair-twist resembled a furry brown animal on her head.

"On Wednesdays I go upstairs to sew. What is your name?"

"Gertrude Weber. Eddie certainly likes to chat about you."

Mary climbed the first step, then the second, but instead of budging, Gertrude said, "I should thank you for discarding him."

Mary's bladder suffered a twinge, as it often did when she was confronted. She replied, "Congratulations, he is very nice, Gertrude. I'd like to go upstairs."

"You'll refer to me as 'Miss Weber.'"

"Miss Weber, may I go to my sewing machine? Edward and I do a business together, we—"

"Fascinating." Gertie backed up a step, as if she required a better launching point to tackle Mary in her attempt to ascend. "This ends at once, this free and easy nonsense of pretending you live here. You will move your"—she waved as if horseflies were circling—"items elsewhere. I'll suggest to Ward that you find other lodgings entirely."

"I don't have room for the Singer machine in the cottage, always I have the room upstairs. I can plan a time when it is acceptable with you, Miss Weber, also Mr. Moore. I lived here with my father, and he died, and Mr. Moore never has required me to leave, I stay with Perpetua, my friend."

"The genius fragile father. What kind of absurd name is 'Perpetua'?"

Mary wholly met Gertrude's watery eyes. "She is Perpetua because that is who she is. When my John returns from war, we will get married and move to a home, and I'll have a place for my Singer, and I'll come to this house only to work with—"

"Beginning when I live here, your presence will no longer be required."

"Miss Weber, I am alone but soon I won't be. I need this job, my papa and I have done it since we arrived. I can live in the boarding-house for women. Today I need to sew the bags. Mr. Moore will expect that." She moved forward, but because battles for territory have a way of bloating women, Gertrude seemed to expand sideways. "Gertrude," pleaded Mary, "please let me go upstairs."

"*Miss Weber.* Next Tuesday, Eddie and I shall throw a party, and you'll clean our kitchen prior to that."

"Cleaning women show up on Mondays. That is not my job, Miss Weber."

"It is now."

"It isn't. It is not." Though shaking, Mary kept her retreat at a saunter.

That evening, she cross-hatched a serpent onto her tablecloth, giggling when Perpetua suggested they barricade themselves in the house with rifles until Gertrude signed a document stating Edward and she were the ones who must inhabit the cottage. His knock on their door was one of the few of Mary's tenure there, and he wanted to know why the usual basket of stitched, filled sachets had not been left on the porch for the middleman to pick up for shipping.

Mary gave the reason, adding that Gertrude had demanded that she leave, and residing at the boardinghouse might not sufficiently define being gone. Perpetua pretended to be reading a newspaper. Edward's reply was for his shoulders to sag.

Mary indicated another problem besetting her. Could they step into the yard?

In the frigid air, wrung out, he said impatiently, "Can this wait?"

"I noticed cuttings off my plant. I thought at first Perpetua did it, but there is no reason for her to; of course she did not." She hesitated. "Edward, it's Maud, or now I think this Gertrude you spend time with, she did it."

"Why would they?"

"To make a problem. Maud breaks things, we know this. She never has replaced my nutcracker. You haven't either."

His head reared upward and back. "No, I haven't bought you a new nutcracker yet. Are you serious?"

"I do not understand, Edward, why you like so many difficult women."

"Because the woman I know who isn't difficult—excluding this moment—wants nothing to do with me."

"No, we are working together, and that is very much something, and I want you to do the thing for me of telling Maud to leave the plants alone."

She observed tumblers rotating in his mind. He said, "I should mention a few things. Let's get this over with, since your favorite obsession has arisen."

Mary stared in disbelief as he spoke, until she interrupted with, "What?"

"I *said,* if you thought of her as human, and a resource, instead of an ogre, you would appreciate how her father is a major distributor for southbound shipping. I've sent cuttings to my farm with his assistance."

"What?"

"Archie Dieterman gets two and a half percent of what we earn wholesale with anything going to Saint Louis and south in general. To get the first thirty cuttings to Florida, he took a ridiculously small fee. That I paid."

"Maud is making two and a half percent *off my plant?*"

"No, her father is, only on the routes south. He gives her an aught-point-five tip out of his share—*his* share, mind you—since she set things up for me. She calls it her new-hat money. A pittance."

"Edward, you took cuttings without telling me. They were hacked in a wrong way."

"I knew you'd act like this."

"Then why do it?" she shrieked. The strawberry-rocks painted with Papa were the sole things keeping this spot of earth pinned in place.

"What do you mean 'hacked'? Are you accusing me of not knowing how to take cuttings properly?"

"I am!"

He performed a strange twisting of his full self. "Again I remind you that everything you brought to Illinois would have died without me, and more luck for you, I own a place that's hospitable for your plant to thrive in the open. Ten out of the thirty cuttings made it. My laborers there confirmed that. I've been waiting for a good time to share the news. I thought you'd be thrilled."

"Other distributors ship to the South!"

"I used a major one known to me, and at a reduced rate. You are overreacting, as you love to do." He weighed stopping there, and then he did not. "Who cares if someone named Archie Dieterman greases the wheels, and takes a puny fraction, and his daughter makes barely a thank-you amount, a former fiancée—we were engaged for only two weeks, Mary—who helped out and whom you detest so much you can't see clear to using what she can do and being done with it. She's marrying spoiled Billy Mars. Who has twice my money."

"Meanwhile she found a way to sink her claws into you."

"Despite your past hardships, you think everyone and everything should be flawless, and that's why you've made John into this paragon of romance, when he's just a handsome boy who lets you wallow in nostalgia and who will never have enough money to keep you happy, and you know it."

Her legs were swift but wooden in trotting her to the interior of her lodging. She unearthed her carpetbag as Perpetua watched, and Mary said, "I apologize again for thinking you cut the plants."

"Don't worry about that. What are you doing?"

Mary threw random items into her bag and pried up the floorboard where they kept their money and took some coins. "Use boron to kill those worms, Pet. Were you listening at the door?"

"I could have been at Nell's house and heard you both. He's a bobo about Maud, but he's never been jealous before. He loves you and doesn't know what to do. Also, you love him and don't know how to act around him either, Cat-Cat."

"You're my smart friend. I won't be gone forever." They hugged, and Mary said she would try the boardinghouse since she might get banished there anyway. Papa would warn, *Do not rush into things, querida, guard against your rash hurling tendencies.* But she trooped to the three-story Illinois House for Women and Girls eight blocks away, and in a dining room with escutcheons and swords, bizarre in a female fortress, she met Adelaide Oscar, the proprietor. Mary believed that women either turned into apples or sparrows as they grew older, and Mrs. Oscar—she went by "Addy"—was gone sparrow. The tablecloths bore indelible stains, and a dustpan was abandoned in a doorway, as if a maid had fled an attack.

Addy welcomed her to what she called "our city of women" and described herself as a gold widow, her husband having abandoned her for the West, where he was rumored to have a new family that almost certainly had no idea about childless Addy.

At first, Mary reveled in the solitude of her tidy room with a window and horses clomping past, resting within the unencumbered feel of needing so little. Her mind gave off sparks as it argued with Ward: *I don't need a lot to be happy. You're wrong,* aware that this chant would alter when her money ran out, and startlingly in tune with that, he sent a note apologizing but referred to her decamping as "stubbornness." And by-the-bye, it made no sense to pay her salary while Perpetua did the work.

How she worshipped the morning bustle of the girls with their buttonhooked shoes as they scrambled out to work in the shops. She sat on her bed, listening. The world broke her in twain, it did, the enormity of it.

———

A FROZEN CHARLOTTE DOLL STOOD ON HER SHELF, AND SHE COVERED it so it would not burst alive and knife her to a bloody pulp. In old age, she was to remember this doll and think: Why did I not merely remove it?

———

THE ICE CHIPS ALONG HER OUTSIDE SILL WERE SHAPED LIKE ANIMALS, a bear, a dog, and a spread-winged pelican. They were tiny and belonged on a charm bracelet. The mere thought of wearing it stung her wrist.

———

PET DELIVERED A LETTER AND PARCEL FROM JOHN:

20 December 1860

Maria-Cat,

So much time has fled since the sound-machine night, & our other outing, but since then Ive felt silence from You. I dont blame You but I want to say Mother is sorry. She is only human after all, & theres so much history of hatred between Yr faith & mine, though isnt it strange, b/c neither You nor I have much to do w/ any of that. She wants another chance w/ You, isnt that good news? With our Great

Man elected, w/only weeks—7, 8—before he goes away, our meeting-place has already been taken over by men-of-decision & has started to be gone from us forever.

On the 3rd of January, therell be an art exhibit at the School for the Blind near the J'ville station close to Ray's General Store, so You could arrange a delivery of Yr crop & meet me at noon at the school. As w/my children being told to use their ears however they want, the blind students are encouraged to draw & paint.

Also on that date . . . I hope itll mean celebrating w/ You. The "Boosting the Spirit of Jacksonville" competition closes in 4 days & I have a good feeling about suggesting a garden because there is none in busy downtown esp. w/a greenhouse to give out free herbs/medicines the way Yr father did. Think of what the prize could mean for us!

Come here for Christmas, I must warn You many Protestant church things will happen plus Madeira Hill friends will offer the usual shot birds and candied fruits. Im sending a gift in case darling You cant make it or want more time—?—Ill understand but pls know Mother wants to do better.

Today the news came that South Carolina left our Union. If we cannot see one another b/c of many reasons, work, distance, (mother), awkwardness w/Edward, etc., we can at least WRITE, & that will be practice for what could be weeks or months, but I hope not that long, of my being at war. I cannot survive away from You w/o at least Yr words. Ill say this once to get it over w/should I die in the service of my country, I can be at peace in heaven being certain that Edward would take You back & grant You not only ease but affection, but let me stop there, my power to say such things is limited. Youre my heart & soul, & I love You, Mary. John.Alves.

His gift was a packet of threads that she knew at once, without reading his tucked-in note, were his best effort to match the rare colors she had described as being in the cabinet in Funchal, the ones Papa had sold to buy their passage to America.

She bought linen scraps to fill while residents in the Illinois House were at their jobs: Blue, red, and green lanterns. New York buildings with Josephine knots and reticello for windows. Turkey stitches for midwestern suns like blood oranges. Guimarães cutwork was perfect for snowflakes. She designed flowers white-on-white like the ghosts of flowers, and filigree tracks, and she whipstitched a replica of the Dorflinger crystal of the Lincolns.

Abruptly she stopped, paralyzed. She curled up in bed, ordering herself to write to John, to send a Christmas gift, to get on a train and embrace Serafina Alves, to check that Pet was having a decent holiday, to admit to Edward that she was afraid to discuss how they could run their business . . . except . . . she felt like a lone soul who sees a mirage in the shape of a loved one and walks toward it and walks toward it, and the mirage-person is doing the same, but before they black out from thirst, they realize it is an illusion, that despite their mad efforts they were not drawing any closer.

She quit visiting the dining room and used a totality of effort to travel to the water-closet and back but mostly relied on a chamber-pot. A knock—she summoned her voice to chime out, "It's open"— revealed Lucy Brattle, who set down a tray and approached Mary in her bed to scold, "Honeybee, you missed Christmas! Addy said, 'I leave you girls to do as you please, but I know a cry for help when it done cry out.'" Floating in the barley soup were carrot rounds that someone had fringed so they looked like daisies. Lucy said, "I get this, too. I call it going into the Well. Are you sad so's you're in the Well?"

Mary answered, "I don't know what you mean." Someone had taken the time to pare the skin off a tomato in a spiral and to curl the peel into a flower for her tray. That made her burst out sobbing.

"There, there!" cried Lucy. With eyes spaced wide and a gap between her front teeth, she looked about fifteen but held Mary as if Mary were the child. "A gent stopped by on Christmas and said to tell you he was sorry, but Mrs. Oscar don't let men in. There're meringues for dessert if you want. Mrs. Oscar made them 'cause she fired the cook, wanna know why?"

"Yes." Mary let Lucy feed her soup.

"The cook used paper to thicken a white sauce. Paper!"

That made them laugh. Mary told her that where she came from, meringues were called suspiros, or sighs.

"That's right pretty."

Mary described Papa, and Madeira—Lucy had never heard of it—and Lucy said, "I'm from Kansas and sure didn't have angels around me." After Lucy's mother hanged herself, her daddy had sold her to an old man, and she ran off, ran this far. She loved Addy's women's house. "My job is serving lunches at Mr. Farnsworth's hotel, and he is so kind. Did you stitch those things? You need to get up and use the gifts God gave you, but first you need a bath."

Lucy hummed what sounded like a hymn while stripping Mary and washing her. Mary said, "You had a difficult life," to which Lucy replied, "That's all put down like a crazed dog, it's over. I'm happy, but that don't mean I don't at times go into the Well."

Mary handed her all the stitched pieces, and when Lucy said she could not accept them, Mary pleaded, "I'd like you to have them, please."

The next morning, she paid her bill, hugged Lucy Brattle, and Addy and a few others, and returned to the Moore estate. Was she really going to stock shelves in Maisie's grocery store and stumble to a dormitory afterward to risk eating white sauce made with paper? In a contest with Edward of who would give in first, she was guaranteed to lose. This infuriated her, and she revived a notion of climbing into a wagon bound for California, to grow her plants on a western range, but also she rather admired his refusal to beg. When Edward saw her in the yard, they exchanged stilted greetings.

But then he took her to the Sangamon Bank to open an account in her name. Women could not do this without a man signing for them.

"I wish you had not spent the holiday away, Mary," he remarked, "and dare I say how much I've missed you? I spoke rudely, and my description of John was unfair and has troubled me. He's learned a third language and cares for children. And for you. He is of pleasing aspect and with a capacity for devotion. He is inventive, and a self-trained man of science. Both of you come from oppressions I cannot imagine."

She apologized for not appreciating his bigger thinking about the business, and for his investment, and she didn't mean to go insane about the women Ward knew.

"No, you're right. Gertrude will be informed, everyone will be informed, that you may enter my house as you wish, and no one is permitted in the greenhouse without your consent. I should have asked if I could take the cuttings. I wanted to see how many would survive on the farm. I did intend it as a pleasing surprise. I've already found another distributor. Leonard Otto, of Otto & Wharton. No more Dietermans."

"Maud will be upset."

"I don't care. It's painful having you around, but worse with you gone." When he mentioned having a Christmas gift for her, she pleaded, "Ward. Please. You opened a bank account for me. You give me too much."

"You'll like this."

She took his arm as she had during that first arrival in the dead of winter over a year ago. A package was on the table in his foyer.

She let the wrapping fall, crinkled-tissue snow. Her present was a nutcracker, metal, shaped like a toucan, and she released a gale of laughter. "Thank you, Ward. You didn't have to."

"I couldn't find a parrot."

She kissed the side of his face, startling him. "I forgot a gift for you," she said.

"Just now, that is the best present I could hope for. If it means you forgive me," to which she replied, "I do."

———

ALWAYS IT WAS MEDITATIVE WHEN MARY KNEADED SOIL WITH BOTH hands, sifting, breaking it down, clods and stringy nexuses, creating an easy banquet for the earthworms so roots could unfurl. She did not hear anyone enter the greenhouse.

She veered as Gertrude seized Mary's head and slammed it into the waist-high bed, shouting, "Dirty tattletale," grinding Mary's face into moist crumbs until her mouth filled, and so did her eyes and nose. She flailed, but Gertrude shoved harder, clutching Mary's hair. A recollection of John's breath-holding saved her—*You can survive without air*—but panicky at the approach of nothingness, she landed a kick against her assailant's knee. It made no difference ... as Mary was choking, blacking out, she sensed a scuffle that caused her release. Gertrude was grabbed away, and Edward bellowed, "Have you lost your mind?" Mary, wearing a mask of earth, saw him gripping Gertrude's elbow as Pet raced to Mary gulping humid air, holding the ledge of the bed before slipping down.

That night, Mary would have bolted upright had she possessed the strength, but she was able to blurt, "Pet, what is today?"

"One step closer to Doomsday."

"Yes, but what day of the year?"

"January the third."

Mary had utterly forgotten about meeting John at the school for the blind, to view the ethereal paintings offered by children with unlit eyes.

Edward was tinkering with his graftings the following dawn when she entered the greenhouse, and he said, not glancing up, "I ended everything with Gertrude, though what we had wasn't much. She will not be bothering us."

Mary sat on a ledge near him as he tightened the threads binding slant-cut stems. "I'm having luck with hybrids of your miracle plant, but a thornless rose is beyond me."

"My plant already exists, and what you're trying to create doesn't, Edward."

"Your father would know how to develop what I'm after."

"I imagine he would. Edward, why are the women you know some of the worst I've ever met?"

He found a chair to rest with her in the artificial warmth. "In my defense, let me point out that I haven't been in Illinois all that long, and men like Sullivan Conant, William Farnsworth, and Philo Beers, and women like Nell Clark, and other exemplary types, count themselves as my friends. My father was a crook, my brothers are depraved. My mother mocked the stutter I spent years overcoming." He touched her shoulder briefly. "I'm learning I don't need to replace their nastiness. I confided in Maud about my failures at Princeton and swindling father. She threatens sometimes to tell everyone. I wanted to keep her happy to prevent such gossip. Now I'm tired of emotional blackmail."

A burst of benevolence toward his flaws scared her. Even so, she doubted she could explain being in the Well to Edward, though that morning, in her letter to John, she had explained it as best she could.

"Contact John and wish him a good new year," he said. "I'm guessing you disappeared from everyone for a while."

"True." She shared that John had invited her to an art show, but yesterday's horror had erased it from her mind. She had sent him a note, trusting all would be healed.

"Good." He pointed at the slants cut into the rose stems. "Have I cut these wrong? Are these sutures terrible?"

His knowledge about cuts and grafts was fine; she regretted her ire about that. The lacing-up of the two varietals was very good indeed, excellent. "No, Ward," she said. They were glad for half smiles. "You know what you're doing."

THE CLOUD TRICK

20 January 1861

Minha querida, Didnt You receive my letter? In it was the news that I WON THE PRIZE, & it is You, You who inspired it. Mr. Ayers said my proposal of a garden w/ greenhouse, & benches to congregate, promises "a haven for the spirit, and merchants will applaud." Ill receive $1000!

I could buy You a house right now & give some toward the church Mother desires. Ill make sure it is under the wing of an honorable holy man. Ha that will be a search. Pls give her another chance? Her stomach ails her, & Nikka & I must attend to her, & I have to teach, else Id race to You. Maybe (Your silence means) Youre in a mood to be left in peace a little?

But 4 more states left our Union, & I long to see You. Should You be in Your Well, Ill pull You out if You are ready & if not, Ill sit against the outside wall of The Well until You are. I want to show You the spot where the ("my") Jacksonville Public Garden will be, & we can celebrate as my mother gives You—us—her blessing. My heart would split the red sea it floats in in me to get to You if You would pls send word. John.Alves.

Repetition Day was designed to loosen the bodies of his deaf students, to thrust them into vocalizations, letting them claim membership like everyone else in the world of din. Many of them worried about making noises, attracting stares. *But here,* signed John, *we are free!* Lillian Wyatt often started the racket by jumping in a rhythm that unblocked her throat. Setting a toy cow on Nathan Schmidt's head, John shouted and signed, *The cow sits on his hair!* The pupils were dancing, arms reaching, knees bending, with Sammy Byrd releasing the version of yelling originating in his gut.

John signed, *Louder! The cow sits on my desk!*

Lillian sits in a chair with the cow!

The children devised fates for the toy cow, spinning her, tossing her to Hiram Lattimore, while John's own mix-and-repeat chorus thrummed. After his repeated pleas for a response, Mary had sent a chilly, succinct note that upended his plan to run to her. She complained of a head cold, too contagious for her to travel or to receive him. Plus she had hurt her hand with shears, and Pet was the impatient scrawler.

Why no congratulations about the contest? When he was at war, picturing his garden would enhance the consolation that he was fighting for everything worthwhile.

Mary, I do not care if I catch Your cold.

I won, Mary. Why so cold?

Claire Clearwater had never spoken, but today the little songbird let out a rasp. While signing, he hollered, *Claire has spoken!*

Wild cheers! The never-to-be-forgotten teacher wants pupils to profess: *I am no longer terrified! You've taught me that education is all about love in the end.*

He was savoring these victories later in the library, puzzling over how to cast impressions of the grooved imprints of whatever the stylus of his Sound Machine recorded, when Superintendent Gillette relayed word that Augustus Ayers had summoned John. Likely to advise him about when he could expect his cash award.

A maid welcomed him into the banker's Italianate masterpiece of a domicile. Mr. Ayers was conferring in his parlor with a crepe-skinned woman of humor-free visage, so bundled in outerwear that if she fell off a building she would bounce. "Mr. Alves, my friend, join us," said Augustus. He was not his usual ebullient self and lacked the demeanor of someone eager to discuss a new fortune with a winner.

John lowered himself into the most comfortable chair he had ever inhabited. A cabinet displayed porcelain figurines arrayed in a pastoral scene. Augustus said, "A complaint has been registered, Mr. Alves, it grieves me to report."

Responding to a knock, the maid admitted someone with a voice that sank John's life force so low it was pounding in his shoe. Into their midst stepped Edward Moore. After their stares linked, the connection snapped. Edward took a chair as far from John as could be managed, clutching his hands with a vehement tightness as Augustus introduced Sarah Brink as the contest's runner-up. Unable to censor himself, John asked Edward, "How is Mary?"

"I might ask you the same." Each word was a chop in the air.

"Her head cold. Her injured hand. Is she better?"

"I'm not aware of any ailments. I prefer not to speak of her with you."

"As to the issue before us," interjected Mr. Ayers.

Sarah Brink stated that it had come to her attention that John had violated the rules. She fumbled in a handbag large enough to facilitate kidnapping an infant, extracted a flyer, and thrust it like a court summons at John, who declined to read it and said, "I thought up an idea and wrote it down. I won. Weeks ago. What's the meaning of this?"

"I can only react to information when I receive it. During a casual conversation," Sarah warbled, "your sister mentioned assisting you in honing your entry. The rules unequivocally state that essays are"—she shook the flyer as if it had sassed her and bleated—"'to be the sole work and bear the hand only of the contestant.' The definitive words are 'sole' and 'only.'"

Why was Edward here? Cranelike, he set an ankle on a knee the way American men did to fashion huge extra triangles of space out of themselves.

John said, "My sister fixed some punctuation, some spelling, but everything I wrote was from my own spirit and mind, Mr. Ayers. Miss Brink." Should he add "Mr. Moore"? No. "There's nowhere downtown to rest and talk except within places of refreshment, and I said nature requires sanctifying, that we err in seeking only to conquer it." A drop of fluid was hanging, refusing to fall, from one of Sarah's nostrils.

"Your idea was the best. I personally agree that minor fixes aren't an egregious wrong." Mr. Ayers's tone was sympathetic, and John flashed a look of gratitude.

But Sarah gassed onward. "You omit contractions, according to your sister, and on occasion your sentences require ungnarling. Mr. Ayers, you are exquisitely fair-minded. But the quality of the prose was one of the determinants." She directed her attention toward Edward, who seemed to have wandered in from the street and was contemplating an exit from a tension of no concern to him.

John weighed darting to Washington, to interrupt the Great Man, who had a thing or two occupying him, to beg him to take on this legal battle.

Augustus muttered, "Let me reaffirm that your essay was superior, Mr. Alves. But we have the problem of a technicality. Mr. Moore donated the lot but had nothing to do with selecting the winner. Mr. Moore, care to venture an opinion?"

John detested throat-clearing, and as if to plague him, Edward treated them to a drawn-out session of it before asking Sarah to summarize her second-place proposal.

"A chapel that would welcome all Protestants. It is an idea inspired by a marvel of a preacher I heard in the town square. I was spellbound."

John's head tipped onto his chest. "No," he managed to utter, even before she bandied the name Isaac Unthank. "No, no, no." He had been powerless to dissuade his sister and mother from joining the packs listening to Unthank's open-air rantings. A casual conversation with Nikka could easily produce a thread that Isaac would pull until he unraveled a minor comment about aiding John slightly. If Sarah were among Isaac's acolytes, he would then impart this detail to her, the second-place finisher, to seize a chance to have his chapel.

"The lot could contain a garden, but with a limited-size greenhouse instead of a large one, to allow room for a small chapel as well," pronounced King Solomon Moore.

"That would not be objectionable," said Sarah. "I wish only for justice."

Edward said, "You could split the prize money and share the installation."

John eyed him, the pettiness of him, pretending to be reasonable but slicing John's ability to care for Mary in half, and he said, "Isaac is a seducer and a fake."

"Then he is a fake who salves the souls of many who hear him," said Sarah.

"Nikka would never say anything to hurt me." John could not stem his groveling. "Her speaking freely of assisting me in the smallest way—and others probably got helped a lot more—proves I did nothing wrong. She changed no wording, offered no suggestions. Isaac would twist a chance comment by her to his use."

"Nevertheless," proclaimed Sarah.

Exchanged were further pleas, rebuttals, and suggestions, topped with pacifying comments by the host, who wished to keep everyone happy, but in the end, half of John's prize would go to rule-mistress Sarah, and construction would commence on her come-one-and-all Protestant chapel on the Edward-donated lot—a double taint.

Neither man was glad to fall into step upon leaving, but John said, "Edward, could you ask Mary to contact me?" to which Edward replied, "How self-effacing am I supposed to be, John? I have no idea what she does most of the time. You took her from me, and now I'm your messenger? Bad enough that your idea is going to be on my property. Former property. I'm late to my class at the college. Good day."

———

THE FIVE GENTLEMEN WERE WREATHED IN CIGAR SMOKE, AS IF THEY had ordered clouds to descend from on high. Capes and top hats were hanging in the entryway. John attempted to mirror their demeanors. This kingly dining parlor in College Hill featured a mermaid in a stained-glass window, her tail resembling Neptune's trident.

Jeduthan Walker, the cattle-baron homeowner, would start as
the dealer. The others were high-society men from Chicago, passing
through on their way to St. Louis. John had learned about this match
from the Dane after slinking behind the tannery to earn back a fraction of what he felt he had lost. For 10 percent of whatever John won,
the Dane was glad to recommend a game with meaningful cash and
would advise Jeduthan that John had an unexpected five hundred in
addition to skill and uncanny luck.

So here he was, violating his vow to Mary never to gamble. But he
might in an instant replace the difference confiscated thanks to an insanely strict interpretation of rules. Through an archway, he glimpsed
a gray marble mantel and, above it, glazed tiles depicting a spider in
a web. At what seemed to be the head of the table—despite it being
round—Jeduthan riffled a deck, the cards purring, five-card stud, hole
cards facedown, door cards faceup, John with a low four of clubs to
start the betting at five dollars, child's play for these men. He had silver dollars and random coins and a few twenty-dollar gold pieces and
one gold nugget worth one hundred dollars, a stunning fortune, and
the others also had gold and silver dollars and appraised gold pieces.
"Out," Jeduthan said, clipping a cigar after a second and third card
suggested defeat. Two others folded.

The round granted John three knaves, one hidden; his victory
increased his ante times five within minutes. From his competitors,
nothing emanated, not a flicker. This was a pastime, not life and death.
Jeduthan reshuffled. In the next round, John lost thirty. Jeduthan took
the third hand. But as the dying sun angled orange through the mermaid, and the men seemed to require neither food nor water nor liquor, John entered a streak of winning.

When he was two hundred up, he showed two tens and two
queens, with another ten hidden. He was a card-counter, a reveler in
numbers. Jeduthan had a pair of kings showing but folded. John par-
layed the betting by a confident waxed-mustache man into his own
high risk. Even with three nines, the waxed-mustache man lost, and
so did someone with a diamond stuck in his tie. They all lost to John's
miraculous full house.

When he reached an astounding four hundred up, almost the

amount redirected into the scaly hands of Sarah Brink, John squirmed. He should go home, letting them call him a yellowbelly. But a man gets the delirium: *I'm one hand from full recovery, one unrevealed card from everything.* What if he not only secured a house for Mary but took these men for enough to ensure a church for his mother? The Dane had drawled, "Those games are too rich for my blood," making John determined to prove he could cross the finish line, to where everyone he cared about would have everything. This also went against his assurance to Mary that he would let go of his brain's preoccupation with cash.

At an hour of starvation, when the Chicago men and Jeduthan showed no signs of craving a late supper, starlight impaled the mermaid's chest, and John's winnings dribbled away, near to depletion, before veering sharply upward to leave him where he started, right at even. The exhaustion overtaking him felt monstrous.

The sun tapped the moon's shoulder to send it on its way—it was already Sunday—as he plunged down a greased chute toward the bottom. The string-tie man was a bully, going all in on every bet, forcing everyone to follow his lead, barely concealing his contempt that John should have an invitation. John was the rabbit hopping near the trap, as daft as Isaac had seemed back when he displayed actual gold. In the company of men of limitless resources, a chorus infected John's bleary mind: *I'll get it all back, Mary, for You and for me.* He left to use the water-closet for a third time, passing by the tiled spider over a barren fireplace. People murmured in the reaches of this tremendous house, a wife and children who allowed Jeduthan to game with associates to buy rocking horses, copper fittings, and undersea designs in glass thickly bubbled and blurring what now appeared to be snowfall. John went massively up in the next rounds, seeing every bet, raising it.

In the final match called as dawn burst—crack of day, yolk poured—Jeduthan ended with a nothing hand. Two Chicago men, including the one with a diamond stuck in his tie, had random face cards and dropped out, too.

In the showdown, the waxed-mustache man revealed a nine, for a jack of spades high and pair of nines. He was ahead one thousand, the lead of the night. The string-tie man smiled for the first time in these godforsaken hours and displayed a pair of queens. Same configuration that saved John's mother from the gallows, queen of Portugal, queen of England.

John eyed him and revealed his hand: king of clubs and king of hearts hidden. He raked in a solid, substantial final win. He would be leaving with two hundred dollars beyond the five hundred he had risked.

"Gentlemen, it is the Sabbath," said Jeduthan. Winnings secured, they stood as one. Outside, with Rammelkamp's spire visible, the men in their capes and top hats headed to carriages, though the man with the diamond pin in his tie paused to remark to John, "You play well, son, and you had luck, but you weren't in your element. Word to the wise." He tipped his hat and bid him a fine if wintry day.

Stewing with annoyance, John figured he was hallucinating until it became apparent that yes, the Reverend Isaac Unthank was strolling toward him. God Almighty.

"Alves," said Isaac, fists shoved into pockets of a thick coat. "Word reached me that I was painted in an unjust light. I never mentioned to anyone about Nikka correcting your illustrious prose. I heard about it from Sarah, but who cares? The shared-chapel-garden thing is sour for me now." He grinned. "I can't help it if I'm so charming that the riotously cheery Miss Brink begged me to run her edifice. But I'm innocent of scheming with her. She is the spy who extracted usable facts from Nikka. Why Nikka would give her Brinkshipness the time of day is yet another piquant stitch in God's rich tapestry."

"Why do you follow me everywhere?"

"I was preaching during the Dane's Friday match, which earned my heave-ho. I've repented of my sinful ways and aim to inspire others, you included. I asked if you'd been around, and he suggested toting my Bible here. Well, he recommended I do something else with my Bible that I shall not repeat. I was loath to call upon your home or place of employ. I've been out in this snow a spell."

"The Dane had no business betraying me like that."

"Don't get ruffled up. He's a worse snake than I am."

"If you're here to pester me about my mother being your ally, I'm not responsible for what I may do."

"Alves, your mother insisted God asked her to build a place high into the sky where He could live, and she wanted my help. I swear. I'll profess again, your sister is of enchanting aspect. Nor do I object to a bit of the sauce such as she concocts. But her romantic interest in me is nil."

"It's the Lord's Day, Unthank. Don't you have plans?"

"Want to hear what my father forced me to do when I was nine? Come on, I'll walk you partway home." Isaac spoke to the air more than to John. "I had a wolfhound named Gracie, and he ordered me to shoot her. She wasn't old or ill. My lesson was that I needed toughening up, and anyone can shoot a dog that needs putting out of its misery."

Feeling black stubble sprouting on his face, John stared at Isaac.

"Took me five bullets to kill her. My mother left him that day. But guess what? She left me with him. There are other episodes, too numerous and luscious to relate."

"Jesus Christ."

Isaac shrugged, and after they trudged farther, he said, "I taught your mother the cloud trick. Want to learn it? You decide what you want to erase overhead. Believe you'll do it, and stare at a cloud until it's gone." He pointed upward at a bank of white, chockful of sleet, shaped like a lamb.

"This sounds Catholic. Ma didn't object?"

"Your mother is searching for answers that embrace us all. She is attempting to conquer her own tendency, shared by the many, to distrust papists."

Isaac stared at the cloud, and God wiped it away. The fleece got shorn, the body eaten. He wished the lamb away in under a minute. From his pocket, John extracted five twenty-dollar gold pieces, half his night's profits. He said, "Take it. It's over twice what I took off you that time you went crazy about. I owe the Dane twenty, and I've got that for him. I'm buying peace between you and me. Got it? That's the reason for this."

"I accept," said Isaac. He handed over a small coin of his own. "Get your mother that cheese she likes. I used to bring it to my sermons so I could give it to her."

"Probably the reason she tolerated you."

"Probably." Isaac shook John's hand, and said, "Give up money sport. The gate to life is narrow, and few find it, and we are punished for seeking easeful ways, Matthew chapter seven. Know why a chapel on that lot doesn't matter? I'll have to join the army like everybody else or get called a lily liver. My idea of a haven for non-conscriptionists was one of my franker absurdities." With a wave backward over his head, he left John near the farrier's.

The wind was sweeping over the poppy-mallow cowering in its burial spots in the prairie until spring, when it would deposit perfumed skeins over the separate quadrants of town, Little Africa southwest of the square where the freedmen dwelled, the Patch with the Irish, and northward into Madeira Hill and west over College Hill.

Even John's beloved Jacksonville, for all its vibrant forward-thinking, was divided, and divided again.

NOT KNOWING WHEN,
OR WHETHER EVER, I MAY RETURN

January 27, 1861

Miss Freitas. Your attachment to my brother is cause for concern, as you already live with a man of means and by all appearances in a state of sin. Your demands would remain excessive even if you ceased your unseemly arrangement and entered wedlock with my brother. I do not approve of a Catholic joining a family that has suffered from Rome's stranglehold. Confine your lusts to where you exist.

Sincerely, Rui Alves

—

2 February 1861

Dearest John,

At last I saw—I located The Morgan Journal—that you won that contest, and I sent congratulations, how proud I am, sweetheart!—parabéns!—but you have not replied. I almost got on the train, but no matter her change of heart, I dread your mother's reaction to seeing me. I have also received—sorrow cracks me, I am made brittle by winter, by our nation's "divided house," by so much—your brother's violent disapproval. Hatred from a brother—who seldom shows himself!—shall not keep me from you, but it grieves me. I regret destroying his poisonous note; I should have confronted him with it.

Shipments of berries are on the rise, though soon the demand will be more than we can supply, an enviable problem! Except I am no good in the world, each upset or harsh word spins me. What a nervous-nellie you are, Mary, said Nell Clark (our neighbor). I've befriended someone named Lucy Brattle, who took me to buy a "grave cover" for Papa. Such a thing, John, what a thing! It is a blanket of fibers that looks like grass so a slab does not crack in winter.

Pet is truly in love! Henry Kingsley, whom you glimpsed from afar at the fair, takes her on walks at dinner-hour. I am happy for her, despite loneliness stealing over me. Henry lives nearby. I wish you did too, but I boast of your work at one of the best schools of its kind in this country. Henry also wants to return from wartime before marrying Pet. An uncle in Los Angeles owns a paper company and has offered him an office job—he is now a stablehand—and Pet speaks of going where it is warm. I try not to be saddened by how much I will miss her.

On the tablecloth I am stitching, I did cutwork to look like your sound-machine. I am not sure it is a good likeness. I stitched a plow that Lucy assured me looked like the real thing, but I think she was just being a friend.

Sometimes in the garden in Funchal, when Papa ran errands, I thought I would die waiting for his return. Once I wept when he arrived home, and he said, "Cat-Cat, there's an extra happiness that can only happen when someone goes away and then comes back." John, so many people I love have left me or will leave me. Do you agree that the longer one is away, the greater the joy upon a reunion? Then please come see me, so we can share that. Please, I have written several times. Are you angry with me? Maria-Cat

She ferried the note to the post office. Edward went there frequently, and it was tempting to ask if he might be confiscating anything addressed to her, but such a pointed accusation would draw blood, and subterfuge did not seem in his nature. On the other hand, things were strained, owing, he reported, to "the worsening chatter about you."

The post office was run by Taylor Seeger, whose pocked skin resembled overcooked custard. He exercised his adeptness at rolling his eyes as she handed over her letter. After tucking it into a mailbag while droning that there was nothing for her, he suggested she quit besieging him daily.

"Are you sure, Mr. Seeger? From John Alves. In Jacksonville."

"Young men have more on their minds these days than tail-chasing."

People fidgeted behind her as she asked, "Would you check again, Mr. Seeger?"

His reply was a blur of unpleasantness.

She accepted Edward's invitation to dine while Perpetua was on one of her strolls with Henry Kingsley. While observing her reflection in the consommé, she was about to announce, *Edward, everyone has moods, certainly I do. Business is good, and there's no need to apologize for your shortness with me these weeks,* but he beat her to a declaration by unleashing, "I want you to consider moving to Addy's."

She asked if Gertrude might be back, if Gertrude demanded this.

"No. On my own, Mary, I can sense that it's inappropriate to have on my property a single woman to whom I was engaged. With Perpetua Roderick now absent many evenings, the gossip has increased."

"Move out?" Had John's recent win of a thousand dollars changed him? Interpreting his silence was mystifying. She pushed aside the shallow dish of pale liquid. She hated consommé, a refinement of scalded bones. Edward set down plates of pork chops, and she heard the pig as a knife rammed into it. They let loose a distinctive hell-screech when mortally wounded. In Madeira, pigs were eaten but also kept as pets, and the gardens where they roamed bloomed more brightly, azaleas, favas, hydrangeas. She whispered, "But you said it was worse having me gone than having me around."

"I did, and I'm sorry to go in circles about it. I'd pay for your lodgings."

Alarm pushed her off a cliff, no landing in sight. "What about Perpetua?"

"She is invisible to gossipers. She can stay here or go with you. I'll pay for her as well." He sawed into his pork chop. "I endure constant taunting, often mild, sometimes not. You don't get any of that, much less the brunt of it. At Addy's, you'll have friends while you wait for your beau to return from God knows what and God knows when. We'll figure out what that implies when it happens."

Meaning: if he comes home alive. The soup and the meat were making her nauseated. She said, "Please, don't send me away, Mr. Moore."

"For God's sake, stop, Mary, and don't call me Mr. Moore. I'm not a judge sentencing you to jail. You can go a few blocks and have company while honoring basic tenets of social decorum. You haven't touched a thing. Dear, you're too thin. I'm only asking that you consider how our circumstance is intolerable."

But she did not provide him with an answer, even after Taylor Seeger forked over a devastating letter:

February 12, 1861

Mary, I cant write much b/c I sprained my hand, Rui is taking dictation. Hes a "wise-acre" hence his leaving out contractions & using "&" etc. so Youll know this is from me, he says, also the capital Y for You. Ive grown close to my family, as I fear the call will soon come to fulfill my solemn duty. Did You go to the station to wave goodbye to Mr. Lincoln yesterday? My mother fell on some ice & sprained her ankle & needs constant attention. That will keep me here & Im afraid she not only "slipped" on the street but she has "slipped" back into anti-Catholic talk. Best not to see You for a while. John.Alves.

What she replied:

17 February 1861

John, I'm posting this to your school rather than risk having it fall into the hands of your family. I'm sorry you hurt yourself, but I'm shocked at your note. Rui has made it clear he does not approve of me. Did you check what he wrote after your "dictation"? I'm less surprised, alas, that your mother has withdrawn her wish to embrace me, but how is this different from how we began, and do you not recall saying you would, should it come to this, choose me? How infuriating that she persists in disputing something that is a matter of my birth! Come see me, as I am far too hesitant to run to you for the purpose of humiliating myself. Yes, I went out in the rain to wave farewell to Mr. Lincoln, who somberly told us that he did not know if he might ever see us again. It felt like an omen about you. Tell me I am wrong.—Mary

What he wrote:

20 February 1861

Maria-Cat, Im confused by a note from You today saying You might be planning to go on a trip & therefore You cannot see me . . . ? Im losing count of the times Ive written to tell You so many things, about a contest "win" that was judged as a tie w/2nd place busybody Sarah Brink due to Nikka's aid w/my grammar ONLY, but never mind sweetheart I won, therell be a garden & $500, it doesnt seem right not to celebrate w/You but last I heard You wanted me to give You time & Ill do that but our time is sad to say

*running short as war is certain now. Rui surprised me by
saying that Nikka & he are not likely to have a love story
so pls could I have one WITH YOU "for the rest of us"!!
I love You, I want to pull You out of the Well b/c I think
Youre in it, & weeks are passing us by. John.Alves.*

*And what she wrote upon receiving no reply to her February 17 com-
plaint:*

4 March 1861

John, Maybe the upset in my last note offended you. I am
once again posting this to your school. Four, five times a
week, how I write, and yet no answer comes to calm me! Mr.
Seeger at the post office thinks me quite mad. If the injury to
your hand persists—that sounds odd, but the wording is so
clearly yours—can you not ask Nikka for help? Don't you
see that I'm reluctant to go to your home and afraid to show
up at your classroom? Is this setting yourself apart from me
due to a fear about soldiering, a distancing of yourself to
prepare for the uncertainty to come? Can you not see the
better wisdom of letting me comfort you in that, convince
you that my love will help you survive?

A shop in Alton placed a large order, and—oh, why
pretend to care about berries, when all I can think about is
how far you have gone from me! What did I do? Why push
me away? If you are upset because I live on Ward's property, then tell me, so I can assure you that I love you. Have
you met someone else? You mentioned once an American girl
named Julietta.

The Wide-Awakes keep marching through. Our story
seems small compared to the nation's terror, and yet war
is a reminder that daily kindness is the least we can do. I
would not have guessed you to be cruel. Or are you hurt,
in a hospital? Once in New York, Papa went missing, and
Mrs. Jamison and I searched until we found him. All will

be forgiven if something has befallen you. But I wrote to
Nikka asking this, and she did not reply either. I am at a
loss. If I did not feel abandoned and afraid, I would go, as
I say, to Jacksonville and insist on an explanation, but I am
too heartbroken to go through much more. Your birthday is
one week from today. What am I to do?—Mary

What he received:

March 11, 1861

Dear John,

Ward and I work night and day. We spend many dinners
together, and our business grows by leaps and bounds!
Happy Birthday. My hand does not hurt as much, but Pet
is writing as I pack in haste, dictating to her, and she'll
post this. I am heading to Alton for the foreseeable future.
Pet will manage the greenhouse and yard, with assistance
from a young woman named Dilly Witherspoon, who fled
the horrors in Kansas. Edward and I have many opportu-
nities in Alton. Forgive me for going there, especially as the
threat of war grows and time seems more pressing. But we feel
we should meet shop owners, rail workers, and the like.
Forgive me for not being able to pass up this opportunity.
With affection—Mary.

What he wrote:

26 março 1861

Dear Mary,

I was about to conquer my shyness at showing up at "Yr"
house for fear of running into Edward. But now I learn
Youre not even there? Where are You to stay in Alton? Is
it necessary, when our time is so short, for You to be there
bodily? Im obligated to teach during the week but would

take a train to Alton on Saturday if I knew where to find You. Your note took me as they say "aback" b/c Ive begun each day to think: Today I should go to her, or she will come to me, & the day passes, & the next one. Im sending this note possibly in vain, b/c it would require Pet to collect it, open it, & write to me herself w/Your location.

Theyre preparing the Fairgrounds for our training. Youre pushing me aside to lessen our approaching saudade, to test whether we can love each other during the absence to come, or else Youre realizing that You cannot wait for a return that now seems farther in the future than wed hoped. Please dont let that be so, Mary.

The Secesh adopted their "Constitution" on my birthday, happy birthday to me. I thought Youd show up, that You & Nikka had put together a surprise, & You would sweep away the anguish about why You havent replied to my notes, & the answer would make sense. Ive suspected of course the mails are bad, but every single thing not going where it should? And then to hear You are in another city without telling me where & for how long. From Frank & Elizabeth I received Traite des Maladies de l'oreille et de l'audition by Jean Marc Gaspard Itard. Itard pioneered the use of a copper ring to make hearing devices more acute & I added a copper ring to my Machine. I wanted to show You!

On my 23rd b'day, I had a gift for You, a perfume made by Rui out of ghost orchids he found in the prairie, a miracle, it isnt their season! But he found a lot & pressed them, & mixed that with "labdanum," an oil from a cistus shrub, though Rui said it can also be combed out of the beards & thighs of goats. He added oil extracted from bergamot, which cost him mightily . . . but Mary, he has made a fortune! I spoke to him once again about You, & he remains very happy for us. Something happened to him in Trinidad that Im sure is romantic in nature, & it has made him a loner but softhearted, I couldnt bear to tell him I havent seen You in a while. He doesnt care about money & insisted I take 1500 dollars, Mary. Mary, I want to use it to buy a truly wonderful house for You. (My prize money for my garden was reduced to 500, I told You that in an earlier note, & Ill explain how that happened, but now Im as rich as Ive ever dreamt of being, sorry to talk about $.)

What if I buy a house in Springfield? I can live in it w/ You when I return. Ill take the train daily if I must, or I'll get another job. I cant live w/o you. I ran to You before & Ive longed to do that again, but I CANT IF YOURE IN ALTON W/O SAYING WHERE & its bad enough that You said Youre busy night & day—the "night" part troubled me, & I sense Youre in a state that would not welcome me. Ive never felt such heartbreak, Im out of my mind. If Youre falling in love w/ Edward, Ill be destroyed but let me know the truth. John.Alves.

What she received:

March 30, 1861

Mary, Rui is back to helping, my hand got infected. Ive hidden myself from You all this time out of shame at the scandal: I was caught cheating in that contest. A mercy, they let me keep ½ the award. (Nikka helped me prepare my submission, despite the rule that we alone are responsible for our entries.)

Then I barely escaped w/ my skin (& a small profit) after large-stakes gambling w/ Chicago elite types. I miss You but now it seems Im being reassigned for the oncoming month, to a school for the deaf starting up in that city of slaughterhouses and near occasions of sin. I dont know how Ill avoid gaming now that I know of these men. Sorry Ill be in Chicago & unable to see You.

Im driven to all this by the thought that I cannot begin to equal what You enjoy with Mr. Moore & Ive decided You must put an end to tormenting 2 men by marrying the

one w/the greater ability to satisfy all You seem to need.
I love You but I must face truth as I further face my near
summoning to war. John.Alves.

She staggered into the Illinois House for Women and Girls, to
the same room with the Frozen Charlotte doll and Connie Partridge
crying herself to sleep on the other side of a thin wall. Connie's husband
had abandoned her for Nevada, making her a silver widow. Mary rose
the next morning and walked to the cemetery as if summoned. Was
this due to her feeling dead herself, or was it because being in a con-
fined space echoing with the sobbing of an unseen woman would kill
her? She was only clear about needing her father.

She encircled Papa's headstone with her arms. A battalion of ants
marched over her wrist, a writhing bracelet. If he were alive, he would
be running the greenhouse with her, and if she married Ward, her
father and she would claim triple, quadruple God's earliest vision for
her. Papa would have had a guest room. They would have discovered
the delights of Florida—postwar, so *heated,* Papa, look at our fields, at
us, and there is my husband. She might even be of a forgiving disposition to welcome John some year, back from his heroics, free of vices or
not, vows broken large and small, his discarding of her absolved, allowing them to marvel at the era when they had been so awfully young.

Her better grasping of what Edward called "the gossip" occurred
when she decided to buy saltwater taffy at Watson's Confectionary for
her fellow residents in the boardinghouse. As Mary exited the shop,
a woman with a hat the size of a tugboat grabbed her arm and whispered, "So you're the vixen. Quite a morsel, aren't you?" She had one
of those smiles that revealed her gums.

"Ma'am?" Whispers swirled into miniature tempests, and the stares
from passersby found Mary as their target, especially the glaring from
one couple and two ancient women. A man grabbed himself in a way
that shocked her.

The boat-hatted woman said, "I'm all for letting men caress our
knees under the lap robe. We women must win however we can."

Gales of derision pursued Mary as she dashed back to hide at Addy's.
A last effort, a last brave push to shout at John for cheating, for

gambling, for breaking so many promises, to exclaim she would forgive all if he professed that he loved her still: She unearthed his address from the roster of those who had been invited to her engagement party, took the train to Jacksonville, and ventured to the Alves house. But no one was home. She waited; no one came.

At the institution for the deaf, they thought, at first, she was seeking a job, now that women were being hired to replace the army volunteers. They asked how she had missed the military camp on the Morgan County Fairgrounds.

Not far from his school, men swarmed, mostly young ones, smoking and rolling dice. Buttons gleamed on their jackets. One leered at her so avidly it seemed to strip her of clothing. She bellowed, "John? John!" Two men with his name approached, asking who she was. She hastened the width and depth of the grounds, through this gigantic male party with meat boiling in cauldrons, and when she tripped, a commander—she could not identify the ranks—helped her up, regarded her as kindly as her father might, and said, "Young lady, this is no place for you. If you've got a feller here, he's lost in the crowd, so I hope you said your goodbyes." To which she replied, "Yes, we've said goodbye."

THE PECULIAR FATE OF
LONG-BILLED CURLEWS

JOHN STOOD AT THE COURTHOUSE FOR FRANK AND ELIZABETH Hampton after a delay, because many couples were tying the knot prior to the soldiers mustering in. George and Teresa Meline hushed Hugo for protesting that he was old enough to go off and fight, too. As John handed over the rings, he shook off distraction for the sake of his friend. Elizabeth wore a dark jacket and light dress of a material that Mary would easily identify, having first explained why she had gone to Alton, but now she was back, and all was well. He pictured her laughing, him laughing, any obscuring nonsense swept away.

He had even written to Perpetua to ask where exactly Mary had gone, but Pet had not replied. He suffered with the vision of Mary and Edward at some distance together.

Everyone ate the iced fruitcake that Teresa had baked after reading that it was the traditional wedding cake of the British royals. Frank told him, "I still think we won't be gone long, Alves, and you just need to find her, and say goodbye, and you'll be fine." Frank shook his friend's shoulder. John needed to reclaim alertness if he hoped to learn how to live outdoors, to use a gun, and to shoot the boys born to other mothers.

After the firing upon Fort Sumter in mid-April, Frank kissed his new wife farewell and reported with John to Camp Duncan in Jacksonville, with Max Jeffers from the school for the deaf joining them. When John went to thank Rui again for giving him a jackpot of money from the Ghost Orchid perfume sales, and to ask if he planned to join the army, he found a note affixed to the door of the shuttered perfume shop: "Gone to War, in an Ohio troop—Rodrigo J. Alves. Ghost perfume in Ray Silva's store."

It was already destroying John that Sammy and Claire had sobbed while hugging him. It was another mistake to visit the site of construction on that Edward-donated lot, a miniature greenhouse appearing next to a cursed chapel. It seemed so hope-dashed.

On John's papers, he recorded his birthplace as New York City.

In mid-May, Company 14-A of Illinois received orders that they would be moving out to Missouri. John visited home and brushed Mother's hair, a mat of white wires. Her translucent fingernails had red dots under them like the ones egg-candlers look for to detect life. On their table was the Sound Machine, outfitted with a new roller and crank. She said into the feather, *"Falai comigo, O Meu Senhor,"* but nothing happened, no syllable was caught. *Maybe God doesn't speak Portuguese anymore, Ma.*

Her forehead had collapsed into lines spaced like a musical staff, and her thoughts were spilling out to where he could almost hum the notation of her anguish. She wailed, "Forgive me!" and lamented anew having made an issue about Catholics. *I don't want to die without seeing you again.* He replied, "You'll live a long while, Ma, and I'll come back. Mary and I have gone apart from each other, but I have faith it's not forever."

"It is my fault."

"One day," he said, kneeling, grasping her hand, "I'll make sure you have at least a chapel, and Mary and I will wed there, and meanwhile, you'll go to the library at my school. You can look at the Kircher book, and when I come home, we'll copy his eavesdroppers. We haven't tried to figure out how to hear through solid walls."

She pressed her Bible, the family Bible, into his possession, and he kissed her goodbye and left quickly, because she was working not to dissolve into lamenting.

Rabbits raced through the sagebrush as Nikka tended their garden, and she echoed their mother's hope, promising, "I won't die before you show up to wave me on, John, wherever you decide to be." A time lapse overtook her face, giving him a vision of his Nikka grown old. Upon her saying she deserved her aloneness, he replied, "Nikkie, Miguel hit you all the time. Please, lie about him when you meet someone right for you."

"I'm sorry things fell apart with Mary."

"Things got in our way, but that won't be forever."

He was due to leave on Saturday, the twenty-fifth day of May. Elizabeth Hampton Meline went on book business to Springfield, and unabashed Lizzy took it upon herself, without telling her new husband and his best friend, to find "the largest greenhouse in the city, on a triple-lot in Aristocracy Hill," where she hoped to locate Perpetua for an address but instead found Mary, ill-looking but gathering berries. Lizzy conveyed John's desperation to find her. She had thought, based on the note John had shown her, that Mary might be still in Alton.

Elizabeth reported to John that for some odd reason, Mary had gotten it into her head that he was in Chicago and not of a state of mind to seek her. Elizabeth had suggested to Mary that she meet him in Springfield's American House on the Thursday two days before he would muster out.

John appeared at the hotel at the appointed hour. The gathering-place had breakfronts and polished buffets, with the legs in dishes filled with cobalt-water to kill the ants. It was a shrine to Turkish splendor, the wallpaper and fixtures proving that the Midwest was not drab. Hordes of men in Union dress, women clinging to them, filled the massive rooms. John wore civilian clothing to reaffirm that every second since meeting in Funchal, and everything since, including their many Saturdays at the Lincolns', would carry them through to normal life, to the time of his return.

Silk songbirds nested in her hat. She wore a springtime coat embroidered with Chinese fans, and a midnight-blue dress stitched with birds-of-paradise. She was already deep inside the dining room with its swirl-laden carpet, wandering and searching. She looked bereft, worried, oh darling girl, it's all right now.

She veered to face him. No distance was felt in getting to her. Her face was in his hands, and he saw himself reversed in her eyes, preserved tiny but whole.

"Mary." He could not utter, "Where have you been? Why?" without it sounding like an accusation.

"Why did you go to Chicago?" she asked.

"I didn't. I haven't been there at all. Are you back from Alton? We wasted so many weeks! Months. I leave day after tomorrow, but we'll be good, we'll be fine."

She was fully in his arms. They had been only in training for apartness. How does a young man die inside a minute, so it is as forever-lasting as death? She whispered, "John." *Memorize her,* not just how she looks but how she feels, her hat fell, leave it there. He wished he had brought her some Ghost Orchid perfume, and his money from that and from his prize-chopped-in-half, so he could say, "Buy us a house, and write to me of it, from it." He said, "I'll be home soon, and I love you."

She answered, "I thought you'd left me." They kissed. Men and women, in forms of farewell, were in tides surging and ebbing.

They spoke about letters, and Alton and Chicago, about him writing to suggest she would be better suited to wed the man able to provide her with more. *What are you talking about?* The notes they had received were few, and abhorrent, not the flood of anxious ones they had genuinely produced. They looked at each other's hands, and truth descended with pealing thundercracks: No injuries, no need for Pet or Rui to write on anyone's behalf, which had sounded not completely unbelievable only because it was more incredible that anyone would go to such lengths to destroy them.

"It's a nice day in May, let's go for a walk," said John, and he knew—he was clear then, holding on to Mary—that someone had wallowed in an entertainment of not merely keeping them apart but of turning them against one another.

Mute with trepidation, they struck out past majestic dwellings and businesses to traverse where the natural world bordered the city. Rich loam lapped over the road, baked in peaks. Pink-rayed coneflowers poked through. He pointed out a long-billed curlew, astonished, because he thought gunners had wiped them clean out of Illinois. They were wanderers from the shore and wetlands that appeared in unexpected habitats—trusting birds, easy to lure, with a flock prone to staying by a downed comrade, even while hunters hooted and closed in and mowed them down. Mary averred to this being equal parts sweet—the staying part, the trying-to-save part—and horrific.

They quit postponing a figuring-out of who might have wished them the most grevious damage. He said, "Mary, we wrote constantly but heard nothing back except off-putting things."

"An awful letter from Rui warned me to stay away. I wrote to tell you that."

"He wishes us happiness. Mary, he mentioned you by name, wondering what had happened to you and telling me he wanted a love story in our family, and I was the only one likely to have it. Rui never utters falsehoods."

"I should have guessed those strange things weren't from you, John. But everything was in your style. Contractions the way you do them, and the shape like a treble clef that means 'and,' and all the rest. The strange period you put between your first name and last. As if you alone could be directing someone to write like that, as proof it was from you."

Who was the villain? Someone who had seen John's writing or knew someone at the post office in Jacksonville or Springfield. It could not have been his mother. She could not write English well enough, and she wanted to make amends. Certainly not Nikka, who loved them. Perpetua? Impossible. No. Maybe? No.

"Edward," said John.

This put her near tears, and she glanced away.

"That wouldn't be like him," she said, tucking up near John. "But I don't know. I argued with a woman named Dottie Willis who hates foreigners. I backtalked her."

"I wouldn't put this past some rabid Presbyterian, or the anti-rebaptism crowd, but I doubt they'd know my writing or every secret. You've mentioned someone named Maud, that she knows everything about everyone. Would that include my brother?"

"But she'd like nothing better than to have me run away with someone. She was engaged to Edward before and would want to push you and me together. Someone named Gertrude wanted him, too. It makes more sense to drive me toward you, to get rid of me." Mary was beginning to cry. "Did you gamble after promising you wouldn't? With rich men from Chicago? You cheated, in that contest? That's what an ugly letter told me."

It dawned on him, the identity of the culprit. "No, no," he said, glad suddenly. Everything was clear. None of the women around Edward fit the right bill. He explained there had been only minor, touch-up help from Nikka on his essay, all innocent, but the second-place finisher had bent that toward her purposes.

He held her hand and felt her melancholia enter him. "But I did break a vow by attending a gaming match with men of means. Forgive me again, Mary, though I don't deserve it. You." But there was only one person aware of that as well as the misadventure with the contest, and that person was not Edward. Edward knew about the contest, since he donated the lot. They had faced one another—he would describe that grim scene one day!—but Edward had no knowledge of John's card-playing. "I've guessed who tried to ruin us, Mary." Acquiring John's writing style would be an easy matter after intercepting his real letters.

"John, I have to tell you about—"

"It's Isaac. Isaac. He's been trouble from the start. I thought we'd made amends." He told her about the cloud trick, about hearing of Isaac's appalling childhood and giving him some gains from that match with the high-society men. Isaac had heard about it and tracked him down, an occasion when they had discussed the mishap with the contest.

Confused at her resistance when he bent toward kissing her, he gabbed that Isaac had seemed genuine. Buying peace to the tune of half the winnings from gaming had seemed worth it to be done with feuding. "The mystery is solved, Mary. Isaac is always up to no good. Please don't look so sad. The war will be short, and he'll be in the army. I'll write to you, and he can't harm us anymore, and I'll come back. He robbed us of some months but not of our lives. I love you with all my heart."

But she refused to embrace him, and when she told him why, his screaming shook birds from a cottonwood as he staggered backward. How was he expected to recover from what she was saying? He tore away, shouting that he never wanted to see her or hear from her again.

NOW I LAY ME DOWN TO SLEEP

MARY'S WEDDING ON MAY THE FIRST HAD BEEN DEW-DAMP, FULL OF
the wet breeding of most dawns. She had entered a bed with
strawberry-rocks to gather a bouquet of calla lilies with their orange
prongs. Edward would deliver her with affection to an elevated fate,
and Papa had given his blessing. John himself had urged this upon her.
Yes, one day she would forgive him, would be able to see how *being
scared of marriage,* along with *fearing war,* along with *fear of wounding
a mother,* along with his *wrong-headed notions of who she was and what
she needed,* had been too much. She must at least pretend to face facts
and dared not lose the man who dwelled where she did, who was circling an ultimatum. And she did love Edward, she did.

She had exited Addy's Illinois House, entered Ward's study, the
ring back on her finger, and said to him, "All right, Edward."

She had laid a hand on his head, because suddenly he had been
kneeling and gripping her skirts, temple pressed to her middle, his
scalp visible through his blond locks, as if he had cut his height in
half in order to make her view the rapid approach of the baring of his
crown. *I can't be wounded again, Mary. We aren't the world's best Catholics, but I could never endure divorce. It's not wonderful to feel second-best.
But if it means you, I'd take fourth-best, fifth.*

Perpetua had worn a wheat-colored frock and had helped Mary into her gown, beige-white as if dipped in weak tea. "So many buttons!" Perpetua had commented. Mary's veil had been Madeiran lace, Ward having found a refugee who needed to sell it.

In the Catholic church before the priest, Edward had awaited her, fretting because his suit was gray, the color of the enemy, and she had assured him he looked handsome. Addy Oscar had worn a white blouse and purple skirt, and Lucy Brattle had a borrowed green dress. Nell Clark, having sent over the diamond earrings that Mary wore, had been attentive. Sprays of gladioli had beautified the altar. The groom was thirty-one and subdued. An orchid from the greenhouse had been tucked behind her ear, though a tropical flower recalled John. She had turned twenty-one.

To be Catholic usually meant candles, and organ music to vibrate the chest, and frankincense. But this had been a wartime wedding. He had pledged to honor her and not part from her until death, and she had done the same. After they had been pronounced man and wife, he had kissed her with an urgency that shot through her tendons.

The buffet at the house had been thanks to Nell: breads, cheeses, and grapes. Addy had baked the cake, filled with pineapple. Mary had not been fated to recall much from the conversations, other than Perpetua remarking, "Write to Mrs. Jamison. I can't wait to see what she sends as a wedding gift." Pet's Henry had already left for the war.

Mary had given her husband a glass-star ornament for their future first Christmas; he had bought her bolts of jacquard. Mary had hugged Perpetua with a fierceness near to what felt like a holding of John, an intensity she suspected she would fail to produce with her husband. But what could she do, if Edward deserved a decision and John had not only left her here but was about to enter battlefields as if to forget her even more?

The wedding night had involved Ward removing her veil and orchid as she stepped from her pinching shoes, and he had lightly held her shoulders and kissed her, and she had kissed him back. He'd said, "I'm happy to be your husband, Mary," and she'd mentioned her happiness, too. The lights had been extinguished as they undressed, and they had laughed from anxiety. Together in his bed, Edward Aloysius Moore had reached for her hand, and she had gripped it as if they were drifting through space rather than resting on a firm mattress he would later replace with a soft-down one at her request. Inside herself, she had recited the child's prayer that Lucy had taught her in the Illinois House when Mary had gone into the Well, about now I lay me down to sleep, and if she did not awaken, God bless everyone she knew.

To her surprise—he must have consulted Perpetua—he had wished her Portuguese pink dreams, saying this in English, and she had been ineffably moved. She had kissed him, and his ardor had astonished her. Her open mouth had felt his tongue. He had climbed onto her, with enough arm strength not to press on her with his full weight. She had to push aside an image of John, because she did not wish even a mental flickering of him to watch, and because his dismissal of her hurt too much and was unfair to her spouse. There had been pain, sharp pain; she had winced. When Edward lay beside her again and said, "Wonderful, Mary," she had smiled but permitted herself the outrageously indecent thought that John would have known—though few men were reputed to hold such knowledge—how to please her, and please her over and over, but enough, that was done.

She had slept only fitfully on the rise and fall of a chest so thin it had almost killed her, how fragile as a drum it seemed.

A MOTHER'S LAMENT

SERAFINA, IT IS NOT YET YOUR TIME TO COME TO ME.

My boys hold rifles to kill Your children. I am my daughter's burden. Let me fly home to You.

———

GOOD AND FAITHFUL SERVANT, I HAVE A MESSAGE YOU REFUSE TO HEAR!

That's not true! Where is Your Voice? Upon the Rock of myself, You have not built Your church. Is Your absence because I did not welcome Mary in time, did not forgive soon enough a faith I've been taught to find pompous?

———

SERAFINA! LISTEN!

(indecipherable)

What happened to Rui in Trinidad? That afternoon in the marketplace with its aroma of dates, when a stranger whispered in his teenaged ear. That's when Rui changed. Tell me what that man said.

—

SERAFINA, YOUR TASK IS TO FIND GRACE OUT IN THE WORLD. THE LORD SHALL preserve thy going out and thy coming in from this time forth.

( )
( )

I can't hear You. Send me to die in place of my sons.

Let me fix what I did to my son and Mary. She vanished from his life.

I thought of offering my heart to her too late. I ruined them.

I see a shadow of a person entering a place where letters are sent and where they arrive. I can't tell if it's a man or a woman, nor what age, though the person is unstooped. The crime is large. This sinner took my son's letters to Mary and Mary's letters to him and wrote fake notes, including one with Rui's name. Allow me to see who this is!

—

BELOVED SERVANT, YOUR EARTHLY WORK IS NOT DONE.
(indecipherable)

—

SERAFINA IS AWAKENED BY BIRDSONG AT THE HOUR SPLICING NIGHT onto day, a time of soldiers setting out, of women standing alone.

Nightbirds are traveling, a V of them.

This is the hour she was made for.

Five in the morning.

The sky is still a single black pearl so generous it lets all the white pearls crowd inside it, until it bulges with them and lets the white gleam through.

And then its skin breaks.

The Book of the Horsemen

BLACK, WHITE, SCARLET, SICKLY GREEN

Once upon a time, Dutch painters invented a curious way of making their floral masterpieces as real as possible. These highly detailed renderings required a massive number of hours to complete.

They waited for consecutive springs in order to copy only the freshest details of new life.

What strength to bide their time, to elevate waiting itself into an art.

SOWING SALT IN THE LAND OF SHILOH

6–7 APRIL 1862

THE SCRATCHING OF PENS SOUNDED LIKE A NEW SPECIES OF CRICKET. The Tennessee River sent gusts of spring air up the bluffs of Pittsburg Landing and over the hordes of boys ordered to jot notes of farewell. Having finished a letter to Mother and Nikka, John sat next to Frank, who was puzzling over what to report to Elizabeth. In nearly a year of service, the Illinois 14th had not exactly put their bravery to any test. While wintering in Otterville, John and Frank got awakened by an attack on their straw huts, only to find cows chewing their walls. That was as close as they had come to being under siege, and diarrhea was the main killer of the men they knew. At Forts Henry and Donelson, the biggest fights in Company A had been over whose turn it was to plunk down nineteen cents for a clean pack of playing cards—the suits were eagles, shields, stars, and flags. John never joined the games, not out of virtue but because it conjured Mary asking him not to gamble, whereas she had not bothered to gamble that he would return. The other half of his brain argued that she too had been a victim of deception. But had he responded by marrying someone? He had drifted from fury to upset to his current balance between hurt and disbelief.

Through these seasons without a home, often without a roof or floor, it helped to envision Mary in the alien tribe of the housed, to remind himself that men who smelled like rotting vegetables were his family. He loved Mortimer Rice's initial keenness to record each day, but after the same drills and weevil-infested meals, he began scrawling "DITTO!" in his pocket journal and then only: "D°!!!" Dexter Loomis was sharing apples bought from a sutler. It stayed a shock, the number of civilians alongside the traveling circus, the women offering their flesh or begging for laundry to wash for a few cents. The men could ill afford to send home anything from their army pay of thirteen dollars a month. Mary was in such comfort—he still winced at the flash images, glass flowers, a bed warmer with its long handle—that he was grateful how these women pushed her farther away, into a storybook castle.

Other companies were combined with theirs to form a 4th Division, one of six under General Ulysses S. Grant. Word from forward camps had it that the Secesh were battle-ready. The Union was trying to hold off until General Don Carlos Buell's Army of the Ohio arrived from Nashville, to combine with them in a mighty plow through the butternut-and gray-garbed traitors to advance on Corinth, where they would take vital rail crossroads, severing supply lines to the Confederacy.

Then: Victory! War's end. That was the rumor.

Frank paused over his letter to Elizabeth and asked, "Alves, should I say that after Corinth, we'll be heading home?"

"Don't make a promise before you can keep it. Just tell her you love her," said John. Along with writing goodbye letters, the soldiers were pinning their names and addresses inside their clothing, to identify their bodies.

"It feels wrong to have to say it." Frank handed John a hardtack cracker dripping with molasses.

"Describe Alonzo's painting lessons. Let her picture something decent." During their weeks stationed here, after a Maine schoolhouse donated easels and watercolors, Alonzo Gillespie taught them how to enhance reality by creating shadows. Striving to replicate peach blossoms let them pretend that soldiering was nothing more than allowing a liquid flower to flow from a brush.

Isaac Unthank was heading toward them, through the swarms of men. John tensed at this violation of their agreement to stay as far apart as possible. When the preacher-or-whatever-he-was had mustered in, John had beaten him—kicked him, punched him—in a rage. Frank sighed now, too.

Isaac held up both hands in surrender. A stone's throw away, he called out, "I come in peace." He edged near enough to stretch a hand toward John, who stared at it as Isaac said, "If I meet my Maker, Alves, I want to tell Him that you and I achieved an accord."

John countered with, "What you did isn't forgivable, Unthank. I want my hundred dollars back."

Isaac's hand dropped, but he grinned and rubbed his jaw. "My face paid for any misunderstandings, Alves. But I swear, before our collected brethren, I did not steal letters you or your lady-love posted, nor did I invent false ones, nor did I impersonate your perfume-crafting brother."

"Unthank." John was on his feet. "We've gone through why it's you." Any reminder of his last conversation with Mary—trodding through the swampy list of suspects, landing on the certainty of Isaac's guilt—seared him anew.

"I am an absolution-seeking sinner," said Isaac, "and I do things for want of cash, but I am falsely accused. I neither pilfered nor composed any missives."

If John pretended to accept this, would it get rid of his tormentor? He shook Isaac's hand as briefly as he could stand, and Isaac declared, "I detect a lack of sincerity, but this will have to do. I've been contemplating the river and feel afflicted with mal de mer. Might I ask you two of seafaring blood how to combat that?"

Frank said, "Stare at the horizon, you goddamn idiot, not straight down at the water."

Isaac doffed an invisible cap. "Thank you kindly."

As Isaac meandered toward the sutlers selling what could be last suppers, as men lined up at the cook's station, Frank indicated a chaplain with a bulging mail sack wending through the troops. It was a miracle that letters from nowhere could arrive in Springfield in only eight or ten days, and their responses from there to a soldier's outpost.

Frank said, "Write to her."

John gestured at the note to his mother and sister. "Already did. To them both."

"You know what I mean. She got scared, John. She got deceived by that bastard, same as you. Forgive her, or your soul won't be free." Frank held out a blue-tissue page.

What indeed might John say if Mary appeared as he lay dying?

Despite his best efforts to forget her, she still felt like someone meant to stretch him into whatever completion he was meant to have, as if he were a compacted accordion. He finished a letter to Mary Catherine Freitas Moore as the chaplain reached them, whereupon night neglected to descend gradually as it was created to do and abruptly dropped a curtain, its fabric moth-bitten by stars. Occasionally a light rose slightly: a soldier standing and carrying a lamp.

John stirred in the still-dark of morning, alerted by a noise like rainfall through foliage. Stepping from his tent, he did not feel any drops, but there came a rush—and it sounded like the very word "rush"—carrying sonic claps like thunder. Next thing he knew, everybody was jumping up and men in long johns were yelling and Colonel Cyrus Hall was catapulting onto his horse. The Secesh had launched an attack near the Shiloh church.

The 14th tossed up a breastwork on an elevated road, and an hour later the rain-sound grew louder until an enormous cloud expanding into a globe enveloped the woods and exploded outward. "Fire!" Colonel Hall hollered, and John yelled, "At what?" because there was only air white-thick as chowder, and Hall bellowed, "Just shoot!" A kid went down after complaining he lacked a forked branch to set his musket. John fired into the cloud. His haversack held Mother's Bible, and while ducking to stuff it into his shirt, a minié ball whistled where his head had been. A wing of his regiment scattered, jamming against the 25th Indiana, their own lines pushing backward to avoid getting trampled. Hall rode through the chaos and barked that the 14th was under orders to hold the line, and hold it they would or he would shoot them himself.

John lost sight of Frank.

Isaac, swallowed by smoke, was in the act of fleeing.

A bullet whizzed through John's right sleeve but failed to touch skin. Trying to contain the recoil of his rifle, he fired toward men like drones pouring from a hive, as if thinking of it—them—this way might help. A ball shot off his hat, and he rubbed his scalp and found blood. In a hail of bullets, a ricocheting one hit the Bible on his chest. Scaling to a ridge, Dexter Loomis yelled, "We'll get em, boys," then spun sideways, dead. The artillery cranked up, and the cannons blazed. A nick on John's ear was the fourth bullet to brush him, and as the whining from the propulsion of metal increased, he waved his arms with an instinct that survival meant warding off insects, and his rifle fell, and he tumbled as a torrent whizzed over him, and his mouth opened with screaming, but he heard nothing. Men spilled and shrieked that the new orders were to get back toward the river, otherwise it would be a massacre.

Everybody was hammered into a retreat. The fifth bullet to find him carved a groove in his left calf. Men toppled and bullets skidded over the back of one who died on top of someone yowling at him to get off. John grabbed the living one's arm and the dead boy rolled away, face rigid. Where was Frank? John's sleeve, his scalp, his Bible, his ear, his leg seeping blood. The choppy terrain made the companies look like tiers of ants scattering. He had never imagined losing. Were they losing?

His company mixed in with others by the river, and the gunpowder-fogs abated. Everyone's skin was blackened from shooting. Screaming swelled from the woods, out of a tale to warn children not to wander in darkness. A flute played "The Girl I Left Behind Me," but a man with his stomach oozing out begged, "Don't," as he collapsed dead, cradling his guts as if they formed a baby.

General Grant, ambushed that morning, had been driven back at the peach orchard and a thicket so dense probably as many men were killed by their brothers as by enemies. But thanks to men like the ones in the 14th, Grant was smoking a cigar where ravines were protecting his front and flanks, and when General Don Carlos Buell got here shortly, they would read the gospel to the rebs. The rebs were certain he would be delayed, so they had left off fighting and planned to finish the job the next morning. Mark Robertson said, "Don't fret, Alves. They cursed themselves by attacking on a Sunday."

John opened his shot-up Bible. The page was intact that recorded all family names and baptismal dates, including both of Mother's, the Catholic one and the Kalley-decreed one, along with the address in Madeira Hill, but the bullet had marred Revelations. He asked for the repose of the soul of Dexter Loomis and stood to search for Frank, but the severity of an arm tremor pulled him earthward. A boy cried out at a cannon noise that turned out to be, this time, a real thunderstorm.

John was awarded unconsciousness. In illuminated slow motion, caught on a magic-lantern slide, Dexter fell off a bridge made of vines. Mary leaned out a window of a cabin as snow swept past. John walked to her with his wounded leg and bleeding scalp, past the grandfather clock from Rui's perfume shop winding backward. She stretched her arms, but he could not get to them.

Evening surrendered to the bull's noon of midnight and then to daytime, and Colonel Hall brought word that Buell's army had indeed arrived. Together they numbered over fifty thousand. When General Grant unleashed a dawn attack, John's company surged to the front lines near Mulberry Field. As the firing and return volleys went on, Hall shouted that now was the hour for the men of the gallant 14th to screw their courage to the sticking point, and they would boast to their grandchildren of being in the vanguard led by Generals Hurlbut, Mc-Clernand, and Sherman. They flowed onward and got hewn down, but the enemy got hacked in wider patches. This felt like merely a trading of what had happened yesterday, and men expired, but John did not connect any one soldier with his specific bullets, though he recognized himself to be in the sea of blue commanding the slaughter. What felt oddest was lacking any instinct about whether one was winning or losing. That should be clearer, so a man had one sensation to hold on to.

Toward twilight, he heard only a white noise. He was deaf, and his children at the school would need to care for him. *The cure for earaches was to hold hot pancakes over the ears.* A sphere bloomed around him, and he emptied his rifle over and over into other spheres until the enemy bolted and finally someone called a halt. Word trickled down that after being forced back to the Shiloh church, the reb general Pierre Beauregard had managed to withdraw to Corinth. Alonzo asked if this meant the Federals had lost, since the point was to own Corinth.

Colonel Hall said no, it was a Union victory, but they would die of exhaustion if they chased the losers there now.

Nikka was carrying a platter with pancakes.
Boys and girls were slapping warm dough where flesh ailed
them.

As the wounded were carried to a medic's tent, John curled up in a churning rain and awoke thinking the fighting was continuing but realized that his hearing had delayed the registering of the sounds, the percussive artillery, the grapeshot's whistling, which were pounding his eardrums in the morning light, not an echo but the living thing of it, the way shock possesses the nerves after an event, not during it.

His ears repaired fully as bloodcurdling screams, the worst yet, pierced him. A dawning as to the cause: Animals were creeping out of the depths to eat the dead and chew and swallow the dying. He stumbled over men who cursed at him as he plodded toward the woods, desperate to locate Frank. A fox was torturing a boy, and John swung his rifle to drive it off, but the fox sped behind a bush to wait. Men cried out for their mothers. Rebs were also scattered around, with Secesh buttons stamped with pelicans feeding their young. John held the hand of the Union boy attacked by the fox and said, "Brother, I'm right here." A fistful of the boy's head was missing. John flared up with wrath about Edward Moore and the other men comfortable at home. "Tell me your name. I'll get word to your family. You got a sweetheart?"

The boy was already in the other world, and John said, "Sleep, brother."

He checked through the dead boy's clothing and haversack but found no identification and started to scrape a grave with his rifle's butt but stopped because animals were hovering in the foliage and would merely dig him up. John surveyed the moaning, the bellowing where more animals emerged to eat. The screeching compared to the troating of bucks at rutting time, a clamor he had discovered his first year in Illinois. He walked southward through the thicket, swinging his rifle at foxes, opossums, and shrews, and emerged in light and glimpsed a yellow-flagged hospital. What he imagined was a haycock turned out to be a pile of arms and legs, leaking their wine. As a patient on the surgical table shrieked, John wandered among the cots, not finding Frank.

"John?" It was Max Jeffers, his colleague, one-armed. "John, you're alive."

"Max." John knelt near the pallet.

"Gonna be tough, signing at the school." Max took an opium tablet, and John asked if he had seen Frank. Max shook his head as the drug swept him away.

Isaac was quivering on a cot, brown beard crazy-wired and eyes even more like mine shafts, and he grabbed John's sleeve and admitted to turning tail. "Brother John, I'm not good enough to preach His word. I cannot even confront men with earthly weapons!"

John signaled at a nurse, sign language that somehow conveyed *Bring morphine.*

"Isaac, it was bad. But it was our doing. Not God's." He tried to tug loose from Isaac's grip.

"I swear to you, I did not commit the vicious offenses you imagine. I did not!"

John removed Isaac's hand from his arm.

"Why can't you believe me?"

"Go to sleep. None of us is very brave, it turns out."

The nurse fed Isaac a few spoonsful from a bottle, hurtling him toward sleep.

Another nurse was dipping strings into hot wax to make candles, so surgeons could ply their hacksaws through the night. She seemed unaccustomed to smiling at a man but did so at John. "Miss," he said, "any inkling where I could find someone missing?" A basic mission—finding his friend—was the only thing that would keep him sane.

She said, "There's some crawling toward a pond to the southwest."

Bullet-studded trees were spearing black-splotched sky. Rocks littering the distance turned out to be bodies. He cut through clouds of gnats that were no better—merely smaller—than the creatures of the woods gouging out pieces of men. Peach blossoms cartwheeled past, refusing to land, the beauty of fruit trees knocked loose prematurely, before the right number of months, like spindly versions of the victims' souls. The men had matted gore in their beards, but what looked like wounds often were gobs of flies, the dying too tired to brush them away. Housewives—the sewing kits the men carried—were scattered. *Thread* to him was always *Mary*, but he shoved an image of her downward to dissolve in his stomach acids so that he could spare her this sight. He loved her. Deep down he always would. But she was in a world lost to him. At the pond's edge, men were bunched near dead horses. John cupped his hand in the red water to aid a man and a mule.

Drawn to a flickering in a glade, he discovered Frank holding his bleeding arm, slumped against an oak. Rushing, John yelled, "Where'd you go?" while choking off a laugh, because here they both were.

Frank lifted his wounded wing and gasped, "Bullet's still in there."

Rumor was that a man had three days to live before the poisoning of a minié ball killed him, and John's pulse thumped beneath his voice, managing, "There's a medic's tent a ways back." Better to be one-armed but alive, like Max.

"I'll die near this tree, if you don't mind," said Frank. He had staggered here after hearing about the pond but found it too horrific, and red, to drink from. John had been right, only shyness kept Frank from telling his wife he loved her. If John could please let Elizabeth know, he was saying it now.

"Shut up," said John. "You're not leaving me here by myself."

He got out his army knife and handed Frank ammunition to bite, but Frank said thanks, he had had enough of bullets, just go ahead, Dr. Alves. John dug the knife into Frank's upper arm and nicked capillaries but dislodged the bullet. Using a strip cut from his army blouse, he tied a tourniquet. Frank confessed that fright had quivered his legs during the battle. "I didn't run, but I was scared. Don't tell anybody I was scared."

"You're the best brother I've got, Frank. Of course I won't."

It proved impossible to avoid stepping on men, heaped in spots so thickly that there was no bare ground, and John could not always discern who was alive. Once in a bluegrass field in Cass County, his foot had gone through something like parchment, and it turned out to be a horse dead long enough to have become a desiccated drum.

Their company was camped near the river.

Alonzo told Colonel Hall about Dexter's location, because he hated to ruminate on a boy from Lincoln's state stuck in Tennessee. Maybe Dexter could get shipped home. There was a newly invented fluid to put into a corpse to preserve it, so a man could stay a while longer looking like himself, until the earth broke him down.

John wandered at night toward still-alive bodies pocked with glowing blues and greens, as if their wounds had liquefied into tidepools. He thought of little Maria Freitas telling him of her fantasy that her birth-parents were pearl-tenders, and he wept for her, the first time in a year, and for the men with their blotches of sea colors eerily gleaming. He sank near one with a shiny blue spot on his neck and hoped the salt of these misplaced, luminescent, broken-up drops of ocean would cure him. The man revived at the language of John's hand in his. After promising to report this patch of survivors to the medics, John sought the comfort of a memory containing water. The transport boat conveying them to this battle had skirted a riverbank with plants like whittled garlands. The pointed leaves had been green unto black when the sun did not hit them and jade when the boat listed into another grade of light: mistletoe. Unbidden, then and now, he had been and was possessed by: Mary, I learned that from You. It's hard not to hear God declare, *I give you beauty, and you pass it by.*

———

CAPTAIN LUCAS JOHNSON WAS SENT TO OVERSEE THE 14TH'S TASK OF cleaning up. Worn out from hauling bodies, John and Frank wandered far afield, with Frank capturing photographs using a borrowed camera and showing no ill effects of having had a bullet in his arm. By the time they sauntered back to camp, hauling a basket of peaches found in a lean-to, they had missed roll call. Amazed that the captain wanted to confront him for "stealing," John protested, "There wasn't exactly anyone selling these peaches."

Captain Johnson shouted that all laxness weakened the army. When John laughed, the captain ordered Frank to stand on a barrel for two hours while draped with the sign THIEF. And the captain did not like John's failure to salute his superior officer.

Abner Quimby muttered about "superior."

"Private," said the captain to Abner, "you are indicating a problem?"

"Yeah. You, Captain," said Abner.

Abner and John got sentenced to a horse-burying brigade, along with Mark Robertson and Bill Snow for protesting the captain's harshness. Early on, white horses got shot by the enemy in droves, their color an easy target along with their riders. The Federals undertook a massive shooting of healthy but pale ones. John had found that hard to swallow, their corpses like regal ghosts. Now, the ones they shot when they ailed or got past their prime were of every color, and no one liked that, either, but often farm boys volunteered, since they were accustomed to mercy killings. A recent session of this had reduced Isaac to clapping hands over his ears, screaming for it to stop.

Four horses of various shades had been shot that morning and were swelling with the humidity. John, Mark, Abner, and Bill tied bandannas around their faces and dug extra wide to avoid the grisly indignity of breaking those agile legs to fit them in. They worked with spades and pickaxes in a rhythm. Mark bashed his shovel at a vulture and yelled, "Goddamn it, I'd rather lick the latrine. Alves, those peaches better taste good."

They tied ropes to the horses' legs to drag them into the graves, and one curse of making them deep was the thud when the bodies landed, the flies going in to be buried alive with them. John judged horses the noblest of creatures, with their fleetness and the elongation of their heads. At the last shovelful, the undertakers ripped off their bandannas, and John stood near Frank's barrel until his punishment ended, with Isaac yawping that John was breaking another rule, to which Captain Johnson hollered, "Shut your bonebox, Unthank. I am plenty tired of this war."

Souvenir seekers poured in, picking the dead clean of shoes and valuables, using pliers to yank out gold teeth. Wedding rings were prime treasures. Enemy corpses got stacked like rotting firewood in trenches to proceed to hell in a single mass. When individual pits were dug, two bodies got packed in and stomped into mush, the gravediggers screaming that rebs were half men who deserved no better. No one checked for any names pinned inside jackets. No one could explain the sea-colored glowings on some of the dying, nor why they seemed prone to recovery. A woman was sending her children with scissors toward bodies, and they were gleefully cutting the buttons off jackets.

As if to pretend nothing untoward had happened, John's company played the new game with a ball and a stick. He impressed everyone with his accuracy in rifling a ball toward the flour-sack bases and the starting-and-finishing point called home. Contests unfolded nice as pie until, in a burst no one could measure, momentum and power surged in and then came the mystery of how one side got unstoppable. His first time with the stick, he cracked the ball tossed at him so it flew in an arc like the ones over measures on a song sheet, and he steeped himself in a daydream of crowds roaring, Mary standing in applause with them, as he sent spheres sailing to his ancestors.

Corinth, June, 1862:

Mrs. Moore, Forgive my intrusion, forgive how long it has taken me to accept Yr marriage. I dont know where to turn but to You. We buried horses & that carved a dungeon inside me that is perhaps like Your Well. I dont know if Youll get this b/c mail service is poor & You & I know to our sorrow how untrustworthy it is. We send letters via a man discharged, or the Chaplains pick up mail sacks to be sent by rail or riverboat. (If You receive this, & the letter I sent before, it proves Isaac wronged us tho he protests otherwise, as he is in Co 14-A, & all other "Suspects" are in the land of the living.)

In Corinth we discovered Gen. Beauregard had slipped away. Did this mean the Union had won, since a key was owning Corinth? No, b/c we have not wiped out the rebs. Our nation's size allows for continuous hiding. I enclose a drawing of the sound of birds in black oaks this morning. They reminded me that I promised Id go away from You if I had to but I wouldnt despair about a world w/ You in it. If You were to take my drawing & stitch it up in a new way

as a reply, Mary, onward w/my duty Ill go, secure in what
You once meant to me. John.Alves.

WATCHMAN, WHO LOWERED MY DRAWBRIDGE?

COLD-WHIPPED APRIL AIR BLASTED INTO NELL CLARK'S HOME AS guests poured past the acanthus-leaf capitals reversed to form flower-pots sprouting columns at the portal. Mary glanced at Edward lagging behind as they entered the drawing room, where soft lighting lavished golden shadows. Conversations rumbled politely, and decanters with scarlet cordials were lined up with military precision on a sideboard. Diamonds glistened in the coves of the throats of women. Mary's frock alternated cream and mocha stripes, and had Edward not seemed subdued, she would have joked about resembling the trifle in its glass bowl among the array of desserts. The evening was a fund-raiser for the Christian Sanitation Commission to aid an army dying more from disease than bullets. "Let's not stay long," she whispered. Kissing her crown, he replied, "Agreed." Nell, in a dress of changeable fabric that was brown in the woof and red in the warp, burst through a wall of people to exclaim, "Mary, those earrings! Your fine-looking husband needed help picking them out."

Mary tapped her dangling quartz stars so they shook and assumed her party voice to say, "Then I have you to thank, too, Nell." Edward flashed his party smile at Mary, then at Nell, who said, "I hear they're an early first-anniversary gift."

"He spoils me. He shouldn't." Mary put a hand on Edward's wrist, but he was swept, with a reluctance palpable to her but likely no one else, into a lively group—one that included Dottie Willis and Maud Dieterman. Nell said to Mary, "Maud asked me what dwarf fruit trees you might like for the greenhouse or yard as her own anniversary present, so expect some apple saplings soon."

"They would be welcome." Hail to mysteries great and small: Maud had turned a corner into pleasantness toward Mary, bestowing conciliations such as baskets of liquor and cheese delivered to the house (good for guests, since Mary did not indulge in any of it), and once darting to the rescue when Mary was hounded downtown by drunkards. (Was it a marking of territory for Maud to stick a tree into their midst, a gift that screamed MAUD permanently aligned with Mary's one-year mark with her spouse? Mary admonished herself with Nell's anthem: *Be gracious, Mary; you won.*) Dottie Willis waved at Mary from a pack with Edward, Maud, and Bill Farnsworth, and she waved back. Marriage was such an ascension that every former combatant bowed before a wife's power. Mary had ordered Gertrude Weber banished after that greenhouse attack, and Gertie was not present and remained excluded from many social lists.

Nell said, "The cigars are not set out. Excuse me, dear, while I deal with this historic crisis." She trundled off on the mission of being a complete hostess.

Mary could never apprehend what to do during any interval of being solitary at a crowded affair. A player piano got activated, its drum bearing marks resembling Braille as it rotated, the keys depressed by an invisible man. The tune was "There Shall Be One Vacant Chair." She wandered toward the lowboy because it was an action to perform. In addition to cakes, pies, and other confections, including miracle berries and lemon slices, there was a silver coffee service and sugar cubes with icing-piped violets. *John, I've heard when soldiers crumble hardtack into coffee, embedded insects awaken and squirm.* She gazed at Edward listening inattentively to a gesture-laden story being related by a socialite named Phyllis Barksdale, and Mary tried to signal him: Come help me be fascinated by the groaning board, we who are the groaning bored! Was it her own anxiety imagining it, or was his face creased with habitual sadness *because of her*? The outer layer of herself labored to make amends, thanking him, fussing over him, being energetic until it caved her in. His grace was in comprehending all of this and adoring her anyway.

Unfolding was a social ballet of such prowess that Mary could swear she heard faint orchestral music. Maud first tucked herself under Edward's arm, gripping him while bantering with Phyllis but using this half embrace only as a propellant to spin away and dance from person to group to person, a hand on an arm, head back with laughter as she was greeted by men and women lighting up as they listened to whatever she knew to say. She was a queen here and elsewhere, her castles ringed by moats. She scribbled something on a scrap of paper that a woman held to her chest in gratitude. It was the first time Mary had absorbed Maud's connectiveness . . . and how much people liked her, or sought her favor, allowing Mary to perceive how it could happen that Edward had been engaged briefly to Maud and might find her boldness appealing. Nimble with crowds, she blasted holes that he could imagine stepping through.

Mary could not hide from this dexterity, because Maud dragged a gentleman to the lowboy, where Mary was studying a pie as if something very interesting were materializing on the top crust, and she trilled, "Mary, you must meet Jeduthan Walker! I've told him about your strange berries, because he entertains constantly in his Jacksonville home, men from Chicago, Saint Louis, where else, Jeddie? Half the world, at least. The *good* half." Pause for ribald jollity.

"Maud exaggerates. Greetings, young lady."

"This is Mrs. Edward Moore, so guard against any temptation to sweep her off her feet, but you must buy her berry wares, berry-waries. Be wary." Maud pinned herself to his side, grinning up at him.

Where was the elusive Billy Mars, to whom Maud was supposedly still engaged? He never came to any event with her.

"Her plant is thriving in Florida. Mary, will you move there? My father will take you back should you wish him again as a distributor, I'll see to it, but fear not, I won't expect a penny." A wink. "Tell Mr. Walker how he can order a hundred dozen!"

She explained to Jeduthan that if he wished, he could obtain them in Jacksonville at Ray Silva's store or through Julian Barr's in Springfield.

Jeduthan said, "Of course, certainly, you own that remarkable greenhouse. Maud told me about it."

The word "own" in connection with it still jolted her. She said, "I work in it, too, from time to time." Perplexing, her dipping in and out of what had once consumed her. How was a lady of a house supposed to behave, and why was it considered odd that a wife might continue laboring at what she loved? She could scarcely define what was so subsuming about domestic obligations.

"You get those lovely hands dirty?" said Jeduthan affably.

Perpetua and her helper Dilly Witherspoon took care of the plants now, leaving Mary's nails scrupulously clean. How she missed Papa, missed tending the plants warmed with her fevers for a boy. A boy who had screamed he never wanted to see her again. "I like to keep my hand in, so to speak," she replied. He laughed, due to this being such a witty turn of phrase, aren't I clever.

Maud kissed Mary and squeezed her—Maud smelled overpoweringly of tuberose—and said, "Jed, come along, you must meet Stuart Trent." Mary's shoulders relaxed as Maud took her leave, Jeduthan obeying her; despite Mary's social strides, proving she would not run from these women was draining. On the far side of the room, Edward was chatting with Bill Farnsworth and Augustus Ayers, the banker, and Annie Ayers, who wore a plain plaid dress with a white collar and no makeup and seemed more confident than any woman Mary had ever noticed. Augustus was regarding his wife fondly. Mary recognized them from the newspaper, once in connection with that accursed essay contest. Edward seemed in a better mood and beamed at her: Come, come to me. Though lacking Maud's regal abilities, Mary set out. Halfway to that island of temporary repose with Edward, she paused—alas, near Dottie Willis—because a Madeiran serving girl was carrying a tray of sugared walnuts and bumped into a woman who sniped to a companion, "These island darkies are so clumsy."

Dottie declared—Dottie who once pontificated that people should stay in the land of their origins!—"Enid, we're here to be charitable."

Whenever Mary hoped to pretend she was safe, some test arrived. She said to Enid, "If you step aside, her tray won't touch your valuable sleeve."

Enid ignored Dottie but hissed at Mary, "No need to get your own pretty little octoroon nose out of joint."

The serving girl directed damp eyes at Mary while whispering, "Senhora, we're all so proud of you." Mary had, earlier, tried to chat with this girl, who had cautioned she was instructed not to speak to the guests, and once again she hastened away before Mary could answer.

Dottie whispered at Mary, "Enid is upset because your beauty is naturally exotic, and she is like curds in color and disposition."

Maud was signaling from the lowboy, holding up a decanter, and Dottie said, "I promised Maud I'd bend an elbow with her, and her ladyship is issuing a summons. Excuse me?"

Mary said she would. Steering toward Edward involved striking another rock in the form of Maisie Mauzy, who intercepted Mary and declared, "From the looks of it, marriage agrees with you." A salacious nudging. "I envy how you seem to know what to do at these things." Maisie thrust a chin in the direction of Maud and Dottie parsing the liquor options and added, "Neither of us will ever get to the level of those two, though, will we. Maud lives in a circle higher in the atmosphere than everyone here acting so pleased with himself. Dottie worked her way into it, don't ask me how, but her family didn't come from it. Her nephew is our lowly postmaster, for God's sake."

Mary wobbled as if struck on the head. Not because she too could be seen as "working her way" into whatever this was, but because the savage wound stabbed into her a year ago had been reopened. "Taylor Seeger is Dottie's nephew?" said Mary.

"Yes. The Seegers worked the slaughterhouses up north. Some escaped." Maisie patted her tight curls while complaining about her grocer's life, her sealed fate since inheriting the store from her parents.

Often Mary longed to blurt, "I heard you laughing about me, in my sewing room." How to contain her sickish gratitude at Maisie's agility with gossip, leaving Mary to wonder if Dottie's nephew had intercepted the letters to and from John, if *Dottie* had been the schemer, her dislike of foreigners that deep, with assuaging kindnesses now nothing but late contrition? Taylor, who disliked Mary anyway, was a prime candidate to do his aunt a nasty service for a fee. A bonus:

Dottie might curry the favor of Gertie and Maud, and more solid inclusion in their stratosphere, by punishing the gardener—garden*ess*—who stole Edward.

Nell Clark cut off all conversations with a hand clap. Time for everyone to endeavor to prove they could afford to send more cash than anyone else to the troops. "Welcome," Nell held forth, the room quieting as Mary lunged to the harbor of Edward, grateful. He never touched her in public, but it was a near-best thing that his flesh seemed always to relax toward her. "In these troubled times," Nell was announcing, "we must attend to our civic duty, but please enjoy the refreshments, as a spot of jollification is not contrary to our sterner purpose of pledging monies to the Sanitation Fund."

This was code for men's bowels betraying them, and pictures arose of John in agony, mired, furious at her. Edward leaned down to whisper, "Speak for our household, if you would, dearest. I fear my voice will falter."

Sometimes his stutter threatened to surface. He did see women as people, to be encouraged, promoted, left to speak; he was her friend, he was her dear friend. When Nell concluded, "Let us therefore bring succor to our sons, brothers, and husbands," Mary summoned composure to open the donations with, "The Moore household commits three hundred dollars to assist our Union cause."

There was a brief stirring of dismay. Maud proclaimed, "Brava! Edward Moore is man enough to let a woman speak for him. I shall donate nine hundred dollars, tripling this excellent display of womanhood and manhood."

The queen having decreed that Mary's forwardness should not be off-putting, there was discernible relief as comeuppance commenced, one thousand dollars from Mary Fish Matteson, the same from Nell, and onward it went, for Lincoln's boys, until Augustus Ayers declaimed, "Two thousand from Annie and me. Word has arrived that Company 14-A, proud citizens of my model town of Jacksonville, were among those sustaining heavy casualties at Pittsburg Landing. Honor and glory to the defenders of our Union's sacred aims."

John's company. Mary tried to stop the tumbling within herself by not moving a trice, and she sensed Edward's spine calcifying.

———

GOING TO BED ON OCCASION INVOLVED LADEN AIR, OFTEN RESOLVED
by lying side by side and holding hands, as they did tonight. Not long
after their wedding, she had lunged to embrace him, and they had yet to
recover fully from his first instinct having been to recoil. Had he imagined her starving for John, or was it because his own needs were less
fervent? They never spoke of it. About once a week, he reached for her.
He said, "You must seek word, about the Jacksonville troops. Women
recite letters from soldiers at the post office. Notices are posted."

She hesitated, then said, "About the deception. The taking and
trickery with the letters. At the party, I wondered if Dottie did it."

She had never asked Edward if he might have done it, did not believe he could do such a thing. And yet the question existed like a pale
unpleasantness between them, as if he sensed, and found distasteful,
that she might summon his name for the purpose of immediately
dismissing his guilt.

"You told me it was some preacher. I thought we laid that ugliness
to rest."

"Yes." Mary spoke in a feint, to steer them away from her own
state, by intoning toward the ceiling, "You've seemed troubled. Won't
you tell me what's bothering you?"

She was glad he could not see her face as he said, "Your sensitivity
to shifts of mood is wonderful and disquieting. I received word from
the sister of my former fiancée, Rose, that she died in childbirth in San
Francisco and the daughter did not survive."

"I'm very sorry." To his credit, she never sensed Rose in their bed,
in their home. She had had no idea he was in touch with the sister, but
why not. *Nell Clark: Mary, you won.* She added, "My father's wife died
like that. It taught me about sorrow."

"Strange, the phantom paths every life has. But I assure you, I do
not dwell on fantasies, which seem an admission that one's existence
is lesser. You are everything to me, Mary."

"I know." It seemed a plea that she scrub herself clean of any make-
believe. "Wouldn't it be nice not to go to parties and such things?" she
said.

"I'd be happy to stay here with only you, but it would not be viewed kindly if we avoided an event to help the war. It's the least I can do, considering my avoidance of shooting strangers and having them fire at me."

"No. Yes, I mean." Attempting to be full of largesse, she said, "I saw Maud's abilities tonight. She has become decent with me."

"Her father is a powerful businessman, and wealthy, but it's her mother's direct lineage from an English duke that impresses people. America only pretends not to be obsessed with royalty. However, you're descended from a king, so you win."

"*Maybe* from a king."

He relaxed, and laughed, and held out his arms. Early on, she had concealed from him her inquiry about annulment. The priest lectured about wifely duty, and lewd questioning about consummation led to his refusal to consider her case. Edward said again, "Go find out what's happened with Company 14-A, Mary. You should." She did not answer, as if to honor such a paradox that their closeness could deepen on a night with Rose and John, and even Maud, brought into their bedroom.

———

AT THE POST OFFICE, AN OCEAN OF FEMALES INDEED EXUDED DESPER-ation for stray words or nailed-up bulletins. A woman wept over an envelope with its embossed eagle as Mary plowed to Taylor Seeger, nephew to Dorothea Willis. He handed out reports of death; he conveyed letters begging for words of life. Rheumy eyes barely registering her, he said, "Mary Catherine Freitas Moore, it's been a while. Two notes for you."

First, she had to snap out of disbelief. Next, she grasped that if Taylor's paid assignment had been to block notices from her to John and incoming from him to her, then what he handed her—she stumbled aside, allowing others to push forward—affirmed that Isaac Unthank, removed at war, had been his conniving employer.

She leaned against an outer wall as a daffodil birthed its head near a trough to read:

MARY,

You once asked me for a love letter. I tried to write one in our Time together, but everything sounded so ordinary. I hope You dont judge me ill now, b/c I cant risk leaving the world without sending Word. Forgive this note. Forgive my anger as the worst of it leaves me. My breathing is so filled with You & with emotion. All I can think is to say Your Name. Mary, My Dear Mary.

Many women have Your name, but I believe You own it.

Im sorry how we ended, but You were right to move ahead with Life. & yet Ive kept You in my thoughts, b/c so much reminds me of You. When Alonzo Gillespie said he would lead us in a painting class to copy the peach blossoms here, I kept thinking how they looked like Your embroidery on that tablecloth. I know Mrs. Lincoln will ask You to bring it to Washington when time & peace allow. I thought of You when 8 cartons of Borden's Condensed Milk arrived from Springfield, I wondered if You helped pack them. Instead of ripping open a tin with my bare hands, I just held it for a time, & the blue eagle on the white label made me smile quite a bit. The milk had the color & taste of that pudding You once made mixing up cocoa-nut with a glass of rose-water & some loaf-sugar. Dexter Loomis bolted down 6 tins & got to moaning, & I ate a 2nd & a 3rd, & soon we were stumbling around drunk on Borden's.

The 14th Illinois must put down the slave-holding rebels in earnest, after our troop has not had much "to write home about." I do not fully remember my Bible, but we are near a Church with an old name out of Palestine, I believe, & so we are due to smell the powder of the enemy near a meeting-place called Shiloh.

Isaac is here, we steer clear or Id kill him. Should You receive this, then it is true he harmed us & I cant forgive that, but pls forgive me for being upset w/ You, when You too were deceived.

The bones in a bird's wing are a perfect match with the
skeleton in the hands of men. Oh, Mary, I was so excited
when I found this out! If I should die, stop to watch a bird
or flock, in the sky or in a tree, or resting on water. Inside
their wings Ive fit the bones of my hands, so that I might
sign over & over: How I loved You once so well, enough for
a lifetime however short or long. John.Alves.

She scanned his second note—though scrawled, its contents and postmark confirmed his survival—with its page of heavy birdsong notes. If she reshaped the drawing and sent it back, it would confirm that whatever forgiveness they both needed was granted.

She hastened to Julian Barr's shop for paper and pen and drew a response, converting his marks into a lightness that resembled stitching, and she waited in line to have her reply pitched into the unknown.

Afterward she stood on a slope overlooking where a fire had scorched the prairie black, and now wildflowers bloomed with a vengeance—*dutchman's breeches, sundrops, butterfly milkweed.* As the wind rustled the blooms up and down, sideways, and on diagonals, forming pictures that shifted, she hurried to nestle supine on a dragon breathing fiery orange blackberry lilies. A breeze smoothed her hair as if it did not belong to her but to an infinite claim of the earth, and her head was as serenely heavy as a pumpkin, though as she rose to go home, she felt like shocked hay that stands temporarily, gallantly gathered before being forked over to its doom.

In the greenhouse, Perpetua and hired hand Dilly Witherspoon were competing to see who could pick berries the fastest. Dilly rented a room on Fifth but often stayed in the cottage, from which laughter with Pet emanated. Mary kept her unreasonable upset over that to herself. Pet and Dilly were plucking, hooting, filling buckets. Dilly was allowed to use the Singer machine but not to barge in without asking first, so as not to startle Mary, and worry that this was from the Book of Gertrude drove Mary to overdo her friendliness.

Pet and Dilly sensed Mary in the doorway and stopped, like

children caught at mischief, and Mary said, "No, go on. Have fun," causing her to wince: how patronizing. She and Pet no longer conspired; they consulted. It broke their hearts. Pet flashed a shy smile, but their work slowed, and Mary made the further error of joining them, declaring, "Dilly seems to be winning. What's the prize?"

Pet said quietly, "We don't win anything, Mary. We're playing."

Dilly offered, "Were we making noise?"

Mary said no, no, and she lingered to correct the discomfort by adding more of it and then took her immaculate hands and spotless dress to the guest room in her house to weep for John, and for Papa, and for Edward's agony in trying to give her everything.

———

HE PROPOSED A GAMBLE AND SCHEME: WHAT IF THEY DONATED HALF her crop to the war effort? With food wretched or rotten, why not ask Leonard Otto, in charge of their southbound shipping, to help aid the longevity and vibrancy of supplies with Union boys? They would lose money at first, in the cause of excellent charity. But an unavoidable side benefit could well be that soldiers would write home about this unheard-of agricultural marvel, how it turned stale bread into manna, how acidic coffee became syrup, and fading vegetables, the few that appeared, hosanna, turned sweet as corn, and pancakes with bug-dotted flour tasted like the ones from boyhood. "I'll put you in charge," said Edward, "while I work on the new hybrid."

Mary looked up from stitching on her storybook tablecloth and said, "All right."

What she should have expressed was that she viewed this as his apology for being momentarily distracted and distraught about the death of his long-ago love, along with the death of a baby that might, in a world without religious insanities, have been his. But just as he never wallowed in hurt and anger, so too did he want to show that as penance for a lapse, he would bring John into her thoughts, since doing anything for the army invited him there. Such a grace made her want to be a good wife, though she neglected to mention John's letter along with her stitched-bird answer that may or may not have roosted.

Just as she had done in a lavender field in Funchal, she put her head down, and she asked the weeks, then the months, to drown her in a spell.

AU CLAIR DE LA LUNE

THE SANGAMON JOURNAL

May 1, 1862

In Our Age beset by Man's Inhumanity, we seek the Immortal! Felicitously, it has reached us—the news ever there, however tardy in arrival—that five years ago, a French printer and bookseller, and thereby a Worthy Man, one Édouard-Léon Scott de Martinville, gifted the ill-deserving world with the PHONAUTOGRAPH, which claims as analog the human ear, for the purpose of Collecting and Rendering Visible the Shapes of Sound.

Into a funnel, Martinville channeled diction whose vibrations landed upon a membrane stretched over the opposite opening, setting in motion a stylus piercing it. The stylus was agent to scratch and thereby arrest marks upon a coating of lampblack on paper, wrapped around a dowel rotated via a crank to give free rein to the agenda of that stylus, aquiver with Human Voice, images that replicate the air's conveyance of the product of vocal cords.

It is the first physical transcription of Human Sound, a PHONAUTOGRAM! On the ninth day of April in the year of Our Lord 1860, Édouard-Léon Scott de Martinville sang *Au Clair de la Lune* into his phonautograph. Capturing the breath of life thus defeats Time's hitherto usual decree that all is passing.

John folded the weeks-old newspaper that had arrived in the mail sack, absorbing this fanfare about a Frenchman producing something that not only resembled John's efforts but was almost the *exact item*. Martinville had not stuck a feather in the funnel, and John had not used soft material, ash or lampblack, to receive the scratchings (great idea), but the Sound Machine was so similar that reading of someone else's acclaim unto immortality shot a bullet into him.

They were camped south of Corinth, where fish had gnawed a flotilla of swollen bodies in the river. Most haunting was that all the eyes were missing. What stopped John from screeching was the approach of the cook, who handed him a crinkled letter and said, "This got stuck to my pan, Alves, don't ask me how, but I almost fried it with the bacon."

John sensed her hand on the hidden page, radiating through the envelope, with her wisdom about the ways in which art provides comfort.

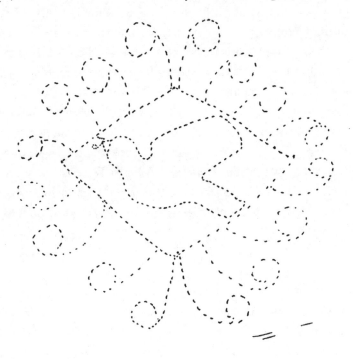

GHOST APPLE

AS THE WINTER OF 1862 TURNED THE BEND INTO THE WINTER OF early 1863, in the era of Mary's anxiety about shipping berries as charity to the Union army, Lucy Brattle took her to view a *ghost apple*. It seemed from a fable with an evil queen. Rain will coat rotting fruit in a tree and freeze. The disintegrating fruit drips through a slit, and a hollow ice-apple remains.

The ghost apple hung from a limb near the Capitol Building. It dripped slightly but did not fall.

Emerging from it was an opaque glimmer, which Mary took as a sign that the irreplacable Edite and Alberto Teixeira had gone into the other world and were sending a message that day by day, not only days but we ourselves drift toward becoming the kind of cold that resembles smoke.

———

IN THE SPRING OF 1863, AS NEWSPAPERS WERE HERALDING THE PHE-nomenon of red berries prolonging the supplies of soldiers—there were surely raves about them in letters home, as evidenced by a rise in sales, a beginning of recovery from the charitable donations—Mary nevertheless panicked. Hoping to prove she could better commandeer not just moderate but immense success, she contacted a western distributor mentioned once in passing by Maisie Mauzy.

Robert White of White Ventures, based in Chicago, responded to her inquiries by suggesting they meet at the American House in Springfield when he came to town. On the agreed-upon afternoon, their coffees arrived with what resembled gibbets for mice—vertical dowels on stands with horizontal arms glutted with what Robert explained was cotton candy—and the cup's steam caused a sugar rain to drip. For the third time since sitting, he stroked Mary's wrist. She had not been here since the day of bludgeoning John with news of her marriage. "Such come-hither eyes," said Mr. White.

She detested herself for smiling. She could ask Edward what this description of her eyes meant beyond triggering visceral discomfort, but that would be a whisker away from admitting she had excluded him from something as gigantic as courting a western distributor. Had they not argued when he neglected to discuss such forays with her first? Nor had she alerted him to the shrinkage of her bank account from the three thousand he had put into it—five years of Papa's working life—to eight hundred. She had been negligent with writing down every expense, as if that would conceal even from herself how much she wasted on domestic and business desires.

"Lunch? You're the size of a fairy child. The mutton stew is remarkable."

"No, thank you, Mr. White. I've dined already, with my husband."

"Wine, then. You have a husky voice for someone so petite."

They were so interchangeable, these wolves. She said, "No, thank you, Mr. White. Do you have the contract?"

"All business." More patting of her bracelet was followed by an inhalation of sugar-cloud-dappled coffee. "My name is Robert, little dove."

She laughed. It was a very Portuguese thing, but pombinha, little dove, was slang for . . . a girl's private parts.

He pulled himself taller, sensing mockery. She could not afford to offend him. Some customers had shuttered their businesses, and sometimes the fruit, despite its desiccation to promote longevity, developed black spot in transit. The trellises needed replacing. Dilly had a salary. Purple spheres ascended from the Turkish carpeting as if from a bog. She went on, "Maisie said you have connections as far as California. Texas. You helped her cousin there? A grocer's outlet." The Far West felt like the ultimate definition of amorphousness.

"Texas is not an easy market, dearie."

The cotton candy had melted off the two little gallows. Granules sparkled on her cup. He removed a document from a carry-all and asked if she could read "legal English," and she assured him yes. In his letters, he had proposed starting with a dozen top outlets amid the growing populations in distant-from-the-war spots, where luxury flourished alongside mining and prospecting. She paused at the contract's final lines stating that his fee was one hundred dollars, and her investment, for reasons unspecified, would be another four hundred. "I didn't realize I'd pay—I'm not sure what this is for, Mr. White."

"Insurance, for one thing. It's for paying off shipping officers, repairing broken crates, and so forth."

"I thought distributors covered those expenses. You get a percentage of the sales."

He produced a patient grin. "You want to reach the West, correct? The West is tough. Bribes, spoilage, miles bordering on infinity. Residents live in a heedless, indulgent fashion. Your product would be welcomed as amusing. What you're selling isn't vital to life." His paper-thin skin advertised his bones. Men like this resembled their own memento mori, and yet they never saw it.

Edward had negotiated the deals with Chicago and St. Louis outlets; she was unsure what the truth was about extra expenses.

"I've been in this game awhile, Mrs. Moore, and you stand to spin an investment of five hundred into several thousand in a year. Perhaps you should consult your business partner. I hear your husband is in charge."

She allowed herself to be pleased with recognizing this as intended to inflame her. "I have my own account, Mr. White, and I make decisions."

"Very—individualistic. I've never heard of such a man."

Was it an error to mention her bank account? Robert asked again if she wanted wine. She stood to gain so much. In a year, she could inform Ward that she had hugely increased the three thousand entrusted to her, that she had led them past their donations to the army and created a fortune. She said, "Maisie never mentioned these fees."

"She paid for my trouble. I arranged for her fruit-leathers to get shipped with ice. I've succeeded in sending dressed meat quite far. I could tell you stories. Ice blocks that tip over railcars going around curves. Frost burns. I don't need your money, but I require compensation for what I provide."

"Yes. I'm sorry."

Robert would be residing in the American House ten more days. She could take that long to sign, with the money due then, after which her coffers could commence overflowing. "I could waive my fee," he said, gripping her sleeve. "My room is upstairs."

Foxes chewed off their legs to escape steel traps. She could twist off her arm, leave him holding it. "Mr. White." Her voice's tremor infuriated her. "I'm married."

"Can't fault me for trying. A gorgeous woman talking business is an aphrodisiac."

She slid the contract toward him and said she understood if his distribution company chose not to promote her products out West.

"Don't get hot and bothered," he said. "You know where to find me." He clinked coins onto the table and said he hoped to "make music together."

———

SHE STOOD OUTSIDE THE SANGAMON BANK. ALWAYS, BEFORE ENTERing it, she steeled herself for the stares from the customers and the male clerks, with the occasional higher-echelon banker watching. Edward ordinarily came along to ease transactions, despite having left instructions that she could conduct them without his signature.

She could draw out five hundred dollars payable in a check to Robert White of White Ventures with his promise of new territory. The passersby arrested her; no one lacked a bloodline connection to someone on a battlefield. What smaller anguishes did everyone carry as well, secrets about debts, or dismay at how to stretch chicken wings into a supper, or glimpses of old age? She could march into the bank or just as easily turn around. Pause. Breathe. And now: She must decide which to choose.

———

THE MOST REMARKABLE THING—SHE MIGHT CONFESS THIS ONE DAY TO someone—was that she had known the outcome with every ounce of her being, with clarion-call vividness, even as she entered the Sangamon Bank and suffered the lowered gaze of the clerk. Though trained not to chide or pity, surely he gossiped with the others stealing glances. *Here's what comes of trusting a woman. They deplete everything.* She had known what would happen even as she traipsed to the American Hotel and met with Robert White of White Ventures, substantially less genial as she paid him and received the executed contract.

She felt the full ringing remarkableness the next day in the same salon as the waiter wondered if the young lady all by herself desired more coffee. She stalled for what would not come: Robert White with the goods he had vowed to bring, the orders arranged with the top outlets that would spin her investment into gold. He was over an hour late. Then two. What a fool she was, not to have insisted upon everything she needed, and had been guaranteed, upon his receipt of payment.

She asked three times at the desk if they were sure there was no message for a Mary Catherine Freitas Moore from Robert White of Chicago.

We've told you already, he left last night.

She should have verified beforehand that Maisie had paid a fee. Instead, a desire for an impossible outcome had led her to believe promises akin to the blatherings of a conjurer. Robert White must have fallen on spare times and plied his past record to prey upon vulnerable types—this was how she appeared to men like that, no matter how smart she was—before hieing from assorted towns and pulling up stakes in Chicago, his victims disinclined to pursuit out of shame and because the amounts were comparatively small.

Botany books were piled on the sofa next to Edward as she stared at him until he said, "Yes, dear?"

After admitting what she had lost, she dropped into a chair and burst into tears. With measured-out tones, he said, "You allowed yourself to be duped rather than ask my advice. Why didn't you simply come to me?"

When she confessed how much she had spent from her account, he reared back with more anguish. "I am not of limitless resources. What exactly cost so much?"

"Everything. I don't know. Besides giving away so much for free to the army."

"What is 'everything'? I've seen the ledger. Didn't you write 'everything' down?"

"I guess I didn't."

"You *guess* you didn't, or you *didn't*? Since I'm expected to make up this difference, at least be honest." He was as furious as she had ever seen him.

She had, as the expression went, no leg to stand on. "I didn't record buying so much ribbon. For the sachets. I needed to repair my spectacles. I don't know, Ward. Perpetua asked for a dollar to go to a show with Henry. *Things.*"

"But why did you not come to me and say your funds were running low?" He added that he was surprised no one at the bank had informed him.

She suggested that that was because they did not mind seeing a woman fail.

"Let's not blame bank workers for your miscalculations, Mary." When Ward said he would take the man to court, she confirmed that Robert White had vanished.

Ward's jaw hardened. More to himself than to her, he went on, "I thought when we married, we were safe from everyone. Including con men. We can dig deeper and take out advertisements for the crop, now that reporters are writing articles. We don't have enough of a supply to include the West right now. I didn't think you'd fail to see you can stretch too thin too fast."

He made his characteristic leap over a chasm, over hurt or upset, into equanimity. "If it's any consolation," he said, "men with high regard for their savvy got taken in by my father. Two-thirds of the human race are killers, Mary." She took his kissing of her ear as absolution, but he made chicken Wellington, and—their sole communication while dining—declared it too milky, and when he preferred to take his turbulent stomach to the guest room, his parting words were "I'm weary of being the understanding spouse."

—

SHE DECIDED TO SURPRISE HIM BY ATTENDING ONE OF HIS LECTURES at Illinois College, since he occasionally wondered aloud why she had never done so. As she touched the doorknob of the theater in Beecher Hall, laughter billowed, and she paused to avoid causing a distraction. Opening the door a crack, she heard her husband midsentence, declaring, ". . . I did catch her at it, talking to the pineapples. Some secret she didn't share with me."

Roars of amusement careered through the audience.

Conversing with plants was the art she shared with her father. Before her rose the specter of the sewing-room gossipers, and she tottered away as if knifed.

Rather than waste two hours in the station, she located the donated lot where a semi-ecumenical chapel was due to exist near a greenhouse in a small park. The two benches were empty, and nothing was sprouting near the gravel pathway. The chapel-in-the-making was a skeleton. The greenhouse was minute but whole, and she found famished rosemary bushes and not much else. Should she *talk* to the rosemary, tell it to perk up and better inspire the person in charge of tending this place that John had dreamt up to embody her? She admired the intensity of rosemary's scent and began pruning, needle by brittle needle. Her meticulousness was her best and worst quality, these self-imposed assignments to do small thing after small thing, because God forbid she sit with her sorrows, free of her checklists of minor actions to keep grief from washing in: Mourn too long, miss someone too much, and it is called *unbecoming*.

Emerging, she blinked at the sight of Serafina Alves on a bench, confirming that John's mother was a witch. She seemed to be waiting for Mary. When Serafina said, "I want to talk to you," Mary dropped next to her and replied, "You could have visited Springfield. You could have asked Ray or Nikka how to find me." Or, she thought, *John,* back when we wanted the chance. Did Serafina know that Mary's husband had donated this lot? To her grave, Mary would take his secret plan to divert an estimated equivalence of his father's profits that were ill-gotten toward good deeds and reparation.

Appraising Mary from her hat to her polished shoes, Serafina said that going to fine places such as her son had described Mary inhabiting would open Serafina to ridicule. "Maybe I deserve that," she said. "Maria, you see, I want to bless you to marry my boy. John, he kept saying we began as Catholics, too. If you tell him you want to marry him, I won't stand in your way and happy like that, it will keep him alive."

"Senhora, not standing in our way isn't the same as wanting me in your family."

"You'll raise the children as Catholics. That is a trouble for me, yes, but no longer is it to upset me that you love my boy."

Mary flaunted her ring in a more obvious manner, since Senhora Alves was electing not to see it. Its sumptuousness felt aggressive. "I married a Catholic," she said. "Happy?"

A Catholic willing to announce, for purposes of entertaining a crowd, her private habit of speaking to plants.

Serafina appeared almost marbled with perplexity. "I do not know how, but you and my boy, one day God will put you together."

"People ask too much of God and not enough of themselves." Mary kept to herself that if there had been no objection at the start, John and she might not have been intimidated, hesitant, allowing those delays and mishaps, would have felt stronger to combat the bald folly of deceptive missives—*my hand is injured,* indeed. Such a clumsy falsehood, and yet it had worked. To Mary's surprise, Serafina said, "You are right. You cannot forgive me, because I cannot fix what I did. But I can say I'm sorry, and sometimes things happen, and the forgiveness can come a little more."

Mary shrugged. She no longer trusted magical outcomes. But it was refreshing that someone believed a pardon should not be easily accorded, that it required more than idle words. She stood and looked at the troubled woman and said, "I'll keep that in mind, Senhora." She kissed either side of a face contoured like John's, and that was enough to think: For your sake, John, I'll let go of disliking her, that at least.

She risked missing her train by detouring to the Jacksonville post office. Maybe the secondary villain was not Taylor Seeger but the postmaster in Isaac's town. Agitated women were amassed inside, and Mary felt lit from within: Sarah Brink! Both John and Ward had mentioned this crow. Contest runner-up Sarah was a ripe candidate to be an avenger. She knew John's writing style, and her nosy ways could have led her to hear about high-society types sullying her town with gaming. She would be prissy about Mary's history of dwelling on a man's property and would know Rui.

But at Mary's turn at the window, she stared at the young man who had been taking his time to offer kind words to customers. His left leg, much shorter than his right—he had cantered out to hug a bereaved woman—was evidence that his body rather than wealth caused dispensation from the army. His brown eyes were like John's. Forces wavering, she said, "I must ask about nondelivery of notes I sent a year ago from Springfield to John Alves, who lived here before going to war. Did you work here then?"

"Mary Freitas?"

She did not correct him with her married name.

"John kept asking if anything had arrived from you, I remember him. He sent you so many letters. I stamped them myself."

This fellow seemed incapable of duplicity. Maybe the guilty party was Dottie after all, using her nephew to punish two refugees with the audacity to try their fortunes in Illinois. What of the *timing* of the horrid letters: *They began right after the incident with Gertrude.* Gertrude, banished, had the most cause of anyone to hate Mary. But would she know about the contest or the gambling? And she would wish to rid Springfield of Mary.

The postmaster said, "He writes from the front to his mother and sister." Noting her wedding ring, he added gently, "A lot goes astray in these times."

She agreed. What did it matter to hear a name of a culprit or culprits, here or in Springfield. That would change nothing.

When Edward arrived home, he asked if she had had a good day. Certainly; how had his been? "I hope you don't mind, dear, but a student read an article I wrote about your father and asked if I spoke to plants the way he did, and I poked a little fun, said that you took after him but I don't."

"Did you now? Poke a little fun." She had not entered the theater, and he could not have seen her. This seemed part of their new ability to sense a truth more often, starkly, in one another.

"Only a little. Have you eaten?"

"Only a little."

When he shuttled her to the underside of his body that night, he spoke about how sorry he was for quarreling about something as ridiculous as money. She was his luminous bride, and everyone made mistakes in business, in life, all a nothingness. Being with her was what granted him peace.

But why did her own idea of peace always feature an image of herself buoyed alone on top of a saline lake?

THE FATHER OF WATERS AGAIN GOES
UNVEXED TO THE SEA

18 MAY–4 JULY 1863

THE 14TH ILLINOIS JOINED THE FEDERALS LAYING SIEGE TO VICKSBURG, and the Father of Waters offered no relief from the heat. The nights were bright red from cannonading. General Grant no longer planned to storm the forts where the Johnny soldiers were trapped on the bluffs. Lincoln's men filled trenches and idled behind lunettes in a twelve-mile ring around Vicksburg as their artillery and gunboats severed the supply lines to the South. Starve 'em into surrender. Men women children. Hundreds of caves were dug into the yellow-clay hills, citizens pocketed inside with quilts and chairs. *Prairie-dog village.* The blue boys crouched in shelters honeycombed under wooden and earthen roofs, not much different from the enemy burrowed in town except for being less hungry. John had survived this far, only to number himself among those responsible for ravenous people being stuck inside cells.

He was haunted by the bloodshed when Federals last tried to storm the fortifications and got so hailed upon that even Grant broke down and accepted a truce. The screeching was so gruesome the rebs could not bear it, either. They put up their weapons and greeted, with affable chatter, the Federals, who were allowed to drag off their dead and wounded. The 14th Illinois had not been assigned to the assault but joined those rescuing their hacked-up compatriots, the stench of ripped-open bowels practically lethal. John had picked up one man under his armpits and watched his lower half detach.

One evening, Cyrus Skylander, who owned Dvořák's Music Shop in Jacksonville, positioned himself so that his gashed face was in shadow thanks to the backlighting of the fires in the city, and he asked John, Frank, and Abner Quimby, "Think we'll be told to shoot women?"

"Not if they starve first," said Abner.

They had been advised to settle in for as long as it took for hunger to occasion surrender. Isaac had been reading the Bible to prostitutes and afterward dispensing fifty cents to each of them toward reform. Soldiers objected to the preaching, but the girls liked the coins and the men liked the girls. Isaac's taste for whiskey had increased. He said to John one sweltering day, "God has given up on me, Alves. I'm meant to be a saloon owner. They are the repositories of confession. I can be a father-listener."

"Unthank, we agreed you'd stay away from me."

A white child with matted white hair, no more than thirteen, wandered into the Union camp, wondering who would hide in the bushes with her for a dollar. John offered her two dollars to leave and barked at some hovering soldiers to go find a knothole in a fence. He gave the girl a tin of beans over the objections of others eyeing the provisions and vowed to meet her with a daily tin near a lean-to on Jackson Road that once held an apiary. She could identify the spot due to the wax smears on the planks. "But don't let these men hurt you," he said.

"Don't hurt me none, mister, they do they business and be quick about it."

She would continue as a prostitute, but he would give her food in the hope that she might spare herself a little. While escorting her toward the camp's perimeter, they passed Isaac railing from St. Paul about women needing to be subservient to men, and he hollered, "Alves, you are with a Jezebel!"

"What ails 'im?" the child asked John.

"No one knows. The lean-to on Jackson Road, noon. Stay away from here."

"Girl of the streets! Hear the admonishments of the Lord!"

"Where I's from we got plenty folk like that 'un," she said to John.

"I was hungry once, when I was even littler than you. Go on now."

He incurred the wrath of men who groused that nourishing the enemy was the opposite of what they were commissioned to do. John nevertheless got the sympathetic ear of the cook and took tins to the meeting point, where the child grabbed them and fled. Once while wandering off his return route, he discovered a cave with an emaciated woman and a beady-eyed grandson. The boy was heating a cauldron over a fire.

"Ma'am," said John. Her eyes clouded with loathing. The boy fished out a strip that John figured was rodent meat before realizing they meant to dine on leather. He teetered backward and kept on until he was at camp, where he stuffed hardtack into his vest and returned to pile it on their cotton rug. They would eat the rug next.

She gathered her strength to spit in his direction. She made no move to collect the crackers but would consume them when he quit watching.

When John returned to his troop, Isaac was hovering behind Captain Lucas Johnson, crabmeat-red in the heat and predisposed to disliking John due to that peach incident at Shiloh, who demanded an explanation as to why John was abetting the enemy.

"Didn't know women and children were that, Captain."

"I had to tell him, Alves, more in sorrow than in anger, that you are a user of Mary Magdalenes and a feeder of same," said Isaac.

"As I understand it, Mary Magdalene was a good friend of Jesus."

When the captain declared John was courting treason, John pulled off his cap. "Look at this scar, Captain." He lifted a trouser leg. "I've got that to show, too."

Isaac suggested those scratches were slender evidence of manhood, and John replied he would be glad to fight Isaac to earn more stripes, and Isaac said that would be practice for breaking up brawling in the postwar Unthank Saloon, that he was being driven to crazed actions and fates due to John's failure to forgive him *for something he did not do*, and the captain barked, "Enough! Both of you!"

The next day, John resolved to bring the woman a tin of corn mush, but the boy was sitting alongside a shape with the rug over it. "I'll help you bury her," John said, offering the tin.

"Git out," said the boy, picking up a glass shard. "Don't you touch her."

Surrender came on the Fourth of July, the day after another victory in a place called Gettysburg. Rather than have thousands of Johnny soldiers fed in prison camps, General Grant released them, hoping they would limp home to warn the South it was defeated in mind as well as body. Such a confounded thing, victory from a hunger siege and not a conclusive battle. The clouds got baked into cracklings, and John wanted to rest his head on Mary's shoulder, to have his thoughts dissolved merely by contact with her.

As if to torment him further, dinner involved the dispensing of red berries to help the men stomach the stale, dwindling provisions. John stared at them in a rusty bucket, picked one up, and set it down. Exclamations about this bizarre marvel swept over the company, but John abstained, as shocked men said one could almost want to fight for this reminder that they were battling for a world with remedies such as this.

CONSIDER THE LILIES OF THE FIELD

FAITHFUL DAUGHTER, SERAFINA! YOU DO NOT HAVE MUCH TIME LEFT. SHOW Me the end of your story.

I am lost. I don't know where to find myself. I had a role in ruining my son's life.

Rui . . . I glimpsed him in that marketplace in Trinidad, a man confiding something in his ear. I recall a smell of ginger and—what else?

Sarsaparilla? I'm not sure, Serafina.

Seek to make amends with those you have harmed, even if you fail to fix what you have done.

And build a sacred place to house Me, one that stretches to the sky.

I am very confused. I tried to do that. Why can't You ever be clear?

(indecipherable)

I was charmed by Isaac, his preaching was fire, but he hurt my son and Mary with false letters, John wrote to tell me of this harm. Why did You let that happen?

(　　　　　　)

—

GOD FELL PAST SILENCE INTO ABSENCE. SERAFINA GLANCED AROUND her cabin in Madeira Hill, with its Joseph Capps–factory rug and the piano with missing teeth from the Presbyterians honoring the commuting of her death sentence. Instead of improving the Sound Machine, she wanted to devise a tuning fork large enough to send messages to her boys. Apologizing to Mary was the first step toward mustering a new brand of courage. She had rested on the laurels of a bravery that was now long past.

Widespread hunger was hurtling at her from far southward, causing people to wail in the heat of summer. She packed a bag, adding her new Bible, since she had given the family one to John. She would bring bread and cheddar, the best taste on earth. Though the Reverend Kalley had tried to teach her, she did not know how to write well. Like the Lord, he too had deserted her.

Nikka was at Ray's store, delivering crates of her homemade wine. Keeping things unadorned, Serafina scratched out words and pictures that she hoped conveyed: Do not worry. I go to look for God.—Mother

———

SERAFINA SET OUT WALKING. SHE FIGURED SHE WOULD STARVE. INstead, she got fed. No one knocked her down to steal the money sewn into her hem. She sampled "clabber" with cherries and "burgoo stew" with squirrel jerky and asked strangers to point her south. And let it be so and so be it, they did. She got better at reading the shadows, the sun's height. She nursed a craving for the dairy foods of this country, reason alone to feel grateful. Nothing prepared her for the spread of the land under skies bird-thatched. God had been vexed at her not trooping out before now to meet her fellow citizens and revel in magnitude magnificence manifold man-made and God-made real paradise.

She pressed a sacred petal from a profusion of asters inside her Bible.

Old men slowed their wagons to utter, "Grandmother, where art thou going? The world is not safe."

"To find my boys before I die, or at least one of them," she would reply.

She was supplied with water, salve for cuts, bread heels, a nail for her shoe, and, once, a tisane of hibiscus. An elderly woman invited her to bathe in a creek, and they had a bawdy chat about men. One horizon was so gloriously multicolored she was smashed to pieces. She rested in a meadow, pestered by gnats, and her shawl around her Bible made a pillow. The July sun baked her, cracked her face. She had to find John and give her blessing about Mary, to hold him when he forgave her. She missed Nikka and Rui. Most of all, she had to go back to the beginning of the meaning of herself: The howling of distant hunger grew louder.

When she reached the southernmost part of Illinois, a finch chorus sang and a boy took her home, and his mother served broth when Serafina mentioned stomach pains.

How much farther to the land of the rebels? She knew the war was in that area, and America was a giant, but she had not reckoned on such distances. While following the Mississippi River, she saw three enslaved men chained together at their feet. All those sermons of Kalley's smacked her bodily, her first actual sight of his declarations that this was humanity's gravest sin. These men sat on a wharf. When she spoke with them, her accent got in the way, and one of them asked, "Where're you from, Granny?" She replied that God had sent her, and why didn't they take off their chains?

The men said they had fled bondage and got caught and were being sent back. That was the purpose of chains, and the padlocks needed a key not in their possession, and you might reason further that this situation did get in the way of free motion.

Serafina pulled her shawl around herself, since the air was rising off the water. "The man who he trap you, where is he?"

At yonder trading post, and he would be back lickety split.

No assistance arrived from God. He was on His own walkabout.

Into one of the locks, Serafina inserted a stick found close by. She explained she was from an island called Madeira, and people born there were escape artists. "I lived in jail for years," she said, adding that she had been sentenced to die for her religion and had dreamt every night about freedom. Her ear was near the lock around the ankle of the first man. She resembled Christ washing the feet of his disciples.

One of the runaways said that was a sad story well told, but if she did not run along, she would upset the man due back, as this part of Illinois was not friendly to all God's children. But the lock clicked; it sprang open. The men stared at one another. The next lock was easier. The third seemed to give way on its own.

"Mercy, Granny!" said the first man.

Run, be safe, hurry . . . God had been waiting for her to thank Him for her freedom by springing other prisoners into the wide kingdom. *Go on!* She spoke the anthem that had accompanied her own fleeing as men came for her with torches.

One of them kissed her gray head where the parting was burned from exposure.

The freedmen ducked past people, racing past carts carrying goods, spinning folks unprompt in clearing out of the way.

A man grabbed her and shouted, "That was someone's property! Goddamn hag!"

This was how Serafina got jailed again. The bounty hunter delivered her to a household in the town of Cairo in Illinois, where the husband agreed to guard her for a fee. His wife and small son watched. The once-enslaved trio had not been located. Serafina would be a house-prisoner until she could be put on trial at a time to be determined, when the judge renowned for returning contraband showed up from his travels. They put her in a windowless room that locked from the outside.

Serafina sat on the cot and bounced a little. She prayed, "Lord, stop sulking and tell me how I get out of this one." No answer came, but she imagined, could hear, the dashing of the men she had helped. She would not know their stories, but thanks to the Reverend Robert Kalley, she had a guess about the ones they had avoided. O world! That I might put a story like this into you!

———

LILY, THE WIFE, ROUTINELY SHOWED UP WITH A BRUISED FACE WHEN she unlocked the door to remove Serafina's bucket for "the necessaries" and set down chunks of bread smeared with lard. Winston took

ten-year-old Christian with him to work in the Cairo foundry. Serafina pointed at the husband's violence and said, "Slap him back. Or
I'll do it."

Lily suggested that would not be required.

"Let me outta here. I need to find my boy, he is company fourteen,
letter A of Illinois." She pronounced the final "s," because it did not
make sense not to.

"Can't. You're in trouble. I think we're not on the same side,
opinion-wise. We come from a slave-favoring part of Missouri, and
Winston brung us here to change the leanings, or something, of y'all."
Lily's instructions were to avoid speaking to their prisoner, but as the
waiting for the judge tipped into a week, vigilance left her; she was
lonely. She explained that Serafina might as well have robbed a bank,
because three enslaved young males cost about—land sakes, she wasn't
sure. Five hundred Federal dollars? Confederate ones? "I've heard two
thousand apiece, sometimes."

"That is a sin." Serafina was truly shocked.

"Maybe," said Lily. "But Winston says we got this storeroom,
might as well earn money, and the sheriff agrees. That jail is full of
desperadoes. No place for a woman."

Serafina snorted and said she had known far scarier jails than this
room or the threat of a midwestern cell. Lily seemed offended. "I was
in a real prison," said Serafina. "I had to fight the guards off, and God
He helped me. We talked a lot."

"You and the guards?"

"Me and God talked. He got quiet now. I only to read the wrong
Bible, it was this my crime. They were going to hang me."

"Junebug bells, darling." Lily set down the washed-out bucket and
collected Serafina's plate. "God don't talk to me or Winston. How
come you're special?"

Serafina shrugged and said God and she used to have lively dis-
cussions, and sometimes He just sang to keep her company, but right
now the person she wanted to speak to most was her son in the Union
army.

"Where're you from, sugar pie?"

"Portugal." An island of Portugal's.

"Where's that be?"

She said it was like Spain, except not.

"Never heard of that, neither. I've got to lock you in now, hunny bunchy."

Serafina asked when the idiot judge was due.

Lily was too young for a face that looked as if a rake had been dragged over it. "He's taking his time, grant you that," she said. "I need to tidy up before Winston and Christian get back for lunch. My ankles hurt. The water in me goes to my feet and my feet don't let it out."

"Make him stop hitting you."

"You have a husband who don't punch you? Where's he?"

Serafina said he got buried far away long ago, and he had been a nice man.

"You miss him."

"Not so much. I miss God and my boys. I live in Jacksonville, and they all know where's to find me."

Nights arrived when Winston sallied out on undefined business. Serafina was not naïve; she suspected some dribble-brained girl was receiving the gruesome scything of her major root by lordly Winston. Trusting Serafina not to bolt, Lily let her out so that Christian could show off his magic tricks. On one such evening, Serafina pointed at a mystifying piece of furniture and asked what it was.

"That? It's from my childhood home in Missouri. My older sister didn't want it when she moved to Iowa, so Winston and I claimed it after my folks went into the ground," said Lily. "It's a piano that unfolds into a bed." Upon detecting Winston's footfalls, she hastened Serafina back to her cell.

When the women were again alone, Serafina said she did not have much longer to be among the living and had never slept in a piano. Would Lily let her do that?

Lily pried open the back and extended a plank like a shelf, and Serafina lay on it, the metal harp with its strings and keys like an awning. There was room for two, so Serafina said, "Come in, the water's perfect," an expression she had heard in Jacksonville, and Lily found that incongruous coming from this foreign old bird and therefore hilarious.

"I've got a rock in my stomach, and I should be dead," declared

Serafina, staring at a fly tiptoeing overhead. She said it must be nice to have sticky feet and be able to walk upside down. Lily said, "With my fat ankles, I'd drop." Serafina offered to massage them for Lily, and she did, getting the stagnating water to flow. They stretched out again, and Lily admitted she had not lain here since doing so at age eight with her friend Franny Porter, playing a game they had called, plainly enough, Wedding. Lily was always the bride, donning her mother's bonnet. As the groom, Franny wore a black outfit. One day Lily's mother found them nestled in the piano-bed, naked on Wedding Night, and she unleased a conniption fit and forbade the friendship.

Lily stole a pecan pie cooling on a sill and snuck it to her groom. There were secret meetings for years and strolls in the woods. Then Franny became pregnant at age fourteen but would not reveal the identity of the father. Lily refused to see her, because shouldn't best friends confide everything to each other?

Franny died of the complications of birthing a boy who survived scarcely a week. Lily had asked the corpse of her friend, on its bier in the chapel, to tell her something, anything. Not about the father of her child; he mattered not a whit. Was heaven real? Why was grass green? What if people were like flies, listening everywhere to what was said about them?

Since Lily knew how to get hit without making a sound, it took Serafina extra seconds to realize Lily was crying and to ask, "Do you like womens more than mens?"

It was a surprise that Lily did not spring up, furious. "I don't know," she said.

When that stranger whispered into Rui's ear in Trinidad's market-place, had it been a declaration of love? Straining, she tried to detect the words, circling in the atmosphere. She wished she could ask her lost boy if her devoutness had hardened into severity, frightening him from his true nature. The world was against him, but a mother should not be. She had applied dogmatic rules to Mary Freitas, too. She joined Lily in crying lightly, but not for long, because Lily leapt up, sensing Winston's return. In lockup, Serafina overheard that the judge was due in two days, and she would be handed over to her punishment.

In the morning, she told Lily not to feel bad and pointed at a hummingbird agitating the bottlebrush outside the window. "The word for that in my language is beija-flor," Serafina said. "That means kiss-flower."

"That is one of the most beautiful words in the wide world, Serafina Alves."

Lily returned her to confinement and left the house. Two hours later, she handed Serafina a piece of paper. "Illinois Company 14-A is still stationed in Vicksburg in Mississippi. They won a battle or something there and are hanging about, that's the word. We have a librarian who keeps track of the troops. I think she's a spy. That is very far from here, sweetie-sweet. How's about I put you on a train?"

"Okay, if Lily you promise to take your boy and go to your sister." Serafina used a knife from the table to rip her hem. She gave Lily all eight of her remaining dollars and declared, "'With a strong hand shalt the Lord deliver thee from Egypt!'"

Christian was due from his schooling—he alternated days of this with foundry work—in half an hour. Staring at the money, Lily scolded that Serafina should not give away everything she had.

Serafina felt wrung out but amid a kind of joy that asks for nothing more, though she was sad to leave the piano-bed, one of the best things ever. "I'll take the cheese that is called cheddar, if you have some." As felicity, serendipity, and whatever else that is glorious would have it, Lillian Devereaux Bobbit, throwing a few belongings into a suitcase, packing grab-fuls of her only child's possessions, said a rind of that was left. "All yours," she cried out. Penniless but with cheddar for her throbbing stomach, Serafina Alves allowed Lily to hasten her to Cairo's train station, pay the fare, and hustle Serafina into a car. Lily hugged her and said, "I promise to get my boy and me to a safe place, and I want that for you, too, Serafina kiss-flower."

It did not dawn on Serafina until almost the end of the route that Lily had put her on a train back to Jacksonville. When she disembarked and glanced around, she bowed her head. She was old, and ill, and would not survive another trip. She could barely stand upright. Her prayer was: *I accept that You wished me to stop hiding, and I am not well enough to roam again. My spirit will fly to John, now that I have released the best of myself into this world. That is how I'll be with him before I die. Lord, You take over now.*

She staggered to Ray's General Store, because it was near the station, and collapsed. He summoned a doctor and Nikka. Tucking Serafina into bed back home, Ray remarked on her seeming as peaceful as ever in her born days, and Nikka quit scolding her. Serafina said she had made a friend who took care of her through a little trick of sending her home after confirming where John was. Would Nikka write to him on their mother's behalf? There was not a second to lose; there is never a second to lose.

KISS

EDWARD'S GAMBLE ON EXPENDING MORE—TAKING OUT NEWSPAPER advertisements—completed their rise out of arrears and toward a bracing profit as Christmas ceded to a boom time in the new year of 1864. They decided to market-test, locally, kits that included a lemon. When Mary conveyed one to Julian Barr along with his standing weekly order, though, he informed her that he was moving away. The new owner planned a haberdashery, so this outlet for her berries would dry up. He said, "I should have told you earlier," sounding so forlorn that Mary set down her sample miracle-set and grabbed his hand, and he did not resist. He added, "My boy died in Virginia. My wife can't stop crying."

"Mr. Barr. Julian, how sad." She released his hand to avoid embarrassing him. "Where will you go?"

He and Carla, now childless, were heading to the Southwest Territories, to be near his brother. "The mountain air is thin, and a person can die of that, I hear. My boy's name was Amos. Have some bread." A loaf was on a cutting board with a serrated knife. "Carla bakes a lot. Starts in the morning. Won't quit." Mary accepted a piece, and it was an effort not to spit it out—too salty, as if Carla had sobbed into the dough.

"I'm sorry I was unkind to you. Back then. Native-born Americans killed my boy, not foreigners. I mean, you're not a foreigner."

"No, I am, Julian. I always feel like that."

"You shouldn't." He rang open his cash register, handed over three dollars, and said, "Buy yourself a hat in Mrs. Aitken's store. You look outstanding in hats. Puts the rest of us to shame. Call it a goodbye present."

He refused to accept the money back, and she promised to light a candle for Amos and two more for Julian and Carla in their high-altitude climate.

The millinery shop was in the main square. Mary tended to walk with a downward gaze, alert to what might trip her, and remnants of an ice storm remained. But when she was across the street from the City Hotel, she glanced at its bay window. Edward had said he was going to run errands, including the acquisition of columbine plants for the yard. She checked an impulse to barge into the City Hotel to ask what was going on, because he was at a table with Maud Dieterman, his hands framing her face. They kissed in full, with their mouths, before sitting back laughing as women and men teemed in high spirits, like carolers on a holiday night, and this included Gertrude Weber, who punched Edward's arm. Maud leapt up and lost herself in this throng, celebrating something other than, clearly, the end of the war, which showed no signs of dawning.

Edward stood, too, and vanished inside whatever was going on during what he had described to Mary as his "busy day."

She stumbled to the boardinghouse of Addy Oscar, and upon hearing commotion in the dining room, she lingered in the shadows as the residents—Lucy Brattle, too—helped themselves riotously to an array of treats on a serving table. Perpetua sat on a folded blanket on her chair to get to the height of the others gabbing with her. Having lost one hand early on, at Bull Run, Henry Kingsley lately spent his evenings training himself to function with one hand so that his job in Los Angeles at his uncle's company would be possible. She would leave soon enough and wed him out West. No one was to blame for Lucy and Mary's not seeing much of one another anymore. Lucy's head turned slightly; did she note Mary on the periphery? If so, she corrected her glance, did not move to greet her and wave her in. (No, stop; Mary was inventing this out of her own shyness.)

Did Mary hope to claim a room here for a night, a week, shivering in January's chill and whimpering about her husband kissing a woman in public view, whereas she compacted everything about John into a pin stuck inside her heart until blood droplets migrated to the boundary of her skin?

She was in her nightdress in the parlor, pretending to read, when Edward entered with cold-flushed skin and said, "You look beautiful. How was your day?"

"How was yours?" she asked.

"Fine enough." He kissed the side of her face. "Mary?" Stepping back, he regarded her.

She asked if there might be anything he wished to tell her, and he replied, "I don't think so. Anything I can get for you?" Sometimes this was code for wishing she would not sink into "one of her moods."

She said no, there was nothing he could get for her, thank you.

SHERMAN'S REHEARSAL FOR
THE MARCH TO THE SEA:
THE MERIDIAN RAID, MISSISSIPPI

14–20 FEBRUARY 1864

THEIR TRAINING WAS AIMED AT PERFECTING THE NEW BRAND OF war.

General William Tecumseh Sherman ordered them to prepare for an operation in Meridian, a major rail junction 150 miles away, still in Mississippi, a dry run for his plan to take Atlanta, then cut a swath to the sea. *We'll end nightmare by using nightmare.* The rebs keep skulking off, playing catch-me-if-you-can. Take no supplies except weapons . . . break into homes if you want linen or ham hocks. Carry no canteens: Houses will have pitchers. Creeks have water. Steal. Cook over spirit lamps. Every ounce of *weight* is your enemy. Destroy your haversacks. Ponder nothing: That is weight, too.

John was reluctant to discard a note from Nikka, received back at the end of a summer that felt like a lifetime ago, before any of them knew they would be stationed in insect-riddled Vicksburg month upon month. The message was brief, and at first it disturbed him that his family had tracked him down in the spot where he had helped to starve innocent women and children. But it was his mother who seemed more tormented; she asked him to forgive her everything, adding, via Nikka's script, "God tells me one day Mary and you shall wed, and John, I met her and gave my blessing, and she kissed me."

He scrawled back: *Be at peace, & may we all be soon at peace, Birdie Mother. Whatever you need forgiven of me, take & hold it to yourself in God's name.*

He had not said: *All well and good, Mãe, but it's too late. Neither God nor man are likely to put Mary and Edward asunder any time soon.* He had not heard from Mary, nor had he written to her, in an eon. As it should be. Enough.

Before marching to Meridian, a captain forced John and his company to tuck all letters under rocks.

Twenty-one thousand infantry, seven thousand cavalry. They bustled out of Vicksburg. Trooping twelve miles a day, twelve days. Math-wise, it was trim and square. Four divisions footing it in two columns, like the front of a Greek theater dismantled and set in motion, swift over dirt roads, corduroy roads. John and Frank looked back at the caissons and men, a dun river. They raided an abandoned farm and dined on chicken and canned peas. Alonzo pocketed a saucer, but a colonel knocked it from him: *Take only what you need, move on.*

Dusk draped itself over them as they camped. Abner said, "I hear we've got to go into houses and punish them."

"I'm not a Viking," said Frank.

"No, we'll just break up the rails," said John.

Cyrus Skylander mentioned an increase in desertions. A man could still get shot for hightailing it. Foragers on both sides were taking what they pleased, but rebs were cutting off the noses and ears of Union thieves. Bill Snow kept asking how come the authorities decided stealing was now an article of faith if it still courted punishment?

Nobody could answer that.

Alonzo had heard of regiments sending commanders full of derring-do to perdition for insisting that everyone march into harm's way. One man got sacrificed so the rest could sit it out until it was time to go home.

"Deserting makes sense," said Frank. "Surviving until the war's called off."

"Don't talk like that," said John. "We've come this far."

"That's just it." Frank's features twisted into animation. "This is like trying to catch a frog with our bare hands. Remember when we tried doing that at Mauvaisterre Creek?" Frank used both hands to mime catching frogs. "You grab one, and it jumps clear. The field's so big you spend hours before you see it—or it's another critter looking the same—and you try to catch it again, but it bounds off." John inhaled a wafting of bayou air, riddled with decomposing crawfish. Frank wanted a camera to take *pictures*, especially of *frogs*, to capture their *motion*.

"We can hear you, Frank," said Cyrus. "You don't need to be so loud. Frogs jump, that is a known fact."

"You're not getting my meaning! They jump, we follow, and pretty soon we're in Indiana! Killing *spirits* instead of *soldiers* means they're making us go to war against families. The fight has to be"—he tapped the side of his head—"up here."

"What happened to the frogs?" asked Abner.

"Who said this was about frogs?" yelled Frank.

"Frank," said John. "Elizabeth's waiting, and you'll get home."

Cyrus stated that no one would want him. Look at his face, torn to butchery.

"You were plumb ugly beforehand," said Abner. "Don't kid yourself."

They laughed, Cyrus, too.

Was it good or bad news that Sherman had no plans to engage the enemy in battle? Perhaps it was better to clash in the manner of Shiloh, and when the smoke cleared, the commanders decided who had won. That form of slaughter instead of ravaging, a new shout of *Wipe everything off the map and scrape up the earth.*

The blue boys swarmed into Meridian on Valentine's Day, their speed and brazenness frightening reb general Leonidas Polk into abandoning the city.

Invent a war in the style of salt plowed so no root can push up. Tens of thousands of men and horsemen embarked on the annihilation of all within eyesight. Depots and storehouses yielded cornmeal and bacon before they were destroyed. The Federals attacked one hundred miles of rails, three intersecting lines, with crowbars and sledges, heating and twisting the metal. Sherman's bow ties. We've cut off the shipping from the foundries of Selma. The Burton House Hotel, disintegrated into ash. John was assigned to the burning of fences. On fire were the silos of grain from the Black Prairie. Citizens streamed away. Let them spread the warning of what's coming. A horde dismantled three steam sawmills and the bridges over the Chickasawhay and at Lauderdale Springs. Men carried the speed of that march still in them, past exhaustion and into exhilaration, cooking food over what remained of a barn. John's vow as a refugee had been to build and preserve in a country that was an engine of constructing. Gone, all of that. The future is about taking what one pleases, about undoing. A flare of wanting his mother was so blistering that he imagined spotting her in every fleeing older woman.

Frank, Cyrus, and Alonzo were sent to level another warehouse while John, Bill Snow, Abner Quimby, and Isaac Unthank were required to troop away from the center, to occupy as a headquarters a house isolated in a nearby field. The dwelling looked like a salt box slammed on top of another salt box. As Captain Manford Pryor was detailing what would transpire, a shot rang out from the upper story. The captain threw himself against the siding and ordered Abner to clear out the sniper. A boy not much older than fourteen, hair haystiff, leaned out a window to squawk, "Bastards." Abner, Colt revolver brandished, entered the house and cleared out the boy and a scrawny woman, her apron faint with pinkish blood. The captain told the woman he had seen mannequins more frightening than this boy her gullyfluff cunt had let loose.

She spat into his eyes.

He blinked, extracted a handkerchief, wiped his face, studied the cloth, folded it, put it into his pocket, and took his gun from his waistband.

Abner said, "Captain, let's send them running like the others. What do you say?"

"I say I got myself defiled."

The citrus sky was going gray. Chickens lazy from never before needing to fly struggled to learn how as they flapped toward the woods that gaped in patches and blazed in others, red teeth at intervals among mossy ones. Shooting gallery. Feathers a blizzard. Birds spun on a bullet's axis before getting roasted in pans. *Beak-hunting:* Same thing during the chaos in Madeira with women jostled, plates smashed, pigs macheted.

I thought we were safe from our old stories, Ma. Mother, lift me away. All of us. I need to get past another crazy guard.

Mother, I don't have your faith, but I know you're with me.

The captain said to John, "Burn this house."

"Captain, we need it for a headquarters."

"After that, you'll choose one or the other of them to die." The captain pointed his pistol toward the mother while Abner, shaking, covered her son.

"Aw, Christ, I don't want to be here. Go on, Alves," said Isaac.

The light around John sailed off to get snagged in some ironwork of black smoke. They were on a periphery. He put pictures to the sounds and odors in the near distance, the corn roasting over flames crackling with shutters and hobbyhorses, with the porcelain heads of dolls popping. Venison was emerging from sheds while bayonets speared butter from churns. Infantrymen whooped and shot into the air as families fled across the winter fields. Captain Pryor directed his pistol at John's face and barked, "You deaf, boy? I said, burn this house, then pick one of these enemies to die. You're a soldier who should pull the trigger, but I'll do it if you're a coward."

Bill said, "Captain Pryor, that's murder. And John's one of us."

John stared into the dilated pupil of the barrel. A tinderbox was on the ground, spilled from a haversack grabbed on the last leg of the march. Captain Pryor's mouth became a sinkhole sucking in fury he then blasted outward, shouting, firearm still leveled at John, "Whose side you on, brown boy?"

Meridian. Madeira. Eerie how similar the names were. Men burning his family out of their home.

Isaac hissed, *Alves, burn the house, you don't have to shoot anyone.*

Captain Pryor turned his pistol back to the woman and her son and said, "Which of you cretins took that shot at me?"

The boy muttered, "I was defending my maw."

The captain laughed and said, "Liar. She'd cut my throat a fair sight faster than you'd piss yourself."

Isaac said, "We'll send them running like the others, Captain. The Bible tells us to smite our enemies, but in this case, I think—"

"I think you should shut your gob."

John inhaled, the Starr revolver slipping in his belt, and said, "Captain, he's right. It's a woman and a boy."

"Bless me, I'm in charge of traitors with their tails down," said the captain.

"That I ain't," said Isaac hotly. "I'm a proud Northerner, same as—"

A bullet from the captain ricocheted off the ground and clipped Isaac's foot, making him leap and yelp, and everyone stared at the blood. "Goddamnit, Alves, don't just stand there!" screamed Isaac. He dropped to the ground to cradle his foot. Bill offered a strip of cloth to bind it, and Isaac yelled at him to shove it up his hole.

"Pipe down, Unthank. You're vexing me." Captain Manford Pryor said to John, "Soldier, either this lovely lady or the two-bit imbecile she whelped is about to leave us. You choose. I'll count to three. *One.* I'm one-third of the way through. Don't look at me like that. You're clearly unaware we're at war."

Bill took a step closer, and his hand rose toward the officer as he stammered, "Captain, I'll escort them out of here. I—"

"Alves is gonna pick one whose time on earth is done."

Isaac finally accepted a strip of cloth from Bill to wrap his gushing foot. Abner quit training his revolver on the boy, holstered it, and eyed the captain. He had been talking about this, men ending the life of an officer and hiding until the war's end.

"I'll burn the house," said John, groping for the tinderbox. The clouds thinned into rugs rolling up because even the heavens were in haste to get elsewhere.

"Insufficient response due to your dawdling. Choose an enemy to die, or you'll get as lame as Isaac. Or I'll hobble his other foot. I'm sick of his Bible spouting."

Abner said, "There are four of us, Captain, and one of you, and these prisoners can run like everyone else."

"*Two*," said the captain. "I'll report you for insubordination, Alves."

He should have torched the house immediately. Now he could do nothing and get injured himself, or he could endure Isaac's wrath at a further maiming at the whim of a raving-mad officer, or he might dispatch a superior and face a firing squad. He would not choose whether a boy or his mother should be dispatched from this world.

A distant cow bellowed as its throat was slit and it collapsed to its front knees.

Past the bonfires and homes dwindling into nothing, citizens continued to flee. Had his mother not vowed to fly to him in need? She was not there in corporeal form, but her strength possessed him. She had taught him to dance, with stomping and whirling, in praise of the God who created all things, mighty and mean, chanting a song akin to a spiritual: *Lift your feet up to the Lord! John, lift your feet!*

He had lifted his knees to twirl with her.

John, lift your heart! Lift it! Open your arms, send up your heart!

Yes, Mother! The Lord saith fling up our hearts!

Lift your voice! Your eyes! Our minds fly to the Lord God!

John could not discern what the captain was roaring and almost cried aloud for her to take from him this burden.

Captain Manford Pryor blasted another bullet, this time straight into Isaac's wounded foot, reducing it to a ribboned stump. He squawled, writhing and cursing John. Bill Snow offered a new tourniquet, kneeling, but Isaac screamed, "Get away from me!"

The captain seized the tinderbox and set the house on fire; flames ate the seams. He hissed, "Think I wouldn't shoot an old woman. Don't you, cowards. Watch." Before anyone could move, he shot the boy through the chest, the powder smell jamming into John's nostrils, before saying to the dead boy's mother, aiming between her eyes, "You next. I wanted you to see him go first."

"Christ!" shouted Bill.

John would treat this enemy mother as his own, years-late reparation for the sin of eating cake instead of readying to die for his fellow Little Bird. He would hearken to Serafina's courage. He reached for his gun. As the captain cocked his pistol, Abner fumbled for his own weapon. Get rid of this murderer so they could seek invisibility and tape their souls together. John lifted his revolver and put a bullet through the captain's shoulder. The captain's screeching sailed toward the woods. John hated not having done it before Pryor had shot the boy.

Bill went for a medic, and Abner yelled at the Southern woman to run. She uttered a curse and looked at her dead son and stalked away. John's revolver pointed downward while the captain, blood streaming over his fingers, gripped his shoulder and shouted that John had signed his death warrant. Abner moved in, pointing his gun at the captain, and intoned, "Four of us here, like I said, and one of you. Want to live, Captain? The sniper clipped you, that's our story, and you'll live, thanks to your men who made sure you got that stitched." Isaac shrieked that if Alves had burned the fucking house right away, none of this would have happened, now he was a cripple because of godforsaken motherfucking John. Captain Pryor obeyed by crouching, then dropping, waiting for a stretcher.

—

EXHAUSTED BOYS WERE SPLAYED NEAR SIBLEY TENTS IN AN impromptu camp. His bones rattling in terror, John spoke inside himself: *Mother, you are with me. You have always been with me.* He pictured her blackened teeth, her distended middle. Not caring who witnessed it, he touched his chest and offered a tossing gesture into the thin air. He imagined her catching his heart. A game they had shared in the jail.

When he spotted Isaac with his mangled foot wrapped and elevated and offered to take him to the medic, Isaac hollered, "What will it take for you to stop torturing me? I didn't wrong you with your lady, I did not, and yet you can walk but I'm a cripple, Alves! You should have been shot, not me! You get away with judging and condemning me! You kept your mother from assisting in my life's aim!"

John lacked a decent reply, and tremors besieged him. He had shot an officer, and a death sentence was not out of the question.

—

BACK IN VICKSBURG, WITH SHERMAN DECLARING MERIDIAN A TIDE-turning success, John tried to apologize again to Isaac about his foot, but Isaac explained in detail where he could put his sympathy. Sugar eaters sat on crates, a tableau out of a woodcut of warriors. Grains got sprinkled on pork belly. Teeth clamped onto white grit. Lift your jaws up to the Lord. Abner was too numb to knock the lice off his sleeve. There was talk of Joshua Chamberlain's past heroism at Little Round Top, and of the valor of Benjamin Grierson, whose lectures on melodic counterpoint at Illinois College were sinking into oblivion.

John told Frank what had happened. Captain Pryor was in a med tent, so far saying nothing, but John would always fear him coming to haunt. Alonzo prepared biscuits, stirring up flour, condensed milk, and lookie, an egg I carried without breaking all the way from the inferno.

John counted the days to the end of his term of service: 118. One and one and eight. Mary, four months before I return to—what?

Feeling called to the Mississippi, he knelt at the riverbank and glanced backward at the current outpost, another repossessed fort, as broken as a pile of stone tablets. The mail hack had come and gone while he had napped. Cupping his reflection, he splashed his face onto his face. A willow's tendrils were like streamers. He noticed Alonzo and Frank not far down the bank with the same idea. Tranquility was ruptured by the lurching into view from the opposite direction of Isaac on a taped-together crutch, foot-stump encased in bloody cloth, who proceeded to rant about wanting to start a business, and since John had turned everyone against him with lies, he was obligated to assist.

"Unthank," said John. "Leave me in peace. I'm sorry about your foot."

"You need to make things up to me!" he yelled. "Maimed men back home won't want to buy *pairs* of shoes! They'll need only *one* shoe, or *one* boot, so I can start a *one-shoe* business, selling left or right ones, not pairs! I need cash."

John made the mistake of laughing; he couldn't help it. He flashed a look toward Alonzo and Frank, who were standing now, watching, and John laughed harder, about the stupidity of the shoes, and the ghastly nightmare of Meridian, and the balled-up endless mess with this shadowy man possessed of constant, amorphous yearning that included a desire to pester John without surcease.

"Shut up!" screamed Isaac. "You almost got me killed! You refuse to admit making up a story about my sins. I did not do you harm, but I should! You got my foot shot twice! I oughta put a bullet in the same place where you put one in the captain!"

John's gun was slightly out of reach. His vision blurred as an insect, out of the South's endless armies of them, bit his shoulder through his shirt. A light exploded from Isaac's direction. The sting hurt. His stomach rattled the white growths sprouting there since his earliest days of hunger. Alonzo and Frank were yelling, their weapons firing while Dexter Loomis was striding toward John, who said, "Dex, you died at Shiloh. I miss you." As blood poured onto John's chest, Dexter scooped up cobwebs and packed them onto John's shoulder. They waved at Mother on the other side of the mighty water. He tried to project his voice to her. She was dancing with penguins, and little lost deaf student Missy Baker, apricot-haired, was with her, too.

The boy murdered in Meridian drew toward him, and his head turned into a cow's skull like the one John had beheld in a field in Morgan County, when he wondered: But where are the bones of its body?

His last image before blacking out was of Isaac curled up like a sleeping baby.

When he awoke, Frank and Alonzo were leaning over him. When John tried to sit, asking if Isaac had shot him, Alonzo pushed him down and said yes, and good thing Frank and he had been there, because Isaac was aiming at John's head after planting the shot in his shoulder. Frank said, "Isaac's dead. You don't have to worry about him anymore. You've been out for three days, and you're getting chills and fever the doctor doesn't like, but he got the bullet out." John touched the bandaging, and the exertion dropped both his arms. They felt nailed to the cot. A haze surrounded Frank, and Alonzo wore an aurora borealis. Fascinating. Very. The air was whipped so thick it was beige. The cot was in a corner opened to the sky, partially sealed with slats from a crate. One slat was stamped MARMALADE. Woozy, his mind slid *to being a teenager in Jacksonville during the advent of those thirteen-year-cycle cicadas. Hatching from the dirt after long slumber, lurching out of the prairie, emerging from gardens. Raining from the sky and the trees, like an illustration out of the book of Revelation. Hooves and carriages ground them into paste. People slipped and fell. Horses broke their legs. Mashes of cicadas, crunching when they got stomped. Boys yelping. Backs cracked, bodies crushed below heels. Buzzing. Screen doors assailed. Green and black and suppurating, everywhere until they died out. Corpses among the flowers and hulls on porches, or in dishes, spinning in bowls of milk, having hopped through open windows.*

And then all clear. All burst. A return to being dormant, invisible pods.

MARY WEDS NORMAN GREER

MARY'S PALM IS THE FINAL NEST FOR A BROWN EGG FROM NELL'S banty hen. She cracks it on the lip of the iron skillet. After her husband warns of a long day ahead at Illinois College, she is alone to a point of fright in a house that will never truly feel like hers.

Edward returns after she is in bed and whispers that the train got stuck. She murmurs. She waits for him to stop touching her hair near the part of her brain inflamed with the question: *What were you doing, kissing someone?* That particular someone. How many weeks have passed by, six, seven? The sword remains stuck through her, the throb undiminished.

They have trouble speaking with words.

They have trouble speaking without words.

Underwater sounds fill her when she sleeps. She dreams of whales perishing, an armada going tail-first to the sea bottom, holding to the majesty of dying upright, chalice-configured. Inside the open mouths of the falling whales, tiny fish swim, as if in pools located in a gyre.

When the whales hit their gravesites fathoms down, the fish dart past the closing jaws. A few get trapped.

Her husband is gone again when she awakens. On the dining table are . . . crumbs, a trace from a tale about wandering children.

Elizabeth Hampton Meline finds her tending the outdoor trees, bringing Frank's grave concern for John, delirious in Vicksburg with a shoulder wound. Isaac was responsible and was shot dead. By Frank and a comrade. "I'm so sorry," Elizabeth whispers, having tiptoed up to shake Mary's shoulder. Frank apologized for not contacting them sooner. He had hoped to convey better news.

Mary's note to Edward was brief. *John might be dying. I must go to a friend. Please understand, love, Mary.* She could not risk him attempting to impede her.

She paused with her carpetbag. Edward would wish no man harm, but she had an inkling that this did not disallow another natural thought he might harbor: *Soldiers die. Hours from home, minutes, they can die.*

Women were entering the fray, going within its magnitude, pretending to be soldiers to remain with their loved ones. Nurses and caregivers dwelled on the edges of fields. Mrs. William H. L. Wallace—Ann—had raced to Shiloh only to hear her husband's dying vow, *We meet in heaven.* He had carried a braid of her hair into battles. What might have redounded, what regret, to have heard of his injury and stayed in the comfort of home, slept well, dined well, and missed a final word?

It was eighty-five miles to St. Louis. Cottonwoods, visible out the train's window, raced with her, liquefying themselves. She was exposing herself to danger, but John had been doing that for almost three years, longer than the time his mother had spent in jail. Forty dollars were in a money belt under her forest-green flannel dress.

She switched trains for the 250 miles to Memphis, where enslaved men were sorting grain into burlap sacks and loading wagons, one tumbling from the weight of a neck iron. The land rumbled with men and women and children fleeing, homeless. The town churned with soldiers, emaciated dogs, and bony women, one puffing a cigar and leering at her, triggering double vision even with her spectacles on. A soldier perched on a pile of cannonballs, whittling a block into the shape of a duck. A woman floated past, plucking feathers off a dead chicken. Boys rolled dice against a store with missing windows.

The Gayoso Hotel, with its wrought-iron balconies, advertised marble tubs, a bakery, and silver faucets. Mary longed for a bath and a hot meal, but blue men poured in and out, and one with tremendous whiskers hollered that the hotel was a Union headquarters, not a brothel. She backed down the steps and bought corn cakes from a woman's cart. Mary quickened her step, toward an outskirt likely to have a barn. The clouds had curdled lumpish as sour milk. She visualized Edward reading her note before burning it in the fireplace.

She came upon a bungalow with an unlocked door and called into the depths, "Anyone home?" There was no answer. A living room offered a library of morocco-bound volumes. A bust of Cicero was on a pedestal in a corner, and a rocking chair was next to a sofa with springs protruding. A side room held a mattress of straw ticking, shafts poking through a gray covering. A Bible rested on a table. It was a man's house. But he was a reading man, a God-fearing one. A pail lay on a counter, and Mary took it to the well. The rope burned her hands as the pulley creaked. Papa told her she had almost been drowned in a well by a Weaver of Angels. From the start, she had defeated assassins. She trudged with the filled pail to the kitchen. A rust-speckled cupboard held a loaf with ants she scraped off. The bread required sawing with a knife, and she chewed slices like teething rusks.

After scrubbing her face and drawing water through her hair, she unbuttoned her dress and untied the drawstrings of her under-blouse to expose herself to the waist, washing rapidly and dabbing with a dirty, balled-up towel as if swiftness would prevent its unpleasantness from touching her. She buttoned up, damp, and rolled down her stockings and bathed her lower half before going outside, certain she heard noises.

A young man with a gourd head approached with a dog, a shotgun cracked over his shoulder. An arrow pierced his flesh below an elbow. He said, "You're on my property." He was not much larger than a child.

"You have an arrow in your arm," Mary said. The far road was empty.

"That is a fact. Hunters. Blind galoots. I was hankering for a partridge and caught none." His dog, fur up, circled her. "Name's Roland."

"You like to read, Roland," said Mary. Think. Speak.

"I'm no bumpkin," he said. "I walked away from the infantry, 'cause

I could not bear how my own people taunted me. I cain't help being short. Cicero got his hands chopped off, head, too, because he wanted to take his smartness to his country place and get away, and the world cain't abide that." Sniffing her, the dog growled. "You are easy on my eyes. But Cicero don't like you."

"That's your dog's name?" If she kept him talking, he might be pacified.

"Yessum. Cicero, sit."

The dog obeyed. Roland's pierced arm hung loosely, and with his whole one he swung his shotgun and cocked the barrel into place. "I look like a Cupid who got awful fraught," he said. "I've no luck with women. This here is smarting me."

Head to soles, she was twisting up. "You have a nice library."

"Inherited my daddy's books," said Roland. "He died of fever, Mama, too. I got no girl and no life but for to read. They laughed at me in the army, so I quit. Y'all set to whup us anyhow. You look south-of-the-border-like. Awful cute."

"Do you have thread? I'm a seamstress. I'll stitch that."

Roland looked at his arm as if he had just noticed the arrow and said, "I know of a feller living with buckshot in his chest." The dog's snarling lowered into indifference. "Kept thinking, I've got a loaf of bread."

"Best not to eat before we care for that. I won't tell anyone you deserted if you'll leave me be." She did not know a soul to whom she could report him, even if she had a mind to do so, but he seemed to consider this.

"I'm inclined toward your stitchery offer." Motioning with the gun, he directed her into the house. Mary was afraid about the bread being half gone. Roland said his departed mama had kept sewing notions under the bed. The arrow knocked into the sofa, and he yelped, and she ran to a cardboard box with virgin needles and skeins spooned together, pinks and whites, like newborn opossums. For the first time ever, she failed to thread a needle on her first attempt. She said, "I'll repair you if you promise not to hurt me."

"I cain't do much mischief at this precise moment," said Roland. "Fix me up, y'all is safe. Ouch." He staggered to Cicero's bust and tapped its pate with the hand of his uninjured arm. "Whether it is our confoundery-federacy or your poxy nation, the problem with folks is they do not do what they swear to. Cicero the man and Cicero the dog are my witnesses. Time was, in a small enough place, a man could hold another man to what he swore. Could track him down. Ouch. This is honest smarting me."

Mary snapped the thin arrow in two. Roland hollered to lift the rooftop, and his dog jumped, almost toppling his namesake. Mary pulled the wood out and used an antimacassar as a tourniquet. "It didn't hit an artery," she said.

"Much obliged, sweetpea," said Roland, doughy faced.

She nudged the dog aside, ordered her vital forces to stay intact, and stitched the arm wound, using a lace runner to wipe away the blood.

"Mama would not approve of her handiwork being used so."

"She'd approve of you being healed. You'll not harm me?"

"Don't blame you for lacking faith. We think if we do or say anything unseen there's no retribution. This is a religious-yakking nation, but we learn quickity to hide from God. People talk about others but smile to their faces. If God is all-powerful, why don't He stop that? Or stop the war. The minister says we chose it of our free will." He cackled. "Jesus, I would like never to die. Yessir, that is what my free will hankers for."

"I don't disagree about folks betraying one another."

"Right!" Roland said, staring at his stitched arm. "God should set up a screen and show folks what goes on behind their backs. Fellers kissing their best friend's wives. Women tee-heeing about so-and-so's clothing. Women never stop with that."

He curtailed her fright by whispering that the milk wagon passed on the high road at dawn, and he never failed to awaken right before that. He promised not to lay a hand on her. "Remember me as a feller from that dying breed of those keeping their word."

At first light, the milk wagon looked like a black-paper silhouette, and she ran to it. It released her outside town. With two hundred miles to go, she hitched a lift with a teamster from Wichita, who chided her for being "calamity-inviting." In Senatobia, she spent four dollars on a fried chicken, itself starved to the size of a glove, and she hunted mushrooms breaking winter's crusts and accepted rides past denuded yellow pines. She bought a tin of oysters in Yazoo City.

Vicksburg astonished her with its vistas and steamboats on the river. Roots poked out of the earth like the humps of sea serpents. The city was ruptured, buckled with gaps and torn cross-hatching. Her impulse was to smooth out and sew the fissures closed.

Bisque heads were crushed on the sidewalk in front of a doll shop, with a sign teetering on one nail: CHILDHOOD'S DEPOT. A Federal told her the hospital was in the Duff Green mansion, with Confederates on the main floor and Union boys in the upper story. A yellow flag flew at its apex, and she found it easily, along with a pungency of ether. Even if this was goodbye, she would hold John's gaze as she had with her father when he died. Men lay in beds on an aproning porch, the stench an intensification of whatever was privately human. A nurse attending to a patient called out, "Don't just stand there. Come here."

Mary drew near a soldier with tunneled-back eyes. The nurse said he was Norman Greer of Ohio, and she was Peg Anderson from Lawrence, Kansas, though after the massacre by bushwhackers last summer, she could hardly return. Norman arched his back, releasing an odor that alerted Mary to the likelihood of his torso disintegrating into the mattress. His paw was sopping. She was so afraid to go inside and find John that she did not mind a lesson in nursing. The patient could not focus his sight, and Mary could not decipher what he babbled.

"Norman," said Peg, "that's not true. I said your fiancée would find you, and here she is, exactly the way you described, pretty as a picture."

Mary stared at Peg, whose kerchief hid most of her hair. Norman reared up at Mary but fell back with a strangled bleating, "I do, I will."

Peg whispered, "Answer him. I promised he'd marry her before he died."

"I take thee, Norman," said Mary, scrambling. The proper words eluded her.

"In sickness and in health." His panting was wretched.

"Her name was Frances Reynolds. From Dayton," whispered Peg. The patient in the adjacent bed rolled onto his side to watch. The air over the porch dirtied into sulfur. Mary said to Norman, "From this day until my last." Her words seemed to satisfy him as Peg said, "I now pronounce you man and wife." The miles were catching up to Mary. Peg crossed his hands over his chest and pulled the bedsheet over his head, soothed it over his crown. "I wanted to be the one to marry him," she said. "Like that, I mean."

"I'm sorry," said Mary.

Peg replied, "No, I've meant something to more men here than happens for most women back home." Peg did not scold her for getting in harm's way; she understood wanting to be inside the country's convulsions rather than cowering outside them. She said, "I'd fancy knowing your name, so I can tell this story properly later."

Mary shared it and rose to go inside, to John. There's a song made of all striving to go back to those we love.

It moves the world on its axis.

This is why the world is said to tilt.

BIRDSONG SHALL SHATTER OUR BONES

JOHN WAS CHOPPED INTO LITTLE SQUARES. THE WIND SCATTERED the pieces, and he loathed being one thousand tiny kites that would make horses shy up for miles. Horses had suffered enough. Fields were divided into checkerboards. Green, red, tan. A fragment of his foot got impaled on a foxtail. A square of forehead was snagged by corn silk. Mary was gathering him up, suturing him with threads drawn tight to pucker him into shape. The needle plunging in and out hurt slightly, but the sharpness told him he was not dead.

Moving on the white screen in front of him was . . . Mary. He struggled to work his eyelids as Frank shouted, "John? John! Wake up!"

Frank hoisted him to his feet. Everything was a hue of gruel. Patients were caterwauling on the lower-floor surgery. His arm was no longer in flames. *Mary.* Your widow's peak, how I love it. Your size is so familiar my arm finds Your shoulders. Your ear is a stethoscope listening to me. You walk me to a window. A scent of orange blossoms flourishes.

Holding You, I beg aloud, Where am I?

And You sob out, With me, you're alive.

—

ONCE, ON THE SECOND FLOOR OF NELL'S HOUSE, MARY HAD CREATED a fantasy of John, inspired by the oak outside a window. The boughs were like a pioneer's idea of candelabra. She had envisioned him below, where the moon had expelled a round cataract. *Step into me,* beckoned this pool of light. *Everyone has the chance to write a love story, to be an actor on a stage.* She imagined dropping a rope made of knotted-together sheets for him to climb. The cataract was itself so excited by his body in the middle of it that the rope wicked up some moon, glowed white also. His strength was arousing to her, and to him, as he scaled upward, hand over hand on bedsheets. When she helped him over the ledge, he toppled onto her, the comedy sparing them, taking them into the trembling of what they had played out in their minds.

Now it is real. He brings her to a house where the owner caught Federals raiding his vegetable patch and brained a sergeant with a brick, for which he was shot. His ghost roams. The property got converted into a Union hospital until the bigger one opened in town. The house is on a blind end, with tobacco leaves in the frieze. After apologizing for his mustache and beard (I love it, she says; you've *sprouted*), John carries her inside.

Always she shall conjure, on the nerve-hairs in her nostrils, the interior paint's smell of fruit and milk, from blueberries smashed into buttermilk, the mixture strained, a formula she recognizes from Nell's parlor, a verdant shade, here pocked with holes. On a table rests a round metal contraption with vertical slats, and inside the circle are pictures of a man in various poses. When Mary spins the ring, a continuous film of a man running appears on the illuminated outside slats. It recalls the pink one with depictions of horses her father gave her in Madeira.

"A zoetrope," he says. It means a wheel of life.

Full of hunger, she kisses him; his surprise excites her.

It is March the tenth in the year 1864, the day before his twenty-sixth birthday, an afternoon in a bullet-notched house, this confiscated spot with its moving-picture toy, and a train set built from corncobs, and yarn dolls, and lace (torn) curtains she itches to darn.

—

IF I COULD HAVE PREDICTED THE NEW CATASTROPHE APPROACHING, MARY, I
would have stayed in this house with its buttermilk-and-blueberry paint
with You, fought never to leave. While inspecting the premises, gleefully,
they find a whalebone hoopskirt. He hates that anything from the sea
might shame women for having legs—but it's just an enormous birdcage; *he forgives it.* As the blinds let in sunlight, Mary and he kiss while
striped black and white before drifting through the rooms, pausing to
embrace, laying bodily claim to the whole house. It confirms for him
that happiness is the purity of not wanting anything else.

This is why happiness is so fleeting.

The worst thing would be to grasp and rush, to cram nearly three
years apart into scant hours. They hasten upstairs, past more bullet
holes, to a bed with a knitted coverlet. This room has cream curtains
that move. He buries himself in her neck, her hair the color of the
black pearl Nikka and he had spotted in the window at Tiffany's in
New York—that pearl had had a glimmer. He undresses her. Mary
seals her mouth against his before releasing him to kiss every inch of
her, and she insists upon doing the same to him. And then he enters
her: She cries out and there is hardly any motion as they lock together,
wrapped tight. And then everything is fierce. They are tender, and she
cries out again.

And . . . *it amazes me,* she thinks. At any diminished point, with its
impetus toward further diminishment, *life pulls up,* fresh and strong.
The cloth pull of the shade, an oval wrapped in thread, taps the glass.
The headboard made of iron swirls creaks.

How long do we have? she whispers. There's kissing like slow-
motion tumbling. A fern sways overhead in a tin hammered with nails
to allow drainage. Her thighs are dripping, her pores sopping. Her
crying covers his chest with a salt he won't wash off for days. They
shift from knowing he must return to final duties in the war to being
startled that they must bear it, and they make love again. John's heart
adheres to her back when he enters her again; then again they cling
heart to heart. She asks softly, "Why does it feel the way it does?"

"No one knows," he says. "We only know that it's so."

He covers her with a quilt decorated with wheels, and he grips
some of the spokes as he hugs her. It's slaughtering him, the fineness of

her hair. He touches a few strands to let her know he wishes he could touch each one. Side by side, they stare at one another. He is months, only months away now, from returning home. She kisses his weather-chapped forehead, where all the pictures he carries are blended.

———

HANDS GLIDE UP AND DOWN EACH OTHER'S BODY TO CONVINCE themselves of solidity. A family once lived here. Wraiths drift past the mirror. Bloodstains mar the floor from when this was a hospital. The cedar chest is imbedded with shot. "Mary, I was in a place called Meridian, and—" He stops. He should guard most of the horrors within rather than spoil this reunion, but he voices an abridged version. "Isaac shot me. Too much history with us. His hatred. He was getting set to fire again, and if Frank and our friend Alonzo had not been close by, I'd be gone. Isaac looked like a crumpled doll. That's the last I know. One day I'll tell you all that happened, about a house on fire, and a dead boy, but not today."

"Yes. All right. I regret how you and I parted."

"We got hurt by Isaac, darling. He even decided to tarnish my brother in your eyes. You and I never meant to hurt each other. How long could you have lived on a man's property before he sent you away? I've been gone years. I understand this now. Your marriage. My mother wrote to tell me we had her blessing, and that she gave it to you in person, for what that's worth."

He cannot speak further, and she tells him he can cry if he needs to.

No, he is far too happy today for tears. He interjects, "Marriage is a vow, and I'm tired of hurting other men. And you're cared for. So I don't know. I'm tempted to ask you again to start over with me in New York." Such a doomed expression: No one gets to "start" a life already underway.

Mary does not bring up finding her husband kissing someone else. Nor does she run through her list of suspects other than Isaac. She replies, "When we met, I wanted everything just so, and perfect, and for right now, I only want to be in this room, John. This time with you."

———

BIRDSONG PENETRATES THE WINDOW. CREATION INSISTS THAT WE note simple graces so profound they break us.

———

THEY ARE IN THEIR FOURTH HOUR. SHE EXCLAIMS, "JOHN!" WHEN HE touches her, as if she has no choice but to name the tenderest parts of herself after him. He strokes for the longest while all the bobbins stacked up to make her spine. They talk while he is inside of her, they want to ensure his being there lasts longer by talking, so that when they are apart and conversing with others, they can feel that behind speaking one can keep on making love.

When she went to the jail as a girl, her singing fed him before they even met, before he was released back to the sort of daylight that is a thing that stretches over the heads of people and hooks itself over the moon, daylight that is not chopped to pieces. She put the thread of her voice into his ear when they were children.

Your cry into my ear in bed with me is my treasure, because it meets the echo I have always known and carried of You inside myself from the start.

———

KNOCKING LOUD AS GUNFIRE WAS ALMOST HAMMERING DOWN THE front door. They scrambled into clothing and sailed down the stairs. A ruddy sergeant studied them and shook his head and barked, "Alves. You're up and hale, obviously, and there's a wall to build. Miss, time to say goodbye."

THE PORTUGUESE NIGHT BLESSING

SNOWFALL CAME HARD AND FANGED TO ILLINOIS, CRACKING ITS molars on buildings. Like a parent awaiting a teenager who had slipped off for revelry, Edward was sleepless in the sitting room the night she tiptoed in. He would make her speak first. She said, "Oh, you're here." Her flannel dress was seeped in her unwashed essence.

"I live here. So do you. I guess you forgot that."

"Edward—"

"There's not much for you to say. Is there."

She stepped toward him, and her hand lit on his forearm, and he flung her off as if her touch burned him.

Despite commanding herself to stop, she brought up overhearing his lecture mocking her speaking with plants. Everyone had been laughing.

He had to work to recall it before jumping to his feet and sticking his face inches from hers to shout, "They were amused because I'd described myself as a bungler needing your father's help, and yours. I heaped praise on you both. You heard a bit of fun at your expense, but you call that equal to running off to be with another man?"

She wrested out of his grip. "Maud," she said. "You kissed Maud. In the City Hotel, and Gertrude—"

He pitched a vase to crash in a fireplace that should be lit except, he screamed, he had been able to do nothing from upset. "You ran into danger and might have been killed, or attacked by men, or injured, Mary. You were insanely careless. Do you care that I was worried? That I sent men and went myself on pointless missions to locate you?"

"I needed to go." She added that she had not been afraid.

"On top of everything, you wish to insult my cowardice. Correct, I dislike the thought of shooting and killing. What I face with you requires a courage you ignore."

"I heard he might be dying."

"Was he?"

"Yes."

"Did he?"

"No."

"No. I see. Maud is a powerful but frivolous girl, for the nine hundredth time, Mary Catherine, and like all the other men there, I kissed her at her party. You have the nerve"—his face darkened to the shade of dried blood as he yelled—"the godforsaken nerve to compare that to going into a war zone for someone? I didn't tell you, because you're crazed about those women, and yes, Gertie was there. It wasn't my party. Should I have asked her to leave? It was a celebration of Maud's engagement. Finally. To Billy Mars, who was necking with Phyllis Barksdale. Stupid Edward. End of story. I lied to you. That's right. I didn't bring you, because you mope and complain when you hate something. How dare you compare that meaningless nonsense with violating your vows to me because you're in love with someone else."

"I—"

"Don't, Mary. Don't try. I won't divorce you. But I don't want to look at you for a good long while."

It was a given that this meant she must be the one to leave.

A new shock came when Mary called on Nell Clark, hoping for refuge, and after relating what had transpired with Edward, Nell remarked coolly, not inviting her in as wind moaned and snow spun in flurries, "I thought you had learned how to rise to your new station, Mary. I'm disappointed. I was at Maud's party, too, and you should have been there and put up with it, but I can't blame Ward for hiding it from you. Maud was not undeserving of cold comfort. Billy is high on the social register and already conducting affairs that make her seem like a nun. You exude anxiety, and untamed passions that you imagine are front and center as a concern to all. Now you have brought scandal upon a fellow who worships you. You are headstrong and immature."

"I went to a friend who was dying, Nell." Mary was pleading. "You know how someone did horrible things, keeping me apart from John."

"Poor little you, with a marriage envied by half the women in Springfield."

"Nell, I care about Edward. You know that, too."

"Then start acting like it. You think Maud is outrageous, and you're not?" She hurled a laugh. "Behaving like a respectable wife might begin by not running like a child to a neighbor. I shan't let you in." And the woman who had supported Mary from the start slammed the door in her face.

Mary took to residing again with Perpetua in the cottage, and Edward communicated via perfunctory notes. Even Pet admitted to dismay at Mary's behavior.

Then, as if her soul's call for an asylum required the original exiles acquainted with desperation, Nikka summoned Mary to Jacksonville.

A dying Serafina was calling for her.

When Mary entered the cabin in Madèira Hill, Nikka directed her toward Serafina stretched on her bed, in a seafoam-colored dress, who rasped at Mary, "Today I go home." She was like the stone inside a peach, scored deeply and consisting of many summers of water and sky, with eyes like John's, made of night. On her table was the Sound Machine. A soot-covered page lay next to it, with gyres and dashes scratched in it: the last words from God spoken through Serafina Alves, and it looked as if she had drawn the waves of the ocean. Nikka explained about John's sending an article to Hugo Meline, suggesting he add lampblack or ash to the paper on the roller to capture clearer markings.

Nikka and Mary stretched out on either side of the great lady and clutched her hands. Nikka tried to joke to Mary, "She won't tell us what the picture says. She wants John to figure that out. Their last sound-study together. Stubborn to the end."

Serafina winced, holding her middle. "It is what God He whispered at me."

To Mary, she said, "Maybe too late, but I want to be your mother. That is not the message from God, it is an asking from me."

"I'd like that, Senhora," said Mary. "Mother. I've never called anyone that." She heard John conveying: *She vowed to grow through the earth to be the wood of sheltering trees, she'll be a table, a cradle holding a grandchild.*

Serafina added, "You can take the machine my boy made, Maria Gato."

Mary replied, "Yes, Mother. I'll guard it."

At twilight came the sobbing of the crickets, and the stars were readying to grate themselves over the yard. "Sonhos cor-de-rosa, Mãe," said Mary, granting her the Portuguese Night Blessing. *Pink dreams, Mother. God bless you and make you a big saint . . . good night, sleep well.* Papa had prepared her to be brave with departures. Mary would see her through the gateway now, walk her down to the river. Serafina, her flesh only on loan from the Lord, seeped an entirety of herself into Mary, molecules of faith, and labored breath, and redemption.

Mama, Mary cried.

Nikka uttered, "Rest, Mother."

A kiss for Nikka, firstborn. A kiss for new daughter Mary. Death can be like going out on a tide. We're people of the sea, children. I understand dying, it is to make room for others. But pain I do not understand. I'll talk to Him about that. Bad idea. And because Mary contained John, John held his mother.

Serafina Alves conveyed without speaking: I'll live in the flowers. Do not call this farewell.

———

IN THE EASTERN CEMETERY, WHILE THE PREACHER LED THEM IN praying over the oak box of her in a cavity in the earth, the Northern Cross train sped on its diagonal through downtown. It was famous for showering ash, and soot settled on them, as if the page with Serafina's last words, the Voice of God through her, had burst loose to

be with her. Mourners from the First and Second Portuguese Presbyterian churches—factions united—concluded with the hymn "Abide
with Me."

Nikka was reluctant to write to John in Vicksburg, fearing what
this would do to him. Mary pointed out he would be home for good
in a short while, and they could tell him the news when he would not
have to endure it alone.

She wrote:

> *Dear Edward, I'll stay in Jacksonville a while. I'm sorry to
> add more pain in mentioning his name, but John's mother
> died, and Nikka needs me and has invited me to stay. (This
> is his older sister.) There are things we must talk about, I
> know. Tell Pet I saw black spot on the camellias. We need to
> send 40 bags to the Treasure Chest Shop in St. Louis. Dilly
> can sew these. Bill Farnsworth wants more pink tomatoes.
> Edward, please forgive me a little first if you can, and then
> we can yes of course discuss our marriage. I am torn with
> confusion, but I am also sorry, I hurt you again, and this is
> unfair. You have been kind from the start, to my father and
> to me. You made me stronger. I care about you, I do. Your
> loving wife, Mary*

She did not receive a reply.

She stitched on her tablecloth.

In the yard, the corn was dead according to the season, no longer
rustling like those snakes that rise out of baskets when they hear
music.

Nikka and Mary saw larks lifting.

Their song was: *We'll fly with her, the Woman Who Talked to God.*

THE BELL TOLLS AGAIN

27 March 1864, Vicksburg

Mary,

Under 3 months before I honorably muster out. Im filled with Emotion about our afternoon but pls dont risk Your life like that again, Darling. Though I didnt want to speak much about Meridian as You know, some day I promise Ill try to do that. Last I heard from Nikka, Mother was not well & Im worried. To bear these final weeks, it helps to relive Your Love as you Held me. I dont know what to do, but Ill sit w/You & Edward & we can sort through how all 3 of us got harmed. If Yr time & mine together was all there can be, I feel braver to endure that. My service to the Country that gave us shelter draws near its close. Ever & Ever, John. Alves.

Unable to post his letter, amid much grumbling that Vicksburg was too major an outpost for such indecent mail service, he stuck it into his Bible.

A scavenging group that included Bill Snow and three others from the 14th was ordered out along the Natchez Trace to clear away any bushwhackers. When the men did not return in a timely manner, Sergeant Phineas Blackwell tapped another party that included John and Frank, along with Caleb Snyder and Patrick O'Donohue from the Illinois 53rd. The orders came too swiftly for John to press his note into anyone's care, and urgency was foreshortened by his being only seventeen days past the blueberry-and-buttermilk house. Its radiance still enveloped him.

They stumbled upon what they figured was the original expedition butchered, the bodies already giving way, in the swampiness, to a decomposition that caused Frank to teeter near fainting. Patrick declared that this climate, with its vermin and no respect for a man's final rest, was as vile as the Secesh. The men barely looked like men. John escorted Frank to a secluded spot, a vantage point near a grove, and Caleb and Patrick agreed to stand guard and tease Frank to keep him from passing out.

John ventured back into the thicket and identified the three men: one via his pocket journal and the other two thanks to the paper slips pinned inside their jackets. Some wayward strides farther, John came upon Bill Snow, a hand over his liver. "Bill," said John. "Let's get you to camp." It was over an hour away. He knelt to assist him, but Bill yelled to be let go, and he wheezed out, "It's not even hurting. I don't want to be mauled by a bear. Bear food."

"No bears around. You shouldn't talk."

"Pryor shooting Isaac, you shooting Pryor, Isaac shooting you, Frank shooting Isaac. Jesus Christ."

"We had a commander who went crazy. Isaac started out crazy and got worse, but I'm not happy about his fate. Anyhow, that's over now, Bill."

Bubbling up under John's hand were Bill's final minutes. Bill panted out, "Daddy was a no-good, gave me his infernal name. Beat my ma black and blue. Killed her, law never found him. God'll confuse us two. Won't let me past the gates."

"He's supposed to be able to tell us apart, though, I think, Bill." John took the Bible from his vest, extracted the letter to Mary and stuck it in his pocket, and said, "This protected me at Shiloh. It was my mother's, and God favors her. Take it."

"Thanks. I want the Good Word with me."

John pointed at his name and address in the front, with the same for everyone in his family. "Shall I scribble your name here too, so God'll know you?" he asked. "I'll put William Snow, Junior." But Bill seized the Bible and held it tightly, wailing out, "How's God supposed to let me in? I've killed people. Just like my daddy did, worse."

"We've done our duty," said John, "and that means men have to die or kill for a good cause." This sounded like the pabulum in the newspapers from people with no idea what they were talking about.

Bill's skin firmed into wax as he perished.

John returned to find Caleb and Patrick with their throats cut and Frank gone. The sky screwed itself onto his head and spun him a few times, bent on pushing him into the earth. He stumbled into the underbrush, past the bodies of the dead, including Bill Snow. Fear of the enemy prevented John from calling for Frank. He tried to get back to the road, but it had slipped off the map. His shoulder wound tunneled through him. Maybe Frank got taken prisoner, but it made no sense that he would be spared and not the others. It would fall to John to find his friend's corpse. A heaving like a sob surged into his frontal lobe. He was having trouble retracing his steps and slid down against a tree. Snipers might still be lurking. The notion of Elizabeth Meline wearing black made him stand. He reread his most recent letter to Mary, then collected his rifle and set out walking. By the fourth day—or was it the sixth?—wondering why he saw no one and no one had come looking for him, he tried not to fret that retracing his steps back to Vicksburg was proving impossible. He ate bark; he roasted a squirrel and found it repellent.

One afternoon in a bog he was sure he had circled before, he had to work not to become hysterical. A songbird called. No harm in heading toward its pitch. He walked until the air grew saturated with a vapor that he hoped signaled the river. Leaves brushed his face because he lacked any strength to push branches aside. As the sun began its descent, he spotted Vicksburg's bluffs.

His reentry into an area outside one of the fortifications was greeted with stares fit for observing a phantom. Mark Robertson said, "What the hell."

John reported to Mark, and others gathering, that the first party was dead in an ambush, and so were Caleb and Patrick, and Frank was missing. Was he here?

"Haven't seen him," said Mark. "John, you got killed."

Sergeant Phineas Blackwell strolled forward, squinting, as the gloaming backlit a sparkling of insects. He whistled and said, "Alves, we buried you. You're Lazarus."

John was spending considerable energy to remain standing despite how the land was rocking. Sergeant Blackwell steered him toward a walnut tree where they could sit, and he explained that a third expedition had stumbled across all the bodies. He said, "Carrion birds found the deceased. Nobody was—distinguishable." He took out a tobacco pouch and rolled a cigarette and swiped a match against the tree trunk. John accepted the offer of a smoke. Blackwell exhaled a plume, and John sent smoke out of himself to meet it. The truth was dawning on him. "You found my Bible on a mauled body and thought I was dead?" A colonel's horse had once galloped into a camp without him, and the newspapers picked up the rumor that he had died. His family suffered for over two months until he recovered from injuries and wrote to them.

"Correct, Alves. You've been gone over a week. The chaplain went out to help bury everyone. Damn."

"But here I am," said John. He cringed to think of Bill Snow with his face and pith—all the soft parts—gone. Or Frank with that fate, though maybe that was better than being captured. One prisoner from Illinois had gotten down to sixty pounds and amputated his own gangrenous leg with a penknife. God forbid Frank had deserted. Surely he would not have run off without telling John.

"Yes, here you are." Blackwell stared into a middle distance as the sun reduced its lamps. "I didn't anticipate the look of dead men. I hate burying them far from home. I hate even more when they don't look human. We didn't study that at West Point."

"Nobody's prepared for that," said John. "You sure no one's seen Frank?"

"Meline? Unaccounted for." They blew rings of smoke. "Listen, Alves," said Blackwell, "there might be a misunderstanding you'll wish to correct. The chaplain who accompanied the last party got reassigned to Georgia. He was fastidious, and your family might soon be sorrowing with bad news. I don't know for a fact if he wrote condolences, but he sat at a desk all night after the burials. You've been gone a long time. He found what remained of you clutching a Bible with your name and address and the information regarding everyone in your family."

The officer's words felt poured down a cone John was inexpertly holding to his ear. From his vest he withdrew the crumpled letter dated March 27th to Mary. It was fibrous with damp. "I've written to a friend, but I should tear this up and send an update."

Sergeant Phineas Blackwell said, "As fate would have it, here comes the irascible cook with the mail sack."

John initiated a debate with the cook about allowing more time to pen a new note. The cook suggested, with ample gusto, that he did not have all day to stand about while an army private wrote a pathetic love letter.

"Send what you've got," said Blackwell. "The postmark should clear up matters, and that's in case the chaplain was efficient. Get a clarification set to go tomorrow."

John scrawled I AM ALIVE on the envelope, the letters bleeding with moisture, and refreshed the address to Mary. The cook snatched it and trudged on his way.

"Affable sort," said Blackwell. "No doubt bolstered by compliments about his trout en croute. Alves, I must bid you adieu and join another regiment near Jackson. Welcome back to life, such as it is." He urged him not to look so unsettled. John should focus upon impressing his family with how capably he could return from the dead, though he might equally have no cause for concern.

He debated writing to Elizabeth about Frank but held out hope there would be no call to worry her yet, and he returned to the barracks presided over by Captain Lucas Johnson. Captain Manford Pryor had vanished into the maw of the war, but John still awaited a night of sleep free of fearing a firing squad for shooting a superior.

Soldiers milled inside cloistering walls as the wind carried in tufts of cotton and stems from bales by the river. Alonzo stepped out of the scattershot to ask John what had happened, and John's words failed, would always build lacunae into the answer. A Jacksonville native named John Harris—his spirit manhandled everything toward giddiness—swatted the cotton blow drifting over everyone. Harris rifled debris at men trying to read, and at John scrounging for paper to write to Mary, and within seconds, most of them were hurling garbage at each other, whatever they could lay a hand on. Abner pitched corn husks at John Alves, whose aim went afoul as he blasted them back, clipping Captain Johnson's head as Harris dumped papers over the officer.

"Cease!" bellowed Johnson. "Alves! Harris! You have struck me with detritus! Quimby, tell these ninnies to desist!"

Harris, ablaze with merriment, ducked more cotton blow and aimed straw at a choleric killjoy who cussed him out. Harris shouted, "What kind of unprincipled fool objects to a little fun?"

The captain hollered, "What did you say, Harris?"

A smattering of crackers hit Harris's chest. "I said, Captain, I find it without principle to object to lads having fun."

While nearly the entire company continued cooking up a version of a pillow fight, Captain Johnson stalked to his quarters to issue the court-martial.

Private John Harris was named as the instigator fomenting the riot, with John Alves and Abner Quimby charged on a lesser count of disobeying the direct orders of a commander. Judge Advocate M. M. Crocker, a brigadier general, presided at the trial in Natchez. Harris pled guilty to throwing debris, thereby fueling the mayhem. Pled not guilty—no, sir—to calling the captain a man of no principle. He had called someone *else* a man of no principle, who in fact happened to *be* a man of no principle.

The trial lasted fifteen minutes, and the defendants were declared guilty on all charges. On came the leg irons. Captain Johnson declared every single numbskull in the regiment equally guilty and stuck everyone with the same twenty-day sentence of hard labor in rebuilding the fort's walls and complete denial of contact with the outside.

7 April 1864, Mary, DO NOT BELIEVE any letter from a chaplain who found my Bible on a dead man. It is possible no such letter was written, but Im worried. I wrote "I AM ALIVE" on the back of an earlier note I sent. A matter has arisen that will put me out of touch a while. Mary, our bond will survive however it is meant to be. I cant send this for 20 days & THEN IT IS 8 OR 10 MORE to get to You, but it is set to fly the moment God & our stern captain allow. John.Alves.

Slow days were made heavier with mortar and bricks. To counter the agony of her thinking him dead, he told himself that soon he would rise up and gladden her. Harris apologized for bringing this on them. Abner replied that the fight was the most fun he had had since leaving home. Isaac's hobbled ghost, single-shoed, a hole in his chest, showed up, but Frank never appeared.

John rewound and replayed his time with Mary in the house with the zoetrope. *Two and a half months before I'm home, love.* A stretch that fits itself over infinity and nothing.

IF I SHOULD DIE BEFORE I WAKE

MARY WAS PURCHASING GROCERIES IN RAY'S GENERAL STORE. HE found it unsettling that his business was booming because people needed soothing items in wartime—candies and doughnuts, and the ready-made dresses he had had the foresight to stock (with merchants grumbling about a foreigner figuring this out ahead of them), and stereopticons, tortoiseshell haircombs, and romance novels that kept flying off the shelf so he doubled their price, which amplified the perception of their value. He had broken up an actual shoving match between two women over a last copy of *Lady Audley's Secret*.

Nikka burst in, without her usual toting of bottles to sell, and the air she conveyed caused Ray's thirteen-year-old Linda to pause in stocking a shelf with blank books. Nikka held a letter at arm's length toward Mary. Ray braced his hands on the counter. Mary would strive to recall wading through the sawdust. When she reached her and took the letter, Nikka said, "Tell me I'm not reading this right."

April the First, 1864

Dear Alves Family of Jacksonville:

It is my privilege to serve as chaplain for the Army of the Tennessee, and though my burden is lighter than that placed upon the shoulders of those serving our country, my heart is taxed when I must bend to the task of informing families that their son, their husband, their uncle, their brother— brothers they are to us all—have perished to this world and attained the glory of heaven.

It grieves me to judge it charity to inform you that one of the Lights of your Life is extinguished, the better to behold the Light at God's right hand. Pvt. John Alves is among the fallen in the cause of our Union. Take comfort that today I found him clutching his Holy Bible, and therein I found his name writ, as if on the firmament, next to the address of his residence in Illinois, the birthplace of so many fighters for unity! The list of those requiring this grim service of mine is lamentably long.

He was buried with his Bible and his fellows with prayers and all due respect for the mortal form with which the Good Lord brought his spirit into the world.

Look up from your weeping, I beseech thee! He served well his nation and his God, and his hold upon the Word in his final Hour is testament to his salvation. He has been summoned by the Master to continue in the Better Land. To your sacrifice all honor and acclaim is also accorded.

Your obedient servant in the Lord,

Rt. Rev. Obadiah Sutton

Even behind her spectacles, her vision grew hazy. Since John was in the arms of sleep, Mary joined him, curled on his former pallet, but his scent was nonexistent, pushing her toward an aspect of rigor mortis. Nikka moved like a one-hundred-year-old woman. Mary had always figured she would be able to sense right away if John died. Was dead. She had been wrong.

Too stunned for tears, Mary was reverse-crying, concentrations flowing inward instead of exiting her eyes.

Yea, thou shalt be as he that lieth down in the midst of the sea.

God was punishing her for reuniting with her first love. Did it hurt when he died, when a bullet tore him open? Her own flesh got jolted whenever she wondered.

Serafina's white shoes exhaled in a corner.

The next day, and the next, John rested somewhere. A dim sense of needing to walk got her up, and Nikka rose, too, a scene out of an early lesson in Illinois: If you are caught in a snowstorm, *never nod off.* Beset by that sinking hunger known as a *feeling of goneness,* they shared a mush of oats.

Nikka failed to complete her wine and brandy orders and stayed on leave from helping in the school for the deaf. She said to Mary, when they forced themselves to consume the bread and marmalade sent over from Ray, "I knew Mother would go ahead to welcome him. Prepare the way."

———

RAY CONTACTED PERPETUA, WHO VISITED AND URGED MARY TO WORK on her tablecloth. Pet bottled Nikka's wine and conveyed it to Ray's. She tempered the usual buoyancy in her step and promised to tell Edward the news. "But stay here awhile," she whispered. Dilly had taken over the work. "John would want you to be all right," said Pet. "Please, go out once every day, and make at least twenty stitches every night."

———

VISITING THE PUBLIC GARDEN HE HAD INITIATED, A FORCED COLLAB-oration with his assailant, on the lot donated by the husband she had grievously wounded, was beyond bearing. She heard the property had grown into a dignified, final form, and citizens were refreshed by it, but she detoured around it.

———

MARY'S SPINE KEPT THE FEEL OF JOHN. A MAN NEAR IVES' JEWELRY Store put his hand with such care on her back to steady her that he feared she was having some sort of attack, *and she was,* because the light touch felt like a hammer sent at the right angle to crack her.

Her abdomen was expanding. She ignored it. She knew what it was.

—

SHE DINED LIGHTLY. DINNER WAS A SLICE OF MELON, OR HOT WATER infused with lavender. Breakfast was elemental—water or air. She stopped in the presence of simplicity. The angle where two walls met a ceiling. A loop of string. The points of leaves.

—

SHE TRIED TO FLOOD HER MIND WITH PICTURES OF JOHN, ESPECIALLY of the afternoon in Vicksburg, but her brain taunted her: *You're not ready to see memories.*

—

MARY ADDED TO HER TABLECLOTH, CLINGING TO THIS ROUTINE. NO word arrived from Edward, and she saw the correctness of that. Her needlework grew frenzied. She must take this art-piece to the Lincoln household in Washington for John's sake, to inform the president that he had given his life for the Union. Nikka advised her not to rip out and fix a crooked crewel line. *Let it speak about the times.*

Mary failed to confide in her (or anyone) that her cycle was late.

Flowers shocked the scene as Mary stumbled to town, their vividness of such a concentration it hurt. Sunflowers shook loose the knobby pointillism of their faces. *The Morgan Journal* had advertised a Revolving Mirror Show, and she paid twenty cents to enter an auditorium on State Street with ceiling-high mirrors. The crowd exhibited polite versions of excitement. Whirring projections surrounded her. Giant mirrors brimmed with lakes and rivers. Cascades ran down the glass panels set ceiling to floor, crashing and booming, a ruffle at each base. A boy in a sailor's hat squirmed; an elderly man with a cane dozed on a bench against his old bride. You, and you, and all of us to dust. The projections shifted into ocean, tides with cutwork froth. Pictures switched from sprinklings of rain to cloudbursts. What flooded into her was: *Bodies of water are doing the weeping for me.*

———

MARY NOTICED A SHADOW CREEPING OVER A CARPET, LOOKING LIKE the scrunched-up darkness attached to a person's heel at noon. A ticking inside her body commanded her attention, a growing awareness that she was with child. She was dead certain. Blood refused to gush from her, to double her over with her monthly cramping. With fury she blazed: How can you leave me alone with our child?

It was not Edward's.

Listen. Grieving is everywhere. It comes from the boy with a slingshot appalled at being fatherless, the widow at the washboard. Billy Fleurville, Lincoln's barber, will soon cry for his son Varveel, who'll perish in the Colored Regiment. Billy will have only three years more before he'll die of grief.

Out of Portugal rises fado music, the laments of the poor and street women, a keening in which the singer attempts to blend with—to become— the music itself.

To dissolve inside notes, never to return.

———

EDWARD ONCE REMARKED, "I PICTURE YOU STANDING BY A WINDOW, gazing out, expecting our child. That pose will tell me I'm a father." He meant it in a lovely way. But for all its depiction of domestic tranquility, it also signaled her husband was granting her a faraway look through a clear pane, her eyes and mind elsewhere, outward, a portrait not every spouse would grant the other. Her telegram:

E. dear: I stand by the window, w/J's child. M

———

A KINDNESS BROKE HER. EDWARD DID NOT IN SO MANY WORDS REPLY to her telegram, but a messenger arrived bearing news that Professor Moore had arranged for his wife and friend to rest in a cottage in Beardstown, owned by an Illinois College colleague, currently vacant. The interior of the gazebo's roof was an intricate herringbone that kindled a sensation shaping itself toward a busy harmony. If Mary could not care for John, it was good to nurse his sister. And country air eased Mary's nausea.

On their fifth day, they concluded that with others in need—as they had once required charity—idleness was worse than grief. They volunteered as helpers at Beardstown's veterans' hospital. A doctor informed them that a patient, Michael Windsor, was so debilitated by consumption that he had been unconscious while bundled into a contingent of furloughed Cass County casualties, even though he was with the New York 14th, veterans of Antietam and Gettysburg.

Nikka murmured, "New York!" The city of sprees with John, like a son to her, gallivanting.

Nikka paced toward Michael Windsor at the far end of the ward, past all the ailing men. Unmindful of contagion, she took the consumptive's hands. Mary was too far to hear the exchange, but they were speaking in a cadence of delight. There it is, thought Mary, cruel bright good thing of it: the suddenness of life, the swiftness of reversals.

A week later, ailments in remission, Michael Windsor of Brooklyn, New York, proposed to Antoinetta Isabela Alves of Santa Cruz, Madeira; Trinidad; Manhattan; and Jacksonville, Illinois, asking if she would finish bringing a man back to life, cherishing him as he would cherish her, if she would marry him the moment his mended chest could produce, with requisite fullness, the right vows.

She explained about being married and not divorced. She was not a virgin. She would be a bigamist.

Michael assured her of the value of private history. They would be lying on a legal document while embracing a keener truth.

When Nikka hesitated for fear of abandoning her, Mary insisted she wed. Though still she failed to tell Nikka she was in-her-marrow sure, deep-in-her-womb-so-accustomed-to-hurling-pain-at-her sure, that she was carrying John's baby.

Mary and Nikka's best friend, Ella King, once Helena Reis, were bridesmaids, clutching bluebird irises at the courthouse. A clerk signed the license. The bride wore a lilac dress with appliqués of tulips, and a gardenia starred her dark hair. An apricot cake baked by Ella featured marzipan fruits and silver dragées and blue-frosting roses.

After a ceremony lasting barely ten minutes, Nikka kissed her new husband and exclaimed, Yes, my love. Yes! I'll move with you to the East! Michael had been offered a return to his profession of patent law at an uncle's firm—Gardner, Windsor & Rice—in Brooklyn.

Mary said it was time for her to leave, too, time to face her own music. Nikka should sell the home where her mother had died, where John would never return. It took less than a week for a widow and daughter of their tribe to purchase it. They had been homesteading on the prairie. They were eager to keep the furnishings.

Nikka desired only the soot-covered page that Mother created at the end, not out of a belief that it held anything from the Beyond but because it would remind her that she was born of a stalwart female unfazed by torment. Nikka Windsor put the sound-contraption into a crate for Mary, and she elected to move with her husband rather than wait for Rui, who might not even notify her should he return, because in a variegated land, even supreme joy must, when an exodus occurs—as a pearl buckles around an abrasion of sand—contain elements of someone, something lost.

———

HE SENSED HER WAITING TO HEAR.

His telegram was succinct: *You are welcome. E.*

———

WHEN MARY TAPPED THE DOOR KNOCKER BUT RECEIVED NO REPLY, she tested the knob and entered. Ward was absorbed at his desk. He had not retrieved her in person. She set her carrying bag outside his study and asked, "What are you writing?"

He glanced up. "I'm sorry for your loss," he said, a recitation. She repeated her question, more tremulously: What was he working on?

"Nothing. I'm writing nothing." He was correcting student essays about Samuel Frederick Gray's studies of fungi. "I'd have contacted you sooner, but I recalled that when you lost your father, you entreated me to leave you alone." He stood and did something new to them. He bolted to her, lifted her, squeezed her. She cried at the strangeness of his capacity to take her back. Both now with dead loves worn like sheens. He set her down, and she touched the side of his face as he said, "I've wondered why you haven't conceived a child with me. I'd like to be a father."

"I'm so sorry." His dignity was killing her.

"I'm in agony, and I was angry, but enough. I've always said we're going to be all right. You don't want to be with child and alone. I don't want that for you, either. I ask only that you let me claim the child is mine, that this is our story."

The exquisite fairness left her speechless. Then she said, "Yes."

"We'll claim happiness again, in time. When is the child due?"

"Early to mid-December. Before Christmas."

Etched physically on him was the cost of forgiving her. He said he wished she could believe she was his star, unlike anyone else, and he stroked her lower back. They made love for the first time outside the bedroom, they made love where they were, in his study, observed by the raven.

—

PET'S ESCORTING HER TO THE POST OFFICE PRODUCED IN MARY A sensation of feeling gnawed by flesh-chewing gazes. The usual crush drove toward Taylor Seeger, and recipients ripped open letters to digest on the spot. In the churning, Mary spotted a morose Dottie Willis with her beauty mark, staring at her.

At the window, Perpetua asked if there might be any letter for Mary Freitas Moore. Hard as it would be to read, Mary sought full knowledge of John's last moments. Taylor said, "I assume you know it's impossible for dead men to send anything."

Did everyone know every aspect of her horror story?

"He might have sent something right before, or his friends, maybe they wrote. Please check again," ordered Perpetua, despite Mary's turning to leave.

"Your friend can't ask herself?" said Taylor. "Is she dumb?"

"No," said Perpetua, "but you are."

While fording toward the exit, Mary was stopped by Dottie, addled as she commented that Mary resembled a walking example of heartbreak. "I'm so sorry."

"Thank you, Dottie."

Without makeup, fingernails bitten, Dorothea was reduced and pitiable. "I haven't heard from my brother. My friends don't have anyone to worry about, so they ignore me. My husband, George, is, shall we say, useless as a comforter."

The always-missing, skirt-chasing, pudgy George. "I'm sorry."

"And I'm sorry for what's befallen you." Dottie uttered something Mary barely caught, about uncertainty. "Could we speak more privately, Mary?" She eyed Perpetua, who snapped, "I'm not leaving her with you."

Had they been near the contest-winning park invented by John, they might have sat at ease near flowers and ever-worried citizens requiring rest. Instead, they paused near the dentistry office, with its display, on strings, of dentures. Mary was glad for the wall's support; her baby, despite being the size of a hummingbird, pressed on her tailbone. She had not even told Perpetua. But her arm flew protectively over her middle as a stammering Dottie said, "It started as a frolic, I swear. Just to make a little trouble for you." Her pleading glance met Mary's dispassionate calmness in putting one and one together, perhaps two and two, even before Dottie Willis admitted to "a role" in intercepting and creating letters along with friends bored enough to smother a love affair.

Why had Mary figured the answer would be one single offender rather than a parcel of people happy to go to war with her?

"Taylor is your nephew. I guess I did figure it out. He went along with you?"

"It wasn't just me," cried Dottie. "I'm terribly sorry. It was—"

Though she would regret it later, Mary put a hand up, to stop her. What did she care for the listing of names, the Maud or Mauds, the

Gertie or Gerties, the Whomever and Sundry Citizens enraged at underclass newcomers edging toward better-classdom while flaunting a physicality of love. Was there a mastermind, or did the game evolve in a chorus as a gaggle lolled around with nothing better to do? That too hardly mattered in light of Chaplain Sutton's note and Nikka's seeking and receiving the official list confirming the dead of Company 14-A. Mary further decided she did not need to hear, from Frank or a comrade, the grisly details of John's sacrifice.

Mary was staggering away, but Pet grabbed Dottie's arm and said, "Why?"

The answer was a bleat. Because Mary knew what she wanted to do in the world, and she was loved all over the map, and she sauntered in with her beauty.

Mary's first impulse was to warn John that they were wrong, totally wrong, completely so, about Isaac, and she plummeted toward a fathoms-down layer of the truth that John was gone. Isaac, too, for that matter. She needed to kick upward, to surface for the sake of her baby. Tread vertically. Edward had pushed off from the shore and was rowing to them, to his family.

The final straw came when Edward suggested a united front in public, a dinner at Bill Farnsworth's hotel. Bill, affable easygoing Bill, was perfunctory in seating them, and a silence descended among the diners as Edward pulled out a chair for his wife and, rare for him when people were watching, he squeezed her hand.

Mary hoped Lucy Brattle might be serving but recalled that she worked lunch shifts. The waiter who collected their menu cards and set down boiled asparagus as a first course was so unobtrusive, he either had orders to be as invisible as possible as a rule, or he, too, was operating in reproach. From a corner of the brocade-wallpapered room, someone stage-whispered, "The nerve." A serviette got thrown onto a table as a couple made a show of leaving. Mary wanted to laugh at the impotent sound of cloth slapping cloth.

Edward conversed about berry shipments. She answered, mournful in her sympathy for the effort this cost him.

Bill appeared and spoke exclusively to Edward, as if to affirm he was sorry that Edward was being accorded a chilly welcome that should be reserved for her. This would be one of the leading horrors out of all the things to destroy her. She was fond of Bill, had shared laughs with him in this very place upon toting in sachets for his front desk! Flatly, Bill remarked, despite her pleading look, "I might recommend the flounder."

"I've never trusted fish in Illinois," said Edward.

Still refusing to look at Mary, Bill said, "I recommend it. I would not impose anything that you would not deem fully worthy of trust, Edward."

A crowning blow came when Nell Clark swept in with a genteel woman Mary did not recognize at the precise moment the plates of flounder landed. Nell paused not far from their table and said, "I can't dine here, Gladys. Come." Mary kept her eyes trained on Nell, who added, "This place is slipping."

The whispers in town were: *He's a saint. Lifting that disgraceful girl right on up, rewarding that hot-blood with so much.*

The night following the debacle of the untouched flounder, Mary knocked at the cottage and found Perpetua Roderick doing her best to write a letter in English. Mary discovered that Henry Kingsley was already on the job in Los Angeles, awaiting her so they could wed. "You're staying here for my sake, aren't you, Pet?" said Mary. She stood there until Pet quit protesting and admitted it, whereupon Mary added, "It would gladden me to picture you in Los Angeles with your fellow."

"But—"

"Dilly can do the job, and I'll do it. But I'll miss you, Pet. It might help you to hear I have a feeling we won't be here much longer."

Mary still did not confide about carrying John's child—hereafter Edward's—but she should have guessed that Pet in a coat and with one bag, ready to go, would have been the razor to gash them into pouring rivers, sobbing and holding on, goodbye, this could be forever, my most loyal—how rare is such loyalty—friend. From the cottage wall, Mary took down the plaque declaring A WISHBONE AIN'T AS LIKELY TO GET YE AS FAR AS A BACKBONE and said, "Uma lembrança. We're wishbones in a world of backbones," and Pet accepted the gift and cried out, "We are, Maria-Cat."

From there, it was the work of a moment for Edward and Mary to leave. Mary herself, as they stared at their breakfast table without focus, suggested that Springfield, because of her, had become frighteningly hostile to them both. For all the vices everyone practiced, nothing was worse than what she—a wanton foreigner—had done. He was ridiculed for putting up with her; she saw that fully. Edward suggested the ready solution of the farm in Florida, saying, "You could restore yourself in the sun." According to the foreman, Judson Stewart, her plant was spreading over the sixty-acre property. "It would be a fresh chance, Mary."

"I thought we needed to wait for the war to end."

"I prefer our chances there to the war around us here. We've been piecing things together, a few hundred berries at a time. The plants belong outdoors. They're thriving. Frankly, it would be prudent to leave before your condition stirs worse speculation and rancor. I have no attachment to my professorship, staring at boys who remind me of my failure to serve." Those battered children knew the truest science of dirt, that it contained a mulch of bones. "I'm a wanderer like you," he said. "I can't stand the cold." He asked if she wanted him to fetch the blueberry jam to relieve the dryness of their toast, and she proclaimed, "It is beyond saving," and they laughed, foreheads together.

———

NEVER COULD WARD HAVE IMAGINED, HE REMARKED TO HER, THAT he would wear a wide-brimmed straw hat and step onto a languorous land of cypresses with Spanish moss, with red-dotted shrubs he could call his, though mostly hers. *His wife's*—another thing he was amazed to be uttering. The sale of his holdings in Illinois had happened almost overnight in such a westward-bound era, the profits already plowed into the farm in Mandarin. The Stewart brothers—Judson, Jacob, Patrick, Brian, and Wyndham—did most of the work and ran the tractors. They lived with their wives and children in cottages on the edge of the property, leased from Ward. Everyone was friendly in a low-key, hot-climate way that reminded her of her childhood. Further clamor for miracle berries was arriving from points reachable by transcontinental trains, and demands would rise at parties, booths at parades, schools, and outposts of recreation. And from a soaring number of households where widows needed to extend their food supply. Mary's child felt solid, something—someone—she could grip with both hands. The heat steamed away Nell, Maud, Dottie, Gertie, Taylor, Isaac; scrabbling creatures in a bad dream.

When she tumbled into the Well after setting out the strawberry-rocks her father had painted—she still could not bring herself to explain to Edward what "the Well" was—she said her state was owing to her condition, and he paid her the courtesy of pretending to believe her.

An awkward moment ensued when he insisted upon placing the daguerreotype of Papa on the mantel, despite her preferring it where she sewed. While repairing the insect-clotted mesh on a screen door, she halted as the reason struck her. Papa's skin was darker than hers, and so was John's. Should the baby's skin be dark, the people who came to call in Mandarin would have an easier time thinking the child was Edward's.

No need to tell anyone Papa had not been her blood-father.

But she loved that Edward loved it, the farm. She rejoiced when a note came from Pet incredulous that California was weirdly brown, brown hills! Henry excelled in his job despite being one-handed, and she had found an apprenticeship with a tailor.

When an offer came from one of Edward's cousins in California, stating that professors were urgently needed at the Saint Ignatius Academy in San Francisco—nine years running, a college-preparatory school—he telegrammed back that he was content where he was, though it was more accurate to say he enjoyed independence in warmth but was not avid about the town, which involved cantering past porch-dawdling Southerners who mocked his attire and his skin burned by the outdoors.

They both admitted to doubts about whether it was safe to make love to a girl so far along in pregnancy. He had no idea whom to ask, nor did she. For now, he would leave her be. He urged her not to labor too much outdoors. A bassinet would soon be on the covered porch, and she would thereafter be hale enough to collect berries alongside

Jacob and Wyndham—she would feel better as a mother getting dirt beneath her fingernails, proof she was happy—and to help the wives packaging the miracle-sets. He had originally envisioned pineapples here, and they might get around to that. She agreed with her husband that shunning all society, except for these amiable Stewarts, was freedom. Enormous shipments of Mandarin Farm sachets went out, conveyed by Brian on a wagon to the depot.

But sometimes Mary's tamped sorrow sprung loose, and it tried Edward's patience. One evening, she burst into their new home piteously undone because legions of mosquitoes savaged her when she walked in the fields. He dabbed on the calamine because she acted incapable of doing it herself. Since the lotion was pink, he quipped about coating her entirely, a rose-colored blessing, but she herself was hard-pressed to explain why she was so upset, and he added, "Mary, enough now, I suspect you'll live."

She was a layered woman. The top layer was cushiony, wrapped over a firm self like a homunculus on a doctor's desk. John lit that human figure up; it blazed, he made it blaze, that replica of herself. Each year the top layer would thicken, and the replica would shrink. But as it shrank, it would glow even brighter, and one day it would be a kernel so intensely hot it might combust all the rest.

She enumerated to herself what was good. Her crop was splendid, her husband devoted, the workers pleasant, her tablecloth expanding. (However. Below this thrummed her wondering why passion was absent from so many lives. Further, why wasn't everyone conversing endlessly about how few people got to claim passion as *increasing* with companionship?) She enacted the image of herself by a window, listening to faraway music. She must be alive for the sake of all her dead, must find joy for them, too. An avalanche of this came when Edward danced with her in the kitchen, remarkably good at it, she remembered this, and he dipped her expanding body.

A sinister occurrence struck as early June delivered sweltering days. The layabouts in town crowed at Edward not just for being a Northerner but for "acting unfriendly-like." He flashed appeasing smiles that they replied to with taunts. One day he came home toting glass plates to repair a cracked side in the miniature greenhouse like a chapel on a rise, where his thornless-rose experiments had restarted. He removed the damaged plates and installed the new ones and brought Mary to admire his work.

Visible in the sunshine, filtering through the glass, were photographic images of heaps of Union corpses. Discarded plates from the likes of Mathew Brady and other photographers were flooding the market, negatives of the images that had brought the war into homes. These awakened people to the fallout of glory: The fighting was a trafficking in mutilated human meat. The wish to own such pictures had receded. A shop owner had sold these to Edward deliberately, tickled that he had not scrutinized them. "I'll knock them out, Mary," he said, aghast at the light illuminating the dead.

She told him to leave them alone. Let the sun slowly melt the specters. "Don't fret," she said. "You had no idea." She was inclined to commune with the black-and-white sacrificial lambs as they blanched in a last bower with fennel, thyme, and the water-fattened melons she craved.

Cry Out the Sea Within

In the Winter of the Deep Snow, snowflakes fell at first like tufts of cloth. Then drifts came six feet deep.

Turkeys compacted into petrified globes. Birds got stuck to branches, their dying calls flaring in fan-shaped icicles. A man grabbed a pump's handle and left his palms behind. People were gutted by white swords thrusting through chinks in their cabins. Bulleting ice hit so fast that animals turned pocked marble in an instant, leaving ice-taxidermies of squirrels in poses of running.

Snowfall buried a child who ran out to find his dog, the two regarded in a hush when springtime's thaw delivered them as a statue, dead dog's muzzle tenderly upon dead boy's neck.

The question: Why can't mayhem be sensed soon enough to get out of its path?

WITH THE KINGS AND COUNSELORS
OF THE EARTH

JOHN'S HONORABLE MUSTERING OUT BEGAN ON THE TWENTY-FOURTH of June in 1864. He traveled from Jackson to Memphis to Nashville, heading toward a mystery. He had not heard from Mary. If his death notice had caused the abeyance, and his frantic subsequent notes had fallen into limbo, he was about to effect a remedy, even if her marriage required his unequivocal banishment thereafter. At the Nashville station, a train rested, black grease buttering the wheels. A lowing issued from the cars, from cattle stuffed in so tightly that a dead one was held upright. The tufted end of a reed blossomed from a cow's ear canal as her head strained out a window. When he extracted the stalk, she groaned in relief.

The animals rolled toward their fate of being chopped into red putty. While he awaited his connection to St. Louis, a noise behind the station drew him toward two men shoving an elderly freedwoman. Hooting, they yanked off her bonnet and held it out of reach. John's look sufficed to make them return it.

"Just having fun, soldier," said one of them, wheezing out bourbon.

"One thing I can't sit still about, it's an older woman made sport of."

As her tormentors stumbled off, she extracted a tiny kaleidoscope from a pocket of her gingham dress and pressed it into his hands.

"I don't need a reward," he said.

"Naw. Yawse."

He peered into the kaleidoscope at a butterfly wing and sequins, tumbling into patterns. When he finished squinting, the woman had vanished.

He rode through the nether tip of Illinois, that arrowhead inflamed with Southern ire in a Northern state, a realm called Little Egypt, its waterways forming an inland delta, its red sea of berries famous for bleeding onto the wildflowers. Frank once said that the width of American rails matched the wheel-span on a Roman chariot. John would have to tell Elizabeth that Frank was likely dead. Corn shocks were drying, and a whiff of lemon monardas and the rumble triggered a physical repossession of that first trip as refugees, starting with the steamship out of New York City.

His last evening in the South, a family had provided a mattress that was a cradling cloud. His hosts were in their thirties, with two children who heated water for his bath in a tub behind a screen painted with the assertive delicacy of cherry blossoms. The man was a cobbler; his wife hailed from a genteel background in Virginia. They were eager, as they put it, to convince him that not all Southerners were lash-wielding beasts. When John listened to the children read from the Bible before the fried-egg hash, he stifled a wail of gratitude, not just for their hospitality but for a reminder that the Bible was a paper summary of his mother. He longed to see her, too.

On Sunday, the twenty-sixth of June, he arrived at the Great Western Depot, as unreal as a papier-mâché prop. The square's buildings, one-, two-, three-, and four-storied, were projections of light, the people diaphanous. Faded awnings sagged. A poster advertised bear-wrestling. Next to an upturned hat, a boy juggled apples. John tossed him a quarter and inhaled a sudsy aroma of barley from a grocery shop. He passed Hathaway's, which sold beaded ceilings and laths and lime and coffins, and he received "Welcome back, soldier" remarks that he answered with pleasantries. His skeleton retained the motion of lifting his revolver to prevent an officer's murder of a woman, would replicate it even at innocent moments for the rest of his days, and his retinas retained images of Isaac collapsing in two blasts of gunfire. John's knapsack was dredged in Mississippi's red dust. *Mary?* Their separation was a torture so extended it was sublime.

A boomerang of geese swept overhead, their migration perilously late. The long-awaited hour was nigh, a Union man desiring only union, but foreboding caused him to detour toward the blaring of a gaudy tune. A merry-go-round was set up on Eighth Street. An elderly man was escorting children onto the animals, the crankshafts visible under the platform. John admired the painted creatures, and the man, pleased, said he had whiled away the time awaiting his grandson's return by carving natives of Illinois: brown bat, squirrel, bison, bobcat, wolf, horse . . . and a smiling rat. John asked if the grandson had come home, and the merry-go-round proprietor said, "God be praised." John chose the white horse. The music started, and the circling began.

When he dismounted along with the children scampering back to their mothers, a little girl in black was holding the hand of a black-clad woman. He took off his cap to the woman, who said, "Matilda is scared to climb up so high, aren't you, dear. But you see this man who looks like Daddy is fine, after it all."

"Would you care to try the squirrel or bat, Matilda?" he asked.

She edged behind her mother's skirts.

As he set out upon the final blocks of his journey toward the full meaning and reward for all his sacrifice, the girl chased him and whispered, "But I'd like to fly in a circle, to play Kite."

"Kite. Very well."

He lifted Matilda and spun, gripping under her armpits, and her legs flew as she happily shrieked. He dipped, reversed her sailing. He had not grinned like this in ages. Matilda's tresses flapped as she kept her skinny arms on his collarbone. When he set her down, she told him, "I know my daddy's not coming back, but thank you. Mama's not strong enough to pick me up." Her mother looked grateful, and he said, "Good luck, ma'am. Goodbye, Matilda." She was jumping up and down, clapping, an American picture of Maria Freitas as a shy but life-seizing little girl.

He beelined to the two-story white house on Sixth Street. Trees in the yard were shedding blossoms. He was braced for the unexpected, but not for the sight of men sweeping up the remains of the razed greenhouse. Must everything of worth be destroyed? A stranger at the door answered his plaintive questions by replying, "We're the new owners and plan to use that space to build a folly." *A what? A folly is an ornamental structure without a defined purpose.* The limbs of plants, miracle bushes, exotic imports, years of careful tending by Mary and her father, the pale-paned magnificent housing, were being carted away, casually consigned to ruin.

Hovering was the arch-eyebrowed wife, too pampered to look so overwhelmed. To John's inquiry, she said, "They moved to Florida. Right, Thomas?" Thomas did a poor job of feigning interest, adding, "The husband said Florida would be healthier." He was possessed by the popular kind of politeness that is really controlled impatience.

Perpetua Roderick could enlighten him. But her name, and John's description of her, seemed even less of interest, other than the wife musing, "A worker who lived in the cottage went to Los Angeles. Anything else, soldier?"

John lifted his hat, wondering if his scalp wound might be visible, and said no, he could think of nothing else.

Desperate to get to Mother and Nikka, he took the train to Jacksonville and stumbled past the cigar factory, its HOME OF THE EL MACCO lettering flaking, and the livery stables and the drugstore advertising anti-bilious pills. Past downtown, two blind boys were knotting cords to chain out a hammock. One blue-dyed end was tied to a porch's pillar, and the boys were nimbly relying on touch to grow the netting beyond where the middle of a man would rest. Dandelion threads blew over the rise into Madeira Hill, surfing toward his youth, over nettles. The cabin with its yard, where a tree was in the season to thrum with fireflies, was occupied by a widow and teenaged daughter. He cried, "Where are my mother and sister?" while gaping at the broken piano.

The widow took his arm and said, "Sit, soldier. I have your sister's address. She married and moved to New York. This is the first house I've owned. Her terms were generous. My Calvin would have been pleased. I'll show you the deed." She and her daughter eased John into a chair as he bawled, "Ma, my mother. Ma!"

Because he knew, had sensed the truth upon his approach. Though she had long been ailing, he had expected to attend her last days. But Nikka vanished, too? Mary, the earth has swallowed everybody. It made sense for all semblance of life as he had been anticipating it to be wiped off the map, and yet he could not have prophesied such laughably utter thoroughness. He wished Isaac had shot him not in the shoulder but through the heart. The widow volunteered to escort him to the Eastern Cemetery.

"Thank you, no, ma'am. You're very kind." He turned down an offer of stew meat and temporary lodging but accepted a glass of well water. When he asked if there might be a plaster funnel with a feather, an art-piece of sorts, he responded to their mystified expressions with, "Never mind." Men of science who dodged the war had been busily striding past the creation he had commenced.

And still the fighting was not done. He should have re-upped.

Alone in his shop, Rui was squinting at beakers on a sawhorse table, measuring items as if he had not missed a beat. A bombardment of balsam smacked John as he asked, "How are you, Rodrigo?"

"Antietam," said Rui, bearded, not looking up. John supposed that, owing to his brother's skills with distillation, he could boil his version of the war down to that. Rui turned frighteningly wordy as he admitted to trouble erasing a memory of bayoneting men who had attacked his company, the Ohio 8th. Cleveland.

Why *Ohio*? To avoid everyone he might know? John asked only, "Mother is gone?"

"To God, yes." He shuffled to a cabinet, extracted a vial, and said, "Good to see you, John. Now. Please excuse me."

John knocked at the downtown apartment where Elizabeth and Frank had made a home for barely a few weeks, and she gasped, and he shook his head "no" to convey that he had lost track of his best friend. He explained the chaplain's likely error. "I'll take you to your mother," said Elizabeth with her wheat-colored, piled-high hair, her ability to evince feelings by summoning necessary actions.

Mother was wearing lilies. He knelt, picturing her stretched among the spiders, and pressed his forehead to her name. Elizabeth had a way of never rushing anyone, a kindness that reverberated through him. Friends sometimes commented that his eating of music to stave off hunger sounded made-up, a prettifying of horror, but it was true. It had been a birdie-mother's special love. Her capacity for such invention had inspired the birth of the Sound Machine. *Ma*, said the vibrations of his heart, scouring away their quarrels. *You said prayer is talking to God as a friend. Begging for things is neither friendship nor prayer. You wanted only for Him to dwell with you.*

I understand this now. I am your house, querida Mãe. Com saudades.

Elizabeth indicated yes, word had it that Mary and Edward had moved to Florida, but she had no knowledge of the name of the town. "Your return from the dead gives me hope," she said. She had baked bread and set it out with tomato preserves, and they discussed her bookshop and nothing else, which he appreciated. She sheltered him for the night, and he slept on a rug from Capps enlivened with cochineal dye.

The completion of the loss of everything came when he was told at the school for the deaf, after much exclaiming about his resurrection from extinction, that they had given his classroom to a leg-amputee veteran conversant with sign language. The teaching roster was filled. He refused to put a soldier out of a job. At the front portal, Claire Clearwater, older now, ran to him, and so did Sammy Byrd, signing that he had drawn a bird recently and asked it to go look for his teacher and bring him back.

The Meline Theater was deserted save for a brocade of mold like green snowflakes. He did not want to run into George, Teresa, or Hugo, who might have word that Frank was dead or imprisoned, and they would charge him with telling Elizabeth.

He took up residence at Latshaw's in Springfield, the boarding-house on Cook Street between the railroad and the American Hotel, jammed pell-mell among warehouses. It attracted veterans incapable of moving swiftly, either because they were not physically able to or because they did not see the point. The dining room reeked of male fare, chops with cornstarch gravy and a penetrating odor of cheap candles. The Ladies' Education Society sent over flowers weekly. At first, he convinced himself that the war would necessitate Edward and Mary's return from Florida, or his spores would call her back while he summoned strength as the world corrected its supreme errors.

Harmonious magic would undo the marriage to Edward in a way that hurt no one. He laughed about that. Summer poured over war-whiskered men in their undershirts, their galluses looping down.

Nikka replied to his letter with exclamations smeared with tears. She had hated being in Madeira Hill thinking he was buried in parts unknown. She would keep an endless vigil awaiting him in Brooklyn, she did not care how long it took him to get to her or how ancient she got. Her husband was aware of her bigamy but cared not a trice. She prayed it would console John to hear that Mother on her deathbed made peace with Mary and bequeathed her the Sound Machine after Mother recorded scratchings on a page of soot that was the Voice of God. *I took that with me, baby brother.* In his law office, Michael Windsor had encountered a lunatic wishing to patent an elixir to raise soldiers from the dead, and Michael had replied, *My wife's brother already discovered it.*

John wrote that she could keep God's message, a wedding gift for her and, at such long last, a husband who cared rightly for her. (What did it matter, with Frank not here to help him decode it, with Mary in the enemy South with a man who had every reason to dash the decrepit Sound Machine into a heap of compost. Who was this God?)

John amused himself upon arising daily at Latshaw's by thinking, *And now to avail myself of the lavishments!:* chipped washbasin, frayed towels, the putrid realm of the water-closet. His dreams were invaded by a leering Captain Pryor, who hissed, *I owe you a bullet in your head, since Isaac couldn't manage to do it.*

He debated traveling to Florida and trying his luck at finding her; he should have asked the location of the farm she had mentioned more than once. He worried about territory dotted with snipers, but this exacerbated his wish to rescue her. But John also had a hideous, debilitating cough, his lungs having picked up bugs in the swamps of Mississippi. At Corneau & Diller's, he bought oil of eucalyptus.

Fueled on chicory coffee and brown bread at Latshaw's, skin inflamed, he slumbered in the hope of his sickness fading. He was frequently lathered into a rage at the thought of Ward getting off scot-free from war and exposing Mary to danger yet being rewarded with her in his bed. In Latshaw's dining room, someone had left a book about trees and flowers—everywhere he turned, things spoke of Mary—that referred to gardening as "the perfection of the art of hope deferred." At twilight, trees suctioned the darkness out of the night, bunching it into corsages on their bark. Evenings brought images of parties in Florida and Ward climbing under her covers, heaped with accolades for forgiving an immoral wife who had run to a wounded army boy. He needed to get back on the road and correct the colossal practical joke that his every breath had become. Next thing he knew, a woman with a stiff white hat like swan's wings was offering him medicine on a spoon, and she scolded him that no, he was not going anywhere until his fever subsided.

A SOUND HEART IS THE LIFE OF THE FLESH

THE SINGER PURRED, HER FAVORED LULLABY. THE SEWING MACHINE was a true friend. The stack of fifty sachets she had stitched so far today alternated sky blue and cream and looked like a puff-paste made of sky; she craved sugar *madly*. Her years in Illinois were fading like fabric abandoned in sunlight, everything was rounded in a mourning, her body was rounded, too. She balanced care for her health, preventing grief from saturating her blood—her baby was the one remnant of John, and she must not hurt it—with a fantastical belief that he would walk through her door. She would settle for his ghost.

She would tell him *I was with your mother at the end.* How often does it happen that all is tied up in a reconciling? She would show him the Sound Machine, battered, still in its crate; she did not know where to put this token from the time of things falling apart with Edward. Upon seeing it, he had commented, "Keep it, but hide it from me." When she imagined John in any form, her eyes shut automatically, as if to view him on the red-black curtains inside her eyelids. Then she had to blink him away, goodbye, darling.

Her knuckles were swollen as if with brine. Good thing that the Stewart women were stitching nonstop, too, to keep up with the demand from shops, homes, and restaurants as far as California, their supply enough for the West now, and heavily north in Ohio, Michigan, Maine—states whose army boys had been aided by berries sweetening their spoiled rations. Last week, thanks to the field's abundance, five thousand sachets had gone into a world chomping at its bit for diversions and solace from the *endless* conflict.

Rousing herself to make tea, bulbous as a globe, she padded into the kitchen, where she pressed her hands onto the pastry marble and again wondered: *What is it in marble that keeps it always cold?* She might, once, have asked Nell. Through the window, she glimpsed the Stewarts at work. *Papa, this was supposed to have been my finale of aspiration.* Much as she was glad to be away from the wild-animal preserve called society, her contentment was flattened by . . . loneliness. *City girl that I guess I am, with Portuguese saudade for man-made realms.* Startled to hear Edward in his study, she set the cozy over the teapot to let the jasmine steep.

He looked up from the ledgers and said, "I should get back outside."

"There's no rush. You work so hard."

He had confessed—learning to confide his fears to his wife—that laboring eleven-hour days, seven days a week, was inducing the end of any romance about farms, despite the tallying books showing profits growing from decent to remarkable.

After the disaster, he would admit to Mary—though not to Judson and his brothers, Southerners themselves—that hecklers had put a dead raccoon in his wagon's seat when he went for groceries the day before, and one of them flashed a pistol and called him a carpetbagger.

"You should rest, too," he said. His books remained in crates. The move had taken so much out of them that they felt mild as children who have run around screaming before collapsing.

"I've made tea," she said, holding out a hand.

She would remember this: Her arm extending and Edward rising to reach for her. They heard the shouts, Brian's and Patrick's in particular, and hastened out to hear Jacob bellow that two boys had shown up with tinderboxes. When the Stewarts realized what was happening at the edge of the field, they had raced toward the arsonists, who escaped without so much as getting snagged by a thorn.

Mary stood stock-still, as forest animals do for a second when they taste the air and see and hear the danger, and they know they must run, again, always there is something to run from. Flames were shooting through the miracle-berry shrubs, and varmints were getting flushed out. Branches were cooking. Embers shot upward and zigzagged, traveling here and there. The field's far end hurled fire onto adjacent rows, and they in turn torched their own neighbors. Mary sank inside herself before summoning stamina. The Stewart wives and children, smelling smoke, were darting out of their cabins, fetching tarps and blankets. Everyone was hollering *Fire*.

Ward snapped to attention. "Go inside, Mary."

She would not. She moved forward, sensing that she would have been shot as a soldier by freezing instead of acting.

Acres got annihilated in a heartbeat, flames chomping. Three, six acres, twenty were gone, fast as ... wildfire. Mary hastened to the irrigation pipes and got them flowing. A few were jammed. Edward hurried past roasting bushes, into the thickets with the Stewarts. Mary headed in, too; her plant had survived the high seas and snowy weather and train travel and confinement only to die because of town boys who hated outsiders. Nowhere—*nowhere*—was safe. Mary and Ward joined the rhythm alongside the men, women, and children, the custodians of this carpeting of the land, but they lacked sufficient manpower, and the fire did its work. At one point, Mary stopped, chest heaving, and thought: Do your worst, take it and be done, finish this already and stop torturing me, I can't, I can't stop this.

The greenhouse—made of the photographic plates of still-dissolving corpses—popped loudly. Under a blackened sky was indissoluble brilliant burning. Patrick stamped toward a rise as Edward and Mary watched from ravaged safety. She prepared to follow, but Ward grabbed her. She had a child to think about. These were plants, and plants died. And she did relent, leaning onto him. Neighbors arrived, employing buckets at the pipes and the well, until the conflagration was contained roughly as it finished its devastation. In the end, it was not an act of God but of men—everything was ruined. Not a plant could be seen alive.

Strange that, at first, she felt a shameful unburdening: This is done, is it? Fine. I've lost people I love; I've been a caretaker of a candied paradise, and one reaches surfeit. She loathed the town, and already her vision had burned clear to images of going slowly mad here. But then she cracked and wept. *Daddy, what should I do?*

Ward broke down in his study. She had never witnessed him shedding decorum; blessings, she bloomed out of herself. Father: Is this the task put to me, to help my husband lose his tight ability to create splendor he only scantily relishes? She would push Ward—though not today, not today—toward accepting joy while allowing him to stay reserved, in his nature, but not constrained. The air stayed gray and thick, and they breathed into damp towels, but even indoors the towels collected the ash they exhaled and left veronicas of mud, soot pictures recording their sounds of exhaustion. His bookcase was bare, and the stuffed raven was still in a box. The glass flowers were in a trunk with shredded newsprint. It felt unsafe to seek refuge in the hostile environs, and their friendly neighbors were also choking on smoke.

"I did this!" he wailed. She could not tell if he clutched his skull primarily due to anguish or to keep her from studying his expression. She soothed his back, streaking his shirt. Her baby kicked. She whispered, "No one got hurt. No one's house burned."

"I was foolish to come here. To bring you here."

She said, shaking her head, "No, we couldn't stay where we were, because of me. The fire? It means we can't get away from the world as it is, Ward. Eddy."

"I don't belong anywhere on this planet," he near shouted. The window behind them was blackened, like smeared night.

"Let's go to California," she said. "It's where my father dreamt of ending up, and you already know it, and your cousin offered you a teaching job, and I have a last move in me, I think." She was not sure this was true, but she was the one who needed to be strong. She owed him that. "Our baby can be Californian, where it's golden." She tipped into her first sensations of being maternal by smoothing down his hair.

"It's my fault your plant is gone. I'm despised wherever I go." He flung back his head as if trying to throw it off his neck.

She smiled, because as she vividly recalled, women had done the opposite of despising him, and therein had burbled the fount of so much ugliness. And she stepped into a fullness of her adult life on this catastrophic day, because it seemed so small a thing to refrain from correcting him, to let him vent, and it even seemed acceptable to sacrifice a plant so she could say to him, and mean it, "That's not true. You are loved. By me, Edward." He stared at her, stunned. She said lightly as an earth-suturing shower, "We'll find where we belong, both of us. I love you." She felt him making sure of keeping his head only lightly against her milk-sore breasts, because he knew how much they were aching.

—

LISTEN TO YOUR MOTHER: PLEASE STOP LURCHING. LIE CALMLY. You're going to live. You're a fish in a red pond of my blood, you can breathe in it. I'm lying down with my hands on you the way healers do. You're an American boy or girl. I have strength to spare; take it. Survive. That is all—you are all—that matters. Your daddy died a soldier, but the daddy you'll know will be devoted to you. I also had two daddies! I've got the blood of exiles and navigators, but I'll give you a home, my Little Fish. I carry knowledge of your Vóvó, Serafina. In her last hours, she was my mother. May you inherit her willpower.

I used to think everyone I loved died, but you'll be my proof that's not so. I'm bathing you with dreams the color of sunrise. Things happen that make us cry so much we get coated with salt, we cry out the sea within, but I'm pushing you above those tears. My papa—your grandfather—told me the ocean is double-salted, because the world over, people sob into it. (Your other grandfather—long story, but he could be a king.) Eternally I love your blood-daddy, with all I was and shall be. We made you a Lusa girl or Luso boy. Your father is named Edward, and he is sorry the land is convulsive and won't let us rest. I'm tired of moving places, but here we go now, one last time, we hope, one last state. California is where my papa longed to be. I'll never stop grieving for your other brave father, but you make me want to be strong, to love everyone I ever had and therefore have, and everyone I will now have and hold.

REQUIEM

"MY GRANDFATHER HAD SOME VERY FINE DUCKS" WAS THE SONG sheet catching John's attention in Cyrus Skylander's music shop, one of the few tunes not about war. His lung ailment had lifted but left a residue, and it impeded his ability to undergo a daft trip to Florida, where he risked being shot dead before he wandered into Mary.

A man entering the store was so skeletal he should not have been able to walk, and while John stared, Cyrus—his jaw healed into a wrinkled pinkness—exclaimed, "What the living hell!"

The apparition said, "John, do I look that bad? Cyrus, good afternoon." He had worn himself out greeting Elizabeth and trying to find John at home or the school for the deaf, where he got directed to Latshaw's, where the proprietor said John mentioned acquiring sheet music so that a resident musician could provide a mealtime concert.

John's fingers encircled the man's forearm. "Christ. Frank?"

"You've been tramping hungry," intoned a gaping Cyrus.

Frank's familiar grin included teeth soft as caramel. A shoulder blade protruded as a ridge. "Andersonville. Let some of us out a week ago. Don't know why they didn't kill me that day. I didn't call out, John, didn't want them to know you were there." A frown. "Hope you didn't think I deserted."

His friend's skin was nothing but cloth over frangible needles. *I don't care if you went on a straggle. But I believe you. Brother, you're a sculpture of sardine bones.*

———

THEY ACCEPTED AN INVITATION FROM MAX JEFFERS, WHOSE SLEEVE hung limply where his arm was missing. His career of signing with deaf students over, Max worked with his wife, Carrie, at the Everybody's Store, though he was slow in stocking shelves. She had taken their boy shopping but left out a teapot. Max poured for John and Frank and lit up a meerschaum and asked if they cared for a smoke. Frank said his chest was too flat, even for East Indian Company tobacco. John asked, "Max, you regret killing men?"

"No. Wish I'd killed more of them. Traitors. They started everything." He added that he had once helped a surgeon scrape a hacksaw through a leg, and now he was holding a teacup with a Dutch couple skating with clogs on an icy pond. And all he could wrap his mind around was the puzzlement of skating in clogs. "I wake up itching to pick up things with a hand that doesn't exist."

"Makes sense," said John. *Close your eyes, you man grown old, and you are drinking tea above the salt with Mary at the Lincolns'.*

Frank took bird-bites out of the loaf prepared by Carrie, nibbling the interior of a slice. Elizabeth was doing her best to fatten him slowly.

"You hear Alonzo Gillespie went to the Utah Territory?" said Max.

"He was a good painting teacher," said Frank.

"All those Mormons out there, though," said Max. "If you're going to start a religion, don't you need a name fancier than Joseph Smith? That's made up by someone on the lam for a robbery. The Jewish folks have Moses. We got Christ Jesus. I don't like the idea of God confiding the big stuff to someone with a countrified name like Smith."

"I might convince Elizabeth to go to Oregon. I want to look at tall trees. I'm tired of these winters," said Frank. "She can bind books while I'm a logger."

"A limit to you seeing trees if you're cutting them down," said John.

That remarkable laugh of his friend was half caliber, as if it too was scraped thin. "Lucky you skipped Vicksburg, Max," said Frank. "The enemy eating horses, and dogs, cats, and rats, and then dirt and rags."

"I'd swallow ten live rats if it'd grow my arm back. I miss the children, I'll tell you. Our students," said Max. He knew John ached for them, too.

Frank appeared sorrowful in appraising John, Portuguese boys who had taken to the sea with notions of safe harbors, but here they were, heaving facedown in the surf. He had told John the business with Mary was a plight for sure, but he hated to see him waiting for life to spell out what to do, since life held disdain for that manner of aid. Frank had said quietly, "I'm in torment about shooting Isaac, but he was fixing to kill you. I don't think I'll ever be able to talk more about it," to which John's manner of reply had been to nod.

As sunset poured its coral syrup, Carrie arrived with their son, Noel, about five years old, who exclaimed, "Daddy!" as if separated from his father for years instead of an hour, and the boy's dashing to Max sliced John in two, what with Max trying to extend both arms, empty sleeve and all.

———

JOHN AGREED TO ASSIST THE MELINE FAMILY IN RESTORING THE theater, and he called upon Ray Silva, who cried the way soldiers do when trying not to, a throat-rattling. They shared amazement that John was alive, and Frank, and Rui, too—producing incredible new perfumes. Such spinning wheels of fortune in America!

Faith and Linda Silva opened a crate and called them over. Sachets had arrived, and attached to the drawstrings were tags with the legend MOORE-STEWART FARMS, MANDARIN, FLORIDA. It was a message in a bottle, tossed from a shore. All would be cured, all fixed, and—John needed to sit. Ray invited him to supper, where Faith offered wine from Nikka's final batch, a full-bodied red. John drained a glass. Its contents shot to his forehead, where it gleamed like an emergent jewel.

2 July 1864 to the Moore-Stewart Farms,
Mandarin, Florida

Mary—I AM ALIVE. Im at Latshaw's in Spfd. Much to say but I share here only the news that Frank is home, in bad shape but E. is caring for him. Im on my way to You. I pray this reaches You. I wrote often to correct the chaplain's mistake, but never mind that now. John.Alves.

Florida was resplendent with bougainvillea and a glare evoking his childhood. He had roamed full spiral: *Madeira, Meridian, Mandarin.* Toothpick people, lean as arrows, were spearing what they needed in nature and holding it up to cook it in the steam. Near a house on stilts, a one-legged rooster was hopping. Isaac-rooster. John ate a tuna steak marinated in lime juice. While waving at a toothless man swinging a machete, he wished Frank were along with his fast new Kinnear camera. He paid for a cot behind a curtain of green beads in a cabana, nervous to the point of illness from lacking any idea of what to suggest to Mary. To Edward. He was near the southern part of another Jacksonville, on the bank of the St. Johns River, with its shine-glazed water, wondering how to ship the currents of citrus in the air—grapefruits, oranges—to Rui.

He inquired as to the whereabouts of the farm of a gentleman named Edward Moore. A wagon ride later, he stared at blackened earth being tended by a family named Stewart. Judson stated that as John could see, there had been a fire, arson, and Mr. Moore, nice fellow, nice wife, sad that they had scarcely settled in only to be hit with this, had sold them the burnt land.

"Everything got killed?" John meant her plant.

Judson told John to stroll alongside him, and they reached a knoll where the scorching had been raked, and Judson crouched and pointed: "See that? And look over there." He indicated another quadrant. "They thought, we thought, the berry plants were all gone. But we're coaxing these survivors back to life. We've got a lemon orchard—yonder—starting out. You friends with Edward?"

"Something like that," said John. "It'd be good to tell them a root or two survived. Mary's from where I'm from. A long while back. She thought I died in the war. I'm of a mind to set her at ease about my fate."

Judson whistled. "Welcome home, soldier."

"Can't say that I have one, but thank you. Did you get the letter I sent from Latshaw's in Mr. Lincoln's state?"

"Yes, but we didn't know where to forward it." They had no idea where Edward and Mary were, except for them mentioning "out West."

"Out West is a big place."

"He was from California. We tend to head back to where we began. Wish I could narrow it down more, soldier." Judson added Mary's mention of a friend named Patricia or Petunia in Los Angeles, so perhaps that was where they all ended up.

John thanked Judson and wished him well. Perpetua, yes, he had heard she was in Los Angeles, but that too was huge as all-get-out.

On the northbound train, he scarcely slept. Instead, he leaned forward, as if to speed his return to yet another place where he no longer belonged.

He stayed at Latshaw's. At the city's Cottage Nursery, he bluffed his way into a job by stating that everyone from Madeira was a born gardener.

He reversed his former life. Instead of teaching all week in Jacksonville and traveling to Springfield on Saturdays, as in the era of courtship, he spent his workweek at the garden center and stayed in Jacksonville Saturday through Sunday, sleepless on Frank's former cot in the Meline cabin. He assisted Frank and Hugo with the theater's shows. They discussed fiddling with a new Sound Machine but had no stomach for the latest experiments. Some of these involved grave robbing, dissecting dead ears to probe the secrets of the auditory canal. As a prisoner of war, Frank had been forced to watch a Maine boy's ear get sliced off to punish everyone for complaining.

———

RUI OFTEN FORAGED FOR ITEMS TO CONCOCT SCENTS, AND AT DAWN on the weekends, John joined his scavenger hunts. Grape seeds. Cinnamon shavings. Bark straining to curl around a bead of an exudation from mown hay. Dirt freckled with rail-rust. Glass, with its pungencies of sand. Droplets of grief, the pervasive emotion, a scent like ginger cut with nutmeg, were collected by Rui's hanging of gauze in oaks. He simmered the gauze with auric oil and used an eyedropper to create a perfume that came close to God, then closer to being *like* God.

A formula that featured Rui's perspiration when he dreamt of bayoneting soldiers . . . that flopped. *John, it's a floral-preferring world.*

Rui advertised customized scents for mourners, with people encouraged to bring items that belonged to someone deceased. He boiled photos, shirts, pipes, pens, suspenders, and letters and dosed the strained results with intensities of his famed neroli bridges. People stretched in a procession a mile long, clutching the belongings of the lost. For the Alves Requiem line, customers chose how much to pay, a generosity that tripled the demand. One Sunday, after the crowd had abated, with John at the cash register, Rui said, "I'll tell you what happened in Trinidad."

Time halted. John feared Rui would clam up should he be assailed with a single syllable.

"I was in the marketplace with Mother. She went to buy papayas. A Frenchman whispered in my ear that he loved me, but he was married, and being with me was impossible. But he loved me at once. He was the only person to know instinctively who I am, and that is my love story. It is so perfect, no other one is worth pursuing. You worry about me. You shouldn't."

John offered a barely perceptible nod and left his brother in peace, and anyway, Rui turned his back to put oils into the cupboard near the walnut grandfather clock, the one with a girl on a swing hung from the rim of a crescent moon.

Rui gave two thousand dollars to John from the Requiem bonanza and the rest to charities. He had no interest in improving his residence or attire. Would that bring him the Frenchman? Would that invent a perfume that was God? Would that locate Mary in the West, John? Money is an abstraction that makes people craven. Rui dabbed on Requiems as he formulated them, on behalf of his brothers and sisters everywhere, and he confessed that sometimes this caused him to break down into the most extraordinary weeping.

—

JOHN VISITED THE JACKSONVILLE PUBLIC GARDEN, WHICH HE CONSID-
ered his own, with a thought of bestowing abundance from his Requiem windfall, but as he beheld people clustering on benches born
out of his essay, the scuffing on the gravel to a chapel with its somber
cross suitable for pinning a giant vampire by its neck to a wall, as
despair over Mary slapped him backward as if to prevent entry into
the pint-sized greenhouse, he recalled that half the prize he deserved
had been confiscated, and he could swear Isaac's bullet-riddled ghost-
corpse was in a heap blocking the entrance to the house of prayer.

—

AT THE COTTAGE NURSERY, HE BEGAN AN APPLE-TREE ESPALIER. OVER
the years, sapling brown arms would reach across the expanse to en-
twine. He set the stakes a decent span apart, with wires like staff paper,
so that the sproutings could be trained upward and horizontally, and
dottings of pink-and-white blossoms like musical notes would arrive.

Word traveled about it. Customers eagerly observed his hooking
of tendrils over wires and raved over incremental progress. Once while
John was working on it, his boss called out, "Alves, you got the shears?"
and John shouted that he would bring them, and the boss volleyed in
return, "Thanks, John." This occasioned the approach of a thin, older
woman—there was a palpable briskness to rich females, a drive to
bustle and arrange—who introduced herself as Nell Clark. Forlorn,
she said, "You're John Alves? Everyone thought you died."

"So I gather."

"That's an impressive espalier. I admire you exiles."

Mary had frequently mentioned a Nell Clark as an ally, and he almost shouted, "Do you know where to find her? Mary Freitas Moore."

"Florida, I believe."

"No. Gone from there."

"That's all I know. I'm upset that we did not part well. Some last
unpleasantness was my doing." Studying the contour of her hands, she
said in a barely perceptible voice, "You were sinned against, as we used

to say. Mary told me that at one point, you and she wrote letters that did not find their destinations."

"I ran afoul of a preacher named Isaac Unthank, who chose to ruin my life. He's dead now, can't do more harm, unless his spirit gets vengeful. I wrote and wrote to explain I wasn't dead." He longed for her to go away and leave him in peace.

She looked ready to cry while murmuring, "Mary's assumption that you died continued up to the time of her departing. I wish I could find her to tell her you are among the living."

"She's probably in California. I don't know where exactly. Ma'am, Mrs. Clark, I need to get back to work. My boss wants these shears."

"I'm glad you have a good job."

"I also work weekends at the Meline Theater. Jacksonville. With Frank and Hugo Meline. They're struggling. Tell your friends to attend shows there, please?"

Nell agreed to do that and muttered about acquiring tomato plants. She seemed ready to utter something and thought the better of it, concluding, "I'm glad to put a face to the awful deeds of others," to which he replied that most civilians had a nose, mouth, and eyes, so he did not understand why his arrangement of these should matter. She offered a peculiar declaration. She said, "I hope one day you and Mary forgive me," and she must have forgotten about her heady goal to be the proud owner of new tomatoes, because she almost knocked over customers as she bolted toward the exit.

ABOVE THE SALT

SHE IS LIFTED ON A STRETCHER LIKE A WOUNDED SOLDIER, RUSHED aloft. Pain is a smoldering white star that bursts her open. There's the gyre-spinning sky. Mrs. Moore, do you know where you are? Agony prevents her from responding, schoolgirl-like: San Francisco. New York in autumn oh that was such a thing, yellow-orange in the trees, art shows, daddy, fish market, stitched leaves on linen. Writhing, she feels the cold assault of a table, who are these shouting people. Edward is sent away, and she lifts her head, come back, but nurses like rams butt him away. Legs split, gut in shreds gushing, who'll be stuck washing what's underneath. *Baby girl,* missus, you have a baby girl, a nose two ears correct number of limbs. Gurgle and scream. My child, bloody wet in my arms, and still my insides exiting between my legs as if there's a fire in my brain to escape from. Cord dripping and violet, cut, funny how I was carrying that coil inside.

It is October 16. She is two months early, or better to say the baby is two months early. People wearing masks stuff cloth up her, baby is hushed, panic, but aha, good, there's cooing, she's too bitty to keep shrieking. Mary fears what the Portuguese call morte roxo, purple death, has come for her, death in childbirth, geyser flood riverbanks broken. She ebbs away, and someone shakes her, the physic when someone is drowsy in snow, *don't fall asleep,* don't, sleep is practice for dying. Baby girl size of a piglet precious one. Swaddled newborn we must take her please mommy let her go, we must put her in a tank if you want her to live, how can such a minute thing breathe with soaked tissue paper instead of lungs.

The foyer, as they convey Mary on a gurney through it, is littered with soldiers trailing bandages, like castaways restaging their ship-wreck. Beds with newel posts—donations—line a wall rather than iron hospital beds. After slumbering in a ward with other mothers, Mary unerringly finds where newborns squirm like tadpoles inside aquariums, spiking her hope that their child—hers, Ward's, John's—will survive, despite hands no bigger than songbirds' beaks. A nurse insists Mary leave, but she will not. If she does not hold her baby, the baby will die, she does not care if the nurse refuses to believe this. Waking or sleeping, in a rocking chair Mary attends her daughter—in a rhythm—hour upon hour—*daughter,* such a lengthy elegant silent-letter-filled English word.

They name her Marcella Augustina Freitas Moore. Edward takes a leave from teaching science at the Saint Ignatius Academy. Her coloration suggests a shade between Mary's skin and John's. Edward asks, marvelously confused, she adores this, poor worldly boy really so limited, "How can she have so much hair already?" He was born bald. Marcella wears a profusion of black strands. He acts as if they'll fall out if handled, this moves her terribly. Mary cradles the sopping mass of her constantly except when sharing her with Ward, hearts speaking to a heart the size of a halved fig: *You're going to live, you'll rise above tears.* Marcella, your blood-daddy did not survive. You need to live, for his sake, and Ward's, yours, mine. I dream of stitching whole the stars like bits of salt in the sky, that my daddy showed me, named for me, so you can have fully outlined creatures to guide you at night, a swan, an eagle a crab a charioteer, and at daybreak they shall descend as guard-ians and absorb the salt-sweat you make as you move along, as you love someone and run and reach, making them twice-salted wonders glistening down when they return skyward, oh look above then and see traces of yourself taken up into the stars, my love my love.

Mary rocks her child, refusing to give up until Marcella is hale. "Marcella" means warrior, and it is a play upon *mar*, sea. *When you grow up, will you be an actress? The audience won't know your power comes from how well you fought from the start. Your papa will attend your performance—see him here?—and this will be the story we'll tell, how we held you so you would absorb our strength, Marcella, our Little Fish.*

A chenille bedspread looks snow-knobbed. *You inherited my arrow of hair. We're under a cover that looks like winter, but we're in a warm state on the edge of the Pacific.*

I'll bring you to the Botanical Garden in Funchal. I'm left to imagine what my father's expression would be upon hugging his grandbaby. Life dear life is confounding, please convince me it's worth it; for that you must be strong.

Babies born too soon, like you, are fussing in their glass cages. They are your first friends. (May they be true ones.)

The plant I brought from Madeira has died. We sold the land to the Stewarts and left them speaking of lemon and orange groves. I must cease mourning the miracle-fruit plant; you must not feel in me a drop of unhappiness.

I swore an oath to honor my marriage, and I want to get better at loving him, and my love for you will help me do that, Marcella. I've been too many places. But San Francisco's air will infuse you with light. Maybe you'll be a writer instead of an actress? I write with thread, but you can use words. You can record the story of your blood-father but also of the man by my side, desperate to guard and keep.

Here now, Marcella. He's holding out his arms, so I can sleep.

NOT THE YEARS IN YOUR LIFE BUT
THE LIFE IN YOUR YEARS

1865–1874

THE SOUND OF THE BLAST THAT MURDERED THE PRESIDENT streaked from Ford's Theater to Illinois, where it formed a cyclone with John in the center. In the grieving crowd as Abraham's body was borne home in a rolling caisson along with the disinterred Willie Lincoln—the casket like a black wedding cake trimmed with white piping, or like a photographic negative of a confection with rosettes—John's eardrums thumped as well with the echo of guns shooting Isaac. And it was then that he grasped the lure of restlessness, the value of having so many places to go in America that one could bury the most daunting clamor below the tasks of deciding where to go next, how to get there, what to do, what it would cost.

He rode an iron horse to the border of Missouri, where, abruptly, the tracks shrank to unconnected jots on maps in the kingdom of Kansas. He hired a teamster to hie him westward, and their sole sustained conversation occurred over a campfire in the Territory of New Mexico, when John wondered aloud, for the sake of comedy, if they might meet the Donner party's fate, and the man snapped, "This look like winter to you?," to which John replied that indeed it did not. The teamster refused to pose for John's camera, a farewell gift from

Frank. They passed horsemen routing beeves in bellowing cascades out of mountain passes. A grass called "blue gama" triggered daydreams of sinking through water shades. A flightless bird sped solo on the ground, too fast for John to photograph. At a hotel, he consumed pancakes with cacao nibs dotted on each one in the shape of a daisy, and this cheerful artistry where none was essential moved him utterly.

Via some veterans who hailed John in a tavern—they recognized one another without need of uniforms—he learned that those phosphorescent blue and green wounds at Shiloh were called "angels' glow" because those men recovered faster, and no one knew why. Everywhere John went, soldiers, some with chunks of flesh missing, or their sweethearts vanished or married, spoke of Sherman's pathway of complete annihilation, Atlanta to the sea, Meridian hundreds of times over. Thousands of dispossessed freedmen and freedwomen and freedchildren had trailed after the general, their cries garlanding the universe as Mother had described it, where not a single noise, thought, action, gesture, or word fails to contribute to the making and unmaking of totality.

He should have asked Mary what town Edward hailed from. The man had merely seemed to embody the farthest reaches of the nation.

The extremely dry, dusty-purple hills of California befuddled him; they suggested the Old Testament. The world seemed flipped so that he was breathing in a drained seabed, and below the land's surface, if it spun upward, he would find families sailing with children in boats. There were olive trees and adobe buildings. A soda-cracker salesman hauled him toward Chino because John had heard Portuguese people dwelled there. Every aspect of every creature in the square looked hardened—the faces of the dairymen, the faces of the dogs. The town was a stopover on the way to hunt for gold and a transient spot for failed gold-seekers to tend cows. Men with money snapped up land and mines and were at war over whether anyone had the right to take possession of anything at all. But he did hear the language of his mother and his childhood, and he shared wine with dairymen plaiting the air with the swallowed sounds and "shh" aspirations he recognized.

He had anticipated that this state would prove sizable, but nothing could have prepared him for its sprawl. No one he asked at random had heard of a Perpetua Roderick or Rodrigues, or a Henry Kingsley, or a Perpetua Kingsley. Attempting a letter with no street address bore no fruit. Despite identifying this as futile, he went on walks expecting her compact size and energy to spark into being before him. He wrote to Nikka in Brooklyn, and to Frank, and he settled into a transients' hotel on First Street, where horse-drawn wagons clopped by in the low-spread frontier and the arid heat cleansed him.

At one suppertime, he was served a yellow-skinned pear so mellow he thought he might burst asunder, because it seemed like a mystery of life solved, that life was a quilt stitched in main of moments containing a little peace, or a little beauty.

This is how a year goes by. Then two.

More. Accordion stretched.

He never happened upon Perpetua. Or Mary. He ventured up and down this state younger than he was until doing so felt pathetic, full of pointless lingering.

While passing through the Wasatch National Forest, he watched a ballerina on a stump of a redwood tree enormous enough to be a dance floor. Before an audience, she twirled on its polished neck.

He helped shear a flock of sheep and caught a parade of vaqueros crossing a plain of wildflowers, the horses tufting up so many they looked ankle-deep in a flaked rainbow.

He hiked the Teton Range and stole a kiss from his first redhead. Courtships never went far, because he could not stop wandering. He failed to locate Alonzo Gillespie in the Utah Territory, but the openness of the land teamed with the blue buckled mountains blocked forward motion enough for him to stop in Fillmore in Millard County because he liked the mathematics of its being the area's exact geographic center. After accepting a job at an apiary, he undertook a marriage to one Edith Wells, fifteen years his senior. She owned the hives. Her porch sagged so much it appeared to be grinning. When he proposed, she said he would do. He thought: *Yes, I'll have to do this; I'll do that. Suits me fine.* The only explanation for this marriage was an impulse to amplify how everything was absurd, a desire to have a home, and an affection for older women who looked beset. She brewed coffee so weak it tasted like water dabbed with beige paint. When he suggested this to her, it was revealed that she had absolutely no sense of humor.

John used a smoker to force bees out of their frames; he set comb chunks onto drip pans. He set queen excluders in place, the mesh wire that drones could pass through but that isolated the queen. If he moved a hive, the bees returning with nectar hovered in the empty spot, which he found unaccountably touching. He measured honey into jars that sold for eight and a half cents per dozen and suggested a peach flavoring that did astoundingly well on a rail route with stops in Reno and Sacramento. He learned that Edith Wells had been married to a Mormon polygamist who had died in debtors' prison, and the house was heavily mortgaged to the bank. This man had burdened her with seven miscarriages, one stillborn girl, and a teenaged son named Charlie who got out a rifle one day and suggested John hit the road. No foreigner was grabbing any deed to any house, and furthermore the thought of what John was up to was disgusting.

Edith seemed as indifferent to losing him as she had been to their vows, and they got a divorce gladly.

He accepted a job at a school for the deaf in Salt Lake City, where he got back to instructing children in how to rise out of silence. He lived once again in a residence for men. He had no religion anymore, but he looked at the violet and brown mountains at times and thanked God. John became patient in his dealings, with barbers, shopkeepers, ranchmen, and the lady who brought eggs to the boardinghouse, his means of acknowledging the quotidian requirements of decency. How to love a world that people so energetically endeavored to destroy? By recalling his mother's counsel to listen to a pervasive song: *Rise up, rise over the weeping bodies on an earth sown with salt. Be consoled.* Salt douses fire, it is a flavor, and if it imparts thirst, bless it for driving you to cool waters. Soar to where lightness resembles the feel of the unions you seek, call it peace, call it a kingdom of love, even if one dwells there alone.

———

IN THE NINTH YEAR OF HIS EXODUS, A FEW YEARS INTO HIS EXILE IN Utah, he returned to his rented room after a day without notable

victories in his classroom, and propped outside his door, where the
paint was weathered, a note awaited him, its cream envelope with
black script, and he backed away, as if it would detonate. He recognized the script with its flourishes, its resemblance to flawless cutwork
and Guimarães stitching.

He bent down and collected what awaited him, and he lifted himself up. He was thirty-six, three years past the time span given to Christ
on the earth, and he held the note just a bit before breaking its seal.

NOTHING CONCEALED THAT
SHALT NOT BE REVEALED

1865–1874

MARCELLA AUGUSTINA FREITAS MOORE GREW UP HEALTHY AND green-eyed, with a fetching widow's peak. Doting upon her, besides Mommy and Daddy, was the staff at Tadich's coffee bar on Clay Street, where servers brought her cups of mocha with a swirled foam heart. She was fond of stone lions, clamshells, bonsais, and Mommy's faraway gaze. She sang to the stuffed pig doll Daddy bought for her. A creature called a "tomato frog" in a city aquarium was a treasured ally, pressing close to the glass to greet her, and she loved the roaring, blubbery sea lions near Cliff House, where Mommy joked that their corkscrewing through the water was like a diagram of what had shot through her skull when Marcella had been a colicky infant.

They lived in the top-floor flat of a four-story building with gargoyles in Russian Hill. The purple trillium pressing from Emily Dickinson ruled supremely upon a wall.

Mary reveled in being an urban girl, dazzled by the streets, the hills, the rush and clanging. The friendly greetings! If there were times when, like many women, she suspected, she wished she could put two men together, one who embodied passion while the other excelled at providing comfort, and if there were times when she studied her daughter and saw John, she likewise felt that Ward was letting go of layers upon layers of reserve, and that was due to her letting herself love him wholly.

She took care of Marcella (she quit thinking of the child as "hers") while he was at the Saint Ignatius Academy, and he tapped into a lecturing circuit. Mary and Marcella attended, in Bolinas, his talk about Central Park in New York City, an example of declaring that nature is our co-resident. No more congregating, as was the current habit, in cemeteries! Mary shoved away the recollection of the little public park conceived by John, ahead of his time. "We stand at our nation's crossroad in deciding who we are," Ward proclaimed, "lest machinery overwhelm our landscape and thereby our souls."

Once during a picnic in the countryside, a mountain lion crept up behind them, and he taught them to get on tiptoe and raise their arms—becoming as tall as possible while shouting—to scare away the danger. The mountain lion bounded away. Marcella declared that Daddy was her hero. "And you're my Marcy-Darcy," he replied.

When she asked if she could have a brother or sister, Mary demurred; the efforts at this had yielded nothing (but this did not vex her). Sometimes Mary held her so tightly Marcella chanted, "Mommy, Mommy, you're loving me too much!"

This once gave her a burst of longing for John. He would agree with her, *some affections shall never diminish with time.*

Edward brought home flowers "for his girls," and Marcella learned to slice stems at a slant to better absorb water. Oh, be more than grateful or content, be fulfilled, be adoring and not just adored.

Mary busied herself with her tablecloth and on a separate square created a dual-sided triumph like one she had seen in a magazine of a peacock on one side, a tiger on the other, *using the same threads.* Hers featured a red-berried plant, with her father on the reverse. Everything was abundant, everything teemed. Recalling that wrecked ships were buried below the streets, she paused over the spots where they were purported to be, sensing their tilt. She thrived on taking Marcella to the Chinese shops with their profusions of reds and golds, where they bought jade elephants for the windowsill to help the birds see the glass, though ones drunk on pyracantha bushes still hurled their inebriated bodies to their doom. At Boudin's Bakery, the men shoveling bread in and out of the ovens gave them extra sourdough rolls. What a taste! It was a city of tastes. Breezes were salted or buttery or crabmeaty. God, but the *produce* of California! To eat here is to swallow sun rays! The food was plumped with chlorophyll and reminded her in a parallel way of Madeiran produce swollen with lava minerals. Who could name it all: Meyer lemons, blackberries, kale, chard, the yerba buena wild on Angel Island.

Mary's visits with Perpetua Kingsley in the state's southern half slowed when demands on their time expanded. Pet had three children within five years, while Henry became adept with his prosthetic hand and entered management at the Acme Paper Company. For a while, before they lost touch completely, their get-togethers were a chance to speak Portuguese. Mary taught Marcella a few words. Mãe. Pai. Filha. Madeira, fogo, faca, foco. Bruma. Bruxa. Beijinho. Alcachofras! O meu coração.

During occasional nightmares about the wiping out of her crop, the flames took the form of locusts from the tales about swarms a mile high and a mile wide sweeping over the prairie, chomping through everything green, drill-buzzing into animals that could not run fast enough.

Edward's cousin who had advised him of the teaching job moved his vigorous, enterprising family to Hawaii to start a tour company, and Mary and her husband and child mourned their departure and pictured them among pineapples and colorful fish. An ongoing dispute involved Edward's refusal to introduce Mary to his mother and brothers, a stone's throw away in Nob Hill. Bizarre to have no communication. But the day came when Edward was with Mary and Marcy-Darcy at Ghirardelli's, sharing chocolate ice cream, when a woman who wore a slipping mask over an aspect ruined by nebulous bile came over from her table to bark, "Edward?" He introduced Mary and Marcella to Andrea Moore, who curled her lip when Mary said, "Pleased to meet you." Andrea said, "Where are you from?" Demanded to know.

Marcella asked, "Who is this mean lady?" and that concluded their one and only association with Ward's past beyond the cousin now basking in Hawaii, to which he said to Mary, "They're not worth fighting for. You are." As consolation for their child's lack of grandparents, he bought a spinet and directed Marcella in dancing, swooping her up to set her on the icebox and proclaim, "Little Fish, you've swum to the moon!" She would giggle, "Oh, Daddy!"

They took wagon rides down the coast to Castroville, near Monterey, where the sea air and heat were so ideal for artichokes that an Italian immigrant had set them to flourishing there, just as Mary had brought her *Synsepalum dulcificum* to new climes (carting it, finally, to its annhilation). Ward announced he had bought five acres with a cabin in Castroville. Mary did not think they needed what he called "a getaway," which sounded as if they had committed a crime. But artichokes were irresistible—teeny ones that a shop sold shellacked as brooches and jumbo ones the size of a cat's head.

Every now and again, lonely there, Mary took Marcella to an oak so they could nestle in a crook edged with leaves. Serafina Alves had promised to grow through trees, to be inside any table her children owned. It stood to reason that John was in the trees, too, holding Mary and their child. Marcella had been born with Portuguese nerves and got easily upset, and the all-encompassing nature of her not infrequent sobbing seemed full of the reminder that John's body lay somewhere unknown while Mary's flesh kept an ember of desiring him still, how impossible, desiring him so.

—

THEN SOMETHING HAPPENED IN THE ELEVENTH YEAR OF MARRIAGE, in 1872. Mary went to buy seafood after Ward promised to make a paella for dinner; he was skilled at crisping the rice on the bottom. He was at the table when she returned from the fishmonger's shack, and his expression suggested that someone had died. Marcella gamboled off to undertake a party with the menagerie in her bedroom.

"Ward?" Hesitant, Mary forced him to look at her. The packages with prawns and mussels smelled as if she had swabbed them in a tide.

"I'm sorry," he said, voice cracking.

For the past week, he had been having an affair, not with an admirer at one of his lectures, as she had sensed might occur—how they gathered afterward, goggling at him, pawing and fawning—but with a shopgirl who had sold him the pinafore for Marcella's birthday.

"What's her name?"

"Why does it matter?"

Foghorns moaned, an otherworldly noise Mary normally associated with tranquility. "I choose to put a name to the picture in my head, Edward."

"June. Only twice. It's over. I was idiotic."

"June. Moon, spoon, tune."

Marcella was crooning to her animal kingdom, with a clatter of toy dishes, and she chanted the lullaby Mary had taught her, about boughs breaking. Mary had not shared the even scarier Portuguese one, about the bicho-bug that ate papa, mama, and now was going to eat baby. This was sung while fingers spider-marched from the baby's sternum to the throat.

"You judge me unfaithful in my heart, so this is my punishment," she said.

"No. I was—I wasn't thinking. You make me so glad. I don't think you should stop loving—you know. Please, forgive me."

Marcella's singing stopped. A worrier, she was alert to shifts in the atmosphere, a girl with questions, a sniffer of mysteries. She appeared, holding the rabbit doll named Bun. "Mommy? Daddy?"

In the night, Mary and Ward slept like a wooden board alongside a wooden board. In a move that would horrify her the full length of her years, she got up and curled like a cat under the dining room table, to sleep there as if under cardboard in an alley. *I have no home.*

Edward left for work at the academy in the morning. She told her daughter that instead of Mommy taking her to school, they would have a holiday. Mary packed a suitcase and hired a carriage to take her not to the cabin in Castroville but to a seaside hotel in Carmel. The dining room served the abalone that the owner pried off the rocks. Marcella wanted to know where Daddy was, and she missed her third-grade school friends. Mary bought her a plush dolphin. She had requested a room near the ocean's roar, where she wept into a pillow to muffle her sorrow, her umbrage, her desire, her never-ending grief over John. Marcella was patting her back, then lying next to her and crying, too, because she wanted to go home. Mary forgave John for dying. Had she never completely done that? She so rued her failure to wed him before he went to war that a storm erupted in her mighty enough to tap out a philosophy on the instrument of her bones: It seemed unspeakably wrong for people to boast of living in a way immaculate of regrets.

Salt-stippled, they strolled along the shore. Marcella cheered up when they ate fried clams in a paper cone with a couple who said they had heard of men firing guns at baseball games to rattle the hurlers and affect the outcomes. This insured a good payday for gamblers. *John is the person I long to tell that to.* They could laugh about his card-playing, which seemed such a minor, hope-addled offense now. She pictured him excelling at baseball, having heard that soldiers played it in camp. His strength, his body—it is so profoundly the body we miss upon missing someone, that thing that hosts everything else we love, too.

In a pink dawn after a two-night stay, she washed her face and said, "Time to go home, Little Fish." The liquid lava eyes of John, Marcella's, regarded her, and Marcella said she was glad. Mary paid the shockingly high tab. Edward had signed her up for her own bank account in California as well. His lifelong capacity to jump toward forgiveness, bounding over stages of brooding and wrath, answered her summons. His mistake was nothing, less than nothing. It was her own heart and its pains that still, still had been tormenting her and therefore him, too.

Distraught after her absence, Ward gave his wife a music-box. Whenever she lifted the lid, a ballerina spun in time with a tinkling of Schubert's *Fantasia*. Schubert, she would come to learn, had nursed a bruising, unrequited love to his grave.

He bought Marcella *Alice's Adventures in Wonderland* and read it to her at night. He told her that her grandpa, Mommy's father, had painted rocks to look like strawberries. When birds knocked their beaks against the masquerade of the surface, they learned to quit attacking a garden. It had been distressing to leave those behind, charred, in Florida. He and Marcella painted new ones, for the geraniums in the window box, and when Mary joined them, it signaled a finality of forgiveness and a cauterizing of wounds. Ward instituted a game of hiding the toy dolphin everywhere, in Marcella's coat pocket, inside her pillowcase, in her school bag, and she hid Dolphy inside his brief-case or dresser drawer and would scream with laughter when he never failed to act surprised. "Oh, Daddy!"

He said, "I love you, Mary, with a strength I didn't know I had." Again he blamed himself for their failure to conceive more children. Evenings grew sedate. Once, with a rustling, he dropped the newspaper that had been shielding his drooping eyelids, and she granted him the face-saving relief of suggesting that despite the early hour, perhaps he would join her in calling it a day. But first Ward proclaimed he would be faithful *now and forevermore, quoth the raven*—he said this as if he had been storing up that line at the ready all his life. John's spirit whispered, *Hold on to the astonishing life you've forged in a united world I fought to preserve.* Edward said he would die to make her happy, if only she would have him.

She would.

———

MOMENTOUS EVENTS STRUCK IN 1874. MARY WOULD TURN THIRTY-four on April 22, what Papa had called a two-swans-swimming day. Edward would be forty-four on June 4. Marcella would turn ten in October. Their thirteenth wedding anniversary would come on May 1.

First, a "Happy New Year" letter arrived from Myrtle Jamison in New York. They went lengthy stretches without contact, but their friendship had never faltered. Myrtle had conversed with an acquain-tance who owned a gallery in San Francisco's Union Square and had agreed to scout Mary Freitas Moore's handiwork and, moreover, to suggest she demonstrate embroidery for visitors for a one-weekend special show.

I insisted you deserve that, Mary! wrote Myrtle. *What to report from here? Teddy's mind collapsed during the war. Lawrence plans an early re-tirement from the bank. Gemma married a lawyer and has a son, and Clarisse works at the Historical Society and seems in no hurry to "settle," as she puts it! I care for my son and continue with my gadding. Our little greenhouse still misses you, as do we all.*

In February, the Cortelli Gallery set up a freestanding case to house Mary's dual-sided rendering of a red-berried plant and her father, with the card legend extolling two compositions with the same threadings ... and she had taken up drawing, and doing watercolors, and these were displayed, while an even larger wall case housed her tablecloth, a length worthy of the biggest banquet in history.

She was given a dais to demonstrate embroidery, with Marcella in her favorite dress beside her. Along its hem was a family of fish, because her nickname was Little Fish, mama, papa, brother, sister, with stitched scales. She proclaimed to the audience, "Mommy did *everything* here!" Mary, snipping with scissors, showed how cutwork was a matter of not fearing the imposing of an empty space. Ward beamed at her from the back of the crowd. Someone bellowed out, "What's the secret to sewing?"

Mary scanned the attentive faces, including her husband's, and said, "My father used to say, 'First one must learn to love the thread.'"

As the event began winding down, a reporter from the *Examiner* interviewed her, and lo and behold, a gentleman named James Righetti handed her a business card and suggested she might consider becoming an illustrator for the children's books he published at his San Francisco firm of Righetti & Leopold. He would send her a manuscript, should she care to audition.

Two months after her Cortelli Gallery event, a letter arrived:

April 10th, 1874, Springfield, Ills.

Dear Mary,

JOHN IS ALIVE! HE LIVES! I'll explain. First, allow me to apologize for the manner of our parting. For years, I have forged an inquiry to repair, inadequately, the damages inflicted upon you, including by me.

When I discovered you were in California, I undertook the perusal, weekly, of newspapers from that state, delivered via the mails, hoping that you or Edward might be mentioned. Though it has taken a decade, what justice that your handiwork should lead to your name in a source I oft

*consulted. The Examiner's reporter would not divulge your
address but agreed to forward anything I might care to send
you. Should this be in your hands, it confirms the fame of
your artwork allowed you to be found.*

*John was spared war's most appalling fate only to suf-
fer a fresh dose of banalities. Shortly before you married
Edward, when you confided in me the full history of your
story with John, I was buying gloves at an emporium when
I happened upon Dottie Willis. Troubled in conscience, she
admitted belonging to a group set upon intercepting the letters
you wrote to John Alves and the ones John wrote in return,
and to the faking of a letter from John's brother, whose
name now escapes me.*

*This enterprise was conceived and kept in motion by
Maud Dieterman. Dottie assumed it was due to Edward's
breaking of his engagement with Maud when you showed
up, even before he attempted a suit with you. Maud engaged Gertie's participation readily after you caused Gertie
to be refused admittance to his house and ruined her chances
with him as well. Maud frequented John's brother's per-
fumery and they quarreled over his refusal to sell her something, apparently, so she included him in what she called
"the sport." Dottie was the sort of going-along-with-things
friend to Gertie and Maud, pressed into "the sport" because her nephew Taylor Seeger, the postmaster, was open
to bribes. He has since been dismissed due to numerous
complaints.*

*They intercepted and absorbed your missives, and
John's, and in so doing adopted his style with words. Here
is my guilt: I did not aid their schemes, I did not condone
them, but I also did not inform you of what was happening, having convinced myself that steering your prospects of
marriage toward an upstanding citizen would better keep
you within reach of me, you in a life that I, in my arro-
gance, pictured as unquestionably the better one. I feared
Maud exiling me from circles I fought my own battles to*

join, when there was chatter about my marrying a much older man "for his money." I did marry Oliver for his money. I also liked him. But let me leave off speaking of myself. I attended your wedding, knowing you had been and were being deceived. I ate your wedding cake.

My next (worse? who can rank these?) sin was that after the death notice arrived from the chaplain, your boy wrote repeatedly, after a substantial delay, and I heard from Dottie that they were back to their old habits. All of us, including Taylor Seeger, were honestly shocked at his notes, as the chaplain's testimonial was authentic. You might have greeted John upon his return from war, that at least, had so many of us not shunned you and driven you away. It is unconscionable to permit you to age yourself with the belief that he is deceased. (Despite my behavior, I admired such a romantic thing, to run to a dying man, and in so doing revive him!) But again I said . . . nothing. I did nothing. My excuse this time? I had an attitude of being your mother, and in the early days, you responded in kind to me, but in marriage you grew up and did not need a mother anymore, and I resented that. I told myself, "She ran to a boy and shamed herself, such a scandal!" I cottoned to the prevailing response. To defend you would be to suffer my own ostracization. I am appalled with my behavior. A further admission: While married to Oliver, I met a young man who wished to provide me with the excitement that had faded in my marriage. Doubtless I thought, "Why should Mary have what I denied for myself?" I too became jealous of you.

There is the strange matter of, according to Dottie, some love letters (one was a drawing?) allowed to pass to and fro during the era of Shiloh, along with perhaps several others over time during the war. Did an angel swoop in, preventing loveliness from being consigned to dust? No, giving these to you, and to John, steamed open and then resealed, would introduce discontent into your marriage, also affecting the man who rejected Maud and Gertie.

The blunt truth: Once you appeared with your long black hair and artistic agility in moving beyond clothing, furniture, and social nonsense, you were marked. I believe Maud's thinking was: Why not relegate you, Ward, and John (another ambitious foreigner) to the common fate of lacking a world-class love? Maud (and Gertie, and anyone else) would be second-best to Ward even if you had not married him. You destroyed any chance of him considering anyone else as your equal, even if you vanished. There was no chance of Ward choosing Maud after you, none. This is why hastening you toward John's embrace would not do. They despised how your beauty and talent found love twice over. (Am I pure in this myself? No.) Your qualities allowed you to step into their social class, and all this together could not go unpunished.

I met John years ago as he was constructing an espalier. Though strikingly handsome, he was a wounded bearer of grace. He mentioned a theater in Jacksonville. Once I had your whereabouts, I secured his by contacting Frank Meline, who clarified that a decomposed man was clutching John's Bible, and thus a well-meaning chaplain erred. Frank indicated that John spent time in Los Angeles before moving to Utah, though he disappeared for spans of time frequently and Frank was often out of touch.

Enclosed herein is John's address in Salt Lake City. I hope it is current. It is up to you whether to use it. One additional curious bit of news is that Frank, upon my explaining the campaign against you both, mentioned John's firm belief that a preacher named Isaac had wronged you. Whatever else that man might have done, he is blameless in this matter, having neither manufactured nor undertaken a plot to keep you apart. Frank appended that Isaac was among the Union's fallen.

When I think of my cold treatment of you, and my doing and saying nothing while telling myself I was only an observer, I am aghast. My comportment told me I did not know myself—or rather, it told me that when put to a test, I was petty and common. No wonder I sought civic projects, to convince myself I was good. I deserve your lasting opprobrium in the name of a friendship that was so dear to me.

From, Nell Clark

My darling is alive. Waves of shock visible in rippling lines entered Mary's arms, horripilating her flesh. After dashing the note to the floor, she cradled her head in her arms on the table. Despite Nell's explanation, it still confused her: Why would Maud and her ilk not *want* to shove Mary out of sight? Was it as simple as John and Mary as a deliriously devoted couple being unbearable to Maud coupling moodily with Ward (if by some errant impulse he would have her)? Mary had already endured Dottie's revelation, but pinpointing a ringleader's name brought it home as carved-in-stone. Oh, as if there were logical reasons for the constant need to scald and level, to equalize, to reduce, to size up and compete at every second over everything, to keep pounding a rival into pulp. Those kindnesses Maud foisted upon her were part of keeping her off guard for the purpose of scrutiny. Even those deliveries of liquor and cheese that Mary gushed with thanks about but had never sampled: Get fat, get drunk, get imperfect.

My love, you're among the living?

Mary had bitten into a roll slathered with gooseberry jam, and the half circle left by her teeth and the whiteness of the plate fascinated her. The numbers of John's address swam on the page. Her child was at school, and Edward was at work. Her task that day was to buy watercolors at the art-supplies shop. A children's book needed flamingos, and she was eager to practice controlling the amount of water on her brush. Initial commands to rise from her chair failed.

While she was treading down the staircase, one knee buckled on a landing, and she could not get up from genuflecting, and for a moment she stayed an animal on all fours. Then she stood, went out, and bought her paints, and near a cabinet in the store with an array of colors, she spoke out loud John's full name.

While applying a first rush of yellow paint to paper, she suddenly moaned and water again flooded her knees, leaving her to hobble to the closet with her tablecloth, and she took it from its linen shroud and clutched it to her middle. She catapulted into space. Eerie how calm she was when she told Edward her news before dinner, barely speaking as she filled a bowl with California lettuce five shades of green. After an intensity of his own shock, he honored her by locating pen and stationery himself and insisting she write to John, and then his shoulders curved, and she sat with him while he went far away inside himself and then came back.

While picking up Marcella from school, she noticed a girl laughing at a tiny child, pointing, and others were gathering to do the same. Her eyeglasses slipping, Mary fled to guard the girl being mocked, and she screamed at the main tormentor, "Go to hell! Go to hell, you little monster! Shame on you!"

The bully backed away.

Mary waited to be arrested or for the school to call, but nothing occurred, because the world can be matter-of-fact about absorbing cruelty into its hide.

One mist-saturated morning, the foghorns groaned especially long and loud, and Mary Catherine Freitas Moore thanked them. Such a symphony. On John's Sound Machine, this might be captured as a ragged circle. We dwell and kindle a short while, our desires spill, and pettiness is a laughable thing, because indeed the earth abides.

APRICOTS

JOHN'S VISION OF THEIR AFFAIR—PICKING UP WHERE THEY HAD LEFT off during the war—was aided by the summer air buffeting him during the train trip from Salt Lake City, baking his limbs. In his fantasy, the backdrop with Mary turned full of astonishing, pounding rain, cooling bursts imparting relief. After their agreed-upon meeting on the wharf in Monterey, getting drenched, they would race to the hotel where he had arrived a day early. The ground cover was wild strawberries. They would laugh as sopping clothes proved difficult to pull off, and with as much fear as yearning, he would carry her to the bed they would make rain-soaked, the ocean's cold front through the open window gentle at first, then tremendous, then easing away.

Monterey's wharf was packed with Saturday promenaders, a watercolor scene. He had brought along his camera. From an old woman on the pier, he purchased a dozen apricots. He loved them as a fruit; he loved them as a color. Mary's note had named this location, where Portuguese people flocked. It was near one of the places she lived, sixteen miles away. This meant Edward had given her not one home but two. John snapped a picture of the apricot seller, the water a shamrock tarp. When he wrote back, he had mentioned taking photographs as a keen pursuit, and that he liked Salt Lake City and his sign-language teaching. He admitted to almost collapsing upon receiving her note on elegant stationery and accepted her invitation to meet. Choose the day, the place.

She advised him that Edward had consented to this meeting in Monterey. She also had news to convey about the old mystery of who had harmed them and would share a letter she had received with the full revelation. He assumed the "revelation" would be a naming of which postmaster or ally (Sarah Brink?) had aided Isaac. Though he did not care to revisit the subject, she might need to speak of it a last time.

Much more important was the stunning news that torqued him into a new shape. There was a girl named Marcella, and she was his, from their time in Vicksburg. He wondered if Mary registered that their child had the word "cell" in her name. His reply included asking if he could meet Marcella, please, even if only this once.

People in summer clothes passed by on the wharf, eating snacks. As he stood with the apricots in their sack, his face shaved with a straight razor, his black hair washed and combed back under a new hat, and his black trousers and white shirt clean and pressed, he expanded his images of an affair into a larger realm that seemed too much to ask. They would go somewhere and have a home. He would plane the floor to make it even and sow the wood curls in the garden. He would install a cedar roof. There would be braiding of a daughter's hair, or the chopping of a piano with an axe if that was all there was left to burn if they lived in unbearable cold.

There would be night-clothing folded, still warm with their sleep in it.

Mary was walking toward him, holding Marcella's hand. He had forgotten to ask if the child would know who he was, and this flustered him. Asking to meet his baby now seemed like a bad idea, his first failure as a parent.

She was nine, going on ten, at the exact midpoint of how he looked and how Mary looked, and this ruined his ability to formulate words.

They stopped a distance apart. His unsteadiness made it seem that the wharf was rocking, same as the riverboat with the wheelchairs dancing. It killed him to note Mary's lemon-colored dress with embroidered cats on the collar. She had worn this at the Lincolns'. She was so painful to look upon that he smiled toward Marcella, who was observing him steadily (serious child, good God was she born of them both).

"Mary," he called out, and he hastened to close the gap between them.

She was wearing her spectacles. The child had her green eyes, and wavy hair with a dark arrow pointing at the forehead. Names were exchanged. *John, this is Marcella. Marcella, this is Mommy's friend John.* Marcella studied the grown-ups while he set down his camera and the sack of fruit full of the western skies. Mary smelled like wintergreen, and they pressed one another close so their hearts could chat. Marcella picked up his hat when it tumbled off. Sensible, she attends to details. She is his and not his. Probably he had begged to meet his daughter so that her presence would confirm what was plain all along: This was a girl who had spent too many years with another man as her father. Add to this the constant truth that Mary was a married Catholic who—and she had reminded John of this in her note—had vowed not to wound her husband again. But her arms stayed around him. Her glasses shifted as he squeezed her and heaved his tears backward. But she was crying.

After all the imaginings, and up until moments ago, he had thought: *She will come away with me. We'll live in Salt Lake City, or Los Angeles, or where she wishes. We'll pretend we have no past.* This was impossible. He said nothing, but she nodded very hard, eyes shut. *All right, O Meu Mais Do Que Tudo,* he whispered, people funneling around them. *All right, my love. I know. I know.* It was incredibly noble of Edward to give them this. That's all there was to it. This was how John and Mary would love each other: They would give one another up for good. He would not take a girl, even his own, from the papa she knew. He would not hurt a decent man. His body against Mary's conveyed to her all this, and upon his soul: He knew she knew he knew she knew. He said only, "Want some great news, Mary? Mary, dear." He held her face in his hands. "Your plant might have survived, in Mandarin. I went there. The Stewarts showed me two straggling new plants."

She said she had no more strength to raise a crop of anything. They laughed, just a touch. Her shoes were a pearly blue, like the inside of abalone shells. She burst out, "I'm so sorry. John, I'm so sorry."

No. No, darling. Nothing to be sorry for.

"I've missed you so," she sobbed. "I thought you were dead." Marcella—a fully formed and forming child—was leaning against his side. He put an arm around her and said Mommy and he were friends from the far place where they were born, and old friends got all worked up when they saw one another. Speaking in Portuguese to conceal her words from their girl, Mary said, "I should have married you the first time you asked."

"Listen, darling," he said. Marcella was like those auditory devices he remembered from the school for the deaf in Jacksonville—the clever, highly sensitive inventions that soak up the tiniest sound. He took out his handkerchief and dabbed Mary's face, would preserve salt tears dried in the cloth. He spoke in Portuguese, too. "Edward was right to marry you. He'll keep taking good care of you, and I thank him." And he broke, because he was broken. He wept, and it was her turn to offer comfort as he heaved out, still in their first language, "I'm no good. I can't care for anyone because of the war. Even if you were free now, I couldn't give you anything." Marcella stayed glued to him. He would pull himself together now, he must, and he would go to pieces later, alone.

Did his undoing begin in Meridian? Mary asked.

"No," he whispered. And in Portuguese: "What destroyed me was helping to starve those people in Vicksburg. Meridian was madness, and a boy got murdered by a crazy officer, and I maimed the officer to stop him from killing the boy's mother, but that sort of tragedy happened all the time."

"What are you saying?" demanded Marcella.

He inclined toward her and asked, "What is your full name, Marcella?" She carried a little purse, a child wanting to be like a grown-up. This one had sparkles.

"I'm Marcella Augustina Freitas Moore," she said. The foam on the sea beyond the railing was puffed large, as if clouds had descended hoping to live on the rock-bottom bed but the water was blocking them, leaving them to agitate.

In their first language, Mary said that she had not fully explained his identity to Marcella. One day she would. But for now, Mary repeated in English that this was a friend from Mommy's youth who helped children speak when they could not hear with their ears, and look, he has a camera, because he is an artist who takes pictures.

Marcella was an old soul, not a young one. John was an old soul, Mary, too. Edward, definitely. He told them to keep the apricots, and he would be on his way. He bent to kiss Marcella goodbye, and in his embrace, she laughed that she liked his mustache. He said to Mary, "You had a letter to give me?"

"It's not necessary. We've been hurt enough."

Still, he said, if there were a truth to bear, he preferred she not suffer it alone, and she searched in her handbag and pressed an envelope upon him.

She mentioned being with his mother as she passed into spirit. "She gave me the Sound Machine. Shall I ship it to you? She said something that got scratched on soot-paper at the end but wouldn't tell us exactly what it was. Nikka took it. Isn't that good?"

Yes, it was good that Nikka owned the last recording. As for the Sound Machine, Mary could keep that fossil or throw it away.

Mary, full of grace. All decorum would shatter if he expressed the peace it imparted to him to hear that his mother's soul was bathed by forgiveness in the end, so he said merely, "Thank you for being good to Mother. That helps repair me so much, my dear."

He took their photograph. Mary, blue-shoed, lemon-wrapped, cat-collared, cracked a smile. They kissed in a way that had to last forever, goodbye, but not in a way that would alarm their daughter. His hands clutched her hair a moment when he lost himself.

He told Marcella he would teach her the best thing in the language used with deaf children. He pointed to his chest, then to hers, then he crossed his arms over his chest.

She did it back to him. Bright child. She understood *I love you.*

Hand in hand, with the apricots, Mary and her daughter turned to leave. The problem with a wharf is there's one exit, and he meandered to the railing, to steady himself while they vanished first. His sole consolation was to be still in the same world, the sky above, land below, and waterways in between, as the person he loved most, would forever love, where he knew she trod and took care of a child hurtling into his wonderment: He was a father. He paused near some fishermen with their sunken lines.

And then he heard the clamor of someone dashing toward him.

CUTOUT

The image she carried:
While she embraced John on a wharf, her desires etched the contour
of them together.
They turned invisible, leaving only the outline of holding one
another.
That was the cutout she stamped everywhere she looked.
That hole in the shape of them melted together.
Bruised apricots, broken skins. She will devour them.

Marcella declared, "Mommy, that man looks like me!" She shook off her mother's hand and grabbed the sack of apricots and stampeded down the wharf to where John had a foot on a railing like a sailor on deck. Mary's carriage awaited. Edward had arranged for it. She had wanted to do the right thing by giving Nell's letter to John, but in her one time seeing her old love, she had handed him more pain. She should have said she had forgotten it. What might it do to him, to discover that they had been mistaken about Isaac, especially with Isaac dead?

No, she owed him full truth. They had reached a point of being able to handle that, nothing concealed. They could bear anything now.

She trusted—knew to trust—that John would allow Mary and Ward to decide when to tell Marcella who he was and therefore who she was. Mary stayed put, watching them. John seemed to be insisting that no, Marcella must keep the apricots. For her! All of them. Then he appeared to laugh and accept one.

What snapped Mary in two was that John lifted Marcella—small for her age, as Mary had been—so she could stand on the lowest bar of the railing and see better as he pointed toward the water. Mary inhaled when John touched their baby under the chin, the instructive tap from their youths to teach the seafarers' lesson about keeping an eye on the horizon, so as not to get seasick. Their child squealed—Mary heard it faintly—and John acted amazed, too, shouting; and Mary saw, from her angle, what their excitement was about.

A flying fish! Another one! And another! Three!

She was from an island, and now a dweller near the Pacific, and these were the first she had seen of this breed. She must not return to his presence, because she would cling and beg for the three of them to run away.

Flying fish!

The only creatures that marry a little bird that flies with a little fish that swims.

He had exclaimed once that her berries were the sweetest taste of his life, but apricots were a close second. Apricot was a shade as exotic as the ones in Papa's color cabinet.

When, years from now, Marcella announced the profession she intended to pursue—one centered upon questions asked, answers sought—Mary would be convinced their child's desire had sprung from this hour.

Her daughter raced back to her, the wharf creaking, and Mary led her to the carriage, not looking back, Marcella swinging her purse decorated with glitter starfish. Marcella said, "I gave him one of the apricots, Mommy. It isn't fair for him to have none." She asked if Mommy had seen the fish with wings, called up by the man from her island, and Mary said it was indeed the rarest sight in all her life, and chances were that it would never come her way again.

GUARD ME AS THE PUPIL OF THINE EYE, O LORD

WHEN IS MOUTHING FORGIVENESS MERELY A FAILURE TO BEAR something forever ruined, to endure what is beyond repair? He was so flattened by the sight of Mary and Marcella, and by guilt over Isaac, that he lay collapsed in the hotel. The news of Isaac's innocence, of John having done his part to drive the unanchored oddball toward death, combusted with a vision of hurling a potted evergreen through the window of this Maud Dieterman, *whom he had never even met.* She had even sought to set John's only brother against him for refusing to sell a perfume to her, probably due to detecting her odor as that of a monster (or simply by being his taciturn self).

It had been *Mary's wars* that had killed them.

And then everything made sense: those Chicago barons, or Jeduthan, would flit through Maud's upper-echelon world, mentioning, for laughs, John's attempts to score a fortune from them. He and Mary had not weighed this, the intersecting circles of the society above their heads. Edward, having donated that lot, might have told Maud about the contest fuss. It might equally be true that Augustus Ayers, pleasant as springtime, would remark upon agonizing over the dispute, and word would spread in the lofty world Mary had invaded, trundling over the drawbridge, John stumbling toward it behind her. Add a postmaster aiding the evildoers, offering access to letters revealing John's style, and onward the nastiness could prevail.

He wrote to Frank spelling out his plans for his Requiem fortune from Rui. They both owned Kinnear cameras and should start a stereoscopic-card business. A person held up a stereopticon's wooden arm with viewing blinders to peer through optical glass at a picture secured at the end of the arm, where the depiction got converted into three dimensions. John would travel, capture one-of-a-kind photographs, and send them to Frank to process into stereoscopic cards with Elizabeth's know-how. Frank could wire John his share of any profits.

Further, John would invest most of his money toward restoring the theater, buffing it to a gloss, and attracting the best acts, illusionists, ventriloquists, and high-paid actors in well-produced plays.

As expected, Frank protested about John pouring so much of his windfall into the Meline Theater, but John insisted. George and Teresa required that he sign a contract whereby he would be entitled to 5 percent of profits but would assume no liability for losses. After all these agreements, cash wire transfers, and business plans, it was time for John to live on the road again.

The first photo for the Alves-Meline Collections was his donation of the Madeiran Beauties of Monterey. The second, one of an Apricot-Seller.

Flying fish: He caught some on film after his return to wait and wait for them.

A Food Series was a hit: whole roasted fish; pyramids of apples; cakes with jellied interiors displayed in cutaway. Some collections—prairie pictures and stories, an Animal & Bird Series—sold modestly, while others, especially Lakes of America, exploded like azaleas in Madeiran heat. No secret, this was his bread crumb trail for Mary: Here I am. Alive. Capturing a world that has You in it.

His Civil War Veterans Series caused a minor sensation. Despite the back of each stereoscopic card being stamped with ALVES-MELINE COLLECTIONS, MELINE THEATER, JACKSONVILLE, ILLINOIS, he heard nothing from Mary and accepted that as justice. Once, in a thought redolent of Catholicism, he felt silence was the penalty for whatever he had done wrong about Isaac, whereupon it struck him that he had turned, like Isaac's twin, into an unfortunate man with an appalling childhood who did not understand why God should overcondemn him, the punishment not fitting whatever human follies were his.

Frank and Elizabeth, after their second son was born, moved to West Orange in New Jersey, where he took a job in the laboratory of Thomas Edison and left Hugo in charge of the now-thriving Meline Theater in Jacksonville.

Their correspondence would grow haphazard, but John met Frank in New York to witness Edison lighting up a square mile of the city. John got the idea of setting portraits of people between pictures of burning lights. Through the stereopticon, his subjects seemed to hover between stars. This series made a lot of money that John did not know what to do with. Buying a home was impractical for a man who kept moving, though he sometimes paused a while in towns with deaf people, teaching for spells.

It became harder to stay in touch with Nikka, but he pictured her strapping on ice skates to cross the frozen East River, Michael Windsor beside her, this man John might never meet. Three children would arrive as the years went on, nieces and a nephew.

A time came when instead of dismissing thoughts of Mary as too wrenching, he allowed himself to contemplate her as frequently as he desired. When students learned from him how to feel music in their bodies, or used more of their full beings to sign words, he heard in his head that she was proud of him. She would, he hoped, do as he did, which was stop at times, many of them unexpected, in an orchard, or upon rising, or while birds sailed in a V, or after convincing a boy not to become frustrated in his soundless prison, and John would shut his eyes and see her in that darkness visible only to him, and his healing sped onward because she was sending the love that had begun in their youths.

A last move occurred right before the turn of the century, in 1899, when John was sixty-one and produced photos on the effects of the Great Blizzard that swept the vertical length of the nation. No longer wishing to run from himself, he conceived a notion of how to spend the rest of his days. He liked Florida; returning there felt like destiny. After calling upon the Stewart Farm and finding *Synsepalum dulcificum* flourishing, he talked his way into a job at a school nearby, founded for children of all races by Harriet Beecher Stowe. After tutoring only two deaf pupils, his reputation grew, and he began instructing a whole room of deaf boys and girls and adults two days a week, performing as vigorously as ever when he signed.

The rest of his time was spent either reaping in the fields after convincing the Stewarts to hire him, or ranging with his camera, though in a more restricted radius.

He absolved himself about Isaac, a little. He let go of the lucid daydream about hurling a potted tree through the plate glass of Maud, just a bit.

He fell into the company of a lively, crop-haired widow his age named Melissa Kaye Bennett, who taught at the Stowe school. When they married, she became technically his second wife (the fiasco with Edith Wells had seared him like a cattle brand, but he supposed he had to count it), though Melissa was his first real spouse. He was grateful for her sense of humor and for nights in a balmy climate where she loved him, and he loved her, and they would awaken entwined like a caduceus in a hammock.

—

HE RESTED.

—

BUT ONE SUNNY SPRING DAY, IN 1906, HE TURNED HIS HEAD SHARPLY, pinching a nerve as he spaded a hillock teeming with berries. He sensed a disaster had struck Mary, and he sank down—O Meu Mais Do Que Tudo, are you hurt?—while chiding himself not to be ridiculous. But he worried she might not be alive, and sure enough, the next day's headlines screamed about a cataclysm rupturing San Francisco, an earthquake that was an act of God. The letter he wrote to Mary, at Melissa's urging—his wife had endured much herself and was enormous of heart—got returned mutilated and with a boldface stamp: ADDRESSEE UNKNOWN.

SOME THOUGHTS ALWAYS FIND US YOUNG, AND KEEP US SO

APRIL 1906

WARD INSISTED THAT EVERYONE DYE EGGS, AND HE WOULD HIDE them in the apartment. There was much to celebrate! Mary would turn sixty-six in a week, and how often did Marcella visit from San Diego? Granddaughter Catharine was going to debut in three days on the stage in the Central Theater, at age fourteen! A walk-on part, but still . . . what a beginning, what a marvelous Easter morning.

Catharine whispered to Grandma Mary that Papa Ward was doing this to distract her from stage-fright jitters. Mary agreed and announced, "You'll get half an hour, Ward. If we miss an egg behind my books and it rots, you'll never hear the end of it."

He laughed and so did she, and Marcella complained that her lack of skill in painting eggs made hers look like the product of birds drunk in a dye factory.

"Off we go, ladies," said Mary, but she turned at the door to regard her husband. Morning brightness cast a spotlight on the tremor in his hand that worried her. Since his retirement, he bent over pages, writing articles for botany journals, and she would kiss his balding head and gently suggest wording when his mind faltered a bit.

San Francisco's streets were cool, and she linked arms with Marcella and Catharine because her eyesight was dimmed. It used to grieve her that this foreshadowed the end to stitching her tablecloth or doing her children's books, but today she set this aside. Her girls were present. Marcella, slender and energetic, was a working woman, a journalist with the *San Diego Union*. Catharine was feverishly set upon acting! Passersby in fresh dresses and hats, on their own promenades, greeted them. A neighbor's phlox bushes susurrated with a convocation of bees. Marcella said, "I'm sorry Francis can't be here." How fitting that Mary's Portuguese daughter had married a navy captain. He was stationed in San Diego, but it was an era of peace.

Catharine added, "Grandma, do a book with the ocean as a setting."

They paused to gather breath at the crest of a hill. It was standard amusing practice to pretend one was taking in the view rather than letting the heart stop pounding. "All right," Mary replied. "Animals at sea aided by dolphins until they reach the shore." With an illustration of their tears increasing the water's swelling to buoy them forward.

When Marcella paused in an oblong of light, John was in her profile. Mary had written to him twice in Utah, but the letters had bounced back, and she had thought: Leave him be. Let him find a new life, as you have. And she no longer yearned desperately for her father's ghost. She carried his spirit. Because he had believed that women should have unusual lives, she had found a husband who thought that, too, and this kept her father as an illumination, phantomhood replete. She also preserved within herself the child who had clung to the fable that she was a sea-creature, born of parents eternally in the ocean. Now that little girl walked on a mermaid's tail split into legs, and she had conquered that pain, above the salt sea.

When they laughed that Ward—Daddy, Papa—had had ample time to hide the eggs, they returned and ascended to their top floor. Excited as a child, Ward cried, "On your marks, get set, go." The winner would be awarded a panther paperweight from Chinatown. Easter breakfast was laid out, tangerines, linguiça sausage, and Portuguese sweetbread with criss-crosses of flat blades off a plant that, thanks to her father, Mary referred to as Our Lady's Grass.

Mary found two eggs behind her array of Righetti & Leopold

books, and Catharine threw open a window to claim a polka-dot egg from the window box.

Mary was asking Marcella about her most recent pieces for the San Diego newspaper, on the expeditions of Roald Amundsen, when Catharine, digging through a trunk in Mary and Ward's bedroom, shouted, "Mama, is this you?"

Mary, Ward, and Marcella hovered in the doorway and saw the stereoscopic card from the wharf in Monterey. Catharine said, "Mama, Grandma, you look so young." Catharine was going to be a good actress, because she could read the shift in the air. Ward looked at Marcella and said quietly, "You never told her?"

Marcella said she would tell her daughter, who was old enough now, about her birth-grandpa, and she went into the room with Catharine and shut the door.

———

MARY AWAKENED VERY EARLY, AS WAS HER HABIT, ON WEDNESDAY the eighteenth. Marcella and Catharine were asleep in the extra bedroom, and her husband slept longer hours now. Ward himself had discovered that stereoscopic card in an antiques shop and bought it for her. If he had a flaw, it was that he was still distressed by her melancholia despite how often she explained that it was not exclusive of joy *at the very same time.* The only good thing to have come from the Maud-led horror story was that Ward had identified the blind spots he created from a wish to placate. He still wanted everything at ease if it could be achieved, but he had given up trying to convince her to forgive Nell Clark, to write to her. Finally, this year, this season, recently, Mary had felt a lightening, a pulling out of the pearl-handled knife embedded in her chest. Had Nell not provided the truth, not offered herself up to be reviled, Mary might never have known the full story that she could then treat as solid and graspable enough to cast aside. She had written, after decades, to Nell, who had replied in a quavery hand: *Bless you, my friend.*

Mary reveled in this hour of pretending to be the only one awake for miles. She padded into the kitchen for coffee, dark-roasted.

Leftovers remained from Easter breakfast. What a meal that had been, Catharine emerging from the bedroom wide-eyed after hearing that her mama had a daddy who was not Papa Ward. Her Portuguese grandma was movie-star-beautiful and a bold illustrator but hardly seemed capable of racing into a war zone to make wild love—!!—with a soldier.

Mary brought her coffee to her drafting board, where she began the story of a penguin, tiger, pig, and hyena who never stops cackling on their boat. The tiger will not stop weeping. They are lost at sea. Mary swept a wet brush over the pan of canary-yellow and paused, glowing with such contentment she wanted to stop and live in it a little.

She felt a rumbling she ignored. San Francisco's ground was temperamental. As a Californian, she paid it little notice.

But then the apartment building rocked, and her family shot out of their beds. Catharine screamed as a wall cracked and books tumbled from the shelves.

Marcella yelled, "Run!" She had grown up in this lofty dwelling but feared earthquakes. Edward ushered Mary down the stairs, everyone taking them two at a time, their neighbors on the lower floors charging out ahead of them. The ground quit shaking as they reached the street, but houses were caving in, and fires—again fire, always—spread in the distance. Edward said, "Wait here, all of you," and dashed back in. Mary shrieked, "No! Darling, come back!" and when he did not, she ran after him, saying only, "Cat, Marcy, stay put. Get away from walls. Stay in the open."

Catharine Miles Webb and her mama, Marcella Moore Webb, watched items fly from the top window: Grandma's books, flying open-winged. The framed purple flower from some poet in Amherst, given by Papa Ward to Grandma Mary eons earlier. The street buckled, more fires ignited, houses fell in on themselves. Catharine shouted, "I have to save them," and prepared to run into their cracking apartment building—the gargoyles plummeted—but her mother grabbed her and said she could not risk losing them all.

Drifting down from the window was Grandma's tablecloth. Marcella pointed, glimpsing her daddy—the one who'd raised her, her truest father—as Grandma Mary was trying to pull him away. Their edifice collapsed on one side as if it were kneeling. Marcella screamed, "Come out, now! Daddy! Mama!" Her father had raced in to rescue the work of Mary's life. Catharine picked up the tablecloth—so gigantic it seemed a shroud for the homes incinerating, everything in flames, the Central Theater and the city she loved burning—and she wanted to holler that the books could be found elsewhere, the cloth was unique but so were they, come to us, escape, hurry, perishing in fire is the worst of all fates.

New World Symphony

1919

A hummingbird drops into view outside your pane.

The bird darts away . . . & it is not a trick of the eyes: There really is a stroke of emerald that lingers, even after the bird is gone.

It thins to a green hook.

The sky writhes on the hook.

You call out.

The hook crashes through your window, and once embedded in Your heart, it explodes back into the wild bird.

CATHARINE

PINK BUBBLES WERE BURSTING IN CATHARINE'S BLOOD FROM THE illegal champagne *spraying in a fountain*—!—inside Grant Fordham's mansion. To hell with Prohibition! He was a motion-pictures producer. Girls were brandishing flutes under the spray. Three of them in court-of-Versailles attire and feathered fascinators giggled at Catharine milling awkwardly, and one shouted, "Penny for your thoughts!" which was uproarious, side-splittingly funny, because the mocker had lost out to her in an audition for the minor role of Penny Apple, a pastry chef, in the film *Bella*. The triad-gaggle wanted to roast and eat her and spit out the gristle. Grant was surrounded by actresses. He had a view of Santa Monica Canyon and boasted palm trees—indoors! Waiters carried trays of caviar and toast points. Dinah—the wife, the faded star—was puffing her cigarette in its cigarette holder, staring daggers at Catharine, because Grant had run a finger down Catharine's arm to suggest what might be required to win the lead in his film about a Spanish princess. Catharine had backed away (not that this mattered to Dinah).

In scuffed mules and an emerald burned-velvet dress with a moth hole, she tried signaling Zachary—let's flee!—but he was engrossed with a man who owned a coveted painting. Zachary worked in art acquisitions for the Los Angeles Museum of History, Science and Art.

The girls envious about her *ridiculously teensy role* were making sotto-voce comments about her clothing. . . . She had to escape *at once*.

Out in the night, she got trapped in brambles on the slope downward from the Fordham mansion, where stickers scratched. She would no more have slept with Grant for a ludicrous part, or even a non-ludicrous one, than she would torch herself. Let those girls with cherry lips and pearl chokers spread their legs for him. Was that howl from a coyote? Superb!

It was frustrating to be (attempting to be) a dramatic actress when Zachary had survived the war's trench-and-flak horrors. Compared to that, who cared about her chirpy radio spots or bit parts in silent films, once playing a damsel tied to railroad tracks who gyrated against the ropes? Gawd, she had even practiced Pained Looks in the mirror. Would it be all downhill after the mighty pinnacle of playing cake-baker Penny Apple in a middling film? *That* was enough to arouse the furies of the Furies in the fangy acting tribe? She agonized about whether to try Chicago and be near her parents, or to push all chips to the center and investigate theater work in New York.

"Cat?" Zachary, grinning, was angular and fit, brown hair in a shock.

She knew he would find her. They were magnets. "I don't think I'll be playing Teresita, the Spanish princess," she said. "My half-Portuguese blood forbids it."

He laughed because that was their salvation, they made one another laugh. She wanted to deliver him from his nightmares about the war. He slapped a mosquito against his chin. Cat dispatched a dive bomber on her elbow and improvised a skit about being attacked by bugs, a shimmy-dance that had them in hysterics. "Should we move to New York, Zach?" she said.

"I'll go anywhere with you, Cat."

"Is that so, fine sir? What will you do for work?"

"Ask the Metropolitan Museum to hire me and keep asking until they say yes. Now I have a question for you. Shouldn't we get married?"

God struck the dome over the Californian night repeatedly with an ice pick, because the darkening sky was heavy, and He was frantic to watch them. Heavenly light flooded through the holes.

She said, "You must ask me in the proper, old-fashioned way."

And so, in a ravine scented with honeysuckle in the Santa Monica Mountains, he knelt and said, "I, Zachary Vogel, will take thee, Catharine Miles Webb, to be my lawful wife. Will you, Catharine Miles Webb, take me?"

Upon her shout of "Yes!" they released echoing sounds of glee as he took her clear of the brambles and whirled her about in a space under the constellation Cygnus at its eternal end of the Milky Way.

—

CATHARINE HATED DRIVING ZACHARY'S MODEL T, A RATTLING DEATH-trap, but she couldn't wait to tell Grandma Mary and invite her to the wedding. In New York! Zachary was excited about moving where they'd dreamt of being—bonus, *zero driving* there! Cabs! *Broadway!* Immediately pressing, however: She pictured herself dying in a thousand ways involving twisted metal before she reached San Diego. When she braked in front of the sea-salted homestead, valiant terra-cotta-roofed thing, she thumped her head on the wheel; hallelujah! Survival! She had grown up here with her parents and then with her grandparents when they sought refuge after the earthquake.

Now they had all deserted Grandma Mary.

Bent at her drawing board—her eyesight held on—Grandma didn't hear Catharine let herself in. The walls displayed watercolor exemplars from her children's books and a framed stitching of a man in a hat, with berries on the side facing the wall. Trunks and crates littered the floor, since Mama had finally talked Grandma into selling the house. The options were to live in Chicago with her or, as very recent events would have it, in New York with Cat and Zach.

"Cat, sweetheart, you startled me!" Such a smile. Grandma's hair was streaked black, silver, and white. Forever she was a beauty, billowing out an aroma of gardenia.

"Grams," shouted Catharine, hugging her hard as life itself, oh, Grandma, hummingbird-boned. Her admirable solitude had begun to appear frail. "Zachary asked me to marry him, and I said yes, and you must come to New York for the wedding."

Through her glasses, Grandma's green eyes were shine-coated as she stroked Catharine's hair and said, "Darling, yes. Parabéns." Through an open window, a rhythm rolled in from the sea. San Diego was tranquil, but gawd with the heat and suffocating tranquility, Grams, enough.

"Sit with me," said Grandma, leading Cat by the hand to the raspberry-velour chairs. Catharine refused offers of coffee and custard tarts and said, "Grams, after the wedding, please stay with Zach and me. Since you've lived in New York already."

"Ages ago."

The house was already shrinking from them. Look; there was Grandma's immense tablecloth, folded but not yet packed. Always Catharine was afraid to touch it. It was like a custom wedding dress made for a field of the Lord. One edge had been singed during the great fire and collapse of their home in San Francisco, when Papa Ward had rescued it. His lungs had never been the same. Grandma was staring at it, too. Her left forearm was still scarred.

"Grams," she said delicately. "It's time. He's been gone five years."

"I know, angel."

"I want you in New York, but your being with Mama and Daddy in butt-freezing Chicago is better than this." When Daddy had retired early from the navy, they'd moved back to his hometown to be near his parents. Catharine's mother was now a reporter at the *Tribune,* and Daddy had become an editor there, too. She trilled out, "Papa Warden would want you to have fun. He was such fun, Grams!" Once as a little girl, Catharine had sassed Edward, and when he sentenced her to her room, she called him Papa Ward-the-Warden—said in anger, but the nickname evolved into a joke that tickled him. "Remember when Jenny stopped speaking to me but wouldn't say why, and I was moping, and Papa Warden took me whale-watching? He said the whales were my friends, and they were bigger and better than some brat named Jenny."

"He loved you very much. And he loved me."

Catharine thought but did not say: And he loved Mama, even though she was not his natural child. Sometimes it still upended her, the ardor of this soft-spoken older woman, because even Catharine, much less a stranger, could look at her and wonder: You had a king for a father? The man who raised you was a magician with plants? Mama's middle name—Augustina—was in his honor, but Catharine knew very little about him. But most of all, what about the teacher and soldier with whom Grandma had been crazily passionate, who took camera-pictures and was lost to them?

Grandma asked, "How's the acting going, querida?"

Cat decided to risk saying, "Whatever roles I get, it's because I remember you telling me how John Alves taught his deaf students to gesture with their full bodies, to put all of themselves into what they said, and I do that, Grams. I figure, audiences can't hear people in silent movies, so—"

To Catharine's everlasting shock, stoical Grams burst out sobbing.

Catharine held her, rocked her, oh, Grammy, forgive me, I'm so sorry, I didn't mean to make you cry.

Grandma Mary led Catharine to her drawing board. When Catharine began seeing Zachary Vogel, Grandma had started a children's book about a bird family as a surprise, because of his German surname meaning "bird" . . . but it had stalled, with her tripping over a remembrance of John's family being called the Little Birds on account of their singing in jail when they were starving. "I get the birds into trouble with hunters, but I can't figure out how to finish the story." She dissolved in tears again. "I don't even know if John is alive, Cat. I once thought he was dead and he wasn't, but now I have no idea."

Catharine declared, "Grams, let's find him and ask his help in figuring out an ending!" What good is being the daughter of a Portuguese magician and a king if you can't command your heart: Call out to him, and tell me if he is gone, or not, whatever the truth may be.

Didn't you tell me that always works? That kind of summoning?

And Catharine wept because she was one in body and mind with her grandmother, always had been, and she whispered: Don't cry, Grandma Mary, you won't be alone here anymore, I won't let you be alone.

QUIET-LIKE, SOME STILL DAY

JOHN USED THE FLY-OFF METHOD TO SEND AWAY AMIE, HIS HOMING pigeon named after the brave bird of the American Signal Corps whose foot got shot off by the Germans. He shaped the bird into a pulsating ball, and upon release, Amie combusted upward. John tossed millet toward the rock pigeons and satin-tie doves, including Dough-boy, named for the soldiers of the recent war. The Civil War had apparently not been grotesque enough, so humanity had smeared slaughter across the globe and was punchy now with the end of it, giddy and appalled and blanketed with jumpy music, jumpy colors.

He had turned eighty-one in March. It was late summer, and Adam Stewart—Judson's great-grandson—had bought everyone out and would be the sole owner of the Stewart Mandarin Farm. The original brothers were dead, and their children, and most of the children's children, preferred to embrace urban versions of the exuberant new century. The clothing in glittering cities was beaded; the nation's mien was pocked with jazzy daring despite the air being riddled with influenza, racial discord, and scandals. Bizarrely—correspondingly—it was all this, and the World War, that caused a surge in miracle-berry sales, a rabid appetite for something purely marvelous. Pockets of adherents sought to slake a thirst for joy, and this got wed to the spirituality craze. The demand for the fruit's powers of entertainment and magic had over-shadowed its medicinal properties.

He strolled through the miracle-fruit fields—or hobbled, since the Shiloh wound on his calf ailed him—to wave farewell to Amie and to bid a last goodbye to the sea of vegetation. He could not endure the labor anymore, but as he greeted the shrubs, he was glad that curiosity as to whether those two straggling plants had survived had transported him back here to divide his time between teaching and putting his hands into the earth that Mary Catherine Freitas Moore had altered and Edward Moore had financed and the Stewarts had restored out of conflagration. The red and green of the Portuguese flag stretched to the horizon!

Amie was winging to Adam Stewart at a family compound with a dovecote in Sarasota. The slip of paper on Amie's leg read: ALL YOURS. John would be the last to leave. He would miss their shared fascination with the pigeons crossing immense distances to go home. Iron flecks in their beaks likely helped them detect the magnetic vectors where they belonged. Adam and John were equally obsessed about the in-vention of radios, the discoveries of Tesla and Marconi regarding the capture of sounds cloaking the globe—*frequencies.*

He returned to his cabin to finish packing. His residence had re-mained plain, a cot, a desk, a washstand. He rued never buying a house, and since this had not exactly been a delirium-wish of a blissful hearth, Melissa had moved out long ago, but they remained friends and still spent some nights together. Tomorrow they would go to the movie palace and ice-cream parlor to celebrate the finalizing of their divorce.

A file cabinet was filled with every note and news clipping ("Teacher, here's what I've done!") his students had sent over the years. Tucked away was the kaleidoscope from that freedwoman at the Nashville station when he mustered out of the army, next to a copy of *The Wizard of Oz* by L. Frank Baum. What memories of reading to Stewart grandchildren about the travelers with their green-tinted spectacles in the Emerald City, and about Dorothy's Silver Shoes car-rying her home! He wrapped the kaleidoscope and book to take with him, though he was unsure where to go. The Reverend Robert Kalley had spent a preponderance of days in Brazil but was buried in his native Scotland. *Mother, I'll heed what he's telling me: In the end, we go homeward.* But how to define that? Utah? Jacksonville? New York? Should he start afresh near Frank and Lizzie with their brood in New Jersey? And—surprise—nature-bejeweled Madeira beckoned.

His stereoscopic negatives and card prints formed magpies' nests in boxes. The Mandarin Collection—alligators, teal storefronts, palm groves—had sold well. He had taken off on weekends with his camera, another nail in the coffin with Melissa. Had it been worth it, this photography mania as recompense for trailing too far behind men in substantial laboratories pursuing the science of sound? It had ended up being Edison, among others, who captured tones and words *and* played them back. Pictures were set in motion, too. Frank was proud of his subordinate role with Edison, and that helped John feel his own fumbling pursuits represented doing his own part, however much unheralded, in humanity's striving toward discoveries.

He kept a separate folder for the photo of Mary and Marcella on the wharf, wanting it near but finding it too incandescent to gaze upon. He had preserved the letter he sent after that horrendous earthquake. When it got returned, he wrote again, in a panic, with only "Castroville, California" as the address. That too might have fallen by the wayside. He tracked down the list of the dead and did not find their names, which he took as a sign that they were likely safe but lost to him again. Edward had wreathed Mary with a grand life, even if their footing got undercut when the farm burned and again when the earth split on the opposite coast. John stayed convinced he would disintegrate into powder if she were dead.

By now Marcella would be just shy of fifty-five.

A letter from Frank had been staring at John since early August without his knowing how to respond. What it contained was astounding.

22 July 1919
West Orange, New Jersey

Dearest John, Lizzie sends her love. She is ok except for the arthuritis. I annoy my sons with advice on taking photos at their studio, truth is they're better than I am but don't you tell them.

You've also been God's own gift with pictures, but Brother, wish you'd sent one of YOU so I can see how you're looking! Hugo says the stereoscope-photo sales have slowed but the Theater in J'ville is BOOMING, God bless moving-pictures. Though retired I'm still friends with Edison lab workers past and present. Hugo and his kids are ok in J'ville, the theater shows everything from Theda Bara motion-pictures to Chaplin's "latest drollery" as Hugo puts it.

I'm not much for letters as you know so as my boys say, Pa, get to the point. Hugo's son (Frankie Meline he goes by) has hit the JACKPOT in Calif. and feels indebbted to how you saved my mother and father, God rest their souls, with our Theater bills and its falling apart ages ago, with that Requiem perfume $. Nobody can find the contract so we don't know what $ exactly should come to you, but Frankie and all of us know you saved our sorry hides.

Frankie went to test his luck in Los Angeles. He started as a window-dresser at Hamburger's Department Store and put the Meline nose to grind-stone and leapt at an offer to enter the real-estate business in Castellamare, Brentwood-Gardens, Beverly-Hills, and Bel-Air. One allotment of his will soon boast a mansion for Douglas Fairbanks and Mary Pickford!

Drum-roll. He wishes to give you $20,000 to honor that vanished contract. I read the average salary in the U.S. of A. is $750/yr! Now that you're leaveing the farm and MOVING AGAIN, Frankie isn't sure where to send it. (Face it, Brother, you and the mails have a curse.) Should he get it to me, so you'll be forced to come see us? We won't hardly recognize each other. Even if I haven't seen you in thirty years or more, you're truley my Brother and Brother in arms. Lizzie and I wish you could meet our boys and grand-childs before you and I, you know, croak. She found some magic-lantern slides in the attic . . . remember those?? I've enclosed one you should have:

(1) Boy and his mother in jail;
(2) Birds come to set them free;
(3) Out they go! Through the window.

Yours truley, Frank

It would be childlike, even hazardous, to imagine that fate regulated a system of justified rewards. Yet here it was: Requiem perfume, the stereoscopic success, the farm's bounty, and now a thank-you from Frankie that had been, unbeknownst to John, an IOU agitating the universe.

He had written sporadically to his loved ones, but why had he never gone to see them? Work, money, time drifting unseized. (They had not come to visit him, either.) Too many moves had dissolved some starch in him, and he could also admit that the berries flooding out nationally meant either they had not reached Mary, or she had chosen never to respond, and this had caved him inward. Rui was alive, according to Linda Silva Marquardt, daughter of the late Ray and Faith of the General Store—the sachets still sold well there— but was hardly one for responding. Nikka was ninety and had raised two daughters and a son who gave her four grandchildren. Michael Windsor was long retired from the law office. They had moved to midtown Manhattan, and John tried to imagine New York, having seen glimpses of it in newsreels. The Public Library with stone lions. Model Ts zooming. Women in harem pants. Immigrants in splintery high-rises. Alfred Gilbert, a doctor, magician, and champion pole-vaulter, took the city as inspiration and invented Erector Sets. Carlike speeds everywhere and in everything. Trumpet riffs. Up, down, zig, zag. Necklaces flapping. "A Pretty Girl Is Like a Melody." "How Ya Gonna Keep 'Em Down on the Farm."

He slept in the hammock under the star-script and told himself that he had reaped great worth by helping rebuild this place. By *staying*, by stopping to repair what had been ravaged, by cheering on children deprived of hearing, and by taking undying images of hanging moss, fishing nets, a Komodo dragon. He was a contributor in an apical moment, in a petri dish of a nation attempting to grow the spores of charity and art alongside the spores of commerce to see which, or which combination, might generate its character.

He sat up with a start alone in the night. Had a culminating beneficence come to a man who began as a Little Bird? A roseate spoonbill was wafting overhead with its lime-tinted face and its gradations-of-pink body and wings. John had always desired to see one, ever since spotting Audubon's rendering of it on John Jacob Astor's walls. And here—having taken its sweet time—oh, here it was.

———

MELISSA WAS ALREADY IN THE ICE CREAM PARLOR, ITS FLOOR A black-and-white checkerboard. Cheerful and sturdy, she reminded him of Frank's Elizabeth. He too was of sound health, despite his war wounds. His scalp's scar was concealed by luxuriant white hair, and his white mustache was full, and his shoulder only throbbed in chilly temperatures, rare in Florida. "Hello, dear," he said, kissing her.

"Hello, handsome."

Claude Mayer, the owner, asked what might please them on this summer's day. They agreed on the blancmange, a taste that conjured his initiation into this country's pleasure in cold, smooth things. Mr. Mayer said, "I hear you're off to Idaho, Melissa, to live with your daughter?"

"She'll help me fend with my aches." She had instructed John to let people chatter. How he and she dealt with their friendship was no one else's business.

The blancmange was made of almonds and cream. Young people flooded in, and while waiting for their orders, they teased each other and tapped their feet and flung their arms in the modern way of not being able to be quiet.

"Happy divorce, Johnny," said Melissa.

He shared everything with her and therefore had shown her Frank's letter. "Since you won't hang on to inherit anything from me, Mel, I'll insist you accept some of Frank's nephew's fortune. It's more than I can spend in what's left of my lifetime."

"I won't say no to a taste of Hollywood cash, though I don't require it, Johnny. But please grant the divorce. I might want to woo a codger." They had a laugh, and she produced the documents, and they signed, and kissed again, and that deed was done.

They strolled on the herb-laced main street to the Mandarin Movie Palace, passing their old school. Founder Harriet Beecher Stowe had described Florida as stitchery with two sides; John pictured one with arabesques and the underside ragtag. Buying a citrus farm for her alcoholic son Frederick had proved a debacle, and finally he vanished. Harriet had ended her days in Hartford, constantly checking her mail. John was not without sympathy for that.

The pianist to accompany the showing of the film *Bella* was a retired sea captain who made up for many wrong notes with spectacular glissandos. He saluted John and Melissa. A smattering of attendees had gathered, and the projectionist lowered the lamplights, and with a whirr and sprockety clicking, *Bella* began. The local paper provided synopses of the films coming to town, and this was a Romeo-and-Juliet thing among the pie-and-cake set, rival bakeries.

John felt drowsy despite the piano's dissonant hammering, and he faded in and out of the story. But at one point, a character named Penny Apple was frosting a three-tier marvel. She had abundant black hair and a widow's peak, and moreover she seemed the very contour and presence of his long-lost love. John almost tumbled from his seat. He gripped Melissa's arm and cried, "Mary!" The pianist stopped. The audience stirred. The music resumed as the movie kept rolling.

The final credits listed Famous Players-Lasky Productions in Hollywood, and the actress playing Penny was revealed as Catharine Miles Webb. She could be anyone. But he exclaimed to Melissa that he had just seen his granddaughter.

"All the more reason to go to Los Angeles," said Melissa. Without fail, she had been kind beyond belief about his history with Mary. "If you find Catharine and she's not yours, maybe she'll have a sense of humor." The worst that could happen is he would visit a place he once called a temporary home and meet his best friend's nephew.

———

ON BROADWAY AND HILL IN LOS ANGELES, JOHN DODGED DELIVERY wagons heaped with goods, but even worse were the goose-honking cars nearly smashing into the horse-drawn buggies. Nothing resembled what he had known in his era of wandering the West. Rattled, he staggered into the stacked-high labyrinth that was Hamburger's Department Store, the bear flag at its apex as if planted by the lad who cried "Excelsior!" He had agreed to meet Frankie Meline, Hugo's son, at this spot that had launched his career. On a whim while communicating with Frankie by letter, John had asked about locating Perpetua and Henry Kingsley. Frankie reported using the magic of a telephone directory to achieve voice contact with Henry and to secure a home address, the data relayed in a note from Frankie to John. John had sent a telegram asking if Perpetua would meet him midafternoon at Hamburger's but embarked on his cross-country trip before receiving her reply.

It had never occurred to him that a store might total thirty acres, and it took a while to locate the soda fountain, where shoppers presumably celebrated surviving their purchases. How jarring to behold a dapper fellow wearing not only Hugo's face but Frank's. The hallucination propelling him—Catharine on a larger-than-life screen—was redoubled as a fairy tale, the missing people he loved grown not old but youthful. "Senhor Alves!" shouted Frankie. He wore a double-breasted suit, and his wide-of-wing American-born body sprawled on a perch at the counter. Families and couples bustled, and photographs of motion-picture stars were framed on spring-green walls. With a tone of authority, Frankie ordered root beer floats and cherry cobblers. Waitstaff in starched aprons moved rapidly, sweeping away dishes, slapping down menus, and motioning to new customers like waves of eager warriors replacing casualties. He had taken the precaution of wiring the twenty thousand to Uncle Frank in West Orange, to be guarded until John decided where to settle. "I hope you don't feel you came here for naught, but I wanted to thank you in person. Uncle Frank tells me you've roamed around."

"I've lived in Florida quite a while, though." But true enough, that was ending as well. He spooned ice cream out of the tall glass of root beer. Frankie said floats had been invented by someone named Wisner in Colorado. This nation loved to cajole its citizens, "Go on, entertain me."

"Uncle Frank told me to order you to attend the GAR Encampment in Columbus. He wants to see you there."

"I'm at loose ends, that's a fact. Might be good to see who's alive from Company 14-A," said John, ashamed to admit that he was chasing a wraith from a screen. Frankie had finished his cobbler, though John could swear Frankie had not lifted his spoon. He was the new sort of American, swift and absorptive. John added that he wanted to see people he knew, and people attached to people he knew, and he should visit his mother in her grave in Illinois, overdue pilgrimages. "I didn't reckon on the globe trying out a worse war than the one I was in, Frankie."

"I'm lucky I was too old for the recent massacres. Do you not care for the cobbler? A vocal faction of habitués at Hamburger's judges it too tart."

John could not eat much anymore, though once upon a time he had always been hungry. A mother was quieting a baby, bouncing him on her knee. Teenagers at a table erupted in laughter. The world soldiered on, and it was wild and fine and full of strangers. He asked, "Is it true you know Mary Pickford and Douglas Fairbanks?"

It was. He had sold them the lot where they would build some mansion for cavorting.

Frankie added, "Don't you realize you saved my family? The theater was going belly-up until you gave them that money. I grew up believing, because of you, Senhor Alves, that remedies can come, often out of friendship, even at a point of doom." He paid the bill, refusing to let John set out a nickel, and he wrote down his telephone number and address: 6767½ Gower Street, Hollywood. They joked about that "½."

Unsure if Perpetua had received his invitation, John wandered in this temple to plenty, kicking himself for not confirming a precise time and exact spot, though he could try to figure out how to telephone or get to her home. A display of Crayola crayons entranced him until the clerk, ringing up his box of All Colors, her lips the shade of red-oxide, said, "Charge it?" He had heard rumors about this. Own goods not fully paid for? She explained that he could make a deposit and pay a 6 percent fee over time, and this alarmed him. The shopgirl grew restive.

He spied a shopper who made him drop the Crayola box and give chase. He spotted her near porcelain tureens, where a teenager sneered, "Watch it, ya hoochy old jane," as the woman bumped into her and stepped onto the moving staircase to a higher floor. So many shoppers were riding it just for the thrill that John got caught in the muddle at the top. After a detour, he located the woman near some mannequins, and striding to her, he bellowed, "Perpetua? Pet Roderick?"

Her brown eyes were flecked with gold, and her bearing was alert. She was an apple doll, white hair in a twist. Her grin widened. They stood as rocks in a stream of shoppers, catching up. She had five children, many grandchildren, and lived with Henry in West Los Angeles. He was an ocean swimmer, retired from Acme Paper. She used to do handiwork for hire but was nothing like Mary and regretted losing touch. "Last I heard, Marcella was going to have a baby, but that was well over twenty years ago. Twenty-five. Do you know where Mary is?"

"I was hoping you could tell me." He admitted to being here because he had seen, in a film called *Bella,* an actress named Catharine who looked so much like Mary that he—well, he could not finish that thought aloud. He had come to confer with Frank's nephew, someone who built houses for stars like Mary Pickford and Douglas Fairbanks.

Perpetua perked up and said, "Let's check the children's book section! Mary was an illustrator. I know that much. People are always thanked in books. I miss her, too." She peered at him. "I'm sorry you didn't marry her. We talked about you. When we used to visit, she told me all she knew. She had a good life with Edward, is it all right to say that? Did you have a good life? Everyone was in awe of you two. I loved her and loved living in the cottage with her."

"Yes, I've had a very good life," he said, because it was true.

The room with children's books at Hamburger's resembled a candy store with its vivid colors. What was it like, to guard a human who fit into those tiny chairs? They spent some time randomly checking books. In the "W" section, Perpetua plucked out one about a girl buttoning herself into a cat suit to pursue adventures. The cat-girl's eyes were slit-shut with perfectly Portuguese happy-sadness. The author was a Marcella Miles Webb. The illustrator was Mary Freitas Moore.

The dedication was to "Catharine."

Like the stereoscopic cards he had tossed over America to reach her, like the berries shipped far and wide, Mary had flung a book of watercolors into the ether.

Catharine Miles Webb.

—

THE STAFF AT FAMOUS PLAYERS—LASKY PRODUCTIONS WAS THE OPPO-site of helpful in locating a bit-part actress in one of their films, scold-ing that private information could not be dispensed anyway. Their discouragement was so adamant, their presentation of dead ends so persuasive, that John slunk back to pack his suitcase for the trip east-ward, to attend the Grand Army of the Republic Encampment in Columbus and to visit Jacksonville and old haunts. But a knock struck the door, and before him stood Perpetua and a man introduced as Henry. She bounced in one place while clamoring out, "Didn't you say Frankie Meline knows Mary Pickford?!" Henry put a hand on his agitated wife—his other hand was a hook—and this settled Pet down for five seconds. "Ask Frankie to tell Mary Pickford to get Catharine's address or telephone number! If those crabapples at the studio don't listen to her, their heads will roll!"

This was how one of the great actresses of the era, as John prepared to leave a dingy hotel at the brink of the United States, helped him find his family. In a relay of telephone contacts, Henry to Frankie to Mary Pickford to Jesse Lasky, then Lasky to Pickford to Frankie to Henry: Here are some numbers, and on the other side of dialing them would be John's grandbaby. It was September the first in the year 1919.

—

THE FIRST TIME JOHN SPOKE INTO A TELEPHONE WAS IN HENRY AND Pet's ranch house, where air billowed through minuscule squares of window screens. To surmount being unnerved at talking to someone who could not be seen, he reminded himself that this was how people spoke to God. "Catharine Miles Webb?" he said timidly upon hearing a greeting. "The granddaughter of Mary Freitas Moore and daughter of Marcella Moore?"

"Yes." The voice carried the cadences of her grandmother. The single syllable was enough for his middle to collapse, and he went searching in the pit of himself for where he had gone. "I'm John Alves," he said. "Do you know who I am?"

She cried out (he held the receiver away from his ear, brought it back), "My God! Yes!" She filled him in, Marcella wed to Captain Francis Webb. "Mama met Daddy on a trip to San Diego, where he was in the navy. She moved there when they married, and she wrote for the newspaper. After Grandma Mary and Papa Ward lost nearly everything in the earthquake, they moved in with us. Grandma does children's books."

"I saw one." He could scarcely breathe. "It had all your names."

"Daddy retired early from the navy, and they've moved to Chicago, to be near his parents, who aren't well. Mama and Daddy work at the *Chicago Tribune*. He's an editor, and she writes about the city and does fiction-stories for magazines."

"Is your grandmother still embroidering a tablecloth?" He pictured this young woman, Catharine, having seen her ten times normal size, in black and white.

Yes, it was the most stunning one on earth!

He replied that he had met her mother when she was a child, under grievous circumstances, a goodbye.

Cat knew that story, she said. The wharf in Monterey.

When Catharine said he could call her Cat, John wanted to choke out that this was her grandmother's nickname, but of course she would know that. He said only, "Mary."

His sweeping glance took in the pots and pans, and a pinboard full of the stuff of family life, flyers for church suppers, ocean-swim announcements, grocery lists, and photos of Henry and Perpetua Kingsley and their children and grandchildren.

She was kind, Cat was, as she said, "I know Grandma would love to see you. I'm not sure of the timing, but I think Grandma plans to visit Mama and Daddy after she sells the house in San Diego. Papa Ward died five years ago. Mama wants her to move to Chicago, but I'm trying to talk her into living with me in New York."

Perpetua was doing a wretched job of pretending not to be listening from the kitchen. Catharine said, "I'm marrying someone named Zachary Vogel. He helps museums and collectors acquire artwork."

John would be at the GAR Encampment on September tenth, followed by a visit to Jacksonville, God willing—

"Oh!" she squealed. "That's so Portuguese, to say 'God willing'! Grandma Mary says that a lot!" Catharine planned to stop in Chicago before moving to New York for her November wedding. "You must come to it, Mr. Alves!" she exclaimed. How about meeting in Jacksonville? She couldn't wait until winter to see him. Please! Marcella could be persuaded to come to Jacksonville, too. Depending on when Grandma sold her house and got on a train, well—

She left the sentence, and Mary, floating in the indeterminate near future.

He shared with her Frank Meline's address and phone number as insurance that they would always find each other. How radiant she was through the phone. What an invention! Through it you could feel when someone smiled, or when someone, though silent, was awkward. She was powerful within herself, and he could feel it as she added, "Leave it to me, Grandpa."

What was it that he should leave to her; what, my darling?

It was this: The instant it became possible, Catharine would let Grandma Mary know that John Alves would be at her wedding.

LIFT THE NEEDLE, LAY IT DOWN

MARY FREITAS MOORE STITCHED THE FINAL SECTION: A PIER IN SAN Diego. The tablecloth was done. It included a berry-plant in flames and the crushed hills of San Francisco, and she could not look at it without recalling Edward running into the earthquake-afflicted building to rescue it, her screaming at him to come back. She would not have it now had he not put himself at risk. When he sold the Castroville property to finance the move to San Diego, he had become distraught at imagining her upset over so much uprooting, and she had replied, "You've been my life, Ward, and nothing can uproot that."

She carried peonies to his grave, Marcella's favorite flower. How proud they were of her being a reporter and story writer! Though Mary was glad Marcella enjoyed Chicago with her husband, she missed them. She set down the peonies, saying, "Here, sweetness." She felt bad about leaving Ward behind, as she had once felt terrible abandoning Papa on the prairie, but Marcella and Catharine were insistent, and her house had sold easily. In the end, Ward never bred a thornless rose, but he won regional acclaim for propagating *Passiflora*, passion flowers. He had gripped her hand, and Catharine's, with Marcella's hand on his arm, as bone marrow cancer claimed him, and he told Mary his fear of dying subsided with her near. If their bedroom life had evaporated long before, he had had eyes only for her and had bloomed as a father. He had been remarkably ahead of his time. Not just with bank accounts in her name, but with his applause for her drawings, stitching, and children's books. Most men did not give their wives so much. So much freedom.

Catharine is moving to New York! she whispered, adjusting her spectacles. She had an invitation to attend the wedding and a train ticket. She was grateful for a good, a wonderful marriage. In sorting through Ward's papers after he died, she came across a note: "If I'd been stronger, Mary, I'd have given you up. Please be happy." Within the envelope was a photocopy of the stereoscopic card of her wharf day. It would never cease to move her immeasurably that after finding it in a shop, he had presented it to her. The legend read: MADEIRAN BEAUTY & BEAUTIFUL AMERICAN CHILD, ALVES-MELINE COLLECTIONS, JACKSON-VILLE, ILLINOIS. Mary kissed Edward's engraved name and stood up and stretched. She was seventy-nine. Awake, awaken.

She had finished the book with the Vogel Bird Family: She put them in charge of an orchestra of animals. What to paint or draw next? She didn't know. And what would happen after her grandchild's wedding?

Robins chattered in a fig tree that would be hers only a short while more.

She no longer perceived of the country as massive and unfathomable. It held a web she had spun. She regretted losing contact with dear old fizzy Pet, but that was no one's fault. While setting the last of her children's books in trunks—she would have to decide soon whether Chicago or New York would be (surely!) her final resting spot—the telephone jangled. It was Catharine, yelping, "Grams! Grams! You'll never believe this!"

———

ON HER WAY TO THE TRAIN, USING INFORMATION PROVIDED BY CATH-arine, Mary wired a telegram to John Alves via Frank, suddenly terrified and shy, more than she had been as a girl first arriving in the icy harbor of the East, where the city had sparkled, sparkled silver.

MOTHER'S THERE, EXPECTING ME

ROCKED IN PULLMAN SLEEPERS, JOHN SPED OVER THE LAND, JOINING the white-bearded men limping as befit specters from another era. Some carried swords. Once on his way to the club car, passing people in the current loose, scintillating clothing who toted contraband liquor, John paused to light a cigarette for a uniformed veteran of the Great War who was shaking so badly he could not manage the task.

In Columbus, the Grand Parade went on in a downpour, soaking the Union soldiers ancient as he was, the rain at first like needles, and then the needles seemed to snap, doubling the amount that fell. Time dissolved, so much time. There was wizened Frank Meline. They drank up the measure of one another, his long-lashed, lock-picking, long-wed, Edison-amplified friend, oh, my friend. In his arms, John bleated, "Salutations, you horse thief," and when they stepped apart, Frank, trembling, said, "Took us a while, didn't it, brother," and handed him a telegram. The typed words might as well have been real hand-script, large, excitable, deeply embedded on paper. He had a place and time: Belvedere Castle, New York City, November the first. Mary.

—

IN THE COLUMBUS STATION, A FRENCH HORN PLAYER UNLEASHED AN-
tonín Dvořák's music, and its slow glory roosted inside John's rib cage
as he boarded a train into the prairie to meet Catharine Miles Webb.
The flat land outside his window soon offered trout lilies, bergamot,
and snow-on-the-mountain flowers. Seasons changed in Illinois; his
Midwest embraced fundamental displacement. He had entertained
the notion of finding Marcella in Chicago, Mary perhaps there by
now, too, but bashfulness got the better of him.

In Springfield, at President Lincoln's sepulcher in the Oak Ridge
Cemetery, John muttered it had been a privilege to meet him, though
all tallied, the sum of hours at the Lincolns' was not so much, maybe
equal to the span of a few sundowns to a few sunups. But it felt like so
much more. The simpler stone of Augusto Pereira Vaz Gato de Freitas
took longer to find, and he offered an internal speech that it had been
an honor to have met him in Madeira, the day of Mary entering his
life.

At the house on Eighth Street, he stared at the A. LINCOLN on the
doorplate. Amazing how unchanged the façade was, the paint still a
shade that reminded John of butterscotch, the shutters dark green. It
was open for visitors. Leaves like crabs a child had cut from brown
paper scuttled around his ankles. He mounted the stairs.

How startling, the first time he had seen the wallpaper, proof
that midwesterners could be merrier than they were given credit for.
They were not averse to designs akin to pinwheels. White roses still
bloomed on the burgundy carpet, and he sank into the black horsehair
chair where Mary had stitched almond-colored guest towels.

An elegant woman and a man wearing a worsted suit entered the
parlor. They chatted by the mantel, as if John were invisible. (Had he
forced a film of himself to emerge from another world?) The man's
accent was British. He likely had no idea that John was wearing the
official GAR pin of a melted Confederate bullet.

John pictured Mr. Lincoln tucking in kindling at the fireplace,
Robert studying, home from the Phillips Academy, Tad playing with
his toy train, and Willie and his mother angling their soles toward
the warmth, with Eddie rising from his grave to dance in the flames
curling from the wood, and Maria Catarina Freitas glancing at John as

she darned, her gaze proclaiming, *Can you believe our good fortune? . . .* while stylized foliage floated on the wallpaper *but did not float away,* leaves and boughs gold and silver as Christmas ornaments. *It was a room that stayed Christmas.*

The British man pointed to the cast-iron stove jutting from the hearth and said, "This was used to heat the room in Lincoln's time, was it, then, Mrs. Brown?"

"Just as you see it today." She wore that style of hat with a bell-jar shape. She must be Mrs. Mary Edwards Brown, Mary Todd Lincoln's grandniece, the current owner. "No, that's not how it was," John heard himself say. *They had it wrong, Mary, and I spoke up and told them so.*

The British gentleman turned and said, "Friend?"

John said, "Mr. Lincoln burned wood in that fireplace. All the rest of the house, he heated with stoves."

They squinted at him. Mrs. Brown introduced the British man as John Drinkwater, author of a theater piece called *Abraham Lincoln.* Drinkwater said, "The fireplace has a role in my play, but I was in England, visualizing it." He held out his arm as if to a bride. "May I escort you throughout the house, sir? I would be grateful to learn the extent of my other mistakes. I see also that I should address you as a hero." He gestured at the GAR pin in John's lapel.

John allowed Mr. Drinkwater and Mrs. Brown to assist him in rising. He shook their hands and said, "I'm John Alves. I've been gone a long while."

Everything spoke of You. *Everything.* Pins stuck in the floorboards, that especially, that so much, and Eliza Leslie's cookbook that Mrs. Brown opened. Root cellar and steep steps and the framed hair wreaths of mourning. The upstairs room for the rare full-time hired girl. Always cold. The portrait of Daniel Webster, *still there.* Baseboard scratches from Fido. The golden custard-set. A twig from—though who knows?—a linden tree. Cerulean walls marred by mold. A pen's nib. A plum's pit, an echo of wailing. John gave a detailed tour, picturing the rooms as they had been and answering Mrs. Brown's and Mr. Drinkwater's questions. Mr. Drinkwater in particular enjoyed this quite a bit, and when the hour for departure came, he asked John to join him in writing their names in the visitors' book.

John was presented with the pen, but his shaking hand dropped it. He stared at the guestbook labeled "The Home of Lincoln" and gripped the pen again, but he was too filled with Mary, the epoch of courting her here, and with emotion. Offering assistance, Mr. Drinkwater wrote in tidy script:

John Drinkwater ‖ *Birmingham, England*
John Alves [*written by me, at Mr. Alves' request——aged* 81] ‖
Mandarin, Florida

When John died, he would grow through a tree, as Mother had, as Mary would. They would end up chopped, blended with water, and stretched to form blank pages, Edward, too. A writer like his daughter might coax their voices to fill pages, fill them with heart-songs.

———

PHLOX, YELLOW STARGRASS, AND GOLD-DOTTED HORSETAIL (PRETTY but poisonous) greeted him: my Jacksonville. He ordered a sarsaparilla soda at Ruark's Ice Cream Saloon. Four booksellers; two wallpaper stores; two undertakers; two coopers. Mathers & Wadsworth offered carriage trimming; John Ruf had a banner extolling his soda water. A steel arch decorated West State Street with its boughs of elms, laden with vermilion. Horse carriages were delivering flowers. Cars veered around curves. The Ayers Bank was a four-story skyscraper. If Jacksonville had not entirely succeeded in making itself an Athens of the West, it had settled into itself while yet rising from hallowed aspiration.

He wondered if fading vision caused him to miss the public garden he had summoned into being. He laughed: It was wiped from the slate, nowhere to be found, the benches and the little chapel gone to oblivion, too. In its place was a two-story hotel.

At Mother's grave in the East Cemetery, he put his jacket on the headstone and curled up alongside her. *Do you know how Mother will never leave you? It is so simple, o meu passarinho!* Days come in; nights fade out. He whispered, "I still owe you a structure that houses God. Forgive me for taking forever, but I'll figure it out."

—

WHEN JOHN OPENED THE DOOR TO A SEEMINGLY DESERTED, FALLING-
in-on-itself shop called Scents, Rui was leaning over a beaker at a
sawhorse table but swiveled a wrinkled visage toward John, a ghostly
beard marking him as a veteran of the same war. He croaked out,
"Why, greetings, my brother." Before John's astonished eyes, Rui began
to dissolve, turning into blots of color before these also faded. The only
traces were uncollectible fumes as fragrant as the lilac vapor said to
blossom from the corpses of saints. Rodrigo Jaime Alves had waited to
say goodbye to his brother before departing, culminating his lifetime's
work by turning himself into a tropical scent that doused John. Rui left
no corporal remains, and John muttered, because the Lord Himself
had arrived, "Oh, my God. God."

—

HE WAS SCHEDULED TO MEET HIS GRANDDAUGHTER (WARD'S GRAND-
daughter) in front of the Meline Theater and prayed her transport
from Chicago would not be delayed. The sky was erupting mango-
colored, with clouds like elongated fruits. They seemed a reminder that
the problem with life is that it's a straight line, but the effort of life
is to make it round. He had endured a wakeful night at the YMCA
and hoped he would not nod off during dinner later with Hugo and
his family.

Birds fluttered in his chest at Catharine's approach. She was so
strikingly like her grandmother that the sight edged her with elec-
tricity. The Meline Theater afforded a backdrop of neon. Praise all the
man-made shades. In her feathered hat, a cloth dove nested, and her
peach-colored dress had short sleeves and abstract swirls shining like
salt crystals. Mary's hair, she had it, and the green eyes and petal skin.
What right had he to be here; what was his? Catharine caught his
arm to steady him. "Grandpa? May I call you that? Grandpa John."
She accepted the bouquet he brought, apricot roses. She was agile and
kinetic, open but cautious, *like You, my love,* with the same aspect of
wanting to hold on to someone, onto the world, *both of you* appearing

frail in one light but indefatigable in another, with a muscularity of the arms. Her face caught a plane of midwestern sunshine, that earned thing, that long-awaited boon barreling as the hallelujah out of the cold. "Do you mind terribly," he whispered, the ticket booth for the theater he had helped save flanked by posters announcing the latest silent pictures, "if I ask you to ask me that once more?"

"Grandpa John. May I call you that?" What a storm-clearing smile.

"Again and again."

Marcella would jump on a train after filing a story in Chicago; *yes yes, Grandpa; she'll meet us later today. Grandma arrived in Chicago, but she has a cold, don't worry, she's resting, she's fine, I think she wants to be perfect before seeing you!* Catharine and John looked through a window into the theater, closed in anticipation of the nighttime shows. The chairs had been replaced by banks of seats. Blue velvet curtains were like cascades of water. Catharine mentioned an audition when the producer and director had merely . . . laughed at her.

"Then make people laugh, Catharine," he said. "You were good as Penny Apple, but I noted some repressed comedy. In your expressions." She did not disagree. They were strolling through the downtown. "Try for roles like that. Not drama." She thanked him for his fatherly advice. He pointed out how they were laughing already.

Marcella Moore Webb met them in the afternoon by the entrance to the park. Chic and dancerlike, she was a middle-aged splicing of John and Mary. They did not need an introduction. She said merely, "Papa." In each other's arms, with Catharine nearby, she whispered, "We didn't invite you to my wedding, but we can make up for lost time because you'll be at my daughter's, and my mother will be there, too."

They rode the Ferris wheel built by the Eli Bridge Company, with its bow of red lights at the top and green lights adorning the seats. It got stuck when they were at the apex. John sat with Marcella, Catharine in the seat below. He gave his daughter the highlights of his history. It seemed too much to ask: *How was your life?* But he did ask it.

She replied, "I suppose it was Portuguese of me to marry a man who would go to sea. Francis. Funny thing, Papa, but our separations kept our marriage happy, that missing of each other. It was a reunion whenever he came home."

"That's something I understand, querida." She took his hand. Her nails were like glossy shells.

She surprised him by musing that Mama had been the quiet one. Ward had been a great cook and loved clowning around. He gave up experimenting with plants and seemed content with teaching high school, though a lot of his money dwindled. "I understand why you could never come see us," she said. "My mother told me it was because the goodbyes get rougher."

"She was always right about everything."

Catharine below them was humming, unafraid of dangling this far off the ground. He asked, "What stories do you write, dear? For the *Tribune*."

Often they were about Chicago's architecture, but she also composed news bulletins and wrote made-up stories for magazines. She wanted to write a novel.

"Your mother," he said, as the Ferris wheel jogged back to life, gears grinding. "Are you sure she wants to see me? In New York."

He would spend the time between now and November 1 with traveling, soaking up the beauty and the strangers of this vast country, would leave Mary to become well, leave her to decide in peace if she would live in Chicago, would wait to meet her in a castle in the city he had claimed as his birthplace on the mustering-in papers when he went to war.

Marcella adjusted her modern hat. "She's as nervous as you are, Papa. Why don't we see what happens? She's agreed to meet you." While she kept her blood-father's hand in her own, the iron wheel creaked, and they were soon ladled back onto the earth.

RESTLESS DREAM ALL DONE

YOUR ARMS AROUND ME, MINE AROUND YOU. MY HEART COUNTS YOUR ribs, a musical staff of bone; your muscles are braided. I'm shaking so much the landscape fizzles, explodes into dots. Pointillist city. Cars, buildings, lamplights man-made stars. People rush. There's snow, un-usually early this year, as if miraculously summoned to toss us on a disc back to our beginning, children hurled onto the white blanket over Illinois. I say, *My eyesight isn't the best anymore,* and you whisper, *Good, you'll be spared the sight of me,* and we laugh as if it's the best joke, never let me go. My love. We are old. Diamond ribbons called rivers run on both sides of our city. My face is buried in the side of yours . . . pressed so hard I can't tell where I end and you start. Ever since my granddaughter, Catharine—yours, too—ordered me not to back out of meeting you here in the Belvedere Castle in Central Park, I'd rehearsed saying, "Hello, Little Bird," because it would be clever, but I love you too much to be clever, couldn't have managed it anyway when I saw you, in profile, then turning, our faces breaking into light in our beholding, us together weeping . . . I can't utter a word, but your flesh says, *Mary.* You said, perhaps: *Mary, the rest of my soul.* Yes. Now my dear we rest. And you are the rest of me. I you. The milky-gray air pretends it's from the prairie, racing into our alabaster city. Buried specks of jeweled tints, red, yellow, hibernate within bulbs in their graves.

Kiss me. It's a fantasy castle we're in, with stone walls and turrets. A hawk flies.

You and I step apart to take each other in. I'm in a black coat with a cream wool collar, and a green velour hat with red velvet roses. There are children in this park, families. We hear cries. There's bread shared. A ball gets thrown. A dog jumps. My spirit leaps. You catch it. Keep it. The snow sifts onto my hat and over its sides, a snow veil. I wear the weather. Sugar powder drifts onto my coat until it's covered with ice-sequins. Men from the Weather Service are making a racket inside Belvedere Castle, using scientific advances to harness, and record for the history of this very day, the velocity of the wind, the temperature. Bits of nest soften the granite, dwellings of birds, their wings with their own measurements of the air. Vanes twist on the colored-slate roof, and windows got installed, making it like a home. You declare, "I have a surprise for you," but what more do I need, if a moment rocks me in its arms in your arms, this is eternal, a girl swoops past on a sled that's an orange shade I can dream into tangerine, and there's shrieking, the young do that often, so wonderfully, when it's out of pure joy.

———

THEY VISITED A GREENHOUSE: THE PANES WERE A LIGHT GREEN, more syrup than glass. She smiled back at the orchids with mauve faces on the bark of stunted trees, flowers with feelers so minute that studying them meant leaning close, and if she did not hold her breath they shook. Her father was within and without everything here.

They traipsed past irises with their papery wattles. The afternoon poured through the cutouts made by the spaces between the leaves of plants to form swimming creatures on the floor. Cutouts of light were hurled down as whitish lobsters—and starfish, lots of those, jagged and missing limbs. Light-fish and light-lobsters, calcified, nipped at the ankles of John and Mary. Her hair clip was a strip of glass that caught the salt-small pieces of pink that hide everywhere until glass finds them. All was banished between *then* and *now*, she believes it; she so believes it. Always this is what love is, you're breathing in a sea where you should not have breath at all.

NO MORE LONGING FOR THE DAY,
GOING TO ROAM NO MORE

NIKKA WINDSOR WAS NINETY, PASTE BRUSHED ONTO A SKELETON, HER hair in the style, Mary later told John, of the Gibson Girls in the magazines. A long pearl necklace, knotted, gently chimed. He set down his suitcase, but before he could cast himself into his sister's arms, she said, "Nothing we want to buy!" Mary stopped Nikka from shutting the door and wondered aloud if they resembled religious fanatics bearing pamphlets.

"Nikka," his tenor voice murmured, "I'm selling homemade wine."

Her cloudy eyes swept over them, and her hands flew to the sides of her head as if to keep it on her body. Edging toward them, through a room with burgundy furniture, was Michael Windsor, looking Edwardian, gray-haired, past their golden anniversary. Mary glanced away from the terrible beauty of Nikka releasing a moan trapped for decades, crying, "My baby brother! Now I can die in peace! Maria Freitas?"

Michael said, "No one here's going to die." His handshake with John conveyed *fellow veteran*. He hugged Mary, recalling her from his wedding.

Nikka felt like a stripped tree in Mary's embrace, one woman old and one ancient. Mary whispered, "Sister." There was grappling, every-one requiring tactile proof of one another's presence.

The view was of an atmosphere light-streaked from the theaters. Michael cranked the Victrola, its trumpet gleaming, and the needle scratched out notes of Handel. Nikka took a yellow cake from the larder and poured wine despite Prohibition, announcing, "Old people should be allowed a little stimulant."

Mary did not drink, but she lifted a glass, and a bead of light on the rim of John's glass jumped onto a bead of light on hers.

They would stay awhile with Nikka and Michael. John decamped during the day, with gifts to secure. Teasing him, Mary would chant, "Tell me, tell me." (He was like a boy, she was a girl on her birthday.) They devoured marzipan for breakfast. At suppertime, they spoke in crosscurrents, torrents, and visited the tenements where the exiles had first lived, the house at Twenty-fifth Street and Seventh Avenue for John, and the boardinghouse on Twenty-eighth Street and Seventh Avenue, now a refined apartment building, where Mary and Papa had been exquisitely happy. John and Mary, and Nikka and Michael, and their offspring and offspring's offspring, walked the city, and the city walked them, and was their cradle at night.

John was given the sofa in Michael's study, while Mary had the guest room, and they parked themselves on either side of the connect-ing wall in lovely agony until they emerged to sit in the living room and talk, talk all night. We'll sleep when we're dead! They could not get enough of each other, time was thickening so they could stretch it as a coverlet over their chapters. Tell me about Melissa—and *Edith Wells*, GAWD, as Catharine would say; are you joking, John?—and Rui turn-ing into divine vapor *because you trust me to believe it*. When the topic of the cruel letters came up, and he mentioned by name the high-flying gamblers, Mary confirmed meeting Jeduthan—with Maud—at a party at Nell's. A party to raise money for soldiers like John. Because those types did indeed operate within an amalgamated lofty atmosphere.

She could not stop touching his face. He kissed where her tube of blood flowed from her ear through her neck.

"Did you never see the Stewart Farm berries?" he asked one mid-night.

"I never did."

They laughed that he had labored over her crop, savior-level work, for years—years, darling!—while she had been oblivious in California. (Most messages tucked into bottles conk the transparent fish at the bottom of the ocean.) "Adam Stewart is in charge now. The fruit is in rising demand because magic is what people want."

"They were my life, but they don't need me anymore." The berries were like children in that way. Set free, going where they liked, praise be their success.

One dawn, sleep defied, she asked, "Shall I make toast?"

Why did that make him almost weep? He had never cared for toast, but he reveled in Mary Catherine Freitas Moore asking him something so gloriously ordinary. Another story, so many threads to weave for the rest of their allotted time: She and her papa had cooked it in this city on radiators, adding jam.

———

THE METROPOLITAN MUSEUM AFFIRMED THAT IT WOULD BUY MARY'S tablecloth, a folk-art tapestry the likes of which they had never seen, for the permanent collection. They paid her five thousand dollars. John had been conspiring with Zachary Vogel, their new acquisitions employee. The vow to visit Lincoln in his house in Washington had been transposed into Mary—alive in her masterpiece—residing in this palace with its white façade.

After strolling past Stieglitz, Whistler, and Cassatt, everyone stood awestruck in front of the wall with Mary's legend on cloth, each little square like a page. Present in their company now were the Jamisons (Myrtle tottering; Lawrence gone to God; Gemma and Clarisse aglow; Teddy, mind lost in the Civil War, at home with a nurse). Myrtle said to Mary, "I knew you'd come back to the best gallery," and Catharine, in an Egyptian-style dress and with Cleopatra-etched eyes, stood next to Marcella and Zachary. John's arm was around Mary.

The tablecloth was an America that began in another place, with a black beach, near camellias; birds-of-paradise; caravelas; father braiding vines; a sword stuck through a blonde in a sun hat; a cabinet of exotic colors. Sea bass on a dock; apricots; midwestern horizons; silos, immensity, tininess, and pumpkins, and rail upon rail, and plows, pigs, wildflowers. Prairie sundrops; an eagle for Mary Todd Lincoln. Salt-shakers. Edward with a thornless rose. A riverboat, a riverboat. Musical notes. Sound Machine! Flames; berries here, and there. Marcella wedding Francis, Catharine on a stage. Snow. Hands signing, Saudade. This was barely a third of it; who could describe the entirety? An edge was singed. A gold mine; a basket of dyed eggs; artichokes. A boat with painted eyes to see in fog. Mermaids. Autumn leaves. A king's tilted crown. A greenhouse. Sea lions. Red-white-blue abstraction. A wharf. Flying fish. A black-haired boy cosseting an octopus.

—

IT WAS A STAINED-GLASS MORNING, COLORS EDGED DISCRETELY BUT fixed together, green, silver, gold. New York's skyline shimmered metallic. For the double wedding at City Hall, the younger bride, Catharine, wore a bias-cut ivory silk frock. Zachary and John had bought dark-blue suits. Mary was in a knee-length white lace dress with orchids she had embroidered on the hem. Over her hair was a Spanish mantilla. She carried hydrangeas. Frank and Elizabeth came in from New Jersey, with Frank the best man. Marcella watched the vows next to Francis, who had arrived from Chicago. His face was weathered from his earlier career on the sea, and he straightened the cuff of Marcella's dress sleeve, a gesture that John read as Marcella's husband being attentive over the years. As John and Mary, and Catharine and Zachary, exchanged vows, the Jamisons crowded near Nikka and Michael.

On the street, Mary heard a girl declare, "Mommy, I didn't know grandmas could be brides!" As the mother shushed her daughter, Mary, laughing, gave her bouquet to the child and said, "They can do everything." The best response stayed inside Mary, which was: Here's the wonder of it, I've never felt so young.

For the wedding lunch, they went to the Automat on Broadway and dropped nickels into slots to open the glass doors of the honey-combed cases filled with vegetable pies and pecan bars, chicken wings and egg creams. Marcella shouted across the table, "Papa, shouldn't you be taking those stereo-thing pictures?" He bantered back his agreement. His child was a Portuguese girl fully formed in America, a writer. How had this happened, when his origin had been one of starving in a jail?

Frank got to his feet, volunteering to take photos, saying he would sing for his supper. He and Elizabeth answered questions about Edison. Mary said Perpetua and Henry could not come from California but had begged them by telephone for a wedding portrait. She had John to thank for putting her back in touch with Pet.

A few of Catharine's actress friends bustled in, exclaiming about an upcoming show on off-Broadway they would all do, with Catharine in a comedic role, playing (heavy on pratfalls) a woman who spies on a man who jilted her. Catharine Vogel winked at John: *See, Grandpa, I'll go after comedy!* Mary and he would soon witness their grandchild, married woman, stroll upon a stage, making the audience roar. The Jamisons, all of them, promised to buy tickets.

The manager at the Automat sent over the cake they had ordered, chiffon with strawberries and cream running pink, and sugar flowers, and Frank took a picture of it, quickly, before it melted, and Catharine's running comments had them in stitches as she served it up.

John's wedding gift to Mary was a used volume of Athanasius Kircher's investigation into sound, unearthed in a bookstore in New York. Mary's crossed arms pinned it to her chest. He had vowed to replace the one burned in the fire consuming his Madeiran home, and replace it he had. She said, "I've thought up gifts for you, but they aren't ready yet."

Tell me, tell me, said her husband, laughing, glad, glad, glad to be old.

———

QUIET POSSESSED JOHN AND MARY. THEIR CATCHING-UP CHATTER ebbed toward ever-longed-for silence, the kind fathoms down. This, Mary thought, is why devoted older couples always seem to be mute on benches, their heads inclined together. They are in the hallowed place.

Marcella returned to Chicago with Francis, to tend to her novel underway. John led his wife, and their granddaughter and her husband, to a building at Twenty-fifth Street and Eighth Avenue and handed Mary a set of keys to the first house he had ever owned. He had bid on a *New York Times* promotion of an aerie on the top floor of a five-story building. It had six rooms and a river view, and it cost him thirty-two hundred dollars. He gave Catharine and Zachary three thousand dollars toward a place of their own. When Catharine objected, John insisted. Mary and he had more than they needed.

Lightness suffused him. Rest now. Work is done. Mary. Married.

On the balcony, he started an apple-tree espalier with dwarf Gravensteins, staking two saplings apart and linking them with three horizontal wires. He would keep clipping above the buddings to force growth horizontally and vertically. Starred flowers would open in this striving to meet in the center, one sapling stretching eastward and one westward. When Catharine and Zachary found a flat close by, on Twenty-second Street, he installed an espalier for them, too.

A minute greenhouse was already on John and Mary's balcony, where he showed her the cutting that Adam Stewart had shipped from the farm. She was done with the massive business of the crop, but she could again nurse a stick with a slant cut in a vase with water and seaweed. She asked, "Where am I?" in the wavering tone like the one he used after almost dying from the bullet in his shoulder, when her running to him saved his life.

He replied, "Home."

REVELATION

ON CHRISTMAS DAY, THE APPLE-TREE ESPALIER ON THE BALCONY WAS covered with tarps. Mary handed John the glass-star ornament she had given Ward after their wedding, and he put it on their decked tree. Everyone gathered around the Victrola, their gift from Nikka and Michael, the lid of its cabinet thrown back as they played records, carols and jazz, "The First Noel"; "Baby, Won't You Please Come Home?"; Cole Porter's "I Never Realized." Catharine demonstrated the latest ragtime dance, causing Nikka to declare that attempting it would snap her in two. Mary danced, John circling with her.

Zachary rushed in, shaking frost from his coat. Notes swarmed, career career, like little birds, the coloration of their bodies streaking overhead, leaving garlands, yellows, reds, and greens. Songs from invisible people rose from a circling black platter while a needle ran in its grooves, like a hoe flinging seeds that sprouted in the air. John thought that the greatest thing about America was its *generosity,* with spirit and hope and faith, but also with land and objects and inventions, a culture of magnaminity he would mourn if it were lost. Those souls in Illinois had emptied their cupboards for the exiles, welcoming them. Him. Mary.

Elizabeth Meline's face was a riverbed, and Frank's sinew was dried, but his smile still was blissful. The birds from the notes of the music squawked. Mary assisted Elizabeth with her halting walk while Frank handed John and Mary a flat, wrapped item. Mary pulled the ribbon to open the package.

It was a phonograph record, a ridged black plate. Nikka boasted that she knew what it was, because she had held on to the Voice of God as rendered by Serafina Alves and had given it to Frank after he assisted with Thomas Edison's creation of a Talking Machine. *Phonograph*. What luck, to have survived into the era of pictures streaming with motion, and voices retained the way God must, a cacophony in His bombarded ears. Frank had traced John's mother's soot-marked jots onto a glass plate that he took to his former laboratory to reproduce as a record, planting her drawing into its furrows. Michael set it onto the Victrola but declared that Mary, the artist of needles, should lift the metal arm and put it down to release the sounds.

Catharine framed her jaw with her hands. (John and Mary would remember this whenever their grandbaby on the stage exaggerated her gestures to comedic effect in performances that won ovations.)

How could John have lived this long without Mother's final gift, the greatest promise she'd given him in his boyhood to tell him God's best advice for the world?

Mary lowered the needle. It rode the record, rasping. Everyone was tensed, with Frank's head inclined as if he were searching for the code of a lock.

John shook, and Mary held him. Nikka proclaimed, "Mama!" Because Serafina Alves had come out of the dead to chant, clear as a bell:

John for ate.

Had she been recollecting the days of hunger? Maybe some part of it got blurred in the soot: *Tell me John ate. John needs for to eat?*

"I'm guessing she wanted to confirm your suffering ended," said Frank. "No matter how awful it was, you survived."

"John ate for to save his life?" Mary said. "God said her son got fed?"

"John ate for me, meaning 'on behalf of me'?" offered Michael Windsor, the translation out of ash bound to have missing or inverted notes.

John judged everyone's guesses good, but who could say, finally, what God wanted anyone to know.

———

EVERY NIGHT WAS A WEDDING NIGHT. AT A DISTANCE FROM THEIR bird's nest—this their holy church—were searchlights made of lime. Ouija boards had been set up with planchettes in Times Square during the World War, people needing a needle to spell out if a young man had died clean. John and Mary slept locked together, kisses profound, her stretched on top of him, and then him on top of her, arms, legs, hollows, and organs, round and round as records spin (and as their age permitted, with the attendant afflictions). That was his true Night Blessing: Your body and mine, wearing twilight's lowering.

One night before the New Year, he awoke with a start. He tucked the bedspread over Mary and searched the bookcase for their Bible, quaking as he had in Meridian. Come morning, he would tell her more about those days, conquering them by sounding them aloud.

John 4:8 was:

He that loveth not does not know God; for God is love.

He leaned against the bookcase, this lineup of covers over what the Reverend Kalley had called "ancient wisdom." God had whispered through Mother, and into a feather's quill, "Only love for others will find Me. I dwell within Love, and every dwelling where Love exists may be named a high place and church where I thrive."

———

IT WAS MARY'S TURN TO DISAPPEAR FOR HOURS. SHE LED HIM TO THE Historical Society, where Clarisse Jamison worked. Clarisse, Mary, and Zachary had arranged a small exhibition with the Sound Machine (new feather) on a table, and Serafina's original soot-page set under glass, and a copy of her Edison phonograph record set on a Victrola to be played by visitors. The wall displayed newspaper articles, found via the New York Public Library, about her arrival with the other exiles in America. This was part of a larger display about the scientific developments of sound and acoustical recordings, with cases holding experimental items and inventions to aid the deaf, but all John could see was this shrine, paid for by his wife, to his uneducated mother's triumphs.

At St. Luke's Hospital, where Mary's father had received lifesaving care as an immigrant, there was a nondenominational chapel allowing anyone to come and pray or sit. Not just Protestants and Catholics, but everyone. Mary said she believed that had Serafina lived this long, she would have come to this idea for the church God kept asking her to build. It combined his mother and her father. In this lay all Mary's redoubled forgiveness of his mother, so potent that, if bottled, it could be drunk as antidote to battle-rage. The plaque read: DONATED BY SERAFINA ALVES, BORN IN SANTA CRUZ, MADEIRA, A PROUD CITIZEN OF JACKSONVILLE, ILLINOIS.

Any attempt at words by him would sully this.

Mary laughed and said, "I want to live one hundred years more, to see what the world invents next."

But it seemed to John, whenever Mary's naked form was pressed against his own, that the night pouring pink dreams through the squares of their window might be a pastel softening of the drawing near of their deaths, when one of them would lose the other. They made love so often, in their elderly way, that it seemed a dissolving into sheer desire. Was it fanciful to believe that everything adds up to creation, nothing lost? When the truth to aging men and aging women is that everything vanishes.

One morning, John awoke to Mary yelling from the balcony, and he dashed out to behold the espalier flourishing, grown into a Japanese screen dotted with two dozen Gravensteins. How much time had gone by? Had this happened overnight?

Catharine came by to cook an apple pie while John dozed, thanks to the warmth emanating from the stove, the comforting rhythm of spoons, Mary drowsing, too, holding his hand.... He was awakened by Zachary shaking his shoulder.

The pie was darkened by its sugared crust. "Grandpa, will you do the honors?" asked Catharine.

John cut into the apple pie, and Catharine dished up slices.

None of us shall pass this way again; what is everything *for*? Knotting a mother's shawl, wheelchairs spinning on a dance floor. Bird concerts through the little squares of a window. The bullets I fired, the fires I caused, the bodies heaped from violent excess. I promised never to forget how the red and blue sky drifted through the portholes of a riverboat. I loved You from the start, before I met You. I loved You in a bullet-riddled house covered with paint made out of blueberries and buttermilk, and perhaps *that* was what it was all for: I put that into the world. The Night Blessing is You in my bed.

A souvenir dish advertising Broadway held the keys to the apartment on the hallway's stand, a folded paper tucked to even out the legs. A honeysuckle aroma introduced itself from somewhere. "Oh, Grandpa John! Grandma Mary!" Catharine shouted, bringing him back to the present, her fork clattering down. "I'm sorry! It's a little sour."

Zachary and his young wife grinned.

This was John's home, and he had given another home to Catharine. His daughter was writing in her home in Chicago. Catharine contained the ministrations of Mary and of Edward, all of them alive in this young woman, set to become a comedy star in the first city of his dreams.

It was the sweetest taste of all his life. Apple pie in America. The sky abides. The sea. Sand often bleeds into it, catching a riptide that heaves in a swath with a knife's sharpness. Some of the riptide's sand finds the shells where it will claw its way into being pearls. *This is desire. This is love.* Some of the sand drifts at random, or it ends up in a riverhead or a lake with children swimming. Some sinks, sifting over whatever is mighty or mean teeming below a surface knocked into prisms by the gales. In longer history, the sea dries up, leaving its salt to reside in the stillness of beds of crystalline beauty, unvanquished by the molten core far below. But all of the sand, churning in a tide, travels for a while surging and seeking, and for a moment it might lift a lost boat harking to light that dots the water when the stars hurl down their eyes, the better to join forces bodily in near-jealous solidarity with the rhythms of magnificent imperfect creation. In waves, under lunar or solar influence, despite the scattering caused by the foraging seabirds, in its howling and yearning, so onward and always the sand carries itself toward its brethren waiting in multitudes on the unseen shore. Home, air, marriage, and gladdened work, and promises to make and promises to keep. Hail to the breaking of bread, the violet bath—O, Mary!—approaching as another day is gifted, and ended, and laid away. *It is the sweetest taste of all my life.* Did he repeat that aloud, or was an echo resounding past fireplace and mantel, past brick and mortar and out the windows? Death is kept at bay; I'll never want to leave a world that has Mary in it, our nights blessed, dreams pink, this beloved earth, this hand in mine, this story of our lives. Thine eyes, Catharine dear, and those of the husband at your side: They glisten and bid me thanks and affection tempered bright as steel. I know that you are born of me, and I treasure that you are mine.

ACKNOWLEDGMENTS

FIRST THANKS GO TO DRA. IÊDA SIQUEIRA WIARDA, FORMERLY WITH the Hispanic Division of the Library of Congress, who recorded my work for the archives after a talk I gave in 1997. She directed me to Ron Grimm in the Maps and Geography section to discover a curious exhibit: "Celebrating the Portuguese Communities in America: A Cartographic Perspective, Presented by the Library of Congress and the Embassy of Portugal," where I was introduced to the immigration story of the Madeiran Protestants of Illinois. The following year, Iêda invited me to present "From Madeira to Illinois: Stories of Survival and Disappearance of the Portuguese Protestants" under the sponsorship of the Hispanic Division. I owe dear Iêda a debt of gratitude.

Enormous thanks forever to my stellar agent, Ellen Levine. This project that has taken over fifteen years would not be alive without her, and her care and passion for my work never wavered. Audrey Crooks was an absolute delight to work with, too. Ellen delivered the manuscript to an ideal home at Flatiron Books/Macmillan. Upon reading my book, executive editor and publisher Megan Lynch wrote the sort of note writers dream of getting, and from that moment, her support of my story and of me has been a life-renewing joy. To the entire Flatiron team, unending thanks: Bob Miller, president/publisher; Marlena Thorsen Bittner, vice president and director of publicity; Kukuwa Ashun, editorial assistant; and Greg Villepique, copy editor. Thank you, Cat Kenney, Katherine Turro, Emily Walters, Jeremy Pink, Eva Maria Diaz, Donna Noetzel, Elizabeth Hubbard, Kelly Gatesman, and Stephanie Torres. Thank you, Rex Bonomelli, for such a gorgeous cover. Thanks as well to Rich Green of the Gotham Group, Ana Ban of Trident Media, Carmen Serrano at LeYa in Portugal, and Tânia Ganho. I'm grateful to Leslie Shipman, longtime friend and founder of the Shipman Agency for authors.

This work is supported by the Radcliffe Institute for Advanced Study at Harvard University, where I was a Fellow (2006–2007). My research assistants, Jason Lazarcheck and Ece Manisali, created the birdsong communications for, respectively, John Alves and Mary Freitas Moore. Jason did invaluable sleuthing on Ancestry.com. What a fine group of Radcliffe colleagues: Rebecca Goldstein, Allegra Goodman, Megan Marshall (who suggested making anagrams with John's surname), and Major Jackson, my kid brother. (Allegra, I'm grateful for your reading of fortune cookies.) Thanks to the late Judith Vichniac. Liz Bradley, thank you for your computer assistance and for mentioning my godmother, Clementina Vaz, from a generation not allowed to marry legally, when you wed your wife.

As serendipity would have it, I came to the fellowship with a copy of Don Harrison Doyle's *The Social Order of a Frontier Community* (Urbana and Chicago: University of Illinois Press, 1983) only to find that fellow-Fellow Marjorie Spruill, a brilliant scholar, especially on women's history and suffrage, was married to him. Many of Don's tenets in this beautifully written volume opened my eyes to a fresh look at the myth of American culture being about community rather than the ability to move on. He directed a spotlight on the tug-of-war between individualism and commerce versus boosterism, community, and charity. This theme in my novel would not exist without his enlightened work.

How I miss the late Lindy Hess, who ran the Radcliffe Publishing Program. Not incidentally, her ability to point people in the right direction included ushering me toward Christopher Cerf, and marrying him remains indisputably the best move of my life.

It took some years from viewing the exhibit in the map room of the Library of Congress to writing first pages, which I did with the support of the MacDowell Colony for the Arts (January 2005) and during my tenure as a Briggs-Copeland Fellow in Fiction at Harvard University (2003–2009).

Drew Gilpin Faust, a renowned Civil War expert, spent her final year as president of the Radcliffe Institute when I was there. When I discovered in the papers of the Veterans Administration that John Alves had, along with others in his company, received a twenty-day punishment, without any mention of what they had done, she directed me to Trevor K. Plante of the Old Military and Civil Records at the National Archives and Records Administration in Washington, D.C. In yet another uncanny gift from the universe while working on this novel, I arrived at almost the same time as double-Pulitzer-winning historian Alan Taylor, whom I've counted as a friend since the time we were both professors at the University of California at Davis. He voiced a variation of Trevor Plante's comment that my trying to find what my character might have done was a needle-in-a-haystack search. Except that after three hours of undoing the pink ribbons around the documents I requested somewhat at random about Illinois companies, I found it. Boys who had survived Shiloh and Vicksburg were throwing "cotton blow" and other debris at each other and refusing an officer's command to desist, and they were court-martialed and sentenced to twenty days of incommunicado punishment. A singular moment was getting to wave this document under the nose of a friend who happens to be one of the best historians and researchers in the world. Alan said, "Welcome to the dark side" and wondered if I would give up being a novelist in favor of history. I told him no, I would rest on these once-in-a-lifetime laurels. The "Wishbone-Backbone" plaque is an Easter egg for him.

My research made substantial headway because of David J. Langum, Sr., who awarded me a Foundation and Travel Grant via the Langum Project for Historical Literature, allowing me access to the Langum Family Papers and de Mattos Family Papers at the Abraham Lincoln Presidential Library. Among the treasures this yielded was a diary of the Reverend Doctor Robert Reid Kalley. David is a

descendant of one of the key ministers during the difficulties in the
Portuguese Presbyterian community over baptismal doctrine and is
the author of *António De Mattos and the Protestant Portuguese Community in Antebellum Illinois,* published by the Morgan County Historical
Society and Production Press (Jacksonville, Illinois, 2006). He put me
in touch with Deborah Kleber, who ran a website on the Madeiran
exiles, whom I met at the Hotel Campo Grande in Lisbon.

I was warmly welcomed in Madeira, especially at the Arquivo Regional da Madeira, by Dra. Fátima Barros and Leonardo Pereira, who
did ample work with the Xerox machine. Dra. Alexandra Canha and
her staff at the Biblioteca Municipal do Funchal unearthed key material for me. Both these departments were housed in the Palácio de
São Pedro in Funchal. Thanks also to the historian Dr. Alberto Vieira,
Director Regional dos Assuntos Culturais at the Região Autonoma
da Madeira and Centro de Estudos de História do Atlântico, where I
was referred by Dr. Gonçalo Di Santis. Additional help was provided
by the Centro do Emigrante, Quinta Villa Passos, with Dr. Gonçalo
Nuno; O Departamento de Cultura da Câmara Municipal do Funchal, with Dra. Teresa Brazão; and the Biblioteca Estrangeira, with
Dr. Carmo Santos.

What are the odds that Illinois College would offer a teaching
fellowship to support writing projects? They exclaimed in surprise
over my sending them work featuring their college and Jacksonville
in general. Thank you, Cindy Cochran, for driving me around town,
and thanks to her colleagues Lisa Udel, Bob Koepp, Betsey Hall,
Nick Capo, and Beth Capo. (Thanks for the entertaining tour of the
haunted sites.) Thanks to my allies in the Illinois College Bookstore,
Linda Cunningham, Robin Oberg, and Candy Norville, who dug into
their own supplies of printing paper when the orders ran late.

I received huge help in my research, with special thanks to: Greg
Olson of the *Jacksonville Journal-Courier* and Steve Hardin, owner of
the Samuel Adams House on West College, a classic example of Greek
Revival architecture, one of the historic homes of College Hill. Steve
and I talked about the town's history for hours. (I believe the house
has since been sold.) Sharon Zuiderveld, director of the Jacksonville
Public Library, and Chris Ashmore were paragons of patience. Director

Carolyn Eilering facilitated a story-changing tour of the Illinois School for the Deaf, a moving institution that continues Jacksonville's old aim to be an Athens of the West by creating prominent facilities of care.

Welcoming me to their homes were several descendants of the original Madeiran immigrants, including Mary Hathaway, Jean Bowen, and William (Bill) DeFrates. Jean set up meetings with descendants and put me in touch with tour guides of the town's Underground Rail system. Mary was generous with letting me copy pages from original Portuguese Bibles and hymnals and other newspaper clippings. Bette DeSilva, Wallace (Jack) Pat Jackson, and Barb Baker also enlightened me about the original colony.

Thanks to Rand Burnette, chairperson of the publications committee of the Morgan County Historical Society, Dan Dixon of the Springfield Genealogical Society, Jane Van Tuyle at Jacksonville High School, Loretta Widdows, caretaker at the Duncan Mansion, and Mary Francis Alkire of the Jacksonville Historical Society. Dr. Lawrence W. Zettler, professor of biology at Illinois College, engineered trips to the prairie to spot orchids, showed me the ghost-orchid perfume experiments in the IC lab, and educated me about the environment. I was stunned by the raining down of cicadas, and he remarked on my good fortune to be there for their hatching after thirteen years of dormancy, a reminder that research requires presence, that the feel of a place on the skin, as Walker Percy once put it, cannot be acquired at a computer. In a further instance of that, Guy and Edie Sternberg at the Starhill Forest Arboretum in Menard County, the official arboretum of IC, led me on a tour and gave me the impressive tome *Country Life: A Handbook of Agriculture, Horticulture, and Landscape Gardening* by Robert Morris Copeland (Boston: Dinsmoor and Company, 1866).

One more instance of the magical turns that enlivened my research: At John R. Paul's Prairie Archives Bookstore on the old Capitol Square in Springfield, I stooped to tie my shoe and came eye level with a mimeographed booklet listing the businessmen of 1849, a surprisingly lighthearted source of names, personality details, and occupations.

Among the many sources in Springfield was Wayne C. Temple, chief deputy director of the Illinois State Archives, who met with me at the Capitol Complex, did research even after I left Illinois, and gave me a copy of his useful *The Taste Is in My Mouth a Little . . . : Lincoln's Victuals and Potables* (Mahomet, IL: Mayhaven Publishing, 2004). I received an in-depth private tour of the Lincoln household thanks to historian Tim Townsend and curator Susan Hakke. Thank you to Linda Garvert for assistance with the Sangamon Valley Collection at the Springfield Public Library and Heather Tennies at the Lancaster Historical Society. The Illinois State Historic Preservation Society in Springfield was a moving source of actual letters, diaries, and assorted materials from Union soldiers; I delved into the Wallace-Dickey Collection, the Augustine Vieira Papers, the Preston Shumway Papers, and the diaries of Mortimer Rice.

At the Abraham Lincoln Presidential Library, Cheryl Schnerring, the manuscripts manager, Debbie S. Hamm, manuscript associate, Dennis E. Suttles of Genealogical Research, Mary Ann Pohl, Lincoln Collection cataloguer, and Glenna Schroeder-Lein of the Manuscripts Department were extraordinary participants in my discoveries. The 1849 issues of the *Illinois State Journal* had numerous articles on "The Coming of the Portuguese from the Island of Madeira, Portugal," found in the Doris M. Sanford Memorial Collection. When I asked if I could see Mary Todd Lincoln's authentic cookbook, it was eagerly brought up from the vault. We admired that the dessert pages were sugar-stuck together. Most significantly, I asked to see "The Home of Lincoln" guestbook from October 1919, to verify (citation of newspaper source is in the next paragraph) that John Alves was so overcome as an old man visiting the Lincoln household in recalling a love named Mary that his hand shook too awfully to sign his name, and the playwright John Drinkwater did the honors for him. There it was, verbatim: His memory and testimonial were impeccable.

Eileen Lynch Gochanour and Wanda Warkins Allers are bracing examples of the value of organizing and compiling historical materials even if they are not mainstream-published. Without their many volumes on the Portuguese exiles in Sangamon and Morgan Counties, I would not have stumbled across the history of John Alves—they faithfully gathered items about the original exiles and their descendants and included a featured interview with him in a 1920 *Salt Lake*

City Tribune. Some of their compilations include: *The lst Portuguese Presbyterian Church of Jacksonville, Illinois 1855–1860, The 2nd Portuguese Presbyterian Church of Springfield, Illinois,* and *The Gathering of the Portuguese.*

Thanks to the staff at the Newberry Library in Chicago, where I found useful articles and maps.

A partial list of other useful sources: *O Apostólo da Madeira,* by Michael Testa (Igreja Evangelica Presbiteriana de Portugal, 1863); *An Island Story: The Scots in Madeira,* by James W. Purves (Edinburgh: Church of Scotland Publications, date unlisted); *Uma exposição de factos,* by Robert Reid Kalley (pamphlet); *Perseguição dos Calvinistas da Madeira,* by João Fernandes Da Gama (São Paulo, Brasil: subsídio para a História das Perseguições Religiosas, 1896); *Sherman's Forgotten Campaign: The Meridian Expedition* by Margie Riddle Bearss, (Baltimore: published for the Jackson Civil War Roundtable by Gateway Press, 1987); *Sherman's Mississippi Campaign,* by Buck T. Foster (Tuscaloosa: University of Alabama Press, 2006); *The History of Hurlbut's Fighting Fourth Division . . . of the Fourteenth Illinois Infantry,* by James Dugan (of Company B.,14th Illinois), (Cincinnati: E. Morgan & Co., 1863); *Thoughts, Essays, and Musings on the Civil War,* an excellent blog on the Meridian Raid by bobcivilwarhistory.blogspot; *Soldier Life: In the Union and Confederate Armies,* edited and with an introduction by Philip Van Doren Stern (New York: Gramercy Books, 1961); *Illinois in the Civil War,* by Victor Hicken, foreword by E. B. Long (Urbana and Chicago: University of Illinois Press, 1966); *One Year at War: The Diary of Private John A. Shultz,* compiled by Hobart L. Morris, Jr. (New York, Washington, Hollywood: Vantage Press, 1968); *Civil War: A Narrative, Fredericksburg to Meridian,* by Shelby Foote (New York: Vintage, 1986); *The Story of a Common Soldier,* by Leander Stillwell (Kansas City, MO: Franklin Hudson Publishing Co., 1920). This touching volume aided my Shiloh scene, including his amazement at the sight of mistletoe.

Also consulted: *Images of America: Springfield: A Reflection in Photography,* edited by Edward J. Russo, Curtis R. Mann, and Melinda L. Garvert (Chicago: Arcadia Publishing, 2002); *Images of America: Jacksonville Illinois: The Traditions Continue,* edited by Betty Carlson

Kay and Gary Jack Barwick (Chicago: Arcadia Publishing, 1999); *Historic Morgan and Classic Jacksonville (1885),* edited by Charles M. Eames and Harvey W. Milligan, with an introduction by Professor Harvey W. Milligan (printed at the Daily Journal Steam Job Printing Office, Jacksonville, 1885); *Faces & Places: A Morgan County Family Album,* by Vernon Fernandes (published by the *Jacksonville Journal-Courier,* Production Press, Inc., 1995); *The Hymnal* (Philadelphia: General Assembly of the Presbyterian Church in the United States of America 1933, reissued in 1940); *The Hymnbook of Northminster Presbyterian Church of Jacksonville, Illinois* (Richmond, Philadelphia, New York: Presbyterian Church in the United States, 1955); *A Window on the Past: Residences of Jacksonville, Illinois: Their History and Design 1833–1925,* by Philip H. Decker, with an introduction by Helen Walton Hackett (Jacksonville, IL: published in cooperation with the Morgan County Historical Society, 1990); *Jacksonville: A Survey of its Past,* compiled by Dr. Ernest Hildner of Illinois College (Jacksonville, IL: Elliott State Bank, 1966); *The Portuguese of Morgan County* (publication of the Jacksonville Area Genealogical & Historical Society); *Where the Sky Began,* by John Madson (Boston: Houghton Mifflin, 1982); *Morgan County, Illinois: Its Past and Present* (Chicago: Donnelley, Loyd & Co. Publishers, 1878); and *Morgan County: The Twentieth Century* (Morgan County Board of Commissioners, 1968). It is significant that I found these last two volumes in Madeira.

At the end of laboring on a lengthy book, many things land on the cutting-room floor. The byways about the birth of baseball are gone, but thanks to John Thorn for his *Baseball in the Garden of Eden* (New York: Simon & Schuster, 2011), and for his generous, fast replies to my inquiries. Likewise, many asides were cut about Billy Fleurville (his surname is spelled in different ways in various sources), the Haitian-immigrant barber who tended to Lincoln, developed a remarkable bond with him, and bought property with Lincoln's aid, and who died only three years after losing his son Varveel in the war. I leave it to some enterprising writer to delve into the friendship of Lincoln, Fleurville, and Elias Merriman, a fascinating physician, inventor, and wanderer in the manner of men seeking fortunes in that era—another cutting-room victim along with his wife, Susan.

A disclaimer used on the TV show *Tokyo Vice:* "*Tokyo Vice* is a fictional program inspired by real events. Certain characters, incidents, and elements were fictionalized for dramatic purposes and are not intended to reflect on an actual person, history, entity, or incident." That adheres to the fictionalization from a springboard of real events envisioned here, based upon the real person of John Alves, born in Madeira to a Maria Joaquinha Alves, who was indeed condemned to die for heresy and with whom he was a little boy in jail, as I discovered him in an interview in *The Salt Lake Tribune,* February 1, 1920. As mentioned above, he speaks of returning in old age to the Lincoln household, where he is undone by memories of courting someone named "Mary." It was cited as a place where Mr. Lincoln welcomed them and proved "very democratic," and the visit put John beyond the ability to sign the Lincoln guestbook. More tellingly—or rather, un-tellingly—he speaks of mustering out of the Union army on June 24, 1864 . . . but he does not mention her. He skips ahead to saying that in the fall of 1865, he was in Nebraska City, Montana, and Utah, a period of wandering. It is where a novelist operates: What happened in that blank space? What occurred between courting this woman and the evocation of the trembling she still induced in his old age?

I honor the memory of this real man with the proviso that I invented a life for him that grew out of that blank, and it should not be construed as nonfiction when looking at, say, a character detail like a love of gambling, which stands in for the lottery mentality of all Americans. He was wounded at Shiloh, and I put in the true detail I discovered about his minor offense in the war of not following a cease-and-desist order about tossing debris around. The Lincoln household visit at the end is based on his account, with a slight adjustment made to fit the story I gave him. There is no evidence that any captain of Illinois Company 14th committed the atrocity of point-blank shooting a civilian—this captain is fictional—but given the horrors of the Civil War, it is not beyond all boundaries of belief. John had, in real life, a brother who died in Illinois, but I invented a different brother for him. Antoinetta Alves lived, and I loved her because in his interview he quotes her as saying, during Prohibition, that "old people should be allowed a little stimulant." But the same tenets of fiction apply to her, and I honor her memory, too. It might be said that I gave

John some happier fates than he enjoyed. When I ordered his papers from the Veterans Administration, my eye first fell on his lament, "I have no one to care for me," and this came at a time when I was debating abandoning the book. I made other minor adjustments: For example, what we know as the Battle of Shiloh was more commonly called the battle at Pittsburg Landing when it occurred. A real estate developer named Frank L. Meline was a descendant of the Portuguese Protestants, and I give him a *Ragtime*-style cameo.

My career has been blessed with enormous support from the Luso-American, Azorean, Madeiran, and Portuguese communities—Teresa Alves, Teresa Cid, Diniz Borges, Maria Teresa Horta, Hélia Correira, Joel Neto, Diogo Fernandes, Ambassador Francisco Duarte Lopes, Paula Lopes, Isabel Pavão, Teresa Tamen, Miguel Vaz of FLAD (Fundação Luso-Americano de Desenvolvimento), Vamberto Freitas, Onésimo Almeida, Maria Carmo Pereira (retired from the *Luso-Americano* newspaper), Henrique Mano, Frank Sousa, Millicent Accardi, Lara Gularte, and Katherine Soares and Angela Costa Simões of the Portuguese-American Leadership Council of the U.S. Jeff Parker, Scott Laughlin, and Oona Patrick are at the helm of the Disquiet International Literary Conference each year in Lisbon, and excerpts from this novel have had a platform for years with this group I consider family. To Parker and Arthur Flowers, special thanks—I still owe you dinner at one of José Avillez's restaurants. Thanks to other beloved Disquiet friends, Cyriaco Lopes, Terri Witek, and Tayari Jones. To the Borrela family of Beja—Herminia, Silvia, Miguel, Dalocas, and the late Leonel—sempre na minha coração. Thanks to Maria de Fátima Mendes, former consul general of Portugal in New York; the current consul general, Maria Pais Lowe; and Manuel S. Bettencourt of the Luso-American Education Foundation.

I appreciate the editorial assistance of Alexandra Shelley and Liz Van Hoose and the longtime support and suggestions of Eleanor Jackson. Thank you, Leslie Lehr, for your edits and excellent plot suggestions, not the least of which was the movie scene. May we walk again on the beach at the Pacific. To Randall Klein: This book would never have crossed the finish line without your top-flight guidance, encouragement, and keen sense of character and plot, your talents as a writer and editor. Your input was always fast, clear, smart, and abundant. Tell August that one day I hope he gets to meet the lady who sent the "chocolate-cookie bread" (also known as chocolate babka). Randall, you were a godsend.

Beowulf Sheehan and his team—Jeska Sand, Shilo Gold, and Shirley Breaux—made author's photo day delightful. He is a dazzling artist, and I feel lucky to have worked with him.

Special thanks to friend Philip Graham, (a birthday-sharer), who has long been enthusiastic about my work and who published an early incarnation of the prologue in *Ninth Letter*, vol. 7, no. 1 (Spring/Summer 2010). Vanessa Garcia commandeered a wildly funny expedition to a miracle-fruit farm in Florida before a tour of Miami. I am blessed with so many incredible friends, including authors Varley O'Connor, who has provided immense wisdom and love over the years (and mentioned "metaphoric furniture," the piano that can turn into a bed), and Liz Strout, an inspiration whose affection I treasure. Special thanks in so many ways to Maaza Mengiste. Thank you, Dylan Landis, for our friendship and Pomodoro writing sessions, and to Alexander Chee for a deep bond over the years that included his sending the text, "Be strong!" at the right moment. Near and dear to me are also Dustin Schell—I'll never forget your kindness when my husband was in the hospital—and Patricia Duffy, Ellen Datlow, Suzanne Simard, Christine Evans, Emily Albu, the aforementioned Alan Taylor, Alessa Johns, Chris Reynolds, Gwyneth Cravens, Henry Beard, Astrid Cravens, Gish Jen, Elizabeth Graver, Julia Glass, Cheryl Tan, Michael Rezendes, Eileen Pollack, Jennifer Acker, Annie Liontas, Flávia Stefani, Emily Passos Duffy, and Xochitl Gonzalez. Thank you, brilliant Maria Konnikova, for your love since Harvard days and for advice on the poker scenes, and likewise to Brian Chapman, who kindly spent an hour chatting about historical references as well as poker. (Any error in these regards is my own.)

My brothers and sisters are my champions: Mark Vaz, Maria Vaz Knox, Patrick Vaz, Peter Vaz, and Teresa Vaz Goodfellow. To godson Daniel Duarte, Katelin Labat Jacobs, godson Joseph Labat, Johnny Labat, Alexandra Vaz, Michael Vaz, and Matthew Duarte—love always. Matt: The glitter-tossing scene is for you. Derek, Judy, and Jon, and Priya, Jared, Marianne, Sorcha, Andrew, and Tiffany, I'm glad you're in the family. A warm welcome to Jackson Jacobs.

Christopher Cerf's name is on the dedication page, and he permeates every subsequent word. I'm happy to divulge that men and women of all ages ask how I managed to find such a beautiful marriage. The span of our relationship encompasses the years it took to write this novel. I can't imagine a kinder and more affectionate companion. Here's to many more years, O Meu Mais Do Que Tudo. Our life is beyond my wildest dreams, and thank you for saying that you love me on a daily basis. This book is for you.

My mother, Elizabeth Sullivan Vaz, turned ninety-five in October 2022, and she died on the nineteenth of November. She was an avid reader who remained a vivid, witty model and inspired in me a passion for writing, and I mourn her absence and miss our affection playing out in the visible world. This will be the first book when I do not receive a long letter of congratulations from her.

To paraphrase Cyriaco Lopes, it might be inevitable that we lose our parents, but it is not inevitable that we receive love and loving support. I also wish my father, August Mark Vaz, were alive to see this book's birth. He made it clear to his children, as did my mother, that we should follow our hearts, even if it meant veering around precarious bends into the arts. A history teacher and the author of *The Portuguese in California,* he took immense pride in his roots in the Azores and was so beloved as a teacher that I still get notes or invitations from students who studied with him. On the day he died at age eighty-six, he was wearing the MacDowell Colony T-shirt I'd given him. Since it's where the writing of this novel was launched in earnest, it seemed fitting that I put on this shirt when at long last I finished my new contribution about the Portuguese in America. That relic no longer has the lavender scent it possessed when I was first given it and buried my head in it and cried. Sonhos cor-de-rosa p'ra sempre, o meu precioso Pai.

ABOUT THE AUTHOR

Katherine Vaz, a former Briggs-Copeland Fellow in Fiction at Harvard and a Radcliffe Fellow, is the author of *Saudade* (Barnes & Noble Discover New Writers), *Mariana* (translated into six languages), *Fado & Other Stories* (Drue Heinz Literature Prize) and *Our Lady of the Artichokes* (Prairie Schooner Book Prize). Her work has appeared in many magazines, and she is the first Portuguese American to have her work recorded for the archives of the Library of Congress (Hispanic Division).